# THE BEAUFORT SISTERS

By the same author

YOU CAN'T SEE ROUND CORNERS
THE LONG SHADOW
JUST LET ME BE
THE SUNDOWNERS
THE CLIMATE OF COURAGE
JUSTIN BAYARD
THE GREEN HELMET
BACK OF SUNSET
NORTH FROM THURSDAY
THE COUNTRY OF MARRIAGE
FORESTS OF THE NIGHT
A FLIGHT OF CHARIOTS
THE FALL OF AN EAGLE
THE PULSE OF DANGER
THE HIGH COMMISSIONER
THE LONG PURSUIT
SEASON OF DOUBT
REMEMBER JACK HOXIE
HELGA'S WEB
THE LIBERATORS
THE NINTH MARQUESS
RANSOM
PETER'S PENCE
THE SAFE HOUSE
A SOUND OF LIGHTNING
HIGH ROAD TO CHINA
VORTEX

# THE BEAUFORT SISTERS

## Jon Cleary

WILLIAM MORROW AND COMPANY, INC.

NEW YORK    1979

To
Shelagh
and Freddie

# THE BEAUFORT SISTERS

# Chapter One

◆

# The Sisters

I

'Why are so many tennis players pigeon-toed?' said Prue. 'They're very sexy-looking till you get to their feet.'

'Why don't we just watch the tennis?' said Margaret. 'We've paid for that, not conversation we could have at home.'

'Oh my God,' said Sally and half-raised her walking stick as if she might thump her sister with it. 'Is this another tax deductible expense?'

Prue put on her glasses, looked out at the four men on the court, frowned, pursed her lips, then took off the glasses. 'What was I about to say? Something about sexiness in sport.'

'Is sex a sport?' said Nina. 'All the manuals I've seen advertised, I thought it was a course in bedroom engineering.'

The Beaufort sisters were sitting in the gold boxes, the most expensive, in the Kansas City municipal auditorium watching the World Professional Tennis Doubles championship. Collectively they were always known by their maiden name, even though all of them were married and all four had been married more than once. Sixteen years separated them from youngest to oldest: Prue was thirty-seven, Sally forty-one, Margaret forty-eight and Nina fifty-three. None of them had lost her beauty and together they attracted the eye of any man not suffering from cataracts or a lack of hormones; even college youths had been known to remark that maybe there was something to be said for older women if they all looked as good as the Beaufort sisters. Of

9

course, for those who knew how much they were worth, their wealth added lustre to their beauty and not just because of all the creams, massage and hair styling it could buy for them. A woman is never better framed than when in the doorway of a bank in which she is a major stockholder.

The tennis tournament was still in its early stages and the local citizens had not yet rushed to fill the huge indoor stadium. Only avid tennis fans and the country club set, and the Beauforts belonged, between them, to one or the other or both, had shown up this afternoon. The sound of racquets meeting ball echoed in the cavernous auditorium like the amplified sound of an accountant's gut-string being torn apart. It was obvious that the players now on court were disturbed by the mocking acoustics of the near-empty galleries. None seemed more upset than Clive Harvest, one of the two Australians playing a South American pair.

He was a tall muscular man, some years older than the other three men on court, with blond good looks and a set of expressions that seemed to jump back and forth between temper and laughter. He went up for a smash, misjudged it and put the ball well out of court; he cursed loudly and flung his racquet after the ball. Then he suddenly jumped the net, raced to each of his opponents, grabbed their hands and went through a pantomime of apology, retrieved his racquet and jumped back over the net. A lone spectator in the upper gallery, wanting to communicate with someone, *anyone*, gave him a loud Bronx cheer; Harvest saluted the compliment with two fingers. The two South Americans glowered in disgust and Harvest's partner, a boy of about twenty, just looked embarrassed.

'Mr Harvest,' said the umpire from his throne, 'if you've finished your little act, may we continue the match?'

For a moment it looked as if Harvest were going to give the umpire the two-fingered salute; then suddenly he smiled, a broad flash of teeth in his tanned face, and looked genuinely contrite. 'Sorry, Mr Baker. I'm a perfectionist, that's my trouble. Missing an easy smash like that – '

'We all aim for perfection, Mr Harvest. Let's try for a little less this afternoon, so that we can get this match finished.'

There was scattered applause, but Harvest just looked around and smiled broadly, as if his antics and display of temper had been committed by someone who had already left the court.

He won the next point and the game with a deft interception that split the two South Americans like a guerrilla's bullet. As the two teams crossed over, pausing near the umpire's chair to towel themselves, Harvest looked towards the Beaufort boxes. He had done the same thing several times during the match. It was impossible to tell who it was interested him; his glance was always too quick and casual. He was, however, more than casually interested in *someone* in the boxes.

'I think I'll go,' said Nina. 'This isn't very interesting.'

'You can't walk out in the middle of a match!' Margaret waved a protesting hand. Sometimes she acted as if she were the family matriarch. She was taller than her sisters, no hint of grey yet in her dark brown hair, and she carried herself in what Nina called Missouri Regal style. 'It's an insult to the players.'

'That Australian has been insulting us spectators all afternoon,' said Sally. 'You don't owe him any compliment, Nina.'

Nina stood up, slipping her arms into the sleeves of the vicuna coat she had been wearing across her shoulders. She was the shortest of the sisters, a little too tall to be called petite; her golden blonde hair would have been darker if not for her weekly visit to her hairdresser. She was no better or more expensively dressed than her sisters, but she had just that extra touch of elegance. In Kansas City, Missouri, the Beauforts were *the* family and it was as if Nina had taken it upon herself to show outsiders that the citizens were not all descendants of One-Eyed Ellis, Wild Bill Hickok and other, later rascals.

She left the boxes, stares following her from the other boxes, and went out into the entrance lobby. George Biff, patient as a statue of himself, the light gleaming like points of humour in his ebony face, was waiting there. He touched the peak of his chauffeur's cap with his maimed hand.

'I get the car, Miz Nina. Be but two minutes, out front there.'

'No, I'll come with you, George.'

The old black looked at her, seeing the nervous tension in her, wondering what had upset her. But he said nothing, led her out to the Rolls-Royce in the nearby parking lot.

Going home in the car Nina sat gazing out the window with a face that seemed suddenly to have become younger, as if years had been wiped away from it. But then George Biff, watching her anxiously in the rear-view mirror, saw the frown appear between her eyes, and then her eyes close, but not before he had seen the glistening of tears.

'You all right, Miz Nina?'

'Yes.' She did not open her eyes. 'Just a headache.'

The car purred along, George Biff making no attempt to get out of line in the traffic and overtake other cars. All the Beauforts had expensive cars, but only Nina had a Rolls-Royce, one of the few in the city. Margaret, who cared too much about such things, being political, thought it a little *nouveau-riche* for the Middle West, something one might expect from the new millionaires who wished to make their wealth conspicuous. But Nina had always had her own way and this was her second Rolls-Royce. Her only concession to inconspicuousness was that both cars had been black and that George Biff was under strict instructions not to show any arrogance in traffic. Not that a Rolls would have had much deference from the local wheelborne peasants.

'Be on the Parkway in a minute. You just relax back there.'

'I am relaxed.' Nina opened her eyes. 'Don't be such an old fusspot, George. Sometimes I think you should have been a mammy.'

George grinned. 'Would of got me locked up, a black mammy chasing some of them black gals like I used to. Don't think I ever heard of a gay black mammy. Here's the Parkway. Nearly home.'

2

Ward Parkway runs south out of Kansas City and is lined with some of the more magnificent homes in the nation. There is no consistency of style, unless conspicuous expenditure of money is in itself a style. French Regency, English Tudor, Southern Colonial: the great-granddaughter of Scarlett O'Hara waves across the manicured lawns to a blue-rinsed Elizabeth R of Missouri. Yet even though the homes are symbols of the wealth of their owners, vulgarity, like the weeds in the expensive lawns, is not allowed to flourish. Reticence, if such a trait is possible in a $500,000 mansion set back only yards from a busy thoroughfare, is looked upon as desirable as being white, Protestant and Republican. Some Catholic Democrats managed to settle along the Parkway, most notably the political boss Tom Pendergast, but they appear to have done little to change the ideas of the majority as to what is right and proper for such an address. When a Catholic President moved into the White House, black crêpe was observed hanging in the windows of one or two of the older mansions. It is only fair to add that they did not hang crêpe in their windows when President Nixon moved *out* of the White House.

The original Beaufort house had been one of the first to be built along the Parkway. Thaddeus Beaufort, the founder of the family fortune, built the house as he had built his wealth: solidly, conservatively and to last. The architect, made light-headed by the commission, had mixed his design but somehow avoided vulgarity; the mansion was an amalgam of English Elizabethan manor house and French chateau, without the libidinous air of either. The property had once taken up fifty acres of a whole block and had been known as Beaufort Park; a private park which the public hoi-polloi could only admire through the spiked iron-railing fence surrounding it. Peacocks, avian, not human, had strutted the lawns; Thaddeus, walking the paths of his estate every evening summer and winter, had always worn black. His wife Lucy wore only mauve; walking together, they offered no competition to the peacocks. Sunday afternoons the hoi-polloi would stand outside the iron railings and whistle at both the peacocks and the Beauforts, but got no recognition from either. Late in life Lucy bore her only child, Lucas, and he too was dressed in dark clothes as he grew out of babyhood. Walking their rounds, the father, mother and small boy looked like a tiny funeral cortège trying to find a graveside ceremony.

Lucas grew up to marry Edith Pye, whose father was one of the principal stockholders in the Kansas City Railroad and who also owned half of Johnson County just over the State line in Kansas. When Thaddeus and Lucy died within six months of each other, in 1923, they left Lucas $220 million, which, with what Edith had inherited from *her* parents, made Lucas and Edith the richest couple in Missouri; all that in a day when income tax, compared to what was to come, was no more unbearable than an attack of hives. Lucas and Edith's money continued to grow since, as any Wall Street farmer will tell you, there is no fertilizer better for growing money than other money.

The Beauforts had never been as ostentatious in the display of their wealth as the rich in the East: the caliphs of New York and Newport had had a barbarous bad taste that had both frightened and offended Thaddeus. His granddaughters had inherited his discretion, to a degree; it was foolish to be too reclusive about one's money, because that only aroused the suspicions of the tax men. Part of the land had been sold off, but the estate still covered just over twenty acres. Nina occupied the original big house and beside it, on the northern side of a private street, three other mansions, slightly less grand but still formidable, housed the other sisters. The peacocks had gone and so had most of the fifty servants and gardeners who had once worked on the estate. But no strangers, passing by the empty lawns, would have mistaken

13

the houses for empty museums or institutions. The Beaufort sisters, even when not visible, had their own vibrancy.

The Rolls-Royce pulled in through the big gates that still provided the main access to the estate. The uniformed security guard saluted Nina; as a child she had been saluted, less formally, by the guard's father. The car went up the curving drive, past the big maples and the bright blaze of azaleas, and pulled up in front of the big main house. Nina got out, said a short *thanks* to George, went inside and straight up to the main bedroom that looked out towards the gates.

She took off her dress and lay down on the wide double bed. Even in the years between her marriages, here at home and in the houses she had rented abroad, she had always slept in a double bed. As if the sleeping place beside her would, inevitably, once again be filled. As it had been, and happily, for the past three years.

She had been lying there an hour when she heard the car coming up the drive.

Downstairs George Biff, who doubled as butler on the latter's day off, alerted by the security guard on the intercom, went to the front door and opened it as the tall blond young man got out of the red compact and came up the steps.

Nina slipped on a robe and went out on to the gallery above the curving staircase. 'What is it, George?'

George looked up in surprise: his mistress normally never came asking who was at her door. 'A Mr Harvest to see you, Miz Nina. He don't say why he want to see you.'

'Why do you want to see me, young man?'

Harvest licked his lips, a hint of nervousness that one would not have expected in him. 'Miss Beaufort – ' His voice was tight; he cleared his throat. 'I believe I am your son Michael.'

# Chapter Two

◆

# Nina

I

Nina Beaufort met Tim Davoren in Hamburg in the fall of 1945, the happiest accident of her life up till then.

It was not her first visit to Europe. In the spring of 1936 Lucas and Edith Beaufort took the three children they then had, Nina, Margaret and Sally, on a grand tour of the Continent. Lucas, who had been nurtured as an isolationist from an early age by his father, had not wanted to make the trip; if the family *had* to travel out of Missouri, there were another forty-seven very good and interesting United States to be explored. But Edith, who had graduated from Vassar, a notoriously internationally-minded school, had insisted that she and the children needed more perspective than any Americán trip, even to outlandish California, could give them. So the three Beaufort sisters, aged twelve, seven and three, eager for perspective, whatever that was, left Kansas City with their parents, a governess, a nurse, George Biff and twenty-two pieces of luggage for New York and the maiden voyage of the *Queen Mary*.

Once at sea and committed to the trip, Lucas, a man who cut his losses and made the most of what was left, began to enjoy himself. He smiled indulgently as his daughters paraded the deck singing *Onward Townsend Soldiers*, even though he detested the socialist crank, Francis Townsend, who was the New Messiah to pensioners all over America. He danced with Edith to the tune of *The Music Goes Round and Round*; he relaxed in a deck chair and read an advance copy of a book called *Gone With The Wind* and was glad that his Edith was not like Scarlett O'Hara. He went to the ship's cinema with his wife and daughters and saw Shirley Temple in *Captain January* and wondered aloud why all American children could not be like the cute curly-haired charmer. When Nina threw up in the cinema, everyone put it down to sea-sickness.

Lucas' only bout of sea-sickness came when he learned that Tom Pendergast and his wife were also on board the *Queen Mary*. The political boss' European trip had been well publicized before he left Kansas City; but, careful of the Irish vote, he had neglected to tell the reporters that he was travelling on a British ship. The *Queen Mary* was just passing the Statue of Liberty when Nina brought her father the news.

'Stop the ship!' Lucas ordered his wife.

'I can't,' said Edith placidly. 'Now settle down, sweetheart. It's only for five days. You don't have to walk arm in arm with the dreadful man all the way across the Atlantic.'

Nina giggled and, though she was his favourite, her father glowered at her. 'There is nothing to be laughed at about that man.'

'Is he really so wicked, Daddy?'

Mr Pendergast certainly didn't look wicked. She and Margaret trailed him all across the ocean, spying on him from behind deck chairs, air funnels and lifeboats. He would wink at them and wave, as if they might be Democratic voters of the future, and they would wave back, though they never told their father. The elder Beauforts and the Pendergasts would occasionally pass each other and though Tom Pendergast would smile expansively, Lucas would only nod stiffly and pass on.

Edith had wanted to visit Spain, but the Spanish, not knowing the Beauforts were coming, inconveniently started a war amongst themselves. So the family spent more time in Germany where Lucas and Edith, paying a courtesy call at the American Embassy in Berlin, were offered the chance to meet Adolf Hitler at a reception. Lucas was impressed by the charm and affability of Der Fuehrer and a week later he and Edith, with the children in tow, met Hitler again at a trade fair in Munich. The German leader showed his attraction for children and Nina, Margaret and Sally were photographed smiling up at the man they obviously thought would make a marvellous uncle. Back home the *Kansas City Star* ran the picture on Page One and everyone but the few Jews in the city remarked on the proper recognition that the élite of Kansas City had been given, much more than

16

they got in New York or Washington.

Nina, for her part, fell in love with the old towns and castles of Germany and determined to return some day on her own. As she grew older and moved into her teens she found it hard to believe the stories she now read about Hitler, but by the time she was in college she hated him and the Nazis as fiercely as did anyone she knew. Except perhaps the Jews, but there were not too many Jewish girls at Vassar.

She graduated in June 1945. Her father had argued that she should go to a college nearer home, where she would not only be under his eye but also under the proper influences. But her mother, still talking about perspective, had prevailed and Nina had gone East to Sodom, Gomorrah and Vassar. She came home and told her parents she wanted to go to Europe with the United Nations Relief and Rehabilitation Agency and help re-build Germany.

'Impossible,' said her father and even her mother agreed. 'You're too young for such an adventure.'

'I'm not thinking of it as an adventure,' said Nina. 'I thought of it as something I should do, a social duty if you like.'

'There is plenty you can do right here in Kansas City.' Lucas had missed his favourite all the time she had been East; he did not want to lose her again so soon, certainly not to foreigners who had got themselves into their own mess. 'Returning GI's, for instance. The Red Cross would be glad to have you help them.'

'I want to go to Germany,' said Nina stubbornly.

'Why?' asked her mother.

But Nina couldn't tell her parents that she wanted to escape from Kansas City, from being a Beaufort. 'I've already applied to UNRRA, but they won't have me. They said they wanted older people with more experience.'

'You see?' said her father. 'Stay at home and join the Red Cross. I'll buy you a new car.'

'Don't be stupid, sweetheart,' said Edith, who began to recognize in her daughter something of herself that she had forgotten. 'You aren't going to bribe her with an automobile. She still has the MG we gave her – '

'I'll give that to Margaret,' said Nina, glowing with zeal, feeling like a Missouri relative of Francis of Assisi.

'Darling,' said her mother, who reserved *sweetheart* for her husband, 'these – UNRRA? – people do have a point, don't they? About your being too young.'

'What's wrong with being young? Youth has more energy and maybe more compassion than older people.'

17

'I knew she shouldn't have gone to Vassar,' said Lucas; then sighed because he knew he couldn't refuse his favourite anything she asked. 'What do you want me to do?'

'Write to President Truman and ask him to have me put on the American team for UNRRA.'

'Ask a favour of that feller in the White House? I'd rather commit suicide!'

'You can't,' said Edith, who had her own way of deflating her husband. 'The Nichols and the Kempers are coming to dinner tomorrow night. You can telephone President Truman. He'll always take a call from Kansas City.'

'Not when he hears who's calling. He knows I can't stand him.'

'Just be thankful you don't have to approach him through Tom Pendergast.' The political boss had died six months before, a bright occurrence only dimmed for Lucas by the succession a little later of Harry Truman to the Presidency. 'Call the White House now. Harry Truman is an early riser.'

'*Harry?* When did you get so familiar with him?'

But Lucas rang Harry Truman and the President spoke to someone who spoke to someone and in August 1945 Nina sailed for Europe as an accredited worker for UNRRA.

On the night before she left home the four girls gathered in Nina's room. Margaret was now almost sixteen, Sally was twelve and Prue, the late arrival, was five-and-a-bit. Nina had laid out the treasured possessions of her childhood and girlhood and invited her sisters to take their pick.

'You're not going to be a nun.' Margaret was jealous of her sister's chance for adventure. 'You might want to keep these when you come back.'

'Can I have your car?' Sally was mechanical-minded and not interested in any of the things laid out on the bed. 'I'll drive it around the gardens.'

Prue was picking over what was offered. 'I'll take them all,' she said.

Nina hugged her youngest sister, gazed at the other two. 'I'm just the first. When you are all old enough, we should all go out and help the poor of the world.'

'What's the poor of the world?' asked Prue.

'I think we'd all look rather silly trying to be Sisters of Charity,' said Margaret, practical-minded. 'We can always get Daddy to write a cheque. The poor don't want people like us fussing over them.'

'They needn't know who we are. We could always change our name!'

'I don't want to change my name,' said Sally.

'I do,' said Prue. 'I'd like to be called Mickey Rooney.'

A few weeks later Nina wished she had changed her name before applying to UNRRA. She crossed the Atlantic on the *Queen Mary* on a return trip after it had transported almost a division of GI's back home. The music this time was *Rum and Coca-Cola*, but there was no dancing; Tom Pendergast was dead, but a British merchant naval officer winked and waved at her and got no further than the political boss had nine years before. She landed in Southampton and flew from England to Frankfurt in Germany in a MATS cargo plane. She landed in Frankfurt on the day that the atom bomb was dropped on Hiroshima on the other side of the world; but the bang wasn't heard and nobody seemed to hear or even feel the ripples spreading into the future. The UNRRA people were waiting for her, some of them with quite open hostility. They made it plain that they thought theirs was no job for spoiled rich kids with political pull. For the first time she realized there was a handicap to being a Beaufort.

Her boss was a retired colonel who had worked with Herbert Hoover on the American Relief Administration after World War One. 'Don't worry, Miss Beaufort. I was young then and there was the same opposition towards me. But some day the young are going to take over the world.' Then added, because he, too, had grown old, 'God help it.'

'Am I doing a good job, Colonel Shasta?'

'As well as anyone on the team. I have to go up to Hamburg next week and see the British. Would you care to come with me as my driver and secretary?'

'Won't that cause gossip, Colonel?'

'I hope it does. I'll be flattered. But you'll be safe with me, Miss Beaufort. I'm that old-fashioned sort, a faithful husband. My wife, who lives in Harrisburg, Pennsylvania, also happens to have antennae than can pick up any immoral thoughts I may have on this side of the Atlantic. I believe it is called extrasexual perception.'

So in October, two months after landing in Germany, Nina drove up to Hamburg with Colonel Shasta. She had become accustomed to the bomb damage she had seen around Frankfurt, but it was still a shock to pass through the towns on the way north and see how widespread was the destruction of Germany. They passed queues of people standing outside shops, Germans wearing

19

the wardrobe of the defeated, half-uniforms, thin ersatz tweed, worn fur coats, and all with the same pale, hopeless faces. The jeep was halted by a military policeman at a cross-street and Nina became acutely aware of the people standing on the sidewalk waiting to cross. She was wearing for the first time the camel hair coat that her mother had had made for her and specially dyed a not-too-unbecoming khaki. She looked at a young girl her own age, saw the thin cotton dress covering the thin bony body; the girl stared back at her, face expressionless. Then Nina saw the envy and hate in the dark eyes and she turned away, too inexperienced in the expressions victors should wear.

'Don't show pity,' said Colonel Shasta, who had been watching her. 'That's the last thing they want.'

'It's difficult not to show it.'

'Tell that to the men who fought them.'

They drove into Hamburg, crossed the Lombard Bridge and after getting lost several times at last found the office Colonel Shasta was looking for. It was in a large house two blocks back from the Altersee; next door to it was another large house that was a club for British officers. Except that they needed a coat of paint, neither house looked as if it had suffered at all from the war.

'Rather grand, aren't they?' Nina said. 'I wonder if any Germans still live around here?'

'Every house in the street has been commandeered,' said a voice behind her and Colonel Shasta. 'The fruits of victory. I was told you were due here today. I'm Major Davoren, Commanding Officer of the unit that's taken over this house. I'm afraid UNRRA has been moved to a larger but less attractive place than this.'

He was dark-haired, good-looking, with a black moustache and dark eyes that might have been tired or just bored. He was tall, with heavy shoulders, and a certain ease of movement that suggested he might have been an athlete before the war. There was a row of ribbons on the breast of his battle tunic, including, Nina was to learn later, the ribbon of the Military Cross.

'Could you have someone direct us?' Shasta asked.

'I'll take you there myself.' He got into the back of the jeep and, it seemed, looked at Nina for the first time. 'Straight ahead, driver, then second right.'

'This is Miss Beaufort,' said Shasta, grinning. 'I don't think she is accustomed to being called Driver.'

'Awfully sorry.' But Davoren's apology sounded perfunctory.

'Shall we go, Miss Beaufort?'

Nina let in the gears with a crash and the jeep jerked forward. Out of the corner of her eye she saw Shasta grin again, but Major Davoren was behind her and she couldn't see how he had reacted. She hoped she had snapped his head off.

Five minutes later they drew up outside a large block of apartments that had been converted into offices. Shrapnel marks pitted the walls and there was a huge black scorch mark stretching up a side wall, as if someone had tried to burn a hole in it with a giant blowtorch. The block had none of the dignity of the house they had just left.

'Blame us English,' said Davoren. 'I'm afraid the army is claiming all the best for itself. As I said, the fruits of victory.'

'You don't believe in rehabilitation for the Germans?' said Nina.

'The young and idealistic,' said Davoren, who couldn't have been more than eight or nine years older than Nina. 'Could you spare me a few minutes with Miss Beaufort, Colonel?'

'I'll be inside.' Shasta climbed out of the jeep. 'Don't scratch his eyes out. I think we're still supposed to be allies.'

He went into the apartment block, carrying his valise, and Davoren slid into the vacated seat beside Nina. 'Well, we seem to have got off on the wrong foot.'

'You have, not me.'

'I've been fighting these bloody Germans for five and a half years. I'm not naturally vindictive, but I haven't yet got round to feeling magnanimous. I lost my parents and my only sister in an air raid on London, wiped out by a V-2. What are you doing for dinner this evening?'

She was surprised to hear herself say, 'Nothing.'

That was Friday and he took her to dinner at the Atlantic Hotel. The dining-room was full of British officers in khaki, Control Commission personnel in blue and German women in tow. There appeared to be no German men and only a few British women, all of whom looked with hatred at the *Fraulein*, none of whom was less than good-looking and most of whom were beautiful.

'Fraternization doesn't seem to worry you men. What would happen if one of those English girls came in here with a German man?'

'She'd be shown the back door. We have to have standards, you know.'

'Double standards, you mean.'

'Of course. What else makes the world go round?' But he

smiled as he said it and his charm almost persuaded her that he only half-meant what he had said.

He took her home early to the billet where she was staying for the weekend. 'There's a curfew on and some of the MP's can get a bit bloody-minded if they catch an officer with a good-looking girl. Pity you're not staying here at the Atlantic, you could have invited me up to your room.'

She let that pass. 'I stayed here with my parents when I was a child.'

He raised an eyebrow. 'You did it in style. I came to Hamburg for a week before the war. I stayed in a dreadful sleazy little room over behind the Reeperbahn. Girls kept knocking on my door all night.'

'Poor you.'

Saturday night he took her to a cabaret in the cellar of a bombed-out theatre. This time there were plenty of Germans, men as well as women; some of them looked remarkably well-fed for people whose official food ration was supposed to be only 1000 calories a day. Nina peered through the cigar and cigarette smoke, listened with her Berlitz-acquired ear to the conversations going on around her.

'They are making business deals!'

'Black marketeers,' said Davoren. 'This cabaret is the sort of stock exchange for it all. If you want to make any money on your PX issue, this is the place to come.'

'I don't need money.' He knew nothing about her or her family; she revelled for the first time in anonymity, as if it were some sort of vice. 'Do you come here and sell things?'

'No. I'm not really interested in money. I shouldn't say no to a fortune, but I don't care for this piecemeal way of getting rich. Oh, I daresay in ten or fifteen years' time some of those jokers will be fat, rich pillars of society – that is, if Germany ever gets off the ground again. And some of our own chaps are making a nice little bundle. But it's not for me.'

'Don't you have any ambition? I don't mean for this sort of thing. But – '

'Not really. I'm a day-to-day type. I'll probably stay on in the army and if I don't blot my copy-book I'll retire as at least a brigadier. All that without having to fight another war – I'll be dead before there's another one.'

'My God, what a limited vision!'

'Oh, it has its compensations. You, for instance. Would I have met you if I'd been back in some office in London trying to make my fortune?'

'What did you do before the war? Had you any ambition then?'

'I had just come down from Cambridge when my country called me. I started out to be an archaeologist, studied Arabic, was going to dig up all Tutankhamen's relatives. But I grew tired of that and I read History instead. One of the things I learned from that was that ambitious men usually finished up dead ahead of their appointed time.'

'You should have met my grandfather. He was ambitious at ten and he lived till he was eighty.'

'Ah, but did he succeed in his ambitions?'

'Up to a point,' she said and he smiled, mistaking her caution.

Then a man came to their table, bowed to Nina, clicked his heels and shook hands with Davoren. He was small, blond, tanned, athletic: ten years ago Nina could see him springing off vaulting-horses into posters extolling the Youth Movement. Or spurting out of starting-blocks in pursuit of Jesse Owens and the other black Americans at the Berlin Olympic Games. Davoren named him as Oberleutnant Schnatz, late of the Luftwaffe.

'A good German, aren't you, Rudi? Well, not a Nazi. But his morals aren't the best.'

Schnatz smiled, unoffended. 'Morality is only a matter of degree, Tim, you know that. After what we have been doing to each other for the past six years, what is a little black market?'

'Rudi went to Oxford,' Davoren explained. 'They always had less concern for morality there than we at Cambridge. We played tennis against each other, each of us got a Blue. Baron von Cramm once tried to seduce him at Wimbledon, but I never got that far. What can I do for you, Rudi, though the answer is no, in advance.'

Not even Vassar, let alone Kansas City and the Barstow School, had prepared Nina for the decadence she was witnessing. Two girls went dancing by, arms wrapped round each other, oblivious of the sneers of the men watching them. Three whores came in, sat down and were in business at once; three pink-cheeked British subalterns fell on them like choirboy rapists. Four men sat at a corner table, heads close together, greed giving them a family resemblance. Evil, or anyway sin, hung in the air as thick as the cigar and cigarette smoke and Nina shivered with the thrill of it. She knew that back in the Thirties Kansas City had been known as America's Sin City, but it could never have been like this. Without knowing it she was suffering from the tourist's astigmatism, seeing foreign evil as worse and much more interesting than the home-grown variety.

23

'I understand your lady friend is an American. I'm looking for contacts in the American zone.'

Nina saw Tim Davoren sit up a little straighter in his chair, felt his legs brush against hers under the table as they tensed. A thin blonde girl with a clown's face had come out on to the small stage at the end of the cellar and was singing *Little Sir Echo* in German; or so Nina thought, till she caught some of the words and realized it was an obscene parody that had the audience who understood it holding their sides. But she was listening with only half an ear, more intent on Tim Davoren and Rudi Schnatz.

'Rudi old chap, you're asking for a poke in the nose. British heavyweights have never been much good, but I think I could flatten you.'

'You are twice my size, old chap. I'm not Max Schmeling.'

'I shouldn't have threatened you if you were.'

'You may not be brave,' said Nina, 'but I'll poke anyone in the nose who says you're not gallant.'

Schnatz smiled, taking her remark as encouragement for himself. 'Miss Beaufort, I would not wish to get you in trouble either with Major Davoren or your American authorities. But there is a lot of unrest in the American zone, I'm told. A lot of GI's wish to go home. Some of them may like to make some money to take home with them. If you should hear – '

'Go away, Rudi,' said Davoren, 'and don't trouble the lady. I mean it.'

Schnatz looked at him, then at Nina: neither of them was smiling. The rest of the room laughed its head off at the clown singer; the lesbians rose behind Schnatz, hand in hand, heading for their bed. He bowed to Nina, nodded to Davoren and went away, disappearing behind the lesbians into the smoke and laughter.

Davoren took Nina's hand, pressed it. 'I know Rudi wasn't a Nazi and I don't think he's a criminal, not at heart. But if he should try to get in touch with you again, give him – I think you call it the bum's rush. Those chaps are going to get into an awful lot of trouble one day.'

Sunday night he took her to bed, in his room in the big house where he was billeted with seven other officers. He was surprised when she told him she was a virgin and he lay back on the pillow and scratched his head as if puzzled and worried.

'You mean you've never had a lover?'

'Depends what you mean by lover. I don't think I've actually been *in love*. I had crushes on several boys I met at college and I had what I suppose you call affairs. But all I did was some heavy

24

petting. I never went all the way.'

'All the way. It sounds like jumping off a cliff.'

'To a girl, losing her virginity *is* like jumping off a cliff. You only do it once. Lose your virginity, I mean. After that I suppose it becomes, um, a habit.'

'Don't ever think of love-making as a habit. The postures of it are ludicrous, but it's still a beautiful experience. And beautiful experiences are not the result of habit.'

'How many girls have you made love to? You sound like Casanova. Where are you going?'

'To get the international defence weapon – a French letter. You obviously haven't come prepared.'

'I think my father would die if I got pregnant.'

'I don't see the connection, unless American fathers have some sort of umbilical union with their daughters.'

'Would you marry me if you got me pregnant?'

'Are you proposing to me?'

'I don't know – am I? Good God, how things sneak up on you! I think I am in love with you.'

He kissed her gently. 'You're far too honest, darling heart. And too forward. You should have let me speak first.'

'Shut up and get back into bed.'

But as he entered her she knew she had indeed spoken too soon, that he was not in love with her.

She went back to Frankfurt next morning with Colonel Shasta who asked her no questions but looked as if he had the answers anyway. All he said when they got back to Frankfurt was, 'Take care, Nina. Germany right now is no place to make commitments. You're very young.'

'You sound like my father, Colonel.'

'I'm trying to. I have a daughter your age back home.' Then he asked his only question: 'Does Major Davoren know who your family are?'

'Not yet.'

'You'd better tell him, then. It may tell you, one way or the other, whether his intentions are honourable or not.'

But she didn't tell Tim, at least not for a couple of months. They met each weekend in villages and towns between Frankfurt and Hamburg, finding accommodation in inns and small hotels that had not been requisitioned by the Military Government. By the time she found she was pregnant he had told her he loved her and she believed him. Or wanted to.

They were in a village on the border of the American and British zones. From the inn they could see the white empty fields stretching away under the grey sky; the dark green river appeared unmoving as it curved below the village. Beyond the river a small copse looked like stacked firewood, black and leafless; two blackbirds sat motionless on a fence, like ebony ornaments. It seemed to Nina that all the seasons had stopped forever in an eternal winter. Despite the fire in the grate in their bedroom she felt cold, colder and more miserable than she had ever felt in her life before.

'I didn't expect you to be *pleased*. But I hoped you'd – *understand*. At least that.'

He stood beside her at the window, but not touching her. From the side of the inn came shouts and laughter as some children fought their own war with snowballs.

'I do understand – if that's the word you want. I'm not an utter bastard, darling. And I'd be pleased, too – in other circumstances.'

'What other circumstances?'

'Why didn't you tell me your family is rich? Really rich?'

'Who told you?' she demanded.

'Simmer down. Wasn't I supposed to know? Rudi Schnatz told me – evidently he made his contacts in the American zone after all. I suppose my English insularity is to blame – if I were really educated I should have known that you are right up there with Barbara Hutton and that other American heiress – Dorothy Duke? *Doris* Duke. But I'm not educated. I obviously took the wrong subjects at Cambridge.'

'Oh, for God's sake stop it! None of that's important – '

'You thought it was or you would have told me. Were you afraid I'd fall in love with your money instead of you? You didn't trust me, that's the important point.'

She knew he was right. But she was too worried and upset to make concessions; unaccustomed to crises, she reacted selfishly. 'What are we going to do then? I'm not going to have an abortion.'

'Well, that leaves only one alternative, doesn't it?' He sounded disappointed that she had vetoed an abortion; or perhaps her angry and frightened ear only made him sound that way. 'We'll have to get married.'

'*Have* to? Good God!'

The children had given up their snowball fight and gone elsewhere. The inn was suddenly quiet, listening. She bit her knuckles, stifling any further outburst. Ladies never made a show of themselves: her mother stood invisible in the corner of the room, telling her how to behave. But her mother would never have got

26

herself into this situation and there was no knowing how she would have reacted if she had. All the decorum Nina had been taught in Kansas City meant nothing in a cold room in an inn in faraway Germany.

'I think we'd better spend the rest of the weekend talking this over. I'm sorry I got you into this, darling. Really.' He moved to take her in his arms, but she pulled away.

'No, I want time to think. Don't touch me – please. I can't stay the weekend – Colonel Shasta wants me back in Frankfurt tonight. They are expecting trouble from the GI's – there's a lot of talk about demonstrations. They want to go home. Colonel Shasta wants us all off the streets, just in case.'

'Do you want to go home, too?'

Suddenly she did want to go home. She felt miserable, frightened and selfish; the poor of the world would have to wait. Unconsciously she put a hand on her belly, as if the baby were already apparent. 'I'll have to. I don't think UNRRA would want this sort of bundle for Europe.'

'Stop that sort of talk! Cheapening yourself isn't going to help.'

She did up her camel hair coat, pulled on her gloves. 'We can't talk to each other in this mood.'

'I'd better see you back to Frankfurt.'

'I'll be all right. I'm not the helpless little mother just yet. I'll call you during the week, when I've thought some more. No, don't kiss me – ' She was close to tears: to have him kiss her would be like turning a key in a dam.

'I'll marry you,' he said quickly. 'Despite your family.'

He had made a mistake in adding the last sentence. She shook her head, realizing how much she belonged to those back home. She hadn't escaped by coming to Germany: she needed now, possibly always would, the security in which she had been brought up.

'I'm part of our family and they're part of me. That's something we'd have to understand right from the beginning. They won't be against you – why should you be against them?'

He sighed. 'I wasn't drawing battle lines. But if we marry, I'm marrying *you*, not them. I'd say the same whether they were rich or poor. I'll ring tonight to see if you got back all right.'

Driving back to Frankfurt in the jeep Colonel Shasta had lent her, Nina was only half-aware of the traffic. She did not see the US Army truck that stayed behind her all the way from the village north of Kassel right through to the outskirts of Frankfurt. As she came into the city she had to slow; traffic had thickened and after a few blocks came to a halt. She leaned out of the jeep and up ahead caught glimpses of soldiers spread out in a thick human barricade across the road. She could hear chanting, loud and angry: she had never thought the word *Home* could have any threat to it. At once she felt frightened and looked about for a way to get out of the traffic jam. She was not normally nervous and she wondered if approaching motherhood made one so; then she ridiculed the thought, laughing at herself. The row with Tim had just upset her, all she really wanted was to get back to her billet and burst into tears.

'We'll get you out of this, Miss Beaufort.' The GI, earflaps of his cap pulled down, thick woollen scarf wrapped round the lower half of his face so that his voice was muffled, had come up quietly beside the jeep. 'It looks pretty ugly up ahead. Just back up and follow us.'

She wondered who the soldier was, that he knew her name. Probably someone she had met on one of her visits to a military office; it was impossible to recognize him behind the scarf and earflaps. She put the jeep into reverse and followed the army truck as it backed up and swung into a side street. The sound of the chanting demonstrators was drowned now by truck horns being punched to the rhythm of the chant. Then a shot rang out and the blaring horns and chanting suddenly stopped. A moment later there were angry shouts and the sound of breaking glass. In a moment of imagination she wondered if she was hearing echoes of the Thirties: had the streets of Frankfurt clamoured like this when the SS had been rounding up the Jews? Street lights came on in the gloomy afternoon and the scene all at once became theatrical, a little unreal, a grey newsreel from the past. But the angry, yelling soldiers streaming down through the stalled traffic were real enough, frighteningly so.

She looked back and saw the GI gesticulating to her from the back of the army truck, which had turned round and was facing down the side street. She slammed on the brakes of the jeep, jumped out and ran to the truck. The GI reached down, grabbed her hand and lifted her easily, as if she were no more than a small child, into the back of the truck. The canvas flaps were pulled down and abruptly she was in darkness.

'Thanks. I'm glad you came – '

Then a hand smothered her face and she smelled chloroform on the rag that was pressed against her nose and mouth. She struggled, but an arm held her, hurting her. Then the darkness turned to blackness.

'My name is McKea, Magnus McKea,' said the tall American major in a voice that sounded slightly English; Davoren wondered if he had been an actor before he had joined the army. 'I'm with the legal staff down at Nuremberg on the War Crimes thing. Colonel Shasta suggested I should come up and see you. It's about Miss Beaufort.'

Davoren laughed, leaning so far back in his chair to let the laugh out that he looked in danger of falling over backwards. He was in his office in the big house on the Kasselallee, the walls papered with maps that he no longer looked at. Orderlies came and went in the corridor beyond the open door, all of them armed with the piece of paper that made them look as if they were too busy to be asked to do something by an officer or NCO. He was safe in British Army occupied territory and here was some Yank come to accuse him of something that was the best joke he had heard in ages.

'You mean Miss Beaufort's condition is a war crime?'

Major McKea looked puzzled. 'Don't joke, Davoren. Kidnapping is a crime, period.'

Davoren sat up straight, suddenly sober. 'Good Christ – she's been *kidnapped*?'

'Yesterday some time. She didn't return to her billet last night – '

'I know. I rang the billet, but some girl said she thought she'd seen Miss Beaufort come in and go out again.'

'She was mistaken. Miss Beaufort never got to her billet. Her jeep was found abandoned in a Frankfurt suburb last night. An hour later Colonel Shasta got a ransom note to be passed on as quickly as possible to her father. He signalled Washington and they got in touch with Kansas City. I was brought in to represent Mr Beaufort till he gets here – my father is the Beaufort family lawyer. Nina's father is being flown over by the Air Force. He's expected in Frankfurt sometime tomorrow.'

Davoren was silent, but his face was expressive enough; he was too close to the war, to the cheapness of life, to be hopeful. Then he looked across at McKea. 'I'm sorry I laughed. It was a stupid private joke.'

'You said something about Miss Beaufort's condition. Is she pregnant?'

Davoren nodded. 'Does her father know about me?'

'I don't know, unless Nina wrote him. I don't think anyone knows about you, except Jack Shasta. He thought you should be told.'

'Why didn't he tell me last night?'

'I don't know. I guess he was too concerned with getting in touch with Nina's father.' He lit a pipe, puffed on it. 'I've known Nina since she was just a kid. We were never close, she's about ten or twelve years younger than I, but I always liked her.'

Davoren saw the enquiring look through the haze of pipe smoke. 'I love her, if that's what you're asking me. I didn't think of her as just someone to jump into bed with.'

McKea ran a hand over his crew-cut, thinning red hair. 'I didn't mean to imply – sorry.'

Davoren got up, closed the door against the traffic in the corridor. This was no longer British Army occupied territory: it was his own and very personal, too. He remained standing, his back to the maps on the wall. The maps were pre-war, marked with towns that now were only rubble: they only seemed to deepen the lack of hope he felt. Nina could be buried anywhere in the havoc.

'Is there any hint of who's kidnapped her?'

'Nothing definite. We think it's probably Krauts. God knows, they have enough reason to be asking for money.' It was difficult to tell whether McKea was critical of or sympathetic to Germans. But then he said, 'The country's full of communists and socialists, you know.'

Magnus McKea came from one of the oldest families in Kansas City, Missouri, a family whose conservatism had a certain hoariness to it. The army, and Europe itself, had opened up his tolerance, but he still tended to suspect any liberal thought that fell into his head, as if it might be the beginning of a brain tumour. He had a slightly fruity voice that almost disguised his Middle West twang. He had been fortunate or unfortunate enough, depending on one's point of view and ear, to have had an English grandmother who had refused to speak to him if he spoke to her in what she described as a nasal infection. His grandmother, in earlier times, would have been scalped for her arrogance towards the natives. He had not enjoyed Europe, neither the war, the Nuremberg trials nor the havoc and misery that passed for conquered territory. All he wanted was to go home, but he had too much sense of duty to demonstrate towards that end.

'Oh? I thought they'd all been killed off by the Nazis.'

McKea wasn't sure whether Davoren meant to sound sardonic or not. 'Not all of them. Half a million dollars, which is what they're asking – what's the matter?'

'The Beauforts are *that* rich?'

'I shouldn't imagine Lucas Beaufort would miss half a million dollars. Finding the money is no problem – I believe he is bringing it with him this evening. In the meantime we're looking for leads to the kidnappers, just in case – '

'Just in case they don't hand Nina back to her father?' Davoren tried to keep any emotion out of his voice; but he was suddenly afraid for Nina's safety. 'Are you expecting me to give you a lead?'

'We thought you might have a suggestion – '

Davoren clicked his fingers. 'Rudi Schnatz! Do you have transport?'

'I have a jeep and driver outside – '

'Let's use it!'

McKea, a man accustomed to taking his time, had to hurry to keep up with Davoren as the Englishman led the way out of the house. They got into the jeep, Davoren gave the driver directions and twenty minutes later they pulled up outside a decrepit old house just off the Elbchaussee. On the other side of the street a row of bombed-out houses, like jagged gravestones, was an ugly testimony to the recent past. On a broken wall was scrawled a plea for the future: *Let Communism Re-Build These!*

'You see?' said McKea. 'They're not all dead.'

'It's in English. Maybe some of our chaps put that there.'

McKea said nothing, dismayed that communists might have fought on the wrong side; he had already decided that the Russians at Nuremberg were the enemy of the future. Even the British, usually so reliable, had tossed out Churchill for Attlee and his socialists.

Davoren led the way up the chipped and cracked marble steps to the house. This had once been one of the best areas of the city, but all its smug dignity and prosperity had gone with the bombs. Davoren thought of the ruined sections of London and wondered which would be re-built first. The Yanks were already talking of re-building Europe before the Russians got too strong.

Rudi Schnatz was in a worn woollen dressing-gown with some sort of crest on the pocket: his day was just beginning. 'I say, old chap, it's a bit strong, isn't it, busting in on a chap like this?'

Davoren pushed into the two-roomed flat, away from the prying frightened faces that had already appeared at the other doors in the hallway and on the landing above. McKea, more polite, less belligerent, followed him, closing the door against the curious.

'Rudi, I don't have any time for manners.' Through the open door to the bedroom Davoren saw a naked girl sit up in a big brass-railed bed; then she lay down quickly again, pulling the blankets up over her. 'We're looking for Miss Beaufort – she's been kidnapped.'

Schnatz pulled his dressing-gown closer round his throat, almost a feminine gesture. 'Please, Tim – you don't think I've kidnapped her, do you?'

'If I thought that, you'd be out in the jeep now and on your way to the Provosts. No, I want to know who your contacts are in the American zone. The ones who told you who Miss Beaufort was. Is.' He corrected himself, like touching wood.

'Are they the ones who have kidnapped her?'

'We don't know. For Christ's sake stop wasting time with bloody questions – this has got nothing to do with you! Tell me who your contacts are, where we can find them!'

'I don't know that I can do that, old chap. Honour among thieves, you know – '

Davoren grabbed him by the front of the dressing-gown and lifted him off the floor. The Englishman's face was dark with anger, heightened by his bared teeth: he looked on the verge of a fit. 'Tell me who they are, Schnatz, or I'll break every bone in your body!'

There was a muffled scream from the other room. McKea crossed to the door and closed that one, too. He didn't have the true spirit of the conqueror, he was too much the lawyer. He just hoped Davoren wouldn't try to kill the little German, though it looked very possible. But he wouldn't interfere, not in the British zone.

Schnatz struggled, unafraid, ready to fight the bigger man. He gasped something in German and Davoren let him go so that he fell back on his heels.

'Who are they? Their names, bugger you, *their names!*'

Schnatz pushed back his long blond hair, shook his head. 'You're acting just like the Gestapo, old chap – '

'*Their names!*'

'Burns and Hiscox. They are with the Supply outfit just out-side Frankfurt on the road to Fulda – ' Davoren was already on his way out of the room and Schnatz shouted after him: 'Don't tell them I sent you! If they're not the ones, I'll still need them – '

Outside in the jeep Davoren said, 'Drive me back to my office,

I'll get my own car and driver.'

'I think you can safely leave it to us. After all, it's in our zone – '

'Don't start drawing bloody boundaries! Back to my office, driver, and get a move on!'

The driver looked at McKea: who did this goddam limey think he was? But McKea just nodded and the driver let in the gears and they sped back through the city.

Davoren picked up his own driver and the commandeered Mercedes which was his staff car. He invited McKea to ride with him in the more comfortable car and the American, after a moment's hesitation, accepted. They sat in the back seat while the Mercedes sped down the autobahn after the jeep. Davoren had calmed down, seemed almost morosely quiet. McKea stared out at the passing countryside, now fading into the thickening dusk. He preferred Germany at night, when so much was hidden by darkness. It was a relief from what he read and listened to at Nuremberg during the day.

At last Davoren said, 'What's Old Man Beaufort like?'

'Autocratic. Devoted to Nina – she's his favourite. Until we find the kidnappers, he'll probably choose you to blame for what's happened. We'll have to tell him, of course. I mean, about – ' McKea could see the driver in front of them half-turn his head, one ear cocked to follow the conversation.

'I'm already blaming myself,' said Davoren, careless of the driver. 'For everything.'

## 3

Nina had a headache and felt ill. So far she had had no morning sickness; but she was sick this morning. And cold and miserable and afraid. She sat on the floor of the bare room, wondering where she was. She could hear no sound from outside except the occasional harsh cry of a bird; she recognized country silence, remembering vacations spent on the Beaufort plantation down in the south-east corner of Missouri. The two men who had kidnapped her had fed her army rations last night and again this morning: at least they were not going to let her starve. They had given her two army blankets, but even with those and still wrapped in her camel hair coat, she had not been able to sleep for the cold. She had never felt worse in her whole life and only an

33

effort kept her from breaking down and weeping helplessly at her plight.

The door was unlocked and one of the men came into the room with a mug of steaming coffee. He was the one who had been driving the truck and she had not seen him until she had woken up in this room last night. He was a small man, in uniform and wearing a parka with the hood up; Air Force dark glasses covered his eyes. In the gloom of the room, with the only light coming through the cracks of the boarded-up window and through the half-open door, it was impossible to distinguish his features. He was just a dark body and head with a rough soft voice.

'Get this into you, honey. Sorry we can't give you any heat, but we don't want people coming around asking why smoke's coming outa the chimney. If your daddy don't fool around, you oughtn't to be here too long.'

Nina stood up, took the mug and almost scalded her throat as she gulped down the coffee. The man stood looking at her and she suddenly felt even more afraid: was he going to rape her? She tightened her grip on the mug, ready to hurl it if he moved towards her.

'I'm just looking at you.' The man's voice was most peculiar, as if he had a small bag of sand or gravel in his throat instead of a voice-box. 'We put a price of half a million bucks on you. You think you're worth that much?'

She almost said, *My father would think I'm worth much more;* but she was not so cold and miserable that her mind had stopped working. She suddenly realized how dangerous wealth could be. It was said that kidnapping in America had originated in Kansas City; people must have been abducted in colonial times, but it had been turned into a modern profession by gangsters in her home town. They had even kidnapped the city manager's daughter; Lucas Beaufort had wanted to broadcast a plea that the kidnappers come back for the city manager, too. The spate of abductions had frightened the wealthy citizens and for a while no children of rich families went anywhere without an escort. When Nina had gone to college her father had wanted a private guard assigned to her, but the Vassar board had been firm that their campus should not be turned into a security camp. From her early teens Nina had been aware that great wealth made her and her sisters different from other children, but, despite her father's concern, she had never really thought of it as endangering her. Now, chillingly, she knew better.

'Why are you doing this?'

But even as she asked she knew it was a foolish question, and the man laughed. 'You ain't that dumb, Nina. We're doing it for money. Ain't that what your old man and his old man worked for, screwed people for? We come over here, us GI's, to fight for a better world, that's what they told us. You need money for a better world, if you're gonna enjoy it properly. My partner and me, we been making a little on the side. But you're worth more than a truck-load of cigarettes, more than a whole PX.'

'They might hang you for kidnapping. They wouldn't do that for selling things on the black market.'

'The Krauts spent three years trying to shoot my ass off, but I survived. I think my luck's gonna hold. Nobody's gonna hang me. You work for UNRRA, but you don't know nothing about the real world. The real world is made up of people without money, and I don't mean just Krauts. We gotta take risks, we wanna get anywhere. You're lucky, you're never gonna have to take a risk in your whole goddam life!'

He sounded abruptly angry, though his voice didn't rise. He went out of the room, slamming the door behind him and locking it. Nina put the mug down on the floor, began to walk round the room in an effort to turn the blocks of ice in her shoes back into feet. She heard an engine start up outside and she went to the window and tried to peer out through the thin cracks between the boards. But all she could see was snow, a blank white mockery.

The truck, or whatever it was, drove away. When its sound had faded she stood listening, ears alert for any sound in the house. She could hear nothing; then the house creaked as if to reassure her that she had been left alone. She made up her mind that she was going to escape.

She had always been a resourceful girl, though never as good at practical matters as Margaret and Sally. She hoped she could get herself out of a locked, boarded-up room. One could not be more practical than to know how to escape from kidnappers.

Buoyed up by her own determination, she began at once to seek a way out of the room. Ten minutes later she was as depressed and miserable as when the kidnapper with the husky voice had come in. There was nothing in the room that she could use as a club to bash the boards away from the window; the door was too stout to be broken open and the lock would have defied Jimmy Valentine or any other cracksman. She sank down to the floor beside the fireplace and began to weep.

Then something fell into the grate, a lump of soot, and she

35

heard the flutter of wings in the chimney. She sat up, waited, then crawled into the fireplace and looked up. A film of soot floated down on to her face; but high up in the chimney she could see a small square of light. She withdrew from the fireplace, sat on her haunches and considered. Weighed her strength and size (would the chimney be too narrow and too high?) against the urge to escape. Weighed, too, her determination against her fear that the men would come back, find her trying to escape and vent their anger on her.

She measured the width of the chimney with her hands, decided it was wide enough to take her shoulders and hips. She took off her coat, knowing the bulk of it would handicap her once she began climbing up the narrow space. But she would need it once she was outside the house; she put the belt of it through the loop inside the collar, tied the belt round her waist and let the coat hang down between her legs. She pulled the knitted cap she wore down over her face to just above her eyes, pulled on her gloves. Then she crawled into the fireplace, stretched her arms above her, eased herself upright into the narrow blackness of the chimney and began to climb.

She was glad she was wearing stout winter shoes; she searched for and found tiny crevices in the chimney wall into which she drove her toes. The chimney had not been cleaned in years and she had climbed no more than her own height when she began to feel she was smothering. A bird suddenly fluttered out of the top of the chimney in a panic; soot cascaded down on her and she shut her eyes and turned her face downwards just in time. She lost her grip and went plunging down, scraping against the bricks, taking more soot with her. She hit the floor of the fireplace, feeling the jarring shock go right up through her body to her skull; but she remained upright, unable to fall over because the chimney held her like a brick corset. She held her breath, feeling the soot in a thick cloud about her face, waiting for it to settle. then she opened her eyes and stared into the blackness.

It seemed that every bone and muscle in her body hurt; her knees and ankles felt as if they might be broken. Her arms were trapped above her head; she could feel the pain where her elbows had been scraped as she fell. Her right knee felt as if there was an open wound in it and her right hip as if it had been kicked by a horse. She wanted to gasp for breath, but she was afraid that would mean sucking in a lungful of choking soot. She thought of the baby inside her, wondered if it was already beginning to miscarry. She was frighted, ready to scream, discovering, *now*, for the first time in her life, that she was claustrophobic.

36

But she held on to herself, didn't bend her knees, kept herself upright in the black prison of the chimney. She was on the point of hysteria, but, without recognizing it, something of the iron she had inherited from her parents and grandparents kept her from breaking. She continued to stare into the blackness, smelling the burned wall only an inch or two from her face, willing herself to believe that it was not going to collapse in on her and smother her. She was no longer cold, she could feel sweat running down her face and body. Some instinct told her that all she had to do was survive the next minute or two. If she didn't, if she gave in and retreated from the chimney, she knew she would never enter it again. And the chance of escape would be gone.

Then the hysteria passed, gone all of a sudden, as if wiped away by her will. She started to climb again, feeling more confident with every foot gained; soot continued to float down, but she ignored it, holding her breath till it had gone past. Her body was just one large ache, but she kept climbing, elbows, knees and ankles scraping against the brickwork. Then, all at once it seemed, the blackness turned to gloom, then there was light and a moment later her head cleared the top of the chimney.

She scrambled out, holding desperately to the chimney so that she would not slide off the snow-covered roof. She was on top of a farmhouse that was more ruin than building; the only rooms left intact were the one in which she had been imprisoned and the room immediately below it. The rest of the house was a shell; charred timbers, a tumble of bricks and a big bomb crater told their own story. All around her the fields lay white and empty.

It took her another five minutes to get down from the roof. Twice she almost fell; snow slid down beneath her like an avalanche and fell into the yard. Then she was down on the ground, stumbling through the mud and snow, running like a crazed person, whimpering like a child. She fell down twice before she realized she had tripped over the coat between her legs. She stood up, gasping for breath, giggling hysterically at herself, and struggled into the soot-blackened, mud-stained coat. Then, steadying herself, she walked out into the lane beside the yard and began to hurry away from the farm.

# 4

Davoren and McKea were stopped twice for speeding by military police, so that it was dark before they pulled into the warehouse on the Fulda road where the supply company was headquartered. The place seemed deserted and it took them a few minutes to find a soldier who could tell them where the adjutant was.

'What an army!' said Davoren. 'How did you chaps manage to win the war?'

'We won it, that's the point. It's over and everybody just wants to go home. Don't you?'

But Davoren didn't answer that, going instead to look for the adjutant, who told them, 'Burns and Hiscox? Sure, they're on weekend passes. They went off Friday night. I understand they do a little business on the side.'

'You condone that?' said Davoren.

The adjutant was fat, bald, homesick and not inclined to take any moralizing from an unknown Englishman 'The war's over, mac. Didn't you know?'

Outside the office Davoren spat into the dirty snow in the cobbled yard. But he made no comment on the adjutant, just said. 'Do we send your MP's looking for Burns and Hiscox?'

'We can't go looking for them ourselves.' McKea himself had a sour taste in his mouth at the sloppy moral attitude of the supply adjutant. 'I understand how you feel, Davoren. But I think we have to do this through the proper channels.'

'Bugger channels!' Then Davoren threw up his arms and let out a loud sigh that was almost a moan of pain. 'You're right. But Jesus Christ – '

'Let's go and see Jack Shasta. He may have heard something further.'

Colonel Shasta was in his office, even though it was Sunday night. 'I've been trying to call you, but Hamburg said you'd left, didn't know where you'd gone. It's a helluva way to run an army, I must say.'

Davoren looked at McKea, grinned, looked back at Shasta. 'Nobody's perfect.'

'We've been doing some sleuthing,' said McKea, all at once liking Davoren. 'We think we might have a lead. If you get in touch with the Provost-Marshal — '

'There's no need,' said Shasta. 'Miss Beaufort is safe.'

'Where?' The heart did not leap, said practical-minded medical men: but Davoren felt something rise in his chest. 'Where, for God's sake?'

She was asleep in her billet, a house on the edge of the bombed ruins of the old city. The other women in the house did not try to stop Davoren as he walked in, asked where Miss Beaufort's room was and went straight upstairs and into the room without knocking. He sat down on the edge of the bed and looked at her still asleep. She had been bathed and fed; her muddied and blackened clothes were in a heap in a corner of the room. But even in sleep her face showed the strain she had been under. She whimpered even as he looked at her and her body shook in a quick spasm. He bent and kissed her, feeling weak and empty himself, demolished by relief and love.

Nina opened her eyes, saw his face close to hers and started away in fear. Then she recognized him and her arms, the elbows decorated with chevrons of medical tape, came out from beneath the blankets and went round his neck.

'Let's go home.'

'Just what I had in mind,' he said, thinking of England.

# 5

They went home to Kansas City two months later.

Burns and Hiscox did not return from their weekend leave and were officially posted as deserters and never heard from again. Since kidnapping was not classified as a military crime, armies having indulged in it for centuries, they were not listed as suspected kidnappers. Military authorities, who had not even bothered to start a file on the Beaufort case, promptly forgot about it and went back to wondering what the hell one did with the peace when one had won a war. The black market continued to flourish, becoming a major industry, and the fed-up GI's gave up demonstrating and went back to gold-bricking, fraternizing and all the other important functions of an occupation force.

And Lucas Beaufort returned to Kansas City with his half a million dollars still unpacked. But not before meeting Nina's brand-new fiancé.

'Are you sure of him?' The army had given him a room which they kept for VIP's. Generals, senators, even Bob Hope had stayed in the room, but Lucas was unimpressed. They had left no presence that made him feel he was in better company than himself. 'He seems rather – cavalier, I think is the word.'

'Wasn't that what Grandfather was?'

'Not towards your grandmother. Only towards his business partners.' Lucas had no illusions about his father. 'Major Davoren says he wants to take you back to England. But he admits he has no prospects there, none at all.'

'I have my own money.'

'I'm sure he knows that.' Then, seeing the angry flush in her face, said, 'I'm sorry. I shouldn't have said that.'

'No, you shouldn't have, Daddy, and I'll never forgive you for saying it. Not about the father of my baby.'

'Dear God!' Lucas normally had only a social relationship with the Almighty. He attended Sunday service at St Andrew's Episcopal Church, where he sat in a reserved pew and wondered why God, if there was a God, answered the prayers of men like Roosevelt and Truman. 'You mean you're – ?'

'Pregnant. *Enceinte. Schwanger.* Or as the English put it, a bun in the oven.' Then, because it hurt her to hurt him, she impulsively put her hand on his. 'I'm sorry, Daddy – I shouldn't have said *that.* But you made me so angry – you're not being fair to Tim – '

Lucas took her hand in his. His face had a handsome boniness to it, but only his family ever saw it softened into his true good looks. 'Nina sweetheart, all I want is to be sure that you are happy. It's just that I have to re-adjust – your mother and I always expected you to marry someone from back home – '

'That's it, Daddy. You don't really want me to have a mind of my own. You don't want me to be anything but a Beaufort – '

'All right. I'll talk to Major Davoren.' Lucas didn't know how to cope with a daughter who showed such independence. Already back in Kansas City Sally and even young Prue, only five years old, were showing they had minds of their own. Only Margaret, the one to whom he showed the least favouritism (and was ashamed for his prejudice), seemed content to do what her parents wanted. 'But do you mind if I try to persuade him to come back to Kansas City? There's no future in England, not under that fellow Attlee.'

Nina made the concession, now secretly wanting to go home to Missouri. She had had enough of Europe, or anyway post-war Europe. All her charity had been frozen out of her by her fear for her own safety. She was ashamed of her selfishness, but she was

40

not the first to discover there are limits to one's self-sacrifice; she was even more ashamed that her limits had been so shallow. The older hands had been right: she had just been a rich kid playing at being a do-gooder.

'But don't press him, Daddy. Let him make the decision.'

Tim Davoren had stayed in Frankfurt and later that day Lucas, who had been in the city only once before, took him on a guided tour. 'This is where the Rothschilds began, did you know that?'

'So I understand. Goethe, too.'

'Gurter? Never heard of him.' Lucas had not been interested in the humanities at college; stick to the money subjects, his father had advised him. 'I was here in 1936. The Rothschild house was still standing then. Right over there.'

Tim Davoren knew he was being tested: for Nina's sake he showed interest. 'From small acorns etcetera, as they say in Kew Gardens.'

'Yes,' said Lucas, his suspicions rising again. 'I take it you are not very interested in the making of money?'

'I don't think I have the talent for it.'

'That doesn't necessarily disqualify you. Gamblers have no talent, but they are interested in making money. Do you gamble?'

'Not knowingly. But I suppose everyone gambles one way or another.'

'What are your talents, may I ask? I understand you are a good soldier, that you won the Military Cross. It's not much of a career, though, is it? Not in peace time.'

'I'm getting out of the army. I thought I might try teaching.'

'You'd soon tire of that,' said Lucas, as if he had known Tim all his life. 'You wouldn't think of coming back to Kansas City?'

'What would I do?' Tim kept his voice deliberately flat, a characteristic he had just before he was about to erupt.

'You could take your choice,' said Lucas, not entirely undiplomatic. 'Come back there and see what offers.'

Tim walked in silence letting his anger subside. He recognized that the older man was only trying to do the natural thing, protect his daughter. But he also recognized that Lucas was already trying to assert some authority over his future son-in-law. *And that's just not in your book, Tim old boy.*

'I'll talk it over with Nina.'

Lucas walked in silence, too. Then he seemed to accept that he could ask for no more. He nodded, then said, 'She tells me she is pregnant. How did that happen?'

'The usual way,' said Tim.

Lucas stopped, looked as if he were offended, then suddenly let out a gust of laughter, surprising Tim, who had decided that the older man had no sense of humour at all. 'Of course! Damnfool question – damn good answer. I'll tell her mother that. You'll like her mother. Has a sense of humour, something I haven't got. Gurter? You don't mean Go-eth, the poet, do you? You don't like poetry, do you?'

'Only if it rhymes,' said Tim, and Lucas seemed satisfied.

That evening Tim had dinner with Nina and her father, then took Nina back to her billet. He had sent the Mercedes and his driver back to Hamburg; they walked home through the ill-lit streets, careful of the ice on the cracked sidewalks. They stood just inside the doorway of her billet and, bundled up against the cold, embraced each other like a couple of bears.

'Darling heart, you shouldn't have told your father you were pregnant, not yet. You're too honest. Never be more than discreetly honest with people you have to live with.'

'Will that include you, too?' She kissed him, silencing his answer. She still had not recovered from her ordeal and she was in no condition to suffer lovers' truths. 'Mother would have guessed in time. Girls usually don't have babies six months after they're married.'

'Did what happened to you – there won't be a miscarriage?'

'I think he, or she, is going to be indestructible. I haven't even felt nauseous.' Then in the darkness, unable to see his face, she said, 'You don't mind going home with me to Kansas City?'

His head was stiff and unmoving against the light in the windows of the house opposite. 'No,' he said quietly.

But she wondered if he was being only discreetly honest with her. She was too afraid to ask. She drew the dark head towards her, felt for his lips with hers and kissed him, seeking a true answer there. But already she had learned that lips were no more truthful than the tongue.

Lucas Beaufort went back to Kansas City relieved and satisfied. Nina and Tim were married quietly by an army chaplain a week after he left, with Colonel Shasta and Major McKea as their witnesses. When Lucas arrived back in Missouri it was announced without fanfare that Miss Nina Beaufort, eldest daughter of Mr and Mrs Lucas T. Beaufort, had been quietly married three months earlier to Major Timothy Davoren, only son of the late Mr and Mrs Clive Davoren of London, England. If anyone in Kansas City wondered why a Beaufort girl, the first one to be married, should have wed so secretly, no one voiced their wonder in public. Not even when she arrived home in March 1946 obviously pregnant.

Word of the kidnapping had got out. However, since the kidnappee had escaped unhurt, the kidnappers had not been caught and no money had been handed over, editors gave the story only a narrow spread in their newspapers. Who in the rest of the world thought anyone from Kansas City was interesting? Even Harry Truman was at pains to say he came from Independence, though cynics said that was only a play on words to show he was not Tom Pendergast's man. Anyone passing through the two places wasn't sure where Kansas City ended and Independence began.

Edith Beaufort, adamant that she had to meet her new son-in-law before anyone else in Kansas City saw him, insisted that she and Lucas go to New York to meet the Davorens as they got off their ship. She liked Tim as soon as she met him and he liked her.

'You'll do,' she told him. 'You're much better than I expected or hoped for.'

'A bad advance report from Mr Beaufort?'

'Just say unenthusiastic. You're not American, specifically not from the Midwest, that's the main thing against you. He ignores the fact that he's only two generations removed himself from England. And his grandfather left under a cloud, as they say.'

'No cloud over me,' said Tim. 'The sun shines on me all the time. Especially when Nina is around.'

'Your charm is obvious, but I like it,' said Edith. 'If there is any charm from our local men, it's accidental and biennial. My husband is a good example. But I love him, Tim, and I hope you will love Nina just as much.'

They rode back from New York in a private railroad car. Nina and her mother watched the two men gradually thaw towards each other, but the thawing was slow, like two polite icebergs cruising down from Greenland. They were half-way between Columbus, Ohio, and St Louis before Lucas slapped Tim on the knee at one of the latter's jokes. By the time they got off at Kansas City they were *Tim son* and *Lucas old chap* and moved in a common cloud of cigar smoke. Nina and her mother felt the future was secure.

There were four cars at Union Station to meet the train. One car contained the other three Beaufort sisters and Edith's secretary, Miss Stafford; one car was for Lucas and Edith; another was for the newly married couple; and the fourth took the luggage. They moved out to a fanfare of flash-bulbs from the press photographers.

'Do you usually travel in convoy?' said Tim as he and Nina settled back in the pre-war Packard.

43

'Only for weddings and funerals. Darling, please – take it all for granted. Please?'

He laughed: nervously, it seemed to her, though she had never thought of him as having nerves. 'I'm not *over*whelmed, but I'm certainly whelmed. Even that – ' He nodded at the glass partition which separated them from the chauffeur. 'We have those in England still, but I thought it had all gone out in democratic America.'

'Don't refer to it as Democratic America,' she said, misunderstanding his adjective. 'Daddy is a Republican. This car belonged to my grandmother – you can see how old it is. She didn't believe in servants listening to their mistress' conversation. Neither do I. What's wrong with a car with a glass partition?'

'It's not just the car. It's just *everything*. The private railway carriage, your father bringing half a million dollars to Germany in a couple of suitcases . . . Take it for granted, she says.'

'It's the only way.'

'You were born to it. I'll try, my love, but don't blame me if I occasionally get a glazed look in my eye.' Then a little later he said, 'What's this?'

'Home.'

'Well, I suppose King George has to say the same when someone asks him about Buckingham Palace. Where are *we* going to live?'

'We're having our own suite for the time being, in that wing there. Daddy is going to build us a house in the park. Something smaller,' she added as he looked at her out of the corner of his eye.

'Let it be as big as you want,' he said expansively. 'If I'm going to take it all for granted, I may as well not be cramped.'

Nina was relieved at how her three sisters took to Tim. 'He's absolutely out of this world!' exclaimed Margaret. 'He's *thrilling!*'

Sally, equally thrilled, rolled her eyes in ecstasy. 'And he's got you pregnant – already! He's a quick worker.'

'Most husbands are,' said Nina, wondering how much her mother had told her sisters. 'That's what wedding nights are for.'

'Are you going to have a baby?' asked Prue, already that mixture of shrewdness and romanticism that would plague her all her life. 'You're a bit fat. I'll look after it if you don't want it.'

'We'll look after it together, darling. What do you think of Tim?'

'He's got funny eyes. They're always looking at things.'

Tim's eyes were indeed always looking at things, Nina noticed as the weeks went by. He made no comment, but his eyes were too sharp and observant for someone who was resigned to taking everything for granted. And, as if his eyes were a mirror of her own, she began to see things from a new angle and in a different light. For the second time since meeting him she saw the family wealth as something *not* to be taken for granted. *You think you're worth that much?* the kidnapper had asked her. And she wondered just what she was really worth in Tim's eyes.

He had refused to take a job in the Beaufort bank or the oil company or the lumber business or with the railroad. He considered going to work for the granary company, but that would have meant living away from Kansas City and Nina refused to do that; small town living, or even small city, was not for her. The same reason ruled out living and working on the cotton plantation down-State. So he went to work for the Beaufort Cattle Company in the stockyards.

'What do you know about cattle?' Nina asked.

'Nothing. But your father tells me he knows nothing about lumber, but he's president of the company. Is that right, Lucas?'

'He's got you there, sweetheart.' Lucas smiled at his daughter, telling her how pleased he now was with her husband. He had half-expected Tim to settle for the cushiest job offered him, but he had turned out to have a wide streak of independence in him. 'But I have fellers who know the business and they see I don't make any mistakes. I'm putting Tim in as a vice-president of the Cattle Company and he'll soon learn.'

'I think you misunderstood me, Lucas. I don't want to start as a vice-president. I'd rather go in as an ordinary worker, right at the bottom.'

'Cutting off the bull's knackers,' said Prue. 'George took me down to see the man doing it.'

'I think you had better eat alone in the nursery from now on,' said Edith. 'And, Lucas, I think you had better have a word with George.'

They were in the big panelled dining-room where Lucas insisted that they eat every evening. The table could seat thirty, but two leaves had been taken out of it, reducing it to a size that did not ridicule the family sitting at it. Nina and Tim sat on one side, the three younger sisters on the other, and Edith and Lucas sat at the ends. Thaddeus and Lucy Beaufort had always dressed for dinner, but when they died and Edith took over the running of the house she had abolished that rule. She loved dressing up, but the fun went out of it if one had to dress every night.

'George is only teaching her the facts of life,' said Sally. 'It's the new society. I was reading about it in *Time* magazine. Things

45

are going to be different. Are you going to be a modern mother, Nina?'

'I'm not going to take the baby down to the stockyards, if that's what you mean. And I think I'll do without George's help.'

George Biff, standing in for the butler on the latter's night off, came in with the dessert. He was not a handsome Negro, but he had a broad friendly face and he moved with the light grace of a man who had been both boxer and musician.

'Caramel custard tonight, ma'am. Just poor folks' stuff.'

'It's crème caramel, George. French and not poor folks' stuff. And Mr Beaufort would like to see you in his study after dinner.'

'It's about the bull's knackers,' said Prue.

'Could we change the subject?' asked Tim. 'Otherwise I'm likely to lose my taste for this delicious crème caramel.'

Later Tim and Nina walked round the park, unconsciously following the paths and habit of Nina's grandparents. A warm breeze blew up from the south and the maples that screened the house from the parkway whispered secretly in the darkness. Twice the Davorens passed security guards patrolling the big railed fence, but Tim made no comment on them. Nina now took it for granted that he was taking everything for granted. Including guarding against any further kidnapping of a Beaufort.

'How did George come to work for your father?'

'He's Daddy's favourite charity, though charity is never mentioned. When Daddy was a young man his one passion was jazz –'

'You're pulling my leg. He seems more like Gilbert and Sullivan.'

'No, really. He used to go down to 12th Street almost every night. Even after he married he used to go down there at least once a month. That was where he met George. George used to be a prize-fighter, but he also played trumpet in several bands. He used to stand in sometimes with Count Basie, when the Count was just plain Bill Basie.' She giggled. 'George once told me that Basie's signature tune in those day was called *Blue Balls*, but he had to change its title when his band went on radio.'

'George seems to spend a lot of his time instructing the Beaufort sisters in genitalia. I hope he never showed you his own.'

'That's a dirty remark and I should kick you in yours for talking about George like that. He loves the lot of us and I think he'd die for any one of us.'

'Sorry. Go on.'

'Well, one night he got into some sort of argument with a gangster we had here in the Thirties, a man name Johnny Lazia.

The next night Lazia sent two of his men back to the Reno Club and they shot off all the fingers on George's right hand. Daddy was there and saw it all. He took George to the hospital in his own car, paid all the hospital expenses, then he brought George home and he's worked for us ever since.'

'What happened to Lazia and his gangsters?'

'Nothing. Daddy went to the police department, but they just didn't want to know. Lazia was hand-in-glove with Tom Pendergast and the police didn't want to tread on the boss' toes.'

'I'm getting a new respect for your father.'

'I'm hoping that one of these days you and he will understand each other exactly. You're still getting used to each other. I think he admires you for wanting to start at the bottom. But I wish you'd chosen somewhere less smelly than the stockyards.'

## 6

Michael Lucas Davoren was born on Labor Day, 1946 – an appropriate day, as his mother remarked, since his birth was not easy. He came into the world reluctantly and for the first minute of his life was as poor as he would ever be. Then the two doctors and the nurse and all the trappings took over; his swaddling clothes might have been a coronation robe. Lucas and Edith made sure that their first grandchild, even if his name was not Beaufort, should begin life in proper Beaufort style. The nursery was re-decorated and re-furnished, a night- and a day-time nurse were engaged. Toys that would not be used for months or even years swamped the nursery and Edith even ordered a bookshelf of children's books.

'He has the best library of any illiterate in America,' said Tim.

'Don't be churlish, darling,' said Nina. 'All grandparents get carried away like that.'

'But Christ Almighty – what are they leaving *us* to buy him? I'd like to bring him home something, but there's nothing he hasn't got!'

'You're bringing home the smell of the stockyards.'

'I'm sorry.' He softened, stroked her golden hair as it lay on the pillow beside his own dark head. 'By the time our next one comes along I'll be taking it all for granted again.'

But there were to be no more children for Tim and Nina. Her

gynaecologist, Dr Voss, was a man who delivered babies and punches with the same precision. 'Your uterus is useless from now on. Forget about any more children. Consider yourself lucky young Michael came out okay.'

Tim got over the disappointment soon enough, but it remained with Nina not only for the next few months but for years to come. She reacted by slipping into the attitude of her parents and spoiling Michael unrestrainedly. He was not allowed to utter a yelp without being picked up and soothed; breezes, draughts and heavy breathing were kept from him as if they were gusts from the plague. Tim was the only one who didn't spoil him, breathing anthrax, foot-and-mouth and a dozen other animal diseases all over his only son. Michael survived both treatments.

In February 1947 the Davorens moved into their new house.

'I love it,' said Tim and Nina knew that he meant it. 'It's – comfortable. What a home should be.'

They were walking round the paths, a habit each of them looked forward to, knowing it was a way of being together for a while before going back to the main house and dinner with the family. Now they had moved into their own house Nina decided she liked the routine and they would keep it up.

'I'm keeping the staff to a minimum. I don't want us overrun.'

'Good idea. For starters, could we fire the nurse? I think it's time Michael stood on his own two feet.'

'He's less than six months old. Don't you think he's a bit young for that?'

'Not if his mum and dad stand on either side of him.'

His tone was easy, almost flippant, but she knew he was serious. She was too happy to argue; besides, the idea appealed to her. It would be another way of showing him that she could be independent when she tried. She had begun to fuss less and less over the baby, who was now allowed to cry sometimes for two minutes before being picked up.

'All right, the nurse goes. I'm so happy, darling.' She squeezed his arm and he returned the pressure but said nothing. After a moment she said, 'But you're not. What's the matter?'

He was silent for a few steps, the gravel crunching beneath his feet like the sound of his thoughts being sorted out. 'I think I made a mistake going to work at the stockyards. The chaps I work with in the yards are all right, but the fellows in the office, the manager and two or three others, think I'm after their jobs. My future down there has about as much promise as a steer's.'

'Well, we'd better speak to Daddy – '

'We shan't speak to him. This is between you and me.'

'I didn't mean that he should put any pressure on those men. I meant he can find a position for you with one of the other companies. Something where you don't come home smelling like Buffalo Bill.'

They had reached the house. He said nothing until they were inside and upstairs in their bedroom. Then he took her by the shoulders and pressed her down on the bed.

'Are we going to make love? Before dinner?'

'Sit up. You talk about me being sex mad. *Sit up*.' She raised herself and he sat down on the bed beside her. 'Now listen to me. From now on you don't go near your father regarding anything about me. If I want him to do something, I'll go to him myself. Understand?'

She stared at him, then slowly nodded. 'You're not taking things for granted, are you? Not even now.'

'Certain things, yes. But I'm not going to become your father's puppet. Hold it – ' He held up a hand as she started to protest. 'He doesn't think of himself as a puppet-master, but that's what he is. With you, your sisters, me, everyone who works for him. The only one who escapes is your mother.'

She was about to argue with him, but only out of her loyalty to her father. Then she realized she had no argument: what he had said was true. At least in regard to herself and her sisters; she had no idea how much power her father wielded over those who worked for him. She had been brought up in a private world: even the years at Vassar and the six months in Germany had been only half-opened windows on the world at large. She knew that money, in a money society, was power; there had been a teacher at Vassar who had taunted his students with that lesson. She was all at once conscious of the fact that she was ignorant of what everyone outside the family thought of Lucas Beaufort. The kidnappers in Germany had taught her nothing except that the family wealth could make her father vulnerable from certain angles. But at the same time she wondered how many children in other families, rich or poor, were in the dark as to what the rest of the world thought of their fathers. Public opinion was a prism she had never examined.

'All right,' she conceded, tasting disloyalty for the first time and not liking it. 'What are you going to do? Go into business on your own?'

'Doing what? I told your father once that I thought of being a teacher, but I know now I'd be no good at it. I don't have enough patience to care whether someone would learn anything from me. As for going into business, what could I do? Take off your dress.'

'Making love is no answer. We have a problem – '

He took his hands from her, rolled over on his back and looked up at the bed canopy. It was a copy of a French tapestry: Diana stood with her hunting dogs, like a greyhound trainer who had lost her shirt at the races. Her blue silk eyes looked straight down at the bed, a voyeur who amused him. But not this evening: he was beyond amusement. None of the goddesses, especially Diana, could help him. Except, perhaps, one of the bitch-goddesses and he had never trusted any of them.

'We'll work it out,' he said listlessly.

A long time later she wondered if that was the moment when his defeat began. But right then, the telephone rang. She leaned across him and picked it up.

'Darling,' said her mother, 'I have a wonderful idea! You must have a house-warming party.'

Nina felt the string being pulled: her mother, too, was a puppeteer. 'Mother, I don't think I really want a party just now –'

Underneath her she saw Tim looking at her expressionlessly. His face was close to hers, only part of it visible: his one eye was like a dark marble, telling her nothing. She lifted herself from him, put her hand over the phone.

'Mother wants us to throw a house-warming party.'

He shrugged, his shoulder rubbing against her stomach. 'Why not? We haven't played host to anyone since we got here.'

She sat up, turned her back on him. 'All right, Mother. We'll have a party. Just one thing, though – I want to plan it all on my own.'

There was silence at the other end of the line. At last, with a sigh that was a plain reproof: 'Of course, darling. But if you need any help – '

7

'I hate to admit it,' said the railroad president, 'but there have been worse Presidents than Harry Truman.'

'In some banana republic,' said the banker. 'Not in this country.'

'I believe in the work ethic,' said the banker's wife. 'I don't

50

know what the workers would do without it.'

'Women's rights?' said the retired general. 'If they'd been important they'd have been discussed at Potsdam. Right, Ethel?'

'Yes, sir,' said his wife. 'Permission to stand easy now?'

Nina moved through the froth of party talk, feeling a pride that was new to her: hostess in her own home. The party was already a success, an instant house-warming; Nina took smug secret pride in the knowledge that it had been due solely to her own efforts. She had chosen the caterers, showing her independence by ignoring her mother's usual choice; she had made out the guest list, splitting it between her parents' friends and her own. It had disturbed her that she had created an awkward moment by asking Tim if there was anyone he would like to invite.

'Only Bumper Cassidy. But I don't think he'd fit in. He's my sidekick down at the yards.'

'Darling, invite him!'

He had shaken his head. 'He would only feel out of place and so would his wife. She's a waitress in a joint on 12th Street.'

'My, how you get around when I'm not with you. Sidekick. Joint on 12th Street. You're becoming more American every day.'

'Tell your father. It'll make his year.'

She approached her father now, sliding into his arm as he crooked it out for her. 'Nina, it's the best party I've been to in years. Where'd you get that band?'

'George was my talent scout. I got them specially for you.'

'Great. I haven't heard music like that since I was a young man and used to go to the Old Kentucky Barbecue down on the Paseo. How much are you paying them?'

'That's my business.'

'Don't spoil them. I can remember when you could get Hot Lips Page for three dollars a night. Where's Tim?'

'Out on the veranda dancing with Sally.'

Tim had already danced with Miss Stafford, Edith's secretary, a plump plain woman who was a snob but likeable and who thought Tim was a real-life version of Ronald Coleman. She lived in the past and Tim played up to her with a courtliness that made her laugh but didn't offend her by mocking her. She was only one of his conquests among all the women, family and staff, on the Beaufort estate.

Now he was charming Sally who, at her first adult party, was in seventh heaven and Tim's arms, floating inches above the floor. 'You dance like Ginger Rogers. Or a ballerina. Why don't you become a dancer?'

51

'I hate *indoors*. You know what my ambition is? To win the Indy 500.'

'Sally my love, don't be a racing driver. Stay feminine.'

'I'm not a lesbian, if that's what you're thinking –'

*My God, what happened to the innocent girls of my youth?* 'Nothing was further from my mind. I don't think they allow lesbians into the pits at Indianapolis.'

Sally shrieked, clutching him. 'Oh Tim, I *adore* you! Divorce Nina and marry me!'

'A child bride – just what I've always wanted. But don't they hang a man for that here in Missouri?'

'Daddy would fix that.'

'Just the man I'd ask. Can I tear myself away now and dance with Meg?'

'Oh God, *her*. Look at her – all those boys hanging around –'

'You'll be like that yourself some day.'

'Oh God.'

Tim left her, moved across to Margaret and took her away from the six boys hanging around. 'Thanks for rescuing me. Boys that age are so *gauche*. I think I like older men.'

'We have our uses. Would you mind backing off a little? Your sister, my wife, is watching us.'

She blushed and was embarrassed, proving she was still only seventeen going on eighteen. 'Oh God. That's the way boys expect you to dance.'

'The gauche ones. Some older men, too. But not this one, not in front of his wife.' They danced sedately for a while, Jane Austen set to *A Good Man Is Hard To Find*. Then he said, 'Let's head down towards your mother.'

'Are you working your way through the Beaufort women tonight?'

'All of them. I have a date with Prue at midnight in her room.'

'I shouldn't be surprised. She's man-mad. At six.'

Smoothly as a gigolo he left Margaret and took Edith in his arms. They moved back down the veranda to *There Goes That Song Again*, which someone had requested and which the band was playing as if they had been insulted.

'Tim, we don't seem to talk to each other very much these days.'

'I'm so busy being a bread-winner, husband and father, I don't have time for other women. But let me know when Lucas is out of town and I'll pop over.'

Edith didn't respond to flirting. 'Were you a philanderer before you met Nina? You have a way with women.'

'Would you expect me to admit it if I had been?'

'Unhappy men sometimes do stray, just as a diversion.'

'What makes you think I'm unhappy?'

'Oh, I don't mean you and Nina. That part is happy enough. But you don't really like America, do you?'

'America is a very big country.'

'All right. Kansas City. You don't like it, do you?'

He smiled, took her through some intricate steps which she had a little difficulty in following. 'That would be tantamount to saying I don't like the family, wouldn't it?'

'*Tantamount.* You sound like Walter Lippmann. Yes, I suppose it would be tantamount to saying you don't like us. But I don't believe that.'

'Edith – don't worry. I love you all. I'd love you even more if we didn't live quite so much on top of each other. Offended?'

'No, I just missed my step.' The band, on orders from Lucas, had thrown *There Goes That Song Again* out the window and had started in on *Make Believe Rag*. Lucas stood by the band, foot tapping, face thirty years younger. 'You can't blame me, Tim. I've never tied Nina to my apron strings.'

'Edith, when did you ever wear an apron? I'm not blaming anyone in particular. It's the circumstances – ' He appreciated her intelligence and tact in not asking for an explanation of the circumstances. 'Nina and I should have gone down to live on the plantation. I think I'd have made an ideal Massa Tim.'

'You can still go down there. Do you want me to talk to Nina?'

'Take your apron off, Edith.'

'What? Oh. You mean stop interfering? It's difficult for a mother like me not to interfere. I grew up in a social frame of mind where mothers expected their daughters to marry within their own circle. Their own class, I suppose you'd call it in England.' Despite her respect for perspective, Edith's world was still small and she felt safe in it. The kidnapping of Nina had had an effect on her, the depth of which not even Lucas suspected. She had presented a brave, calm face to everyone at the time, but in her secret self there was wreckage, the realization that the world was full of enemies for people like themselves. 'You've met all our friends – there are practically no outsiders. Some of the younger ones, maybe, have other ideas – Nina, for instance. The war changed things. I try, Tim, but it is difficult for me. Lucas and I are selfish, I know, but we want our family around us. And we think of you as family, Tim.'

*But I'll always be an outsider; but not for the reasons you think.* He had belonged to a middle-class family who had always had

53

enough money to get by, mainly because their wants and ambitions had been small. His father had been a suburban solicitor who had been more than content with his house in Ealing with a modest mortgage on it, the second-hand Wolseley car and membership of the local tennis club. Wealth, real riches, was something the family never thought about, as they never thought about the families who had the wealth, the Grosvenors, the Cavendishes, the Howards. Perhaps it had something to do with the English system: he might have been different had he been an American. Ambition, even envy, was not considered off-side in this country. He was handicapped by his upbringing, by a mother and father who had, without ever mentioning the subject, taught him to be satisfied with his lot. But these days he felt like a man who, accustomed to everyday sunsets, was all at once confronted with the pyrotechnics of Judgement Day. It was an image he never confided to Nina. Something else he also never confessed to her, and only reluctantly to himself, was that he was afraid of the seduction of money. Since coming here to Kansas City he had realized he had a weakness he had never suspected in himself: if he had enough money of his own he would be nothing but a hedonist. That was the ultimate and real reason for not taking the Beaufort riches for granted. It was not something he could explain to Edith.

He handed Edith over to Lucas, collected Nina and took her into the buffet supper. 'It's a marvellous success, darling. We should do this more often.'

'You're really enjoying yourself? Truly?'

'Darling heart – ' He kissed her cheek. 'Truly.'

# 8

The stockyards' strike began on the day the Paris conference on the newly announced Marshall Plan opened.

'Truman should be running this country,' said Lucas, 'instead of trying to run Europe. We've got enough damned Reds here without trying to stop the Reds over there. Let 'em look after themselves.'

'I don't think there's a Red down in the yards,' said Tim. 'Except Red Ludwig, the feed man, and he makes you look like Joe Stalin. I didn't think it was possible for a man to be so far to

54

the right without falling off the edge of the world.'

'Well, someone's stirring up this trouble. Wanting seventy-five cents an hour as the minimum wage – if we give them that, there'll be no end to their demands. You get that now, don't you?'

'Yes. But the minimum is forty cents an hour.'

'Are you supporting the demand?'

'They're letting me stay neutral. The chaps appreciate my position. But there's a lot of solidarity down there, Lucas. You won't employ union labour, but these chaps are as solidly together as if they were a union.'

'You sound as if you do support them.'

'I told you, I'm neutral. But I'm leaning a little your way in telling you just how strong their feelings are. They're not going to back down. I think you ought to meet with them.'

'I'm not meeting with anyone. I've got fellers down there to run the company – I don't believe in interfering.'

'Nonsense,' said Nina, who had been sitting quietly listening to their discussion. 'I'll bet you've already told management to say no to the men.'

'A Red in my own family,' said Lucas. 'Emma Goldman.'

They were sitting on the enclosed back porch of the Davoren house. Tim and Lucas had played two sets of tennis on the court behind the main house, then they had come across for a beer. Even though they had played late in the afternoon, the July heat had been too much for Lucas and he was exhausted and testy. He was also very red, but in the circumstances of the discussion Nina diplomatically did not mention it. She placidly knitted, a pursuit she had taken up in the past month, telling Tim it would not only keep her occupied but would save them money on Michael's clothes, a thriftiness which Tim, with a perfectly straight face which she hadn't missed, said he appreciated. Occasionally she looked out towards the lawns where Michael was crawling around under the benevolent eye of George Biff. The nurse had been got rid of and George, without asking or being asked, had taken over.

'You're behaving like Grandfather.'

'You don't know how your grandfather behaved.' Something more personal than the strike had made Lucas irritable. He had always fancied himself as a tennis player, but Tim, playing at only half-pace, had beaten him without the loss of a game.

'I do know, Daddy. We had a teacher at Vassar who gave us a short course in labour history. Grandfather wasn't quite as bad as Rockefeller and Henry Ford at breaking strikes, but he was bad enough. I was ashamed when the teacher told us what Grandfather did here in, I think it was 1924, some time then, when he locked out the railroad workers.'

'Your teacher didn't show much taste by mentioning that with you in his class.'

'You don't learn history by being squeamish. I knew he was trying to make me uncomfortable, he was that sort of man. But I checked and found out he was telling the truth.'

'There are two sides to every dispute.'

'Maybe you should go down to the yards and listen to the men's side.'

Lucas, still red and sweating, wiped his face with his towel. He looked at his favourite, sensing, as he had for some time, that he was losing her day by day. He supposed this happened to all fathers when their daughters married; he wondered how Edith's father had felt. A father's rival was his son-in-law and all at once he felt a stab of jealousy towards Tim. He stood up, picked up his racquet and headed for the door with the abrupt departure that was an occasional characteristic of his, as if he had heard a whistle that called him to some other place.

'Thanks for the game, Tim.' The screen door banged behind him, a thudding first-act curtain.

'That's not the end of our argument with him,' said Tim.

'Do you think you should take a week off till all this blows over? We could go down to the plantation, you could do some fishing – '

'It's not going to blow over in a week. The men are as stubborn as your father. And I think it would be cowardice for me to walk out before it was over.'

'You're not neutral, are you? You're on their side.'

'Do you mind?'

'Not if you think they're right. I just can't imagine how people live on those sort of wages. They can't live much better than those people I worked amongst in Germany.'

'Oh, they live better than *that*. Nobody down at the yards is starving and they've all got a roof over their heads when they go home. But Bumper Cassidy told me, even with him and his wife working, they've never been out of debt in the fifteen years they've been married.'

'Is he going on strike?'

'He's one of the leaders.'

She folded up her knitting, put it away in the expensive embroidered sewing bag that had cost her ten times the price of the wool she was knitting. 'Don't get involved, darling,' she said and went out to Michael and George Biff, closing the screen door quietly behind her.

George picked up the baby, brushed the grass from him. 'You stopped spoiling him, Miz Nina, he's a good kid now.'

'George, when did you become an expert on child raising?'

'I had six brother and four sisters, all younger'n me. They started yowling, I belt 'em over the ear. They's all grown up, nice people.'

'But all deaf in one ear.'

He grinned, bounced Michael up and down in his arms. 'Miz Nina, a little paddy-whacking never hurt nobody.'

'If ever I see you paddy-whacking Michael I'll knock you down.'

His grin broadened. 'Ain't never gone a coupla rounds with a lady. You want six-ounce or eight-ounce gloves?'

Each of them knew how far their banter could go before she lost her authority. There were always certain hints, which she recognized, that he loved and respected her: he had said 'ain't never gone a coupla rounds with a lady' instead of 'with a woman.' Such small gestures were always there behind his easy cheek.

She took Michael from him, kissed the flushed chubby face. He was blond like her, but there were traces of his father in him, glimpses of the future. 'I'll let my son defend me when he grows up. You just watch out.'

Tim went to work next day and came home that night worried and upset. He showered and changed and went out with Nina and the baby for their walk round the park. She could see that something was troubling him, but she contained her impatience. It was after dinner, when they were having coffee in the living-room, before her patience finally ran out.

'Well, what happened today?'

Inger, the Swedish maid, brought in fresh coffee. Nina had a staff of three helping her run the house and Inger was the brightest of them, a plump plain girl whose eyes and ears were like magnets for every splinter of gossip dropped about the house. Nina waited till she had gone out of the room again, then she repeated her question.

'Nothing happened.' He sipped his coffee, then leaned back in his chair, the big red leather wing-back that she had bought specially for him, and sighed. 'It's tomorrow something's going to happen. Your father is bringing in scab labour.'

'Daddy or the company managers?'

'Same thing. He'd have to okay it. They've recruited them

57

from down in Arkansas and they're bringing them in by truck tomorrow morning. They announced it to us this afternoon, just as if they were asking for a flat-out confrontation. We've been locked out.'

'We?'

'I'm sorry, darling, but I'm with the men. I can't be otherwise – I think they're entitled to what they're asking for. I don't want to be an agitator or anything like that, but I have to support Bumper and the other chaps. I find I have a social conscience, something that's never troubled me before.'

'Do you think you should go over and tell Daddy what you're going to do?'

'It wouldn't do any good. If he doesn't understand the men's reasons for the strike by now, no amount of explanation will convince him I'm doing the right thing. He's living in the past. He still believes in the sanctity of capital, right or wrong.'

'I don't understand him.' She could feel anguish boiling up inside her, less bearable because she was unprepared for it. She had wanted her father and Tim to be friends, though she had known there would always be powder there to explode a division between them. She had not expected the powder train to come from the direction of the stockyards. 'He's basically a kind man. He's charitable – look at the money he's given to charity. The Foundation isn't just something he inherited from Grandfather – he *believes* in it.'

'It could be from a sense of guilt. I don't know, I'm not judging his charity. But he's like a lot of rich men – we have them in England, too – as soon as the workers start demanding a little more, they think they're endangered, they're going to have another revolution on their hands. From what I've read, John D. Rockefeller was like your father. He gave away millions with one hand and with the other hit a worker over the head with an iron bar. I don't mean he wielded the iron bar himself, but he condoned it when it was done by others.'

'Daddy would never allow any violence.'

'There's going to be violence tomorrow when those scabs turn up.'

'You better not go to work tomorrow, then. I don't want you getting hurt.'

But when she woke in the morning he was already gone. Distressed, she couldn't eat breakfast. She tried to bathe the baby, but he was in one of his playful moods and she got short-tempered with him and finally called in Inger to take over. She dressed without showering, careless of what she put on, then hurried across to the main house. Her mother was having breakfast in her bedroom, planning her day with Miss Stafford.

'Where's Daddy?'

Edith looked at her, then nodded at Miss Stafford. 'That will be all, Portia. Tell one of the gardeners to look at the tennis court. Mr Beaufort was complaining about it night before last. He said he got some bad bounces.'

'Another beautiful day,' Miss Stafford said to Nina and went out of the bedroom.

'Now what's all this? You know your father is always downtown by this time. He's in his office at eight every morning.'

'Did he say if he was going down to the stockyards?'

'He and I never discuss his business.' But she patted the newspaper that lay on the bed beside her breakfast tray. It was yesterday's *Star*; it was one of her idiosyncrasies that she always waited till the news was at least a day old before she read it. That way, she said, she got a better perspective on whether the doomsayers of yesterday had been proved correct today. It also buttressed her optimism because the doom-sayers were usually wrong. 'You're worried about the strike? I think you can leave it safely with your father to deal with. He's a reasonable man in business, they tell me.'

'Mother, how would you know? You said you never discuss business with him. This strike is *serious*. And Daddy is being pig-headed about it. I'm worried, Mother. Tim has gone to work this morning – there's going to be trouble – '

'Darling – ' Edith put her tray aside, patted the bed. 'Sit down here. I can't remember when I last saw you so upset. You'll have to *trust* Tim. That's what wives must do – '

'Oh Jesus!' Edith said nothing, but her face stiffened and a deep frown appeared between her eyes. Nina flopped on the bed, hugged her mother. 'I'm sorry – I didn't mean to swear. But you don't know what could happen down there this morning. It's not just a question of trusting Tim – '

'Darling, I know we both live a sheltered life. Me more than you. But I don't think that even out there – ' She waved a hand vaguely towards the windows, towards the green thrones of trees, the pikestaffs of the iron fence, the outer world beyond the moat of wealth. 'Even out there I don't think women interfere in their husbands' affairs. We just have to trust that they know what they are doing, that they are doing the right thing – '

'One of them will have to be wrong this morning, Tim or Daddy. They can't both be right, not about this strike. And I think Daddy is the one who's wrong this time.'

Edith looked at the newspaper headline covering the strike story: perhaps the doom-sayers were going to be right after all. She was not foolish, she did not believe she lived in the best of all possible worlds, only in a tiny corner of it; but she had not been bred to go looking for what was wrong with the world, her plea for perspective was only play-acting and she knew it. Her equanimity was only cowardice genteelly disguised.

'I'll talk to him tonight – '

'It may be too late then.' Nina kissed her mother, slid off the bed. 'Whatever happens down at the stockyards today, there's going to be a hell of a scene here tonight. I'm going to tell Daddy a few truths.'

She left her mother, ran downstairs, out of the house and back towards the stables where all the cars were garaged. She drove her MG out into the cobbled yard and almost ran down George Biff as he stepped in front of her.

'Where you going, Miz Nina?'

'None of your business! Out of the way – please, George!'

He came round, slipped into the passenger's seat beside her. 'You rushing off down to the yards, right? You damn foolish. You ain't gonna solve nothing like that.'

'I'm not trying to solve anything – all I want is to bring Mister Tim home before the trouble starts.'

George looked at his watch. 'It gonna start, it already started. I talked to Mister Tim this morning when he come to get his car. He told me about them scabs coming in. You gonna drive or you want me to?'

She argued no further. It took them twenty-five minutes to get to the stockyards, caught as they were in the morning peak-hour traffic. One or two of Nina's friends saw them, waved cheerfully; they had no problems, none of them had a husband on his way to do battle, scabs, scabs. The morning was already hot, the eye-scalding sunlight an omen in itself. As they drove down towards the yards the smell of livestock hit them suddenly, as if they had driven through an invisible gate into another atmosphere. Police cars blocked the roadway up ahead and beyond the cars they could see trucks and a crowd of men. Nina parked the car, switched off the engine and at once they heard the shouts and booing of the men above the bellowing of the cattle in the yards.

George Biff put a hand on Nina's arm as she started to get out of the car, but she took his hand by the wrist and dropped it back on his knee. 'I'm going up there, George, so don't try and stop me. I want to know what's happening.'

'I can find out – '

60

She relented. 'We'll find out together. Come on.'

As they got to the line of police cars a sergeant blocked their way. 'Okay, you two, this is no place for you. You with the lady, boy?'

'He's with me, yes,' said Nina, squarely facing the thickset, over-weight officer. He had a Southern accent and she resented his calling George 'boy'. She wondered what his attitude was towards the strikers. 'My name is Davoren – my father owns the Beaufort Cattle Company, where all the trouble is.'

'You can say that again, there's trouble, all right.' The sergeant's tone hadn't altered. He knew who she was, even if he hadn't seen her before; but he wasn't impressed by rich girls who took niggers driving with them in imported sports cars. 'That's why you better turn round and go back home. We'll take care of the trouble if it gets any worse.'

A young policeman came running down from the trucks, looking hot, angry and as if wishing he were somewhere else. 'Sarge, you better come on up there. Those pickets, they're not gonna let the trucks through. It's getting rough.'

'You buzz off, you understand?' the sergeant said to Nina, then he lumbered up the road after the young officer.

'We better do what he says,' said George, sweat beginning to glisten on his dark face. 'Looks like it gonna get pretty bad in a minute.'

The yelling had increased and the horns of the trucks had begun to blare; strident echoes rang in Nina's ears, Frankfurt and Kansas City merged, she was suddenly as afraid of the past as of the present. She started to run towards the disturbance, but George grabbed her arm, held her back. Utterly distraught now, as if the yelling and the truck horns blaring were an omen, she struggled against his grip. The cattle in the yards on either side of them began to mill, bellowing loudly, raising dust that blew up and floated across the road like the smoke of an explosion. Down here on the flats beside the river the sun bounced back from the roadway, splintered itself on the windshields of the police cars. The stockyards became a cauldron of heat and dust and panic and anger.

'Stay here! Don't come any closer – you hear me? Stay here!'

George pushed her back towards the MG, then turned and ran up towards the trucks and the yelling crowd.

In the front line of the crowd Tim was struggling to edge towards the side. He had no desire to be a ring-leader in what was going to be an ugly encounter. He had been standing talking to Bumper Cassidy, both of them watching the blocked trucks carrying the scab labour, when suddenly the situation had got out of hand. The pickets had been rocking the trucks, trying to force the drivers to reverse; one of the drivers lost his head, threw a wrench and a picket went down with blood gushing from his face. Next moment the whole mob had surged forward, pickets clambering to get up at the men in the trucks like pirates boarding a convoy of galleons. Whistles blew and the police came in at the mob of strikers from the other side of the trucks.

Tim knew he was in danger. Mob mindlessness had taken over; if there was a cool head among the three or four hundred men it was having no effect. Bumper Cassidy, beside Tim, had responded to the uproar with a reflex action; he was a big, bald-headed man who, if he was lost for words, was never lost for fists. A man fell out of a truck and Bumper hit him on the way down, stopping him for a moment in mid-air as if the blow from his fist was stronger than the pull of gravity. Then a police baton hit Bumper on the side of the head and he fell sideways against Tim, who went down in the stampede.

Tim fought his way to his feet, hitting out indiscriminately; a man he worked with every day, blind with rage, threw a punch at him and he just managed to duck under it. Choked with dust, blinded by sweat, gasping for breath in the stifling heat, he found himself being swept round in the mob as in a whirlpool. Suddenly he was on the edge of the big melée, but in a worse position; he thudded up against the railings of a yard, felt a searing pain across his belly as a steer's horn swept by. He was spreadeagled against the fence, the fighting crowd behind him hammering him there; right in front of him the stampeding cattle thundered by, eyes white-wild, their bellowing as brutally bruising as if they were running him down. Their horns went dangerously close as some of them thudded into the fence; he fought to push himself away from the railings but the crowd threw its weight against him, unaware of him. For a moment he thought of trying to climb over the fence, but knew at once that that would mean almost certain death.

He began to fight his way along the fence, punching and swiping at everyone in his way. He had almost reached the edge of the crowd when something hit him behind the ear; he went down, dazed, had no strength to pull himself up again. Then he felt someone lifting him, a black man who was faintly familiar; he clung to the man as the latter began to drag him out of the riot. He was dimly aware of a policeman appearing out of nowhere, baton raised; the black man let go of Tim with one hand, swung at the policeman and the latter went down. Tim was dragged over the fallen officer, then the black man picked him up in a fireman's lift and carried him out of the yelling, struggling crush and down the road. He was dumped into the seat of a car that was also vaguely familiar, he felt someone kiss him, then he passed out.

'Get going, Miz Nina!'

Nina swung the MG round, ignoring the shouts of the police sergeant as he ran down towards them, and took the car down the road with a screech of tyres.

# 9

'Disgraceful!' Lucas looked as if his bones wanted to blow him apart; all arms and legs and rigid body, he stalked up and down his study. 'The papers have got on to the story! The two of you down there like damned agitators. And George hitting that policeman – Goddam it, what got into you?'

'You can't blame George for anything he did – he was just trying to rescue Tim.'

Nina had never seen her father so angry; but she was surprised at her own total unconcern for his reaction. All she cared about at the moment was Tim, lying in their bedroom in the house across the lawns with twelve stitches in the wound in his belly, two broken ribs and a slight concussion. She was off-balance emotionally, as if there had been a subsidence within her, a breaking-up of levels that had sustained her all her life up till now. There had been worries and doubts in the sixteen months she had been married to Tim, all brought on by Tim's sometimes prickly attitude towards her father: there had never been any open quarrel but at best his attitude had always been one of guarded geniality, his smile not hypocritical but a defence that neither of her parents had recognized as such and had never penetrated. The evidence had been growing in her mind for months, but only today had it all suddenly formed itself into a pattern that she acknowledged. It was no news to her that Tim had never really accepted her father, but it had come as a shock to learn that her father returned the attitude.

'I've had to talk to the chief of police, get him to drop the charge against George. Damn it, you know what they could do to him – a Negro hitting a white officer! And you took George down

63

there with you, let him get into that situation!'

'I didn't do any such thing!' She never had fought with her father like this; she burned with both shame and temper. 'George came of his own accord – to help me. And he went into the mob to help Tim because he had some spark of humanity in him – something I think you've forgotten!'

She had hurt him, she could see that, but he wasn't a weak man: he did not retreat behind a whine of reproach for her betrayal. 'You don't know what you're talking about. The company has always been fair with its workers – it isn't inhumane to object to their greediness. They get a fair share in wages of the profits – '

'It's nothing to the money we have!'

'Don't be naïve. You don't run a business that way. The Cattle Company has to pay its own way – whatever else we have doesn't enter into it. You're talking like some woolly-minded socialist. If you got that from your husband – '

'I didn't get it from *my husband* – he has a name or have you put it out of your mind? He's never attempted any propaganda with me – I think he'd laugh his head off if you called him a socialist. I worked it out for myself – I think the men are entitled to what they're asking for.'

'They get a living wage – '

'A living wage isn't enough! God, Daddy, you're still in the last century – I don't think I've ever looked at you properly. Grandfather must have put blinkers on you when you were born – '

Her voice had risen; she was almost shouting. The study door opened and Edith came in quickly, closing it behind her. 'I told myself I was not going to interfere. But this has gone on long enough and loudly enough – too loud, all the servants can hear you. I think you had better apologize to your father, Nina, then go home and cool down. You'd better cool down, too, Lucas – your voice has been just as loud as hers.'

'I'm not going to apologize! Tell your husband to come into the twentieth century – he just doesn't know what's going on in the world!'

'My husband?' said Edith.

But Nina had already rushed out of the room, past George Biff standing in the hall, his face grey with pain and emotion; then she was running across the lawns, through the afternoon heat, like someone fleeing a catastrophe she couldn't face. Margaret and Sally, coming up from the tennis court, called to her, but she didn't hear them. She ran towards her own house, tears streaming down her face, but even in her distress she knew the house was no real haven, that it had never really belonged to her and Tim. It had been a gift from her parents and she ran now through the strings that bound it to the big house that dominated the park.

Tim lay flat on his back in the bed, a low pillow under his head. He tried to sit up when she came into the room, but winced in pain and lay back at once. 'What's the matter? For Christ's sake – *Nina!* What happened?'

She had flopped on the foot of the bed, hand over her face, her head shaking from side to side. She struggled to control herself, the sobs coming up as great gobs of pain in her chest. He reached for her, but she got up and moved away, waving a dumb hand for him to remain lying down and not hurt himself. She should have stayed downstairs till she had composed herself, but she had come headlong up the stairs to the one true haven that was all her own, *him.*

He waited impatiently for her to tell him what had happened. At last she was in control of herself, had *cooled down*, as her mother had advised; she was tearless now, dried-out and cold, more than just cool. She told herself she owed no more allegiance to her mother and father.

'I got nowhere with Daddy.' She told Tim all that had been said and argued in her father's study; as she talked, she felt the distance increasing between her parents' house and her own. 'He's hopeless – he'll never see things our way.'

He misunderstood her, thinking she was talking only about the strike. 'Bumper phoned me – the men are going back to work. They haven't announced it yet, but Bumper says they've all recognized now that they can't win.'

She had to concentrate to think about the events of the morning: she had been preoccupied with the wide empty horizon of the future. 'Oh – you mean they're giving up? So easily?'

'Don't criticize them. It's too easy for us – '

'But you were hurt – for *them!* Daddy will laugh at us – '

'I don't think he's that heartless or undiplomatic.'

She moved up closer to him on the bed, took one of his bandaged hands in hers. 'Darling, let's go away.'

He stared at her closely, his eyes wary in his bruised and grazed face. 'You don't mean just for a holiday, do you?'

'No, I mean move away from here, go somewhere else to live. Anywhere – I don't care – '

'I think you'd better sleep on it – '

'I don't want to sleep on it! For God's sake, stop being so damn careful of me – I'm not doing this just for you! I'm thinking of me – of *us*, both of us. And Michael –' She was infested with pessimism, was building fears on fears without any real foundation. She had been too well protected, even from the knowledge that her father had another set of loyalties, ones outside that to her and her sisters. 'Let's go to England! You'd like that – '

He searched her face as if it were strange territory: he had never known her to look and sound like this. He sensed the seriousness in her: what she had just suggested may have come off the top of her head, but she felt it deeply. The decision she had made was bigger than her decision to marry him. But he wasn't hurt by it.

'All right, we'll go back to England. But you have to promise me – we tell your parents together and you have to make them understand it was a joint decision on our part.'

'But it isn't – '

'Yes, it is. You may have suggested it, but you're not to tell them you did. You'll hurt them enough just by going – you don't have to rub it in by letting them know you had to talk me into it.'

It was her turn to look searchingly. 'Why are you being so careful of their feelings? They've never been that way about yours.'

'I'm being careful for your sake, darling heart. You may want to come back here some day – '

'Never – '

He shook his head on the pillow. 'You'll want to come back. Perhaps not to live, but you'll want to come back for visits, long ones. There's not just your parents – there are your sisters. You're too attached to them to want to turn your back on them.'

## 10

Lucas and Edith took the news as Nina had expected: as if she had turned a gun on them. Lucas did not speak to her for two days, going out of his way to avoid her. But Edith, after her initial shock, did not surrender her daughter without a fight.

'If we've made mistakes, Nina, then all I can ask is that you forgive us. It won't happen again.'

'It will, Mother. Daddy will never change. He thinks he *owns* us. Not just all of us, but Tim, too.'

'You're mistaking love for ownership. Maybe he shows it the wrong way, but it *is* love. I know him better than you.'

'That's why you can make excuses for him. But I can't, Mother – not any longer.'

Then she tried to explain her departure to her sisters. She got them together in what had been the old nursery and was now a games and television room. But all the artefacts of their childhood were still there: dolls, toys, finger-paintings. It was a museum now for the older girls, but it was Prue's retreat and domain. She was delighted to have her sisters as her guests. She sat playing with her dolls, only occasionally cocking an ear to the conversation. But Margaret and Sally were in tears.

'Oh God!' wailed Sally. 'We'll miss you terribly!'

Margaret wiped her eyes. 'I suppose I knew marriage was going to break us up some day. But not like *this*. Daddy is like a zombie.'

'I think I'd like a zombie doll,' said Prue.

'Oh God,' said Sally; then wiped her eyes. 'If you go, Nina, can I have your MG?'

'How mercenary can you get?' said Margaret. 'Nina, how does Tim feel? We're going to miss him as much as you. He's part of the family.'

'That's just what he's not. Daddy doesn't think so. Will you come and see us when we're in England?'

'Of course,' said all three; then all four of them had another big weep. 'God, it's just awful!'

Later Margaret walked back with Nina to the Davoren house. Purple clouds boiled above then and a wind whipped the trees to life. There were tornadoes further south, but so far no warnings had been issued for this area. It was a good day for being miserable.

'If there's anything I can do to help – '

'Better not take sides,' said Nina, linking her arm in her sister's. She had never been as close to Margaret as to Sally and Prue, but now she was grateful for Meg's comfort and presence. She wanted someone to talk to, and her mother had failed her. 'Just watch out when it comes time for you to fall in love. Please yourself, not Daddy. Is there anyone you're serious about right now?'

'No.' But Margaret seemed to close up; Nina felt her arm stiffen slightly within her own. 'Well, maybe. But we haven't talked about it. I could be crazy about someone else this time next year. Did you fall in and out of love once a month when you were my age?'

'I was crazy for half a dozen boys. It was a wonder I didn't have half a dozen babies.'

'You mean you went all the way with all of them?'

Nina laughed, beginning to feel a little better. Her sisters were indeed a comfort, she really was going to miss them. 'I always said No at the last moment. I must have been a terrible tease. But I was afraid of losing them. I'm – I don't know, I used to fall in love too easily. I did with Tim, all in a weekend.'

'You're not sorry about that, for God's sake?' Margaret pulled up, her arm jerking Nina to a halt.

'Of course not. But I break out in a cold sweat sometimes. I mean I might have missed him, never met him, if I'd married one of the others.'

Margaret nodded. 'I know what you mean. I'm trying to teach myself to be patient. But it's hard, isn't it? Oh, there's Tim! I didn't know he was up.'

'He's not supposed to be.'

But Tim was sitting in an armchair on the wide rear porch, a book open on his knees, a pitcher of lemonade on the cane table beside him. Inger, the maid, hovered over him, a Swedish angel who would gladly have fallen if the master had tempted her. Nina had already decided that, if she and Tim had not been leaving, then Inger would have had to go.

The maid went back into the house and Nina and Margaret sat down on either side of Tim. 'Who helped you out of bed? Inger Nightingale?'

'Only after she'd given me some Swedish massage. They have some marvellous ways with their hands –' He grinned at her, then at Margaret. 'When you marry, Meg, don't be jealous of your maids. No husband in his right mind would ever dally so close to home. What do you think of our news?'

'I'm heart-broken. But I think you're doing the right thing. I just wish you didn't have to go all that way, to England.'

Nina picked up the book from his lap. '*All the King's Men.*'

'I thought it was about your father.' Then he pressed her hand. 'Sorry. I shouldn't make snide remarks like that.'

She kissed him and went inside to supervise Michael's lunch. Tim watched her go. 'I hope she knows what she's doing, Meg. It's going to be a bigger wrench for her than she realizes.'

Tears suddenly sprang into Margaret's eyes, surprising him: she had always struck him as the least emotional of the sisters. 'Oh Tim, why did it have to happen?'

'I don't really know. The fault isn't all your father's. Just learn from our mistakes. Be sure the man you marry will be one your father approves of. You may have to wait till the right one comes along, I mean a chap you love who also meets your father's approval, but it'll be worth it. Don't let some chap bugger up things for you the way I have for Nina.'

'You haven't – buggered up things for her. She loves you – isn't that all that matters? I just hope I'm as lucky as she is.'

'You're sweet.' He put a finger against her cheek. 'Just take care. You Beaufort girls have got everything in the world but a guarantee of happiness. And nobody has that.'

# Chapter Three

♦

# Nina

## I

By the time the Davorens were ready to leave for England, Lucas had thawed out towards both of them. It was not in his nature to beg forgiveness and he could only go just so far in his rapprochement with them. He left it to Edith to make a last-minute effort to talk Nina and Tim into staying.

'I'm sorry, Mother. I'm glad we're friends again with Daddy, but I think we need to get away from him. For a while, anyway. Once we're on the other side of the Atlantic, maybe he'll learn not to be so possessive.'

Edith, standing amidst the Sèvres china, the Persian rugs, the silk drapes, said, 'I feel like a mother must have felt a hundred years ago when her family left her and headed West.'

Nina laughed, a little too heartily; but it was a good excuse to let out some of the emotion in her. 'You don't really think you're a pioneer woman!'

Edith had not lost her sense of humour. She looked about her, then laughed and took her daughter, the pioneer sailing for England, in her arms. 'You know what I mean. I never dreamed I'd be losing any of you – '

'You're not losing us, Mother. You'll just have to get used to the idea that the world has got bigger.'

Even Lucas, when it came time to say goodbye, conceded that fact. 'We're investing overseas – in oil, for a start. I suppose it was inevitable. Can't get used to it, though. I don't like the thought of

70

foreigners telling me what I can do with my money.'

'Why are you doing it then?' said Tim, more at ease with Lucas than Lucas was with him. 'You don't need the money.'

'Washington approached us. I never thought I'd be doing that feller Truman a favour, but he *is* the President, God help us. They want us to expand over there in the Middle East before the Russians get in. Beaufort Oil is going into a place called Abu Sadar on the Persian Gulf.'

'You can stop off and visit us in England when you're on your way to the Gulf.'

'I won't be going out there, I've got fellers to do that. But Edith and I will come and visit you – ' He put out his hand, for a moment looked as if he was going to break down and plead with Tim to stay, not to take his favourite daughter away from him. 'We'll come whenever you ask us.'

The departure was a quiet one, with no farewell parties. Nina went round and said goodbye to her friends, discovering only as she was leaving them that none of them was really close to her. Tim went back to the stockyards only once, to say goodbye to Bumper Cassidy, who wished him well and invited him back for the next strike – 'Next time we're gonna get what we ask for.'

Magnus McKea, home now from Europe, glad to have Nuremberg behind him, came to say goodbye to both of them. 'My father is retiring and I'm taking over the law office. That means I'll be dealing with your father direct, Nina. If there's anything – '

'We'll let you know if there is, Magnus. Will you handle my funds for me, send money across when we need it?'

She was alone with McKea for the moment. There was a tacit agreement between her and Tim that they would need her money to live comfortably in England, but she had become self-conscious about it, as if it were some sort of family birthmark better left ignored. She welcomed the idea of Magnus as her own lawyer, even if he was also her father's.

Magnus himself was a little dubious. 'I'm your father's lawyer first. If there's any conflict of interest, I'm afraid I'll have to take his side.'

'We'll risk that. I'm hoping any disagreement between Daddy and us is over for good.'

The final farewells were said at home, then George drove them to Union Station. Lucas had decided against a public goodbye, in case there should be a reporter or two waiting. It was as if he saw Nina's going away as some sort of defeat for himself: he didn't want it spread across the newspapers for all to see. It was bad enough that people in their own circle knew what had happened, even if they could only guess at the reason for the Davorens' departure.

George carried Michael into the station. 'I'm gonna miss him, Miz Nina.' Michael, a year old now, laughed without restraint, the only one young enough not to feel the pain of the occasion. 'Gonna miss you and Mister Tim, too.'

The Davorens crossed the Atlantic on the *Queen Mary*, a booking that Nina had sentimentally insisted upon. They spent a month at the Savoy while they looked about for a place in the country. Tim raised no objection to their staying at the hotel, even though Nina was footing the bill; she wondered if he was letting her indulge them before they got down to living on his terms.

They found a house to lease and a business to buy at the same time and in the same place, Stoke Bayard, a village on the River Thames near Henley. The house was on a ten-acre island in the middle of the river, connected to the main bank by an arched bridge over a tributary of the main stream. The business was on the edge of the village, a boat-yard which built punts and skiffs and, in summer, rented them out to fishermen and picnickers who came down from London.

The house was a pre-1914 summer pavilion, a seven-roomed folly or, as Tim described it, a family of gazebos. 'I love it,' said Nina. 'It just proves not all the bad taste is in America.'

'It's not practical. We'll freeze in winter.'

But they went ahead anyway, because she insisted, and leased the house for a year and moved in as the best summer England could remember began to turn into an equally beautiful autumn. Tim took over the boat-yard and the one full-time worker as the last of the summer visitors began to dwindle away.

The yard stood at a bend in the river and looked up to the house on the island. Tim would sometimes see Nina on their front lawn with Michael and they would wave to each other; life seemed idyllic, with his work so close to his home and no Lucas to worry about. He even forgot about the prospect of winter in the pavilion built for summer.

His sole full-time employee was an Australian artist who lived opposite the island with his wife and two small daughters. He had done his apprenticeship as a boat-builder back home in Australia and he was still working at his trade while he established himself as an artist in England.

'Australia is a bloody cultural desert.' Steve Hamill was a short chunky man with a thick moustache and a rolling gait that suggested he had been a sailor; but he was scared of the water and couldn't explain why he had become a builder of craft to sail upon it. 'I suppose it's like that in the Middle West, is it?'

'I don't know,' said Tim. 'I was never much of a one for culture.'

'I've got no education to speak of, but I know where the soul of art is. Right here in Europe. All I've got to do is absorb it, get it *into* me, and then I'm going to be the most successful bloody artist ever came out of Aussie.'

'Perhaps I'd better buy one of your paintings now while I can still afford your prices.'

The Hamills lived in a large caravan which Steve had redecorated. It stood in one corner of a field like something forgotten by a carnival that had moved on. Near it he had built himself a small shed that was his studio.

Eileen Hamill was a pretty girl with auburn-tinted bangs and a quiet manner that suggested she took a long view of everything. Her whole life seemed to be Steve and their two small girls; she was prepared to wait forever for him to be the artist he wanted to be. But Tim, who had now developed a very personal eye for such things, wondered how long her patience would survive the cramped, uncomfortable life in a caravan.

While Tim looked at Steve's paintings in the shed, Nina sat with Eileen in the caravan and sipped tea and ate home-made scones. The two small Hamill girls, delighted to have a living doll, played with Michael on the grass at the bottom of the caravan steps.

'I grew up in the slums back in Melbourne,' said Eileen. 'The only time I ever got out of the city was when the local church took us on a picnic. To live like this — it's heaven.' Then she added, 'Though I don't know what it will be like in the winter.'

Nina was still adjusting. Life for her had suddenly been reduced to a much smaller scale. She could not imagine living in the confined quarters of the caravan; she wondered how the Hamills made love, sleeping so close to their children. She couldn't see herself under Tim with two pairs of bright curious eyes peering over his shoulder. She smothered a giggle at the thought, coughed and made out some tea had gone down the wrong way.

'But at least it's our own and it's better than living right on top of each other as they do in London. Even in the slums back home we had a backyard. But we keep hoping we'll have something bigger in a year or two. You have to, when you're an artist. Hope, I mean.'

Nina went across to the shed to look at the paintings. Taking

73

Steve Hamill as no more than a working man with perhaps enough talent to have given him some ambition, she was surprised at the sensitivity of his paintings. His wife and his children were subjects in all his work, but they were not portraits; they were dream figures in a world in which the rough, casual Steve would have looked as out of place as a cubist dustman in a Watteau landscape. There were thoughts in Steve Hamill's head that he could never express in words, that had to come out through his rough, broad-fingered hands.

Nina and Tim bought three paintings and two sketches and Steve shook his head at them. 'I hope you're not being charitable.'

'We're buying them as an investment,' said Tim.

'You want your heads read. My stuff an investment? Well, it's your money. I hope you're not leaving yourself short.' He and Eileen had no idea who Nina was, nor did anyone else in the village; she was enjoying her anonymity, the first time in her life she had not been a Beaufort. 'How about twenty quid each for the paintings and a fiver for the two sketches? Or am I asking too much?'

Going back to the pavilion, Tim carrying the paintings and Nina carrying Michael straddled across her hip, Nina said, 'I wonder what it's like to start at the bottom like that?'

'You'll never know, darling heart.'

'I couldn't live in cramped conditions like that. I was thinking, how do they make love with everything right on top of them? Including the children.'

'The poor have had to do it that way for centuries. They hold their breath, which accounts for the pop-eyed look among the poor. It's only the fortunate who can expose their privates in private. Shall we go in and try a little exposure?'

'It's five o'clock. *Cinq à sept*, as the French say. I've always wanted a lover to call on me before dinner. What shall we do with Michael?'

'Hang him on the wall with the paintings.'

2

Autumn slipped into winter. The river lost its sparkle, the songbirds went south, the sun came out only occasionally as if it too was being rationed by the austerity-minded government. Tim and Nina made friends in the village, but gradually Nina began to feel homesick. Food and Christmas gift parcels arrived from Kansas City like insidious propaganda: come home, said every tin and package. But she said nothing and if Tim noticed any change in her, he also said nothing.

She and Tim and Michael had Christmas dinner alone. The table was loaded, but all the food had come in cans from America. Each of them put on a brave face, but Michael was the only one who laughed and enjoyed himself without restraint. Tim had suggested having the Hamills join them, but they had gone up to spend Christmas with some Australian friends in Earls Court. Despite fires in every room the house was cold; it seemed to have a chill of its own that had nothing to do with the weather outside. A winter wind scavenged the trees, seeking the last of the leaves; yesterday's rain had turned to ice under the hedgerows, like negatives of shadows. When the phone rang at four-o'clock in the afternoon Nina rushed to it as if it were a lifeline thrown to her across the Atlantic, though she knew nobody would call her from Kansas City.

'We're here,' said her mother, sounding warm and comfortable, as if she herself were centrally heated.

'Where?'

'In London, of course. At the Savoy. We were going to surprise you, be down with you for Christmas dinner, but the boat was delayed by storms. We – '

'Mother, who's *we*? All of you?'

'No, just your father and Meg. Your father had to come over on business – '

'What about Sally and Prue?' She wanted to see them *all*. She still couldn't believe her mother was in England, knew this had to be a dream and she might as well dream for the most.

'Sally's been left with a tutor. She's been neglecting her school work for that blessed car you gave her. Can you imagine, she got only nine per cent in history. American history, too.'

Nina laughed and laughed: Oh God, she was glad to hear anything about any of them! 'Prue?'

'Has the measles. How is my grandson? How do we get down to see you?'

'Mother, we'll come up!' All at once she didn't want her parents to see where she and Tim were living; not in this season with the house as cold as it was. She was afraid they would use it as an excuse to criticize Tim, blame him for making her and Michael live in such Spartan conditions. She did not want her

75

Christmas, which had suddenly *become* Christmas, spoiled. 'We'll have dinner at the hotel with you . . . No, we were going to have it tonight anyway . . . No, I don't have enough for us all . . .'

'Two Christmas dinners in a day?' said Tim.

They drove up to London in the pre-war Jaguar SS they had bought when they had moved down to the country. There was still petrol rationing, but Tim got a business quota for the boat-yard and, in the spirit of spivvery of the times, each weekend he filched a gallon or two and it added to the small family allowance they got. Being able to drive up to London was a luxury in itself, another way of feeling rich.

'Why didn't you ask them down to the house?'

'I thought you'd like a break – '

He said nothing and she knew she hadn't convinced him.

But any uneasiness vanished as soon as the family reunion took place. Her parents greeted Tim with the same warmth as they did her. It seemed that all was forgotten and this was a new start. Nina went into the main bedroom of the hotel suite with her mother, Margaret and Michael, the latter swamped with atten-tion from his grandmother and aunt. Lucas and Tim sat down in chairs by the window and looked out on the dark river and the bombed ruins along the south bank.

'Nina's letters said you were doing well with your boat busi-ness.'

Tim himself had never written and he wondered how much Nina had boasted of him as a successful boatman. He said cautiously, 'It's too early to tell. I took over at the end of the season. I shan't really know how things will go till the end of next summer.'

'Well, if you need any finance . . . Or shouldn't I offer that?'

'I'll keep it in mind.' But the last thing he would ever do, he told himself, would be to accept money from Lucas. 'Why are you here? Edith said you were on business.'

'The oil company is expanding. We're setting up an office in London, then we plan to branch out with gas stations all over the country. I'm afraid I'm an internationalist now. Never thought I would be, but a man has to change, I guess.'

'How's the project going in the Middle East?'

'Abu Sadar? The place is floating on oil. Our only problem is keeping on the right side of the Sultan. *He*'s okay, but he's got some sons who want to meddle. We're starting to educate them in America now, you know? Bringing the young fellers to Harvard, Caltech, places like that. A mistake, I think. Educate the natives, you buy trouble for yourselves. Their ignorance is your bliss.'

'That one of your own?'

Lucas laughed, slapped Tim on the knee: the armistice was complete. 'I think it was one of your Foreign Ministers talking about the British Empire. Well, shall we go down to dinner? I guess you're hungry as a horse?'

'A whole stable,' said Tim, wondering if he looked as stuffed as he felt.

The Savoy produced a cot and Michael, worn out by all the fuss made of him, was put to bed in the care of a chambermaid. Then the Beauforts and the Davorens all went down to dinner.

Tim sat between Margaret and Edith; it was the former who engaged him. He had never seen her so animated and voluble; she kept grabbing his arm to turn him back to her every time he attempted to say a word to Edith. She looked beautiful and, yes, sexy (he was surprised to find himself looking at her in that light). It occurred to him as he looked across the table that, compared to Margaret, Nina looked tired and drab. He chided himself, because he knew it was his fault.

'Nina looks tired.' Edith managed to get a word in. 'Has she been unwell?'

'The excitement has just got to her.' But he knew it was more than that.

'We miss her, Tim. I have to tell you that, even though you'll dislike me for it. We miss you, too. And that last isn't an afterthought.'

'Of course it isn't!' Margaret grabbed his arm from the other side, swivelling him round; at least she was preventing him from eating, a relief he hadn't expected. 'We all do miss you! We're here for a week, you've got to spend every day with us – '

'I'm a working man – '

'Oh bushwah! Close your old boat-yard down – give your men a vacation – '

'With pay? That would give your father a stroke.'

But nothing, it seemed, would give Lucas a stroke right now. All his attention was on Nina; he had re-possessed his favourite, if only temporarily. He caught Tim's glance and he flashed a smile, the across-the-table smile, the dental fireworks that mean nothing. Or did the smile mean nothing? Tim wondered if there wasn't a spark of triumph in it, that Lucas was beginning a new battle in which he had already made a gain.

Edith suggested that Tim and Nina stay up in town that night, but Tim, feeling perverse, said they would have to go back. 'But tomorrow is a holiday,' said Nina. 'Boxing Day.'

'You never know, there may be some fools wanting to go out on the river.'

'Business is business,' said Lucas understandingly, nodding in agreement. Then: 'But maybe Nina and Michael could stay.'

*Did he say that too innocently?* Tim looked across at Nina and was disappointed to see how eagerly she had greeted her father's suggestion. He felt suddenly jealous; and then, just as abruptly, didn't care. The other side of the coin of jealousy was indifference; it was his first experience of how the coin could flip without warning.

'Stay a couple of nights,' he said, 'then bring your mother and father and Meg down to our place. I'm sure they want to see where we live.'

Nina's face was blank. 'A good idea.'

Nina and Michael, her parents and Margaret, came down by chauffeur-driven Rolls-Royce the day after Boxing Day. The big car rolled through the village and the villagers stopped and looked after it when they saw Nina sitting in the car. It drew up at the boat-yard and Steve Hamill came into the office where Tim was struggling with a stock list.

'The wife's outside. Yours, not mine. In a bloody great Rolls. I must say she looks at home in it.'

Tim went out to the car. It was a cold day, a wind coming in from the ice-works of Russia, and only Lucas got out of the car. 'Nice little place. Bit primitive though, isn't it?'

'We preserve the primitive here in England. It's part of our tradition.' He tried to keep the acid off his tongue; he wasn't looking for another battle. 'It seems to work.'

'Couldn't work in these conditions myself.'

'Lucas – ' He couldn't resist it; even so he diluted the acid with a smile. 'You've always worked in a board-room. These conditions here are no worse than those I worked in at the stock-yards. Did the chaps there ever get their raise?'

'No. But we gave them a fifty-dollar bonus for Christmas.'

'Your place in Heaven is assured.'

'You're too cynical, Tim.'

'No, just whimsical. You bring it on in me. Shall we go down and look at our house? The conditions there are a little better. Just.'

Lucas and Edith were appalled at the conditions that Nina and Michael had to live in; they didn't appear to worry about Tim, he was English and accustomed to such living. They said

78

nothing to him, though doing a poor job of disguising their reaction; but they had a lot to say to Nina when Tim took Margaret for a walk round the small island. Edith kept her mink coat on all the time, as if to emphasize her feeling that the fires, blazing though they were and supplemented by electric radiators, were useless in such a house.

'You can't live like *this*. You'll have to get a better house. It's not fair to Michael. He'll grow up crippled with arthritis or something.'

'I couldn't live in these conditions myself,' said Lucas. 'We'll have to do better for you.'

Nina shook her head. 'This house was my mistake, not Tim's. I'll look around for something better. But you're not to say a word to Tim, understand? He's working hard and he's perfectly happy.'

Out in the grounds Tim was saying, 'Perhaps the boat-yard is not what I want for the rest of my life. But it's a start.'

'I still think you should have stayed in America,' said Margaret. 'You *liked* all our creature comforts, I know you did. You should have gone out to California, started something there.'

'How did you know I liked the creature comforts?'

'I know you better than you think. Prue used to say you were always looking at things, and you were. While you were, I was looking at you. And you lapped up everything the family could offer you. Everything but Daddy wanting to run you the way he runs the rest of us.'

They had been walking arm-in-arm, but now he moved away from her on the pretext of pulling off a switch from one of the willows that lined the river bank. He swung the switch back and forth, taking the heads off the yellow reed-feathers along the bank, like a destructive schoolboy who, for reasons he couldn't name, had to abuse nature. Then he stopped, regretting the reed-feathers lying like gold dust on the thin snow that had fallen last night. He looked sideways at her, again like a schoolboy.

'What else have you observed about me?' He felt uncomfortable with her; her very youth somehow made her formidable. 'Never mind, I don't want to know. But obviously I should have been looking at you more closely.'

'You could have done worse.'

At first he didn't catch what she meant. Then he burst out laughing, more with surprise than amusement. 'Meg, for Christ's sake – ! I don't play around – '

'I know that. That was why it was all so hopeless.' She said it flatly, with no dramatics.

It might have been better if there had been dramatics: then he could have put it down to a crush on him. But he realized, with sickening certainty and no conceit, that she was in love with him. He slammed the willow switch against the trunk of a wych-elm, a substitute for her. He wanted to whip some sense into her, could feel the anger building in him as he stared at her.

'Jesus God Almighty – Meg, do you know what you're saying? Of course you do –' He saw the pain in her dark eyes. He threw the willow switch into the river, afraid of the angry trembling in his hands. He walked on and she fell into step beside him but did not put her arm in his this time. 'Meg, I'm sorry, but you'll have to put all this out of your head. I'm married to Nina and I'm in love with her and that's that.'

'Don't you think I know it? I shouldn't have told you. But it slipped out.'

'You've got to be sensible –' He sounded as if he were talking to a schoolgirl; and he didn't want to sound that way. This was far more serious, for himself as well as for her, than a fleeting schoolgirl fantasy. He began to wish she wasn't so damned adult. 'You'll be unhappy, I suppose, for a while. But you'll make me unhappy. And Nina, too, if she ever found out.'

'She won't. I'm not a bitch. And I said I'm sorry I told you.'

Out of habit he went to kiss her on the cheek, as he had done innumerable times; but at the last moment held himself back. 'Let's go back to the house. One thing I'm glad of – there are no tears.'

'There may be tonight,' she said. 'But you're safe for now.'

The Beauforts went back to London in the afternoon, Lucas and Edith convinced that Nina had condemned herself to a life of poverty, Margaret angry and ashamed that she had exposed her feelings to Tim. They stayed another week in London but did not come down to Stoke Bayard again. Tim and Nina went up to visit them and Nina stayed at the Savoy with Michael for a couple of nights. Edith and Lucas said nothing more about the way in which the Davorens were living, but when Tim came up on the last day Lucas took him aside.

'I meant what I said, Tim. If you want to expand that boat-yard, call on me. Don't go to a bank. No point in getting into their clutches,' he said with a banker's smile.

*Nor in yours, Lucas old chap.* 'I shan't think of expanding for at least another year.' He returned Lucas's smile, turning the conversation into a joke between them: 'If you want any help with the oil fields out in Abu Sadar, call on me. My Arabic is rusty, but I can always brush it up.'

'Didn't know you spoke Arabic. The young fellers all speak English out there, but the old guys never bother to learn. You'd think they would, dealing with us all the time.'

'Just what we English used to say in our Empire days.'

'You being whimsical again? You can't joke about the Arabs. They're going to be a pain in the ass to us some day. Well, now we're off to Paris – Edith and Meg want to go. Never liked the French myself. They're a pain in the ass, too. Never can trust them.'

'What about the English?'

Lucas winked, refusing to take the bait. 'Time we were leaving.'

Farewells were said. The Beauforts hugged Michael, squeezing affection into him as if giving him blood. Nina hugged and kissed her parents and sister; Tim watched carefully, alert for any sign that she wanted to go home with them. He shook hands with Lucas, kissed Edith on the cheek. Then he had to say goodbye to Margaret.

He took her hand, felt the tension in her fingers. 'Enjoy Paris. I was there only once, but I loved it.'

'Why don't you come with us now?'

He kissed her quickly on the cheek, extricated his fingers from hers. 'I'm a working man with a wife and kid to support.'

He turned away from her, still feeling the tension in her even though he was no longer touching her.

# 3

It snowed heavily during the night and for the next two days. All the pipes in the house froze, and Tim moved Nina and Michael down to a hotel in Henley. He went back to the house and invited the Hamills and their children in to join him; they would be a little more comfortable than in their caravan. Tim stoked up the fire in the living-room, kept it going twenty-four hours a day, and he and the Hamills camped in the room. They boiled ice for drinking water and poured hot water down the toilet to break up the ice in the sewage pipe. Nina phoned twice a day from the hotel and Tim, lying unconvincingly with a half-frozen tongue, told her things were fine. On the third night the snow turned to rain and it rained for the next three days. By then Tim, telling Steve Hamill not to worry about the cost, had insisted that Eileen

Hamill and the two little girls be moved down to join Nina and Michael in the hotel at Henley.

On the sixth morning Tim, who had been dozing in a chair, half-awake all night, sat up as Steve shook him. 'We've got to get out, mate. The bloody river's at the front door.'

Tim hastily did up his boots. He looked around the living-room, at first saw nothing that he wanted to save from the flood; then he noticed Steve's paintings and sketches hanging on the wall. He grabbed them and raced upstairs with them, wrapped them in blankets and laid them on the bed in the main bedroom. When he got downstairs and into the hall Steve was at the front door with a skiff.

'Lucky I got this before the bloody thing went under.' The water was rising by the minute, flooding into the house through the open door. 'We better head for the boat-yard. And pull like buggery. If we can't get across that current, we're going to finish up half-way to France.'

Brown water, looking as thick as soup, was rushing down past the house as they slid the skiff away from the front door. The island had already disappeared; the house stood in a brown swirling waste. The usually placid Thames raged past in swift, yellow-flecked ropes of current. Logs and trees bobbed and whirled like drowning dancers; a panic-stricken dog went by, only its head showing, chasing a sheep's carcase. The rain was still falling, shutting out the slopes of the valley, deadening every sound but the hiss and death-rattle gurgle of water.

As soon as Tim and Steve pushed off they had to start rowing furiously. The current swept them straight at the raised bridge that connected the island to the main bank; but there was no island and no bank and it stood like an upturned long-boat stuck on a hidden reef. Tim saw the bridge rushing at them; he dug in his oar and they skidded past with inches to spare. Then he quickly started rowing again. They had to row diagonally across the river if they were not to be swept round the bend and past the boat-yard. A mile downstream there were a lock and a weir and the thought of crashing into one or plunging over the other made him and Steve row furiously.

The river was normally forty to fifty yards wide at the bend; now it was closer to a hundred. The current tore at the skiff, muscling it off an even keel as it struggled sideways across the wide sweep of the bend. Tim was blinded by rain and each time he opened his mouth to gulp in air he choked on the water he took in. Cold and stiff, he must have pulled a muscle: every time he pulled back on the oar he wanted to yell with the pain in his side.

He had got into the skiff without any thought that they might be in any real danger, but now he saw they stood a better than even chance of having the skiff overturned and their being flung into the river. He saw Steve, the man afraid of water, throwing frantic glances back over his shoulder, looking for the far bank and safety.

Everything flung itself against them as they battled their way across the current: the swirling water, the rain, logs and debris. A dead cow hit the skiff head-on in a blind charge; the boat swung round, tipping dangerously, and for a moment Tim thought they were going to go under. Then the skiff righted itself, the two men dug in their oars and they swept down towards the tiny jetty that ran out from the slope below the yard. They hit it with a thud, the skiff splintered and tipped over and Tim and Steve were flung into the freezing water.

Tim grabbed at the jetty as the water tore at him, pulled himself up on to it. He clutched at Steve as the latter was about to be sucked under the platform. Water was already lapping over the jetty and Tim could feel it moving on its pilings. As Steve struggled out of the water, the whole jetty leaned dangerously to one side. Both men scrambled to their feet and ran.

They leapt on to the cobbled slope as the jetty was swept away by the flood. They staggered up the slope and sat down heavily, exhausted by their efforts, weak with relief at their narrow escape. It was fully a minute before they stood up, both of them wavering on unsteady legs.

'Jesus wept!' Steve Hamill let out a cry of agony. 'Look at that!'

Coming downstream, like runaways down a hill, were his caravan and studio shed. They went past at speed, the caravan a bright mocking note, bobbing and dancing like something on a carnival carousel, in the brown raging flood. As it went past the boat-yard the shed, which had been upright, suddenly tipped over. Its floor opened and paintings and canvases shot out and went skimming down the river, riding the current like gaily-coloured surf-boards that had lost their riders.

Tim looked at Steve. The Australian's face was wet, water streaming down his cheeks, but it was impossible to tell whether it was rain or tears. The look on his face, however, was that of a man seeing his life's work going pell-mell down a huge drain.

# 4

The rain stopped the next day, but it was almost a week before the flood fully subsided. The yard lost two-thirds of its boats, sunk or smashed; all the moorings and slipways and the work-shed went downriver. Tim and Nina, the house abandoned, living now in the hotel in Henley, drove up at the end of the week and took stock of the damage. Eileen Hamill stayed at the hotel to look after the children and Steve drove up with the Davorens.

'It will take us at least six months to get things back to normal,' Tim said. 'We'll never be ready for summer.'

'What about the insurance?' Nina asked. 'Maybe we could buy all the boats we need.'

Tim looked around at the havoc. 'The insurance won't cover everything by a long chalk. You want to stay on, Steve?'

The Australian shrugged. He was utterly depressed, unrelated to the casual, happy man the Davorens had known. 'I'm willing. But I don't know if the wife wants to. Did she tell you? One of my paintings finished up stuck under the bridge all the way down at Henley. She saw some kids chucking stones at it, using it as a target. She's more upset at what happened than I am. I think she'd like to move somewhere else, right away from here.'

Tim took Nina's arm and they walked back to the car. The sky had cleared and the sun was shining; the flood-damaged valley was exposed pitilessly in the pale silver-gold light. Upstream the island was above water again; even at this distance it was possible to see the mark just below the upper-storey windows of the house where the flood had peaked. The boat-yard was thick with mud and debris, all of it beginning to smell as the sun shone on it. It looks like a battlefield, Tim thought. And I've just lost the battle.

'I hate to say it, but I don't want to start all over again. And that's what it would mean.'

Nina felt a mixture of surprise, relief and disappointment. She had never seen him defeated before; or anyway so ready to accept defeat. In the time they had been married he had made compromises, but always with a wry insouciance that let her know he was granting concessions to please her. But this was a surrender of himself for himself: for the first time she saw a weakness of character that she had never suspected.

'What worries me is what will happen to Steve?' He looked across at the Australian moving through the wreckage of the yard; Steve picked up a rudder, looked at it as if wondering what to do with it, then threw it aside. 'You should have seen the look on his face when everything he owned went past here the other day. I think it was then I realized how lucky we are.'

'What do you mean?'

'We could lose a lot. This, for instance – even a lot more.' He gestured at the yard. 'But we could never lose everything. He was telling me yesterday. He has exactly fifty-two pounds in the bank and that's all.'

Her disappointment in him was giving way to relief for herself. *My character is no better than his.* 'I don't want to stay here if you don't. But what will you do?'

He had done a lot of thinking: that was evident as soon as he spoke. 'I could go to work for your father again.'

'Back in Kansas City?' She tried to keep the excitement out of her voice.

'Not just yet, perhaps later. I could work for the oil company now it's set up an office in London. I don't know what I'd do, but I'm sure your father could find something for me.' There was just a hint of sarcasm in his voice, as if he were adding salt to his own wounds.

'We'll have to call him right away. They're leaving Paris for Cherbourg tomorrow, to catch the ship.' She was pushing him, but she was confident now she was taking no risk.

They called Lucas that afternoon at the Crillon in Paris. 'Sure, I can find a place for you,' said Lucas. 'I'm sorry about the boat-yard. You sure you want to come and work for me?'

'Lucas, it wasn't exactly easy for me to make this decision – '

'Sure, I understand. But I had to ask.'

Lucas came to London alone, on the boat train. Edith and Margaret had wanted to come back to London for a few more days, but he insisted that they take their booked passage on the *Ile de France* from Cherbourg. He expected some heated discussion in London and he did not want any interference from the women. He expected he would get enough from Nina.

He was right. 'You can't do this, Daddy! You can't expect us to go out to Abu Sadar, taking Michael to a place like that – '

'You and Michael don't have to go. All I'm asking Tim to do is go and learn the business at the source. He said he could speak Arabic – that's not much, but it's more than he has to offer in the London office.'

85

You son-of-a-bitch, thought Tim, using an Americanism because it had just the right amount of bite to it. There were four-letter words on the tip of his tongue, but he held those back. He was surrendering to Lucas and he was going to do it as gracefully as possible. To do so, he knew, would take some of the edge off Lucas' satisfaction.

'I've given it a lot of thought since you called me, Tim. If I put you into the London office, I'd have to move someone side-ways to make way for you – '

'Why do you have to move someone?' Nina demanded. 'The company is big enough – just make another position.'

'Tim wouldn't like that, would you, Tim?'

*The old son-of-a-bitch is co-opting me on his side while he's cutting my balls off.* 'We don't want any nepotism. At least none that will show.'

'I'm not going to Abu Sadar and I'm not letting you go!'

'Drop your voice, darling heart, or we'll be thrown out of here.'

'We shouldn't have invited her to lunch,' said Lucas. 'Women should be left out of business discussions.'

Lucas had checked into the Savoy again and Tim and Nina, leaving Michael with Eileen Hamill, had come up by train. They were having lunch in the Grill, a setting not designed for family rows.

'Do you *want* to go to Abu Sadar?' Nina said.

'Not really. Certainly not without you and Michael.'

'It's no place for women and children, not yet awhile.' Lucas looked at the dessert trolley as a waiter approached with it. 'I'll try the baked custard. You'll only need six months out there. You'll get the feel of the business and then you can come home to Kansas City, to head office. Don't you want dessert, Nina?'

'And what do I do?' Nina dismissed the waiter and the dessert trolley without looking at either. 'Sit here in London twiddling my thumbs?'

'I think what your father is suggesting is that you should go back to Kansas City. Or is that a wild guess, Lucas?' The sarcasm was as smooth as the baked custard which he, too, had ordered.

'Do you need to go to the ladies' room?' Lucas said to Nina.

'No, I don't! Dammit, Daddy, what are you trying to do?'

'Tim will go into marketing when he comes back to head office. That suit you, Tim?' But he didn't wait for an answer. 'Go and powder your nose, Nina. When you come back we'll have it all worked out.'

'That's what I'm afraid of.' She looked at Tim for support, but he shook his head, a gentle movement that she almost missed. But

86

his message was in his eyes: *your old man has won, darling heart.* Abruptly she stood up, almost knocking over a waiter, and plunged blindly across the room and out to the ladies' room.

'Do you agree she and Michael should come home?'

'As she asked you, Lucas, what are you trying to do? Are you stuffing me and having me mounted like some sort of trophy?'

'This is good custard. Think I'll have some more. Stuffing you? I take it that's a euphemism for a stronger term. No, I'm not. I'll remind you, you came to me asking for a job. I didn't have you flooded out of the boat-yard.'

'I'm glad to hear you say that.'

'Cut out your whimsy. That's your trouble, you don't take anything seriously enough.'

'You're wrong there, Lucas old chap. I know this is bloody serious. You're trying to break up my marriage.'

'That's where *you* are wrong. I'm not trying to break up your marriage. But I don't want my daughter and my only grandchild traipsing round the world after you while you try to make a living at trades you have no training for. I can make a good career for you in oil. You're intelligent and if you can sell oil as well as you sell yourself, you'll be a success in no time.'

'You're a past-master at flattery.'

Lucas ignored the comment. 'I can't bring you in cold and dump you on the marketing vice-president back home. That's why you have to go out to Abu Sadar. While you're out there Nina and Michael can live in comfort back home in your own house.'

'I still feel I'm being stuffed. But as the ladies say, if rape is inevitable you may as well lie back and enjoy it. No ladies of my acquaintance, I hasten to add.'

'You'd never need to rape any woman. You're too good a salesman.'

'No more flattery. It's going to my head. Yes, I think I'll have some more baked custard. I'll probably get nothing like this out in Abu Sadar. Unless you'll send me food parcels?'

Lucas smiled, knowing he had won. 'I'll see if Sears Roebuck send food parcels.'

Nina came back, face made up, spirit repaired. Before she even sat down she knew that everything had been decided, that her father, this time with the acquiescence of her husband, had claimed her back into the family. She was angry at Tim for his surrender, but her anger at herself was only slightly less. She would be glad to be returning home.

'I think I'll have some dessert, after all. No, not baked custard.

I'll have a couple of éclairs. I always over-eat when I'm unhappy. When do you leave for Abu Sadar?'

'He goes as soon as possible,' said Lucas. 'I'll stay on until you're ready to leave, then you and Michael can come home with me. The *Queen Mary* is sailing next week.'

'How appropriate. Just like old times.'

'There was nothing wrong with old times.'

'There is if you persist in trying to hang on to them. I see you're ready for your coffee. I'll have a double brandy with mine.'

'The good life,' said Tim, trying to salvage something out of the lunch, the past and the future. 'I thought we had said goodbye to it, but it seems I was wrong.'

# Chapter Four

♦

# Nina

## I

It was another two months before Tim and Nina got away to their respective destinations. Lucas, an army of staff always standing by to do his bidding, had little idea what faced a man in a one-man business. The boat-yard could not be disposed of by just walking away from it; over the two months Tim gained an education in the failure of a business if in nothing else. Steve Hamill stayed on till the final winding-up.

He protested in strong terms when Tim said he and Eileen and the two children were to stay on at the hotel in Henley with the Davorens. 'I can't fork out that sort of money! I'll spend the rest of my life paying you back.'

'It comes out of business expenses. You won't have to pay it back. No argument, Steve.'

On the last day Tim gave him a cheque for a thousand pounds. It was Nina who insisted that the Hamills be given that much and the money came from her own account. 'Two years' wages!' said Steve. 'What's going on? I don't want charity, mate. I know who Nina is now. The wife did a bit of looking up – she got in touch with the American embassy, they told her who Old Man Beaufort was – '

'It's not charity. It's a down payment on your first painting that has a thousand pounds price tag on it.'

'You want your head read. If ever I get more than two hundred and fifty quid for a painting of mine – ' He looked at the cheque and Tim saw the temptation in his face. 'Money. It drugs you, doesn't it?'

The question was too much on target, though he was sure Steve had not meant it to be personal.

They said goodbye to the Hamills and went up to London by train. The Jaguar SS had been disposed of and a property developer had bought the boat-yard site, wreckage and all. They checked into the Savoy again and Nina went shopping while Tim spent a week in the London office of Beaufort Oil. Nights they spent making love.

'I'll be worn out by the time I get to Abu Sadar.'

'That's the idea.' He was highly sexed, something that had never troubled her in the past. But now there was just the lurking doubt. 'Then you won't be chasing the Arab girls up the date palms.'

'I'd never think of doing it up a date palm. I'm going to miss you. I don't mean just *this*. But you, just being with you.'

She could only answer him with tears, clinging to him as if she were losing him forever. They had not discussed her father; all they talked about was what they would do when the six months' separation was up. When it came time for them to say goodbye down at Southampton, where Nina was to board the ship for New York, she was surprised at how emotional Tim became when he held Michael for the last time. There were tears in his eyes as he kissed the child.

'Don't let your father take him over. He's our son and that's what he's going to stay. He's not going to be known as Lucas' grandson. Promise me?'

'I promise. If he has to have a surrogate father, how about George Biff?'

'Couldn't be better. Goodbye, darling heart. Don't look at any other chaps.'

'Let's make love as a final reminder.'

'Here? I don't think the sports deck was meant for that sort of sport.'

The ship sailed and Tim went back to London and two days later flew out to the Middle East. He hated the place: the desert, the discomfort, the tightly enclosed living among the small oil community. But he hid his feelings from those he worked with and was popular with them. He became acquainted with some of the American-educated young men and idly wondered if, as Lucas had predicted, they would provide trouble in the future.

He had been there three months when he flew up to Beirut with one of the engineers. The engineer, who had a girl friend, left him to his own devices. He met an English dancer from one of the night clubs, took her home and went to bed with her. In the morning she asked him for fifty pounds.

'I don't do it for love, love. When my legs have gone and my bosom's drooping, I want to live in as much luxury as I can afford. I'm the original whore with a heart of gold. Only I have it in a bank and I keep adding to it every week.'

He handed her the money. 'That's penance, not payment.'

She kissed him. 'You married men. Your conscience stands up as your cock goes down. Shall I see you again?'

'I think not. Take care of your bullion.'

He went back to Abu Sadar, wondering how many people in Kansas City would think of him as a male whore when he went back there.

Nina had arrived home with mixed feelings that stayed with her like a dull fever for a month after her return. She missed Tim and she hated her father for what he had done to them. But she welcomed the security and warmth of being back home with her sisters.

'How's your love life?' she asked Margaret.

'She's going out with an *ancient* man.' Prue was now seven, bright and observant; she still had the innocence of childhood but was looking forward to losing it. 'He's a professor.'

'He's not a full professor and he's only twenty-eight, for God's sake.' Margaret, trying to please her father, had elected to go to the University of Missouri instead of Vassar; but Lucas, disappointing her again, had taken her decision for granted. 'He's teaching me politics.'

'Hah-hah,' said Sally, who was beginning to show some of the beauty of her older sisters. She was still a tomboy, still mad about cars, but Nina noticed that when a boy called on Saturday evening to take her out she was as feminine as any of them. She had begun to learn that boys didn't like kissing a grease-stained cheek, no matter how mechanical-minded they were. 'That Frank Minett is more interested in Daddy than he is in you.'

'What about you? Who's your regular boy-friend?'

'She's got dozens,' said Prue, the gossip columnist. 'She goes out with anyone who's got a sports car. She's going to get into trouble some day, that's what I heard Daddy tell Mother.'

'Not in a sports car,' said Nina, winking at Margaret and Sally. 'Where does this child get her education?'

'Reading books. She reads everything she can find. She brought home *Forever Amber* the other day from school. God knows where she got it.'

'I think I'd like to have lived in olden times,' said Prue. 'Men liked women in those days.'

That six months was, up till then, the most drawn-out period Nina had ever lived through. Each day fell reluctantly from the calendar; a week was a long treadmill that never got her anywhere. She attended dinner parties put on by her parents, went to other parties with Margaret, took up with old schoolfriends; but all the distractions were only a way of filling in time and were not always successful. Sometimes, desperately hungry for Tim, she thought of taking off to join him but she knew she could not take Michael with her and she put the idea out of her mind. Once again she began to spoil Michael, lavishing on him all the attention that normally he would have had to share with his father.

That year, 1948, spun itself slowly off the globe and into the fog of history. The new nation of Israel was proclaimed; Arab armies invaded Palestine. Nina suddenly worried that Tim might be caught up in another war; but he wrote her reassuringly, telling her that the Arabs would never be united against a common foe. President Truman announced that the 80th Congress was the worst in history, a judgement that Lucas agreed with, though it gave his Republican conscience a hernia to say so. The Russians blockaded Berlin and some people began to wonder if Germany was to be another battleground so soon. Thomas E. Dewey was nominated as the Republican candidate for the coming Presidential elections and Lucas accepted a nomination to the Missouri Republican committee; Harry Truman was nominated again by the Democrats and Lucas at once gave a quarter of a million dollars to the Dewey campaign – 'It's worth it to get rid of that feller Truman.' General Pershing, D. W. Griffiths and Babe Ruth died within a month of each other, each of them taking a little glory with them into the grave. The New Look, which had come in the year before, turned into an Old Look; but bobby-socks were still fashionable, proving that bobby-soxers were not as fickle as their older sisters.

Dr Kinsey appeared, to tell the world what it had long suspected, that the next door neighbours had their secrets too; people who had thought they were perverts suddenly discovered they were normal and rushed back to bed, some even neglecting to pull down the blinds. Dale Carnegie's *How to Stop Worrying and Start Living* was published and some people, who never looked at an author's name, bought it thinking it was a sequel to Dr Kinsey's *Sexual Behaviour in the Human Male*. Women readers anxiously waited for Dr Kinsey's promised book on female

92

sexual behaviour, hoping to learn something that their husbands, the dirty beasts, had experienced with the whores out at tha place on the edge of town. The months spun slowly away and Nina, careless of news or history, waited for Tim to come home.

He arrived back in time for Michael's second birthday. 'Good God, how he's grown! What's George been doing – stretching him?'

'He thinks George is God Almighty. You're going to have your nose put out of joint for a while. He doesn't remember you, you know.'

'Do you?'

She kissed him hungrily, glad that she had insisted that none of the family should come to the airport with her. 'Don't ever let us be separated again. I've practically dried up inside. I've had such a yen for you.'

'Me too,' he said, the dancer in Beirut forgotten.

Nina had bought a new car, a Buick, which she drove herself. Michael sat between them, looking up curiously at this stranger, not frightened of him but still cautious. 'I thought you said he could talk?'

'Give him time. He's got to get used to having a strange man playing around with his mother.'

'I hope he's not going to be a two-year-old prude.' He smiled at his son, who continued to look suspicious. 'What does he think of his grandfather? Is he God Almighty too?'

She drove in silence for a while, as if concentrating on getting him home unscathed. She wondered if he *felt* that he was coming home, but was afraid to ask him.

'Don't start fighting with him, please darling.'

'There won't be any fighting. I'm a pacifist in family matters now. Totally spineless. I just want the major share of my son's attention and affection, that's all.'

'You'll get it,' she promised, not wanting to spoil a moment of his homecoming. 'Look, he's already smiling at you. He has your smile, you know. Everyone comments on it.'

He looked steadily at her for a moment, then he relaxed and grinned at his son. 'Five teeth. Is that my smile?'

The reunion with the family went off without incident. Tim was kissed warmly by Edith, Margaret, Sally and Prue, Lucas just as warmly shook hands. He was part of the family again and no one seemed to have any doubts that he might want it otherwise. Nina watched him being charming to everyone, but behind the smile and the banter she sensed a certain restraint, a reserve of feeling that he was not going to squander on this first day home.

93

She had been living in their own house ever since she had first returned from England and today she had prepared the place specially for him. He had always liked flowers, azaleas and camellias being his favourites, and every room glowed with their colours. She introduced him to the new staff she had engaged on her return, a cook and two housemaids, then she took him into the living-room. On the wall above the fireplace was one of Steve Hamill's paintings.

'The other paintings are in your study and the sketches in our bedroom. The more I look at them, the more I like them.'

He looked around the room, but in his mind's eye he was looking all around the house and the estate. It was all so much better than anything he had lived in since leaving here a year ago. *For want of a better phrase, let's say I've come home.*

'Let's have a look at the sketches in the bedroom.'

'I thought you'd never ask.'

A long time later she would remember that first night of reunion. It was perfect: the playing with Michael before he was put to bed, the dinner alone for just the two of them, the love-making when they went to bed for the night. She had never been happier, her mind completely wrapped in the joys of the moment; she did not have to make any conscious effort to shut out to-morrow, the world was just this house and time was only now. Even the pain of the six months' separation was forgotten.

Tim went to work in the oil company and, as far as Nina could judge, seemed happy and successful in his job. He went out of town, to New York, Washington, Chicago on business, but he was never away for more than two nights and he always called her each night. September became October; then November and the elections loomed. Republicans across the nation, Lucas not least of all, prepared to welcome President Dewey.

'We must have a party,' said Lucas. 'We'll have something to celebrate – a man of our own in the White House after sixteen years of those goddam Democrats. We'll have the party on Election Night.'

'Mightn't that be a little premature?' said Tim. 'I'm not so sure that Truman won't win.'

'Care for a small bet? I'll give you ten to one.'

It was a moment before Tim said quietly, 'All right. I'll put up five thousand dollars.'

Lucas looked as if he was going to laugh, then he frowned as he saw that Tim was serious. 'That's a lot of money for you. You've never been a gambling man before.'

'No. But didn't you once tell me that this country was built by men who took chances? Your father included.'

'They didn't back losing Presidents. Still, if you want to throw your money away . . . Five thousand. That's half what the company's paying you a year, isn't it?'

'Yes. So if I win I'll be five years ahead.'

'You might also be out of a job,' said Lucas, but managed to smile as he said it.

Harry Truman came home to Independence, worn out by his whistle-stop campaign by train across the country. But on the front page of the *Star*, which had not endorsed him, he showed the old chirpy confident smile – 'The people are going to win this election, not the pollsters.'

'Bull,' said Lucas, tying his black tie in front of the dressing-table mirror; Edith had decided that a Republican victory should be celebrated in proper style. 'The pollsters are right, every one of them. He can't goddam win!'

'Watch your language, sweetheart – you're starting to sound like him.'

Though the word had not then been coined to describe them, the Establishment of Kansas City was there that night at the Beaufort party. The celebration started as soon as they arrived; guests were drinking champagne toasts to victory within ten minutes of being inside the house. There was a television set and a radio in every room; the big house resembled a luxury campaign headquarters. The men looked rather sombre in their tuxedos, but the women provided a look of bunting: gowns of every colour swirled through the rooms, visible symbols of everyone's gay spirits. Lucas had sent George Biff down to 12th Street to recruit a band; it jammed its way through a score of numbers, playing with such verve that one would have thought that every member of the band was a ragtime Republican. The only number they didn't play was *The Missouri Waltz*, Mr Truman's own favourite.

Nina, radiant in pink, was enjoying herself immensely. She had no interest in politics, but tonight's party had all the bright revelry of parties she could remember from her girlhood. She danced with old boy-friends, hugged old girl-friends, raised her glass a dozen times in victory salutes with her parents' friends. Then, wanting a respite, she went out on the wide enclosed veranda with Magnus McKea.

'Where's Tim?' he asked.

She had been enjoying herself so much she hadn't missed him. 'Probably trying to dodge Daddy. He has a bet on, you know. He thinks Mr Truman will win.'

'God forbid. I hope he's not broadcasting it.'

'Tim is more discreet than that. What time will we hear the first returns?'

'Not for another hour at least. By then all the crowd should be pie-eyed, the way they're going. Ah, Mr Minett. Quite a night, eh?'

Frank Minett was a heavily-built, medium-height man who looked several years older than he actually was. He was ambitious and that gave him a certain spurious aggressiveness which not-too-observant people mistook for confidence. But he was out of his depth in this house tonight, acutely aware of the power and money that he would never have.

'Quite a night, Mr McKea. I was looking for Meg – she wants me to explain the trends in voting as they come in.'

'No need for that,' said Magnus. 'It's going to be a landslide all over.'

Then, looking through the wide french doors into the living-room, Nina saw Tim and Margaret come into the room, both of them looking a little dishevelled, as if they had been out in the rain and wind that had sprung up. Margaret said something to Tim, held his hand while she smiled at him, then went to join her mother and father. Tim looked around, saw Nina out on the veranda and came out, patting down his wind-blown hair. There were rain-spots on the shoulder of his dinner-jacket and a smudge of lipstick on his shirt.

'You look as if you've been celebrating already,' said Magnus.

'He's backing Mr Truman,' said Nina. 'What's he got to celebrate?'

Magnus and Frank Minett seemed to retreat without actually moving. Neither of them was married but they recognized the electricity in a marital storm.

'Oh, there's Meg!' Minett was gone as if he had been jerked away by an invisible wire.

'Think I need a refill,' said Magnus, not even looking at his almost full glass. 'Excuse me.'

'Well,' said Tim when he and Nina were alone, 'my deodorant can't be working.'

'Your charm must be working. You have lipstick on your shirt.'

He smiled, unabashed. 'Meg's. Or did you think it might be someone else's?'

Suddenly she felt ridiculous, wondering what had made her so

96

jealous and suspicious of Margaret. He seemed only mildly concerned, as if perplexed that she should suspect him of any sort of philandering with Margaret or anyone else.

'Sorry. I think I've had too much champagne.'

It was only later, just as she was about to drop off to sleep in his arms in their bed, that it came to her that he had made no attempt to explain why Margaret's lipstick was on his shirt. But that was after they had made love and she knew from experience that the mind had a way of shooting off at tangents after sex, thought trying to re-establish itself again after animal instinct.

The party began to wind down around midnight when it became apparent that Dewey was not going to have a landslide victory after all, that in fact President Truman was leading in the early returns. Magnus McKea got on the phone to the *Star* and came back to report that the political writers were now working on second, revised drafts of their columns.

'They tell me that Harry Truman is out at Excelsior Springs, has gone to bed and is sound asleep. The man's too damned cocky.'

'Going to sleep while feeling cocky – that's no mean feat,' said Tim. 'We had a Prime Minister who used to go to sleep, Stanley Baldwin, but that was because he couldn't stay awake once he sat down in the Commons.'

'You're looking cocky, too,' said Lucas.

'Would you make out the cheque to cash, just in case you decide to commit suicide before the banks open? I don't want Magnus as your executor freezing all transactions.'

The men grouped around the television set in Lucas' study. A few women, Margaret included, hovered in the background. Edith had looked in once or twice, but like most of the women at the party she knew better than to intrude too much. When things were going bad politically, men found women a nuisance. Politics, Lucas had told her, was a male disease that the weaker sex should avoid.

It was Nina, inoculated by too much champagne, who intruded. She breezed into the study, looked at the glum faces, then announced, 'Cheer up, for God's sake! It's not going to be the end of the world if Truman wins!'

'Darling heart,' said Tim, the only cheerful face in the room, 'you are risking being scalped. I believe the gentlemen here are just about to join the Indians.'

Frank Minett laughed, then strangled it as several of the black-tied Indians looked at him as if *he* should be scalped. Margaret, sitting on the arm of his chair, cuffed his ear. Lucas didn't even glance at him but looked at his favourite as if she had hit him with a poisoned arrow.

'Nina, we're not worried about the world. It's what that feller can do to this country that concerns us. Now please stop acting like a high school cheer leader.'

'I think I should make a confession – I voted for Mr Truman.' She had not, but she was in a rebellious mood; something had gone wrong with her evening and she wasn't sure what it was. 'I'm disgusted that anyone from the Midwest could vote for a New Yorker like that Tom Dewey.'

'I apologize for my daughter, gentlemen,' said Lucas.

'He feels like Mrs Brutus,' said Tim. 'Darling heart, you shouldn't stab Caesar in this temple.'

'I think you're both drunk,' said Margaret, coming to her father's aid.

'French champagne,' said Tim. 'It wouldn't have happened if we had been drinking domestic stuff. Never trust the French. Remember saying that, Lucas?'

'I hate to say it,' said Magnus McKea, 'but I think it's all over. I shall go home and get drunk. On domestic bourbon.'

'Spoken like an honourable loser,' said Tim. He sounded as recklessly rebellious as Nina; she had never seen him so opposed to her father in public. He was smiling all the time, seemed in high good humour, but he was getting malicious satisfaction from the fact that he looked like winning his bet with Lucas. 'I'll be over in the morning, Lucas old chap. Shall we leave the wake, darling heart?'

Nina took his arm, 'Bear up, Daddy. You only have to wait another four years. Who knows whom you'll find?'

Next day, after he had collected his cheque from Lucas, Tim went downtown to the Muehlebach Hotel and managed to shake hands with President Truman. 'My father-in-law Lucas Beaufort asked me to give you his congratulations, Mr President,' he lied.

The President's eyes twinkled behind his glasses. 'I'll bet. Ask him if he'd like to come to Washington and work for me. I'm looking for someone to run the social welfare programme.'

Tim went across and deposited his cheque in his account in the City and Country Bank. The teller's eyes went up when he saw the amount and the signature; Tim was tempted to tell him what the cheque represented, but refrained. Last night's champagne was now a sour taste in his mouth. There was also another sour taste, the memory of what had happened with Margaret in one of the empty rooms above the stables. His sense of guilt was doubled by the knowledge that he had enjoyed being with her and that he could be tempted again.

He stood outside the bank in a drizzle of rain wondering where he might go. He was thinking of the ends of the earth, but eventually he went home. Or what, in today's mood, passed for home.

## 2

Though they never came to open warfare and they were always polite to each other, the gap between Tim and Lucas widened. Nina only slowly became aware of it, because Tim never mentioned it. She also slowly became aware of a change in him, a retreat into himself. It was not so much a shutting-out of her as that he seemed to become absent-minded about her. He was just as passionate in bed; but then it is difficult to be absent-minded about sex unless one is a professional. But the light-hearted courting of her that had been such a custom of his was now only an occasional whim. She wondered if this was how it was with all marriages, if husbands and wives, though still in love, stopped being lovers. On a couple of occasions when he went off on business trips he neglected to phone her at night. She even, to her shame, began to look for signs that he was having an affair with another woman, but there was none. Her one stab of jealousy towards Margaret had already been forgotten, put out of her mind by the fact that Margaret's time now seemed taken up with Frank Minett.

'Is he getting serious?' she asked one day when she had volunteered to pick up Margaret at the university. 'Prue tells me he's always hanging around the house.'

'Prue notices too much. Yes, he's serious. But I'm not. The trouble is, Daddy thinks he's just great. He wants Frank to leave the university and go into the bank.'

'I thought Frank's subject was politics, not economics.'

'Frank's subject is anything that's going to get him to the top.'

'You sound as if you don't like him.'

'Oh, I like him all right. But I'd like to do my own choosing, not have Daddy do it for me – which is virtually what he's doing. You were lucky. I mean, choosing Tim without any interference from Daddy.'

'Oh, he tried to interfere. He'll never forgive Tim for being independent.' She paused. 'Have you noticed any change in him lately? Tim, I mean.'

Intent on driving, she did not notice Margaret's careful glance at her. 'No. Why?'

Nina took her eyes off the road for a moment. 'You sound as if I shouldn't have asked you that question.'

'Maybe that's how I do feel. He's your husband – we shouldn't be talking about him.'

'We've been talking about Frank.' She knew she had made a mistake. If Margaret herself had been married it might have been different, but Margaret had no experience to draw upon, had, as far as she knew, never been in love, not really in love. 'No, I shouldn't have mentioned it. It's just that – well, Daddy's turned his back on him. Tim's not going to get anywhere in the oil company.'

'How do you know? Has he told you?'

Nina turned the car in through the gates of the estate, nodded to the security guard as he saluted them. 'No. But I recognize the signs. It's going to be the stockyards all over again. I'm beginning to think we should go away again.'

'Where would you run to this time?'

Nina jerked the car to a halt, skidding it in the gravel. 'That sounds so – so *brutal!*'

'It's true, isn't it? If you take Tim away from here again – '

'For your information, I didn't take him away last time. It was a mutual idea – '

'You still went, that's the point, and it didn't work out. You're never going to win your fight with Daddy by trying to beat him from a distance.'

'You're talking about transferring to Vassar next semester. Is that how you're going to win your fight over Frank?'

'My case is different. I'm not married to Frank and not likely to be. I just want to get away from here for a year or two. I'll come back eventually because I don't think I'd want to live anywhere else. But Daddy's not going to run my life the way he's tried to run yours and Tim's. Thanks for picking me up.'

She got out of the car and ran up the steps and into the big house, not looking back. Nor did Nina look after her: instead she looked across the lawns to where Tim, George Biff and Michael were playing with a tennis ball. Tim had been spending a great deal of time with Michael and George; as a mother she was delighted but as a wife she sometimes felt she was in the way. She looked at the man's world there on the green lawns and suddenly wished for another child, a daughter. She drove on down to the stables, garaged the car and walked back up the winding path. The air held the promise of a hot dry summer to come and she wondered where she, Tim and Michael could go to avoid it. Perhaps to Minnesota or even Maine. A long way from her father.

'Two and a half years old and he has the reflexes of Fred Perry,' said Tim, showing his chauvinism when it came to sport.

'And Sugar Ray Robinson, too,' said George, who wouldn't have known Fred Perry from Suzanne Lenglen but knew his boxers. 'He gets beat at tennis, he can knock out the referee.'

Michael was a sturdy child, big for his age and seemingly without fear. He tumbled about the lawn, chasing after the ball when it was thrown to him, falling over and coming up gurgling with laughter. It was obvious that his father had now become his particular favourite, even over George. He saw Nina, threw the tennis ball at her, then rushed at her and almost bowled her off her feet.

'Terrific tackler, too,' said Tim. 'We'll put him down for Cambridge next year. Eton or Harrow first, then Cambridge.'

'He's going to be educated in England?' She meant to say it lightly but it came out tart. Which was her real feeling.

'I thought we'd discussed it.' He managed to get the proper light note; he tossed the ball high into the air and caught it to his son's great delight. 'English education is still the best, despite the socialists.'

Michael saw his aunts, Sally and Prue, come out of the rear of the big house. He screamed at them, then galloped off towards them. Tim nodded at George. 'Keep an eye on him, George. Don't let the girls spoil him.'

'No chance. He's like me, a man's man.'

As she and Tim walked towards their own house, Nina said, 'I don't think we've said a word about Michael's education.'

'No, we haven't. That was why I was surprised when your father told me everything was arranged.'

'Nothing is arranged! Did you argue with him?'

'I no longer argue with your father. In another nine or ten years, when Michael is ready to go to boarding school, your father may no longer be with us. He's almighty, but I don't think he's immortal.'

She changed the subject abruptly. Criticism was not one of her pleasures, especially of him. 'Why home so early?'

'I've decided I'm working too hard.'

'Are you getting lazy?' She smiled, straining to be light.

He bounced the tennis ball on the close-cut lawn as they walked.

'Yes, I think I am. Or put it another way – I ask myself is there any point in working? Daddy, I've learned, is invincible. He is never going to allow me to be sacked from the oil company – he would never let that happen, for your sake. But I'm never going to get very far up the ladder, either. The truth is, I am not a businessman at heart. The thought of selling millions or billions of gallons of oil doesn't thrill me in the least. And the word has got through to Daddy that the marketing division finds me less than enthusiastic.'

'What's got into you? You sound, I don't know, *shiftless*. You were never like that before.'

'I think I was, only you never saw it. Neither did I. Darling heart, don't be offended by this. I've decided I like being a rich girl's husband, but I'm not going to work at it. Steve Hamill had a word to describe me – a bludger. If one can swallow one's conscience, and I've been chewing mine for some time, there's no pain at all in being a bludger. I'm sorry to disappoint you, but that's the way it is going to be, I'm afraid. I enjoy luxury. Just as you do,' he added unmaliciously.

'I was born to it,' she said, as if that were some sort of argument. But he was unimpressed and she went on, 'What are you going to do, then?'

'I'll do what all the other bludgers – '

'Don't use that word.'

He looked at her quizzically, bounced the ball a few times. She felt awkward, somehow naked; this was a crisis in their marriage and she was unprepared for it. From the maples at the rear of the park there came the plaintive note of a mourning dove; but across the lawns the laughter of Michael, Sally and Prue was a counterpoint. Somewhere a lawn-mower whirred and out on the parkway traffic growled, hummed and sighed. In the midst of an ordinary day, surrounded by the security that she treasured, she felt her life falling apart. She stared at him for some help, but he was blind to or ignored her silent plea.

'I shan't make myself conspicuous. I'll fill in my time so that, if nothing else, I'll *look* busy. But most of all I'll concentrate on being a father. Just to make sure Michael doesn't grow up in my image.'

'Whose image do you want for him?'

'Not your father's.' He smiled, but still managed to sound good-humoured.

She felt bewildered, first by Margaret's outburst, now by this casual declaration by Tim that he was throwing in the towel. True, she had orginally wanted him to become part of the family, though at the time she had not really appreciated how much that surrendering of his independence would mean to him. But in the three years they had been married she had come to see his point, to share his determination to be his own man and not her father's. He was not becoming her father's man now. What was worse, he was settling for being *her* man, letting her money keep him. Her disappointment in him sickened her, yet she knew that she was the one who had planted the seed of corruption.

'Don't worry.' He put out a hand, took hers. 'Things won't change between us.'

'But – ' She gestured helplessly. Michael called *Mummy!* across the still afternoon, but she didn't hear him 'Why all of a sudden – like this?'

'Not all of a sudden. It's been creeping up on me, ever since – ' He bounced the ball in his hand, as if he were weighing time. 'Ever since we were flooded out, I suppose. A lot went down the river that day, though I don't think I realized how much till a long time later.'

Then Sally and Prue, dragging him between them while he squealed with laughter, brought Michael across to them. Red-faced and sweating, he rushed at his father, was swept up into the air by Tim. A week ago, even yesterday, Nina would have smiled benevolently at the sight of her husband and son so delighted in each other's company; now she felt jealous, wished again, with a longing that was almost a physical ache, for another child. Both husband and son smiled at her and, jealousy twisting her vision, it seemed to her that they both looked triumphant.

'Have you heard the news?' Sally said. 'President Truman has asked Daddy to go to Washington, chair some sort of committee. Daddy's having a stroke.'

'Mother's already packing,' said Prue.

'Let's go over and enjoy the fun,' said Tim and, still carrying Michael, taking Prue by the hand, set off towards the big house without looking to see if Nina was following him. But she did, linking her arm in Sally's.

Lucas was shouting loud enough to be heard in Washington if the President had his ear turned their way. 'He's doing it to humiliate me! He could have picked a dozen men, but he had to pick *me*! Will I take the job? Of course I will! It's a man's duty when Washington calls. Why the hell does it always have to be a Democrat who does the calling?'

'Relax, sweetheart. How long shall we be there? Shall we live in a hotel or take an apartment? We can't take you girls, of course – '

'Great!' said the girls, even Margaret. 'God, Washington would be just too awful!'

'We can't leave them here on their own,' said Lucas. 'I'll call that feller and tell him I can't take the job.'

'They can stay with us,' said Nina, and Tim nodded. 'Washington in summer is dreadful.'

'That's why he asked me!' Lucas was torn between patriotism, pride and Republicanism. Brought up by a father who had believed that bi-partisanism was the refuge of political cowards, he had none the less felt considerably out of things. Washington had become a nest of Democrats, socialist vipers who were poisoning the country. He had a moral duty to go there and do what he could to stop the rot. 'He won't be there, he'll be down in Florida or somewhere, gallivanting around in one of those dreadful sports shirts he wears.'

'You can wear your grey flannel suit all the time, to make up for him,' said Edith. 'You're being honoured. You should look at it that way.'

'That's one of the drawbacks of the American system, Lucas old chap,' said Tim. 'If you were in England, they'd give you a title and you wouldn't have to be chairman of anything. Sir Lucas Beaufort. It has an English ring to it.'

Lucas' retort was a loud snort. Edith considered, then beamed: she would not have minded being Lady Beaufort. Then, more practical, she said, 'We'd better decide what you girls are going to do for the summer. Mr Truman has ruined your father's summer. There's no need for yours to be spoiled.'

'I thought we might go up to Minnesota, hire a place on one of the lakes,' Nina said. 'We could rent a place big enough for all of us.'

'No,' said Lucas. 'I'm not having you go up there unprotected.'

'We'd take George,' said Sally. 'And there'd be Tim.'

'Thank you,' said Tim. 'I just scraped into the security force there.'

'No,' said Lucas, unimpressed by either of the nominated security guards. 'If you want somewhere cool, there are other places. Where an eye can be kept on you all. We're well-known now outside Missouri. People would recognize our name and there's no knowing whom you'd attract. Crime is on the increase. Socialism breeds crime,' he added, getting in a swipe at the absent Mr Truman.

'The Davoren name isn't well-known,' said Tim. 'We could be the Davoren family. Unless the girls object?'

'Oh no,' said the girls. 'Anything but Beauforts.'

Lucas looked at the deserters, then at Tim. 'How long were you planning to take off?'

'A month, six weeks. I'll call the office every day, but they won't miss me.'

The two men exchanged looks: swords were in scabbards, but a glint of steel showed from either side.

'I don't think so,' said Lucas. 'We can't have a member of the family taking six weeks off, when the most any other executive gets is two weeks. One week at your level.'

Nina waited for Tim to argue. But all he did, after a moment of sitting very still, was to shrug. 'All right, Lucas, if you feel I must set an example. One week.'

'But that will spoil our vacation!' Then Nina saw that this was a bigger battle between her father and her husband than was apparent on the surface; her father had declared war. She looked at her mother for support, but Edith was suddenly rigid and blind with tact. She turned back to Tim. 'Oh, all right. But you can fly up each weekend.'

'You can go to Montana,' said Lucas. 'The Cattle Company has bought a ranch up there on the Yellowstone River. You'll have the ranch staff to look after you.'

'Oh yes!' said Sally and Prue, who welcomed anywhere as an escape.

'I'm not going,' said Margaret, who had said almost nothing up till now. 'I'm taking a summer course at college.'

'You can't stay here on your own,' said Edith, feeling no need to be tactful with an unmarried daughter.

'Why not? The servants will be here. And I'll have Frank and Tim to see I don't come to any harm – '

'Hah-hah,' said Sally.

Margaret ignored her. 'You can't object, Daddy, if I want to educate myself further instead of taking a vacation.'

'You might have mentioned it to us,' said Lucas. 'Or is this a sudden decision?'

'Frank suggested it a month ago. It will help me at Vassar when I transfer there.'

Is she avoiding looking at me, Nina wondered, or am I imagining it? But it was none of her concern: she was not her sister's keeper. She had her own worries, trying to keep the peace not only between her father and Tim but between herself and Tim. She had to resist the urge to declare war on *him* because of his casual surrender to her father. She was ready to rage at all men for their weaknesses.

She picked up Michael just as he was about to pull over one of his grandmother's Sèvres vases; Edith had been smiling indulgently at him, her heart choking her behind her teeth. 'We'd better go home before Michael wrecks the place.'

'A good idea,' said Tim, rising from his chair as if a spring had bitten him. Then added, already on his way out of the room, 'One wrecker is enough.'

As they went back to their own house Nina said, 'What was that last remark meant to mean? Who's the other wrecker?'

'Go back and ask your father.'

Tornadoes rolled across Missouri during the next couple of weeks though none hit Kansas City. But the atmosphere at Beaufort Park had its own storms; the individual presences of Tim and Lucas met like warm and cold fronts. Nina and Edith watched for storm warnings while they made out lists of what to take to Montana and Washington. Edith prepared as if Lucas had been made ambassador to some country where he and she would be foreigners; in the capital of the United States she would not let America down. Nina contented herself with lists of exotic foods that Tim was to bring up each Friday: she was convinced that Montanans ate nothing but T-bone steaks and French fries.

Lucas and Edith finally went off to Washington, where Lucas was surprised and mollified to find out just how much the Beaufort name meant. President Truman, in a blue summer-weight suit, white shirt and plain blue tie, was still in Washington and greeted Lucas like an old friend. Or an old foe who had seen the error of his ways and couldn't resist flattery. But he didn't flatter Lucas to his face, being too wise a politician: you only did that with the party faithful. Lucas was to be chairman of a committee to look into new banking regulations.

'They were all expecting me to give the job to one of those Eastern fellers,' said the President. 'Rockefeller or one of them. But I said I wanted someone from back home and you were the first name came to mind.'

'I'm honoured, Mr President,' said Lucas, overcome by the Oval Office if not its occupant. He wondered why it had never occurred to him to run for the Presidency. 'Really honoured.'

'So am I,' said the President with a grin. 'Tom Pendergast always said you had the best business mind in the Middle West.'

Lucas smiled politely, glanced at the famous sign on the President's desk: *The Buck Stops Here*. It wasn't much of a Presidential motto, but what else could you expect from an ex-haberdasher?

Nina, Michael, Sally and Prue, accompanied by George Biff, went to Montana, where no one knew the Davorens and no one genuflected to the Beauforts. The ranch was far less primitive than Nina had expected; Jim Bridger and the mountain men were long dead and the Montanans had discovered electricity, refrigeration and innerspring mattresses. They did make a fetish of T-bone steaks and French fries, but the mountain air gave all the Missourians such an appetite that anything tasted good. They swam in the cold waters of the Yellowstone and went for long walks through the ponderosa pines on the mountain slopes. It was all idyllic for Nina, particularly when Tim came up each weekend.

'I hate the thought of you slaving down there in that Missouri heat.'

'I'm a privileged slave. The air-conditioner in my office actually works.'

'How's Margaret? I wish she were up her with us.'

'I hardly see her. Frank must be taking up her time.'

'How do you fill in your time at night?'

'Reading – I'm at last attempting *War and Peace*. And looking at Milton Berle on TV.'

'Did you miss *this*?'

'Actually, I've been thinking of taking up celibacy as a hobby.'

'Like hell you will.'

But later, after they had made love, she wondered why he lay awake and did not fall asleep as usual. He lay stiff and silent in the bed beside her. When she sleepily murmured what was keeping him awake, he did not answer but just put his arm under her and held her to him. She was happy enough to accept that as an answer.

## 3

Lucas and Edith returned from Washington after only a month. Lucas was careful to point out that he was not resigning from the committee because of any disagreement with it or the President; he was returning to his home solely for health reasons. Edith, who was enjoying Washington despite the heat and the fact that virtually *nobody* was in town, asked worriedly what was wrong with his health. He assured her there was nothing wrong with him, but she was to keep her mouth shut. He had sometimes told her to be quiet or not to say anything; he had never before told her to keep her mouth shut. She guessed something had gone wrong, seriously wrong, either politically or with business, and she recognized that, worried as he appeared, he was only trying to protect her. But she wished that, even if only occasionally, he would take her into his confidence more about matters that concerned him.

Nina brought her sisters and Michael and George Biff back to Kansas City on the same day. It was one of those coincidences that tie knots in the web of destiny, reassure astrologers and are the despair of cynics and rationalists: there was no connecting reason why Nina and her parents should have returned home on the same day. Nina had just suddenly tired of Montana and of being separated from Tim and had packed up and left, despite the complaints of Sally and Prue who had been enjoying themselves as never before. Recurringly in the future she would wonder what would have happened if she had remained in Montana with Michael.

She came back without warning Tim, was home in the house before she called him at the office. 'I couldn't take a cowboy lover, darling. I need you.'

Even on the phone he sounded remote and when he came home half an hour later she at once saw the difference in him. He kissed her warmly, but she felt his heart wasn't in it. 'What's the matter?'

'Nothing.' But he saw she didn't believe him. He turned away, stood at the bedroom window staring across at the main house. 'Okay, it's the office. Things aren't going well down there.'

'Are you going to have to leave?'

'I don't know.'

'Is that why Daddy's come home?'

'I don't know that, either. But he wants to see me in his office at the bank tomorrow at ten.'

'I'll come with you.'

'No, you won't. I'll tell you all about it when I come back. This is between me and your father.'

'Don't give in to him again.' It was a plea, but somehow it sounded like an accusation.

He looked at her. 'I'll try not to, this time, But I wish you wouldn't expect so much of me.'

They went out to dinner, came home, went to bed and made love. He was as passionate as ever; brutally so and she welcomed it. Her only regret, which she didn't voice, was that tonight, as every other time, he could make not her pregnant again.

# 4

Lucas was standing waiting for Tim as the latter was shown into the big office. Thaddeus Beaufort had built the bank on 11th Street and this corner office had been his; Lucas had changed nothing, not even the old prints on the walnut-panelled walls. The huge leather-topped antique desk, the leather chairs, even the old-fashioned upright telephone on the desk: Thaddeus could have come back from the grave and felt thoroughly at home. For Lucas it was a constant reminder of a past whose values, he was convinced, were truer than those of today.

'We are not to be disturbed, Miss Plummer.' He waited till his secretary had gone out and closed the door behind her. 'You're on time.'

'Punctuality is the courtesy of kings, my mother used to tell me,' said Tim.

'It's a good rule for businessmen, too.'

'I'll keep it in mind in future.'

'That's what I wanted to see you about. Your future.' Lucas was not one to stare out of windows looking for the right words in an awkward situation. Instead he stared directly at Tim, as if sizing up a stranger who had come to him seeking a job. At last he said, 'I've had a private investigator following you for the past month.'

Tim kept his voice level. 'On my business trips?'

'No.' For the first time Lucas looked as if he might be at a loss for words. A big hand moved restlessly on the desk, as if searching for something to pick up; but the desk was clear of papers and finally his hand settled on a heavy brass ruler. He picked it up, tapped it in his other hand. He looked like a school principal, less formidable than the hard-faced, hard-voiced executive he had been a moment ago. Uncertainty invaded him, something Tim had not expected to see. 'You're finished with the oil company. That was decided before I went to Washington.'

'Thank you for telling me.' Tim himself was suddenly beset by all sorts of uncertainty, doubts and fears. He felt himself beginning to sweat, though the room was air-conditioned almost to chilling point.

'You are also finished as far as the family is concerned.' Lucas waited for some comment, but Tim was now the one lost for words. Or hoped, without much hope, that silence would give him some sort of defence. 'The private investigator reported that you have been seeing another woman while Nina has been up in Montana. Do you deny it?'

'How reliable is your private eye?' The *private eye* sounded flippant, though that wasn't Tim's intention. He knew all at once that everything was coming to an end. He had been a good soldier during the war, but now he had forgotten how to attack. Already surrendering, he said, 'But then you employ only the best, don't you?'

'Not in your case,' said Lucas, not meaning to be witty.

Tim held his ground, if only for a moment: 'Was I employed as a junior executive or a son-in-law?'

'No whimsy.' Lucas held up the brass ruler: light from the window shone on it, cold as his own eye. 'The report has the dates and the names of motels where you met this woman.'

'Does it have the name of the woman?'

'No. That's immaterial. I'm not going to bring the matter to court.'

'You amaze me, Lucas.' Tim knew he was whistling into the wind, which was blowing at gale force; but, already defeated, it was still in his nature to be whimsical. 'I'm unfaithful to Nina and you're the one who's charging me with adultery. You're like something out of the Old Testament.'

'You admit you were unfaithful?'

'Yes.' Tim sighed, but said nothing further.

'Do you want to tell me who the woman was?' Lucas couldn't resist his curiosity, like a sneak glance at some pornography.

'As you said, it's immaterial.' There was silence for a while but for the faint hum of the air-conditioner. At last Tim said, 'What happens now? Do you tell Nina?'

'No. Nor will you.'

'I just might, you know – '

Lucas shook his head firmly; he appeared much less uncertain now. 'I don't think you will. You're weak, Tim. You always have been – I know you better than you know yourself. I'll give you $250,000 and you'll disappear. I don't care where you go, but go. With the $50,000 you won on our bet, you'll have enough to stake you to the good life – you obviously enjoy that. You won't be rich, but you won't starve.'

'Nina won't let me go.'

'If you go without telling her, she won't be able to stop you.'

Tim felt his blood thumping, but it wasn't with anger: unless it was anger at himself. Slowly, over the past months, he had been pulling the plug on his own life: he had known it, but he had not been able to stop. Every time after making love to Margaret he had known it; but each time she had called him to make another date he had gone to her. It had not been just sex that had made him go to her, though she had been surprisingly abandoned at that. He was not in love with her nor infatuated by her; but he had met her each time with anticipation and the pleasure only evaporated when all the love-making was finished and he stood under the shower in the motel bedroom and looked down at the swollen traitor between his legs. Margaret would come into the bathroom and kiss him, not passionately any more but tenderly, with love, and every time he would offer no argument, would tell himself that next time there would be no next time. He knew now that he had been unfaithful to Nina for the simplest and meanest of reasons: he was incapable, if another woman loved him, of being totally faithful. *I have been faithful to thee, Nina, in my fashion . . .*

'What about Michael?'

'He stays with Nina and you renounce all rights to him.'

'You make him sound like an oil lease.'

'He's more than that to me, and you know it. I have no sons, but one day he will be the senior stockholder in the Beaufort Trust. I'll have other grandchildren eventually, but he will always be the first.'

'You seem to be talking only in money terms.' Tim got up, began to walk around. He looked and sounded angry, but he knew it was a hollow anger. 'Jesus, what about Nina? She still loves me. You won't believe me, but I still love her, too!'

'It's a pity you didn't think of that when you were with the other woman.'

He wanted to shout Margaret's name; but already he saw the consequences. It would wound Lucas, which would give himself malicious pleasure; but it would not stop there. Lucas would confront Margaret; and Tim knew enough of Margaret now to know what would happen next. She would confront him, demand that he tell Nina the truth. And that he could not do: Lucas had been right. Telling her would not be easy, but he could do it; but he was too weak to go on living the life that would follow. Everyone would have their hold on him: Nina, Lucas, Margaret. And he was not such a bludger that he could stand that.

'You want me to disappear? You mean just go, without a good-bye or anything?'

'What would you have to say?' Lucas had put down the brass ruler: he had won, was no longer uncertain.

Tim sat down again. 'You're asking too much, Lucas.'

Lucas shook his head. 'Not if it protects Nina and Michael. You'll never be worth ánything to them. If you stay, you'll only go on whoring and sooner or later Nina will find out. You can go now, a clean break, and take some money with you – '

'For Christ's sake, stop talking about money!'

Lucas' look now was that of a businessman, not a father-in-law: he had already won the war in the latter relationship. 'You would regret saying that if I said, all right, let's stop talking about money. But you'll need it – you've become too accustomed to it. The money is there – ' He nodded to a large brief-case on a side table. Tim was not to know it, but it was one of two cases that had carried the ransom money for Nina to Germany three-and-a-half years before. Lucas appreciated the irony, but would not share it. 'You can leave immediately. There isn't even any need for you to go back to the house.'

Tim didn't bother to check the brief-case: he knew that Lucas was honest in money matters if not in family matters. 'You're mean, Lucas. Other rich men have paid millions to get rid of their unwanted in-laws.'

'Are you asking for a million?'

'Don't blanch. This will do. But I'm going home first. Don't worry – I shan't give the game away. But I want a last look at them. I'm entitled to that in lieu of more money.'

'Can I trust you?' Lucas wasn't certain how serious Tim was about the extra money.

'You'll have to, Lucas old chap.' He picked up the brief-case. Money weighed heavily when you were unaccustomed to it. 'I just hope Nina forgives you for what you're doing.'

'If I can trust you, she'll never know what I've done.'

## 5

Nina saw Tim drive in through the gates as she drove down from the stables. She pulled up opposite him. 'How did you get on with Daddy?'

'We had a good heart-to-heart talk. Everything is going to be all right from now on.'

'No fight? Or did you give in to him again?' Then: 'I'm sorry.

I didn't mean to say that. But he's so demanding . . . Why are you home?'

'I have to pick up some papers. Where's Michael?'

'He's somewhere around, with George. I'm going into the Plaza, to get my hair done. Can you meet me for lunch?'

'I can't. I have a date. You look beautiful, darling heart.'

'Thank you. A wife loves to hear that from her husband in the middle of the day. Come home more often.'

So, without knowing it, she said goodbye to him in a banter of banalities. She smiled, blew him a kiss and drove out of the estate. She also drove out of his life and that of her son. When she came home in mid-afternoon they were both gone.

'Mr Tim said he was taking Michael to the zoo,' said George Biff.

'Strange. He didn't mention anything to me. When did they go?'

' 'Bout twenty minutes after you went this morning. Mr Tim was in the house, then he come down and said him and Michael was going to the zoo.'

Nina went back into the house and spoke to one of the maids.

'No, Mrs Davoren, Mr Davoren didn't say where he was going. He came downstairs with a couple of bags, put 'em in his car. Then he and Michael drove away.'

Then Nina began to panic. She rang her father: there must be some connection between him and Tim's strange behaviour. He said abruptly. 'I'll be home at once,' and hung up in her ear.

The panic gave way to aching fear, which is far worse, because the mind has started working again. Then, as the hours and the days and the weeks went by, the fear turned into shock and grief and anger. Tim, whom she loved, had murdered her without actually taking her life. And he had taken Michael, for which she could never forgive him.

# Chapter Five

◆

# Margaret

I

When Tim disappeared, Margaret was shattered; though no one would have known. It was then that she showed the control that was later to have some people describe her as cold and calculating. The change in her did not occur overnight and if it had it would probably not have been noticed by the other members of the family. For everyone was shattered to a greater or lesser degree, even George Biff, who had come to have a great deal of affection for young Michael. The worst affected were Nina and Lucas.

'He had no right to take Michael with him!' Lucas raged. 'He had no right to do that to Nina!'

Edith, consoling the weeping Nina, had tried to quieten her husband. 'Sweetheart, *please*. He wasn't concerned with rights and wrongs. He's walked out on us. Don't make it sound as though we had some sort of contract with him.'

'Isn't marriage a contract?' Lucas was ready for murder; or looked to be. 'We'll get him back, Nina – I promise – '

'Who?' Margaret sat aside from her parents and Nina, her senses numbed. But she looked the least upset of the four. They were in Nina's bedroom and she deliberately kept her eyes away from the bed where Tim and Nina had slept together last night. 'Who will you get back? Tim or Michael?'

'We don't want *him* back – '

'Sweetheart – *please*. It's for Nina to decide.' Edith picked up the crumpled note from the bedside table. '*Goodbye, darling heart.*

*Forgive me.* That's all. You would have expected an explanation
. . . Is there an explanation?'

Nina shook her head, sat up slowly and wiped her eyes. 'I told
you, Mother – ' She looked at her father. 'Can you get someone to
look for them, Daddy? Both of them?'

'Both?' Lucas sounded cautious. Or so it seemed to Margaret,
watching everything like a spectator.

Edith said, 'You'll have to look for both of them. You don't
think he will leave Michael somewhere alone, do you? He's a
swine, going off like that, but he did love Michael. He wouldn't
do that to the child.'

'Both of them, Daddy.' Nina sat listless, body slumped; but
her voice was determined. 'Please.'

'Of course,' said Lucas.

'Leave the police out of it,' said Edith. 'If we can get them back
here without anyone knowing, it will be less hard on Nina – '

'I don't care if anyone knows!' Nina straightened up for a
moment. 'All I want is them back! Jesus, Mother, stop worrying
about what people will think!'

Edith's face was expressionless, but Margaret, watching closely,
knew that she was hurt. She gazed at Nina for a moment, then
stood up and looked at Lucas. 'I still think we can do without the
police for at least twenty-four hours. Get a private investigator,
Lucas. Do you know a reliable one?'

Lucas hesitated. 'I think so.'

'Don't waste any time then. Now I'd better go back and see to
Sally and Prue. They are as upset as any of us. No – ' She put a
tentative hand on Nina's shoulder. 'Not as much as you, darling.
Stay with her, Meg. Come on, Lucas. There's no time to waste.'

But too much time had already been lost. At the end of the
week Dave Pedemont, the private investigator Lucas had
engaged, came to Lucas and told him he was certain that Tim
and Michael were not in Kansas City or even in Missouri or any
of the neighbouring states. 'He's fled the country, Mr Beaufort. I
reckon we're gonna have to start looking for him somewheres else.
Canada, Europe, anywheres. That's gonna cost money.'

'Is the job too big for you?'

'Well, it's bigger'n anything I've done so far. But I got contacts – '

'How much do I owe you, Mr Pedemont?'

'Mr Beaufort, my job's not finished – '

'It's finished. If my grandson – and my son-in-law' – an afterthought – 'have left the country, then I'll need an international
agency to look for them. Send me your bill, Mr Pedemont.

115

Amalgamate it with your bill for that other job. Address it to me here and mark it personal.'

'I can handle this job.' Pedemont could see a dream going out the window: a job that might take him all over the world . . . 'I think I deserve a chance to prove I can do it – '

'This isn't some sort of entrance examination. Send me your bill. That will be all. The door's behind you.'

'You son-of-a-bitch.' But Pedemont said it under his breath: in his job you spent half your time working for sons-of-bitches and you never knew when they'd call on you again.

Five days after Tim disappeared Margaret missed her period. At first she thought it might have been due to the shock she felt at his vanishing as he had; but then she knew better. Or worse, if you liked. Her mother was still concerned with consoling Nina; both households, family as well as servants, were subdued. If Margaret's inner turmoil showed at all, and she had no way of knowing, no one appeared to notice it. But for protection against scrutiny, wary of Prue who had recovered more quickly than any of the others and was once more as observant as ever, she said she was going down to Fairfax, the family plantation.

'I want to do some study. I can't concentrate here.'

'I think you should stay here,' her mother said. 'Nina needs all of us to lean on. She may want to talk to you rather than to me. Sisters have confidences – '

Margaret went across to see Nina. 'I'm not deserting you, Nina – '

'I know that.' Nina had lost weight, looked almost plain. God, I wonder if I look like that, Margaret thought. But I'm not losing any weight. 'You've been wonderful.'

'I've done nothing – '

'You've been more understanding, just saying nothing . . . I'd hate to hurt them, but Mother and Daddy are wearing me out with their attention. They mean well, but sometimes I just want to be alone. Or sit with someone who doesn't feel they have to keep talking all the time. That's where you've been so understanding.'

'Well – ' Margaret accepted the compliment awkwardly, feeling the irony of it. If she had been quiet, untalkative, it had been because she had been afraid of giving herself away. She ventured, 'I miss them. Not as much as you, naturally, but I do miss them. I still keep believing Tim will walk in here one day – '

'Me, too. I don't believe he'll keep Michael from me. Not forever.'

Margaret kissed her, loving her but feeling hypocritical. 'I'll only be a few days down at Fairfax.'

'I'm tempted to go with you – '

'Why don't you?' said Margaret loyally; but wanted to be alone.

'No, I'd better stay here. Just in case . . .'

Margaret went down to Fairfax and two days later did the most calculated thing she would ever do. She spent the two days pondering whether she should have an abortion. To do so would mean having to go out-of-state, to some doctor whom she would not know and who would not know her. There were doctors in Kansas City who did abortions; there was one who came to her mother's parties who took care of the country club women, married and unmarried. She knew two girls at college who had gone east to St Louis; they would give her the name of their doctor. But she was too much a Beaufort: she could not take outsiders into such a confidence. In the end, however, she decided against an abortion because she wanted Tim's baby: she knew she had lost Tim forever. It was an emotional decision, totally against the calculated one that followed it.

She called Frank Minett, asked him to come down to Fairfax. He came at once, tearing down the country roads in his ten-year-old Pontiac; the only place Frank ever took risks was on the roads. He swung in through the gates of the plantation and roared up the avenue of willow oaks that led to the mansion. But when he switched off the engine and stepped out he was a different man: it was as if the hellbent driver had stayed in the car.

'Meg honey – ' He kissed her on the cheek, one eye over her shoulder to see if anyone was watching them. 'You look – hell, *worn out.*'

'I need comforting.' She tucked her arm into his, thinking: *Can I really spend the rest of my life with him?* 'I came down here to think about us.'

'Us?' He was no fool: he knew how little real encouragement he had been given.

'I think what happened up home brought it on. Tim walking out – Nina losing him. I started to wonder about losing you.'

'I was beginning to think you had already lost me. Or got rid of me. How much have we seen of each other in the last six weeks? A couple of nights a week and all we talked about was what you were doing in your summer courses.'

Somehow she had expected him to be overjoyed, unquestioning at her sending for him. But she gave him another chance: 'I was trying to make up my mind about how you felt. Sometimes I got the feeling you were more concerned with what my father thought of you than what I did.'

'Meg – ' He was weakening. 'Look – Christ, how do I say this? If I hung back with you, it was because I thought you'd already written me off. When you and I would neck – this is insulting, I'm sorry – I'd think it was just a Beaufort sister's way of having a fling before she settled down with one of her own class.'

She smiled, hiding her annoyance. 'You think too much about class, Frank. You sound like a socialist.'

It was his turn to smile. 'Don't tell your father, for God's sake! Are they coming down here – the family?'

'No, there's just you and me.'

'In a house this size?'

He had never been invited to Fairfax by the family; it was only a long time later that she learned he had come down to inspect it on his own. He had been writing a book on Midwest wealth, naturally starting with the Beauforts. Three chapters into the book he had met Lucas Beaufort and Margaret; and the book had got no farther. But *he* had; and he would go much farther. He looked at the ante-bellum mansion, a little awed to think that it represented only a minor symbol of the wealth to which this girl beside him was part-heiress. It was almost a cliché Southern mansion. An Ionic-columned porch stretched across the front, giant magnolia trees stood at either side like floral book-ends, a peacock, like a bonus grace note, strutted across the broad lawns.

'There's the housekeeper, Mrs Henriques, and her daughter,' said Margaret. 'But that's all. They'll look after us. Can you stay?'

'A day or two, yes.' He had become cautious again. 'What's the matter, Meg?'

'I told you – I need comforting.' She almost lost her temper then; and he almost lost his chance to marry into the Beauforts. 'You're not much help – so far – '

Then, diving off the high-board, suddenly realizing his luck, he swept her up in his arms and swung her round, put her down and kissed her passionately. She had never seen him so abandonedly gay: he was a stranger, suddenly attractive. If he stayed like this she might, *might*, even come to love him.

He let her go, grabbed his bag out of the car. 'Where's the guest-room? There must be a dozen of them in a house like this.'

'We'd better sleep in separate wings. Just to keep Mrs Henriques appeased. She's very Baptist.'

He smiled broadly, happiness making him almost handsome. 'In front of Mrs Henriques I'll be the soul of discretion.'

But he came to her room that night and she made a very good pretence of welcoming him into her bed. He had none of Tim's subtlety as a lover; he was proud of his equipment and he displayed it like a salesman. But she restrained him, telling him she liked to be brought on gradually, while she made her final decision that this was what she wanted as a solution. She would forever be in love with Tim, but Frank was next best. And he loved her, which was something. She opened herself to him and when it was over he took her tears for granted.

'I feel like crying myself, I'm so happy.'

'Oh Frank,' she murmured, choked with guilt and sorry for him. 'Be good to me.'

'Could I be anything else?' he said and was all at once a very gentle and considerate lover.

Later, after he had shown off the size and value of his equipment again ('I'm proud of that, you know'), she said, 'Let's get married right away, Frank.'

He was sated, but he was still shrewd. 'You mean now? Elope or something? Your father would kill me.'

She sat up in bed. Out in the night a hoot-owl challenged the moon; a mile away on the Mississippi a boat-whistle replied. She wondered if they were warning notes, her imagination expanding with the enormity of what she was contemplating. But she had committed herself and all she could do was lay the foundations for the future.

'If we marry, Frank, you'll have to stop thinking about pleasing my father. Nina's lost Tim because Daddy tried to run his life – '

'I suspected that, but I didn't like to say it.' He lay still, waiting for her to go on.

'I shouldn't want to lose you that way.' The salt of hypocrisy tinged her tongue; it was a taste she would get used to as time went by. 'I have to come first with you, not my father.'

He stroked her back with fingers that were surprisingly rough for a man who did no hard labour. But perhaps he did work with his hands, perhaps as a hobby. It struck her that she had no idea how he occupied his time when he was not with her.

'Okay,' he said quietly.

'We shan't elope, but we'll tell my parents tomorrow that we're going to be married right away.'

'We'll tell mine, too.'

'Of course.' She had never met his parents and she had not given a thought to them.

He ran his hands over her like a blind man. 'You're beautiful. I just can't believe my luck.'

She felt him rising again and she rolled on top of him. He would never be the lover Tim had been, but he had his compensations. She loved sex and he was the sort of bull who could satisfy her.

They went back to Kansas City next morning. Lucas and Edith welcomed Frank into the family, though Edith wanted to know why they couldn't wait. 'Nina gave me no chance to give her a big wedding. A mother looks forward to that – '

'It wouldn't be appropriate, Mother. Not now, not while Nina is feeling as she is. I think the quieter our wedding, the better.'

'I suppose so. But why can't you wait? Am I never going to have a big wedding?'

'From what I read in that old edition of the *Independent*, you had a big one, the biggest in all Missouri up till then.'

'One's own wedding is different. A mother gets more pleasure out of her daughter's wedding – it's a law of nature. No offence, sweetheart.'

'None taken,' said Lucas, favourable towards Frank Minett but wondering if a man bought trouble when he took on a son-in-law. He had certainly bought trouble with that English son-of-a-bitch. He had been unnaturally quiet over the past week, but no one commented on it; they took it for granted that he was grieving for Nina, his favourite, who had been dealt such a blow. What he actually felt was guilt, for he was convinced now that if he had not put Pedemont, the private investigator, on Tim's trail, Tim might still be here. Still playing around with the mystery woman, perhaps, but still here. And, more importantly, Michael would still be here, too.

'Get married as quietly as you like,' he said. 'The quieter the better, as you say.'

'I suppose so,' Edith said reluctantly. 'There's already enough gossip about Tim's disappearance.'

The absence of Tim and Michael had been kept from even their closest friends, with the exception of Magnus McKea; there was still the hope that Tim would have a change of heart and would return, or anyway send back Michael. But eventually, they knew, everyone would have to be told something. For the time being their friends, and the rest of the world, had something else to talk about: Russia had just exploded its first atomic bomb. For once Lucas was grateful to the Communists.

Margaret and Frank Minett were married a week later in the main house. The only guests were her parents and sisters, his parents and his brother and sister-in-law from Detroit, and Magnus McKea. They left that night for a honeymoon in Acapulco, a new resort where none of their friends were likely to be vacationing in summer. Lucas gave them the honeymoon as an added wedding present and Margaret noticed that Frank did not make even a token protest. She knew then that she had married a man who, unlike Tim, would take the Beaufort money for granted.

Once committed she determined to make the best of Frank and the situation she had created. He loved her, even if he also loved her money; he was the perfect husband for a honeymoon, ready for bed every time she looked at him. He liked strutting around their suite naked, a habit he would keep up when they returned home. He had a strong muscular frame, like that of an ambitious road-worker; but he had one physical drawback in Margaret's eyes. His chest and belly were covered in dark hair and it took her some time to get used to his hairiness. Sometimes, only half awake in the morning, she would see him standing looking at her and, in her still sleepy eyes, he would look like a mat hung out to dry.

'I get it from my Sicilian grandfather,' he told her when, one day beside the hotel swimming pool, she mentioned it as delicately as she could. 'Our name was Minetta. Didn't you know?'

'Yes.' She didn't tell him that her father had called him a wop when she had first brought him home. It was only later that Lucas, remembering what Johnny Lazia had had done to George Biff, began to see other things in Frank besides his Italian background. 'Who changed it?'

'My father. I was born in Clay County, but Pop wanted to get into Republican politics and a Republican had no hope of getting elected in Clay County. So we moved over to Johnson County and Pop decided that though it was safe Republican territory, an Italian Republican didn't sound right. So he changed our name to Minett and now he's a county commissioner. By the time our son comes along no one will ever think he might have some Italian blood in him. Not even if he grows up to be like this.' He stroked the mat on his chest. 'Sicilians aren't the only hairy men in America.'

She smiled, beginning almost to love him for his simple pride in himself. 'Let's have some more loving before lunch.'

He looked ready to leap on her there beside the pool. 'You're full of surprises. I never dreamed you'd be like this, as hungry for it as I am.'

'Sicilians aren't the only sexy ones.'

They returned to Kansas City at the end of September, taking over the suite in the big house that Tim and Nina had occupied when they first came back from Germany. The atmosphere in the family was still depressed, with Nina silent and withdrawn, still unable to believe what had happened to her.

It was decided that, to dampen the rumours that were now flying like autumn leaves in the country club district, a statement should be released. Roy Roberts, the editor of the *Star* and one of Lucas's club acquaintances, sent out his most discreet reporter. Nina and her mother saw the reporter and next day a small item appeared saying that Mr and Mrs Timothy Davoren had separated by mutual consent. Nothing was said about Michael. Nobody in the country club set believed the story and only scattered more rumours. *Star* readers in the poorer sections of town and the outer suburbs nodded their heads and said what could you expect of the rich who were always getting married and divorced. The rich, of course, didn't give a damn what the poorer sections of town and the suburbs thought.

The day after the return from Mexico Margaret, without telling Frank, went to see Dr Voss. He examined her and then with his usual bluntness said, 'You've missed your second period, eh? How long have you been married – three weeks? Well, you're not the first girl who jumped the gun getting into the bridal bed. Does your mother know about this?'

'No. When it arrives, can you say it's premature? I don't want her and Daddy thinking the worst of Frank.'

'I'll need to take some tests – we're not even sure you are pregnant yet. But if you are, he could turn out to be the only overweight premature baby I've delivered. There's a first time for everything, I guess. Go home and give the father the joyous news. If he doesn't already know.'

'That's another thing.' She knew there was never a perfect secret: someone always had to be told. 'I'm not sure it's Frank's baby.'

Dr Voss was a small thin man with no hair and almost no eyebrows; he had a bland egg-like face that never showed any surprise, the perfect bedside manner. 'Well, so long as it's not black or yellow, we'll try and keep that information from him. But you Beaufort sisters get yourselves in a fix, don't you? Do you love Frank Minett?'

'Yes.' She tried hard to be truthful.

He studied her for a moment, but it was impossible to read his face. 'What about the baby? Are you going to love it, too?'

'Of course.' Even in her own ears she sounded more sincere than in the earlier reply.

'Then that's all we have to worry about, isn't it? The poor little bastard – just a figure of speech – isn't going to starve. Give my regards to your husband.'

Everyone was delighted with the news, though Edith privately confessed she was surprised at how soon Margaret had become pregnant. 'You're sure you weren't pregnant beforehand, darling? I'd hate to think all my daughters were going to arrive at the altar in the family way.'

'Mother, I've never asked you if you and Daddy went to bed before you were married –'

'I'd slap your face if you did.'

'I wouldn't do that to you, Mother. So don't ask.'

'Well –' Edith kissed her daughter. 'I'm happy for you. And for Frank, he's such a nice man. But how will you get on at college, being taught by your husband? You won't go to Vassar now, will you, and leave Frank here?'

'I'm giving up college. I don't fancy being a pregnant senior.'

'It's a pity you couldn't have waited . . .'

Margaret changed the subject. 'Do you think it's wise to let Nina go off to England on her own?'

'I offered to go with her, but she said she'd rather go alone. One can understand it, I suppose. She wants to go looking for Tim and Michael herself. She's taking a maid with her – Rosemary, I think. And George is going, too. Your father insisted that she needed a man along to take care of things.'

All the time she had been in Acapulco Margaret had kept in touch with the situation at home. She had called Kansas City every day, each time fearful that Tim might have returned. How would she react, coming back from her honeymoon with Frank and finding him, her one true love, back living with Nina? But there had been no word of him or Michael, except that the new investigators had traced them to Canada. When she had returned home she had not really been surprised when Nina had told her she was going to England to look for them.

'I can't just sit here waiting,' Nina had said. 'If nothing else, I'll get away from all the silent pity everyone's giving me. God, it's been awful, Meg!'

'Don't cry, darling –'

'I'm not going to. I'm past all that now – I couldn't wring another tear out of myself.'

'You'll cry your eyes out when you find them.'

'Do you think I'll find them? No, that sounds too pessimistic. I've *got* to believe I'll find them.'

'How long will you be away?'

'I don't know. Who knows, Tim might even have gone back to where we used to live, Stoke Bayard, and is just waiting for me to turn up. Maybe all he wanted to do was to get away from Daddy again.'

'Good luck.' But she knew in her heart that Nina would never find Tim in Stoke Bayard or anywhere else where they might have shared memories. She knew him well enough to know that he was not sentimental.

'Take over my house,' Nina said. 'I'll be away for at least six months, though I haven't told Mother and Daddy that.'

'I can't move into your house – '

'Don't be silly. It'll be standing empty. And you need to get Frank away from Mother and Daddy. It just won't work out, living in the same house as them.'

'Daddy's offered to build us a house here in the park. But I'm not sure – ' What Margaret meant was that she was not sure whether her marriage to Frank would last; but she couldn't say that. 'All right. We'll take your house and think about building our own when you come back. Would you mind if I changed some of your furnishings?'

'Of course not. Just take care of my paintings, that's all. The ones by Steve Hamill. They have a sentimental value.'

Nina went abroad at the end of October 1949. Margaret and Frank moved into the Davoren house two days after Nina's departure; but not before Margaret had been in touch with Lucy Drage, the interior decorator, and had had Nina's canopied bed replaced with one of the new emperor-sized beds. She told Frank it was to give them more room for experimental love-making, but the real reason was that she could not bear the thought of going to bed with Frank in a bed where Tim had made love to Nina.

And then Dave Pedemont called her.

## 2

'No, I'd rather not come see you at your house, Mrs Minett.'

'Who did you say you were?'

'I'm a private investigator. I was employed by your father, but I think it would be better if you didn't mention my name to him till after you've seen me.'

'Is it about my brother-in-law Mr Davoren?'

'In a way, yes it is.'

All at once she didn't want to know anything about Tim. She felt a wave of nausea, but it had nothing to do with morning sickness. She was afraid; she could not bear to face Tim again. Yet she heard herself say. 'I'll see you, Mr Pedemont. Where?'

'If you go south on Route 71, just past Belton there's a side road – '

'No.' She was afraid now for another reason, remembering the kidnapping of Nina; she wasn't going to be foolish enough to meet some stranger out on a country road. 'No, you'd better come here to my house . . . I'm sorry, Mr Pedemont. You come here or I don't see you.'

'Okay.' He sounded as if he had sighed. 'You're asking for it.'

He arrived at the house within the hour, in mid-morning. There was no one except the servants to witness his arrival. Lucas was at his office, Frank at the university, Edith at a board meeting of the Nelson Gallery, Sally and Prue at school. Pedemont was shown into the living-room and one of the maids came upstairs to tell Margaret that Mr Phillips was waiting to see her downstairs.

'Mr Phillips? Oh yes.'

She went downstairs wondering why Pedemont was going to such lengths to hide his identity. He stood in the middle of the living-room, feet firmly planted yet at the same time he looked uneasy and ready to run. He was younger than he had sounded on the phone, spare, bony, with a flat face behind horn-rimmed glasses. He looked more like an unsuccessful book-keeper than a private investigator. Humphrey Bogart had made it difficult for private eyes to live up to their image.

Pedemont licked his lips and came straight to the point. 'It's about Mr Davoren, sure. You see, your father hired me to tail you and Mr Davoren when the two of you – You all right, Mrs Minett?'

She sat down, feeling she was about to throw up. The room wavered in her gaze, as if the earth had trembled beneath the house. She wanted a glass of water, anything at all to drink, but she couldn't ring for a servant. She had one clear thought in her stunned mind: she had to keep everyone away from this man Pedemont.

'I'll be all right. Just give me a moment.'

He stood watching her anxiously, his feet apart and still firmly planted, as if he were afraid that if he moved he would fall over. Then, when she at last nodded, he went on: 'It was last July and August. I had you under surveillance every time you met Mr Davoren.'

'When did my father ask you to – to tail me, as you call it?'

'Oh, he didn't ask me to keep an eye on *you*.' He moved his feet at last, looked around for a chair and sat down. But he looked no more at ease. 'I was tailing Mr Davoren. Believe me, when I found out he was spending his time in those motels with you – I mean when I found out who you were – I mean you could have pushed me over, just like that.'

'What did my father say when you told him I'd been – I'd been with Mr Davoren?'

'Ah well – well, that's it, you see. I didn't tell him. I dunno why, maybe I thought it would be too much for him. All he was really interested in was whether Mr Davoren was playing around. He didn't care who the woman was.'

'So nobody knows but you?'

'That's correct.' He began to sound a little more formal, giving even more the impression of being a book-keeper. 'You and me and Mr Davoren. And I gather Mr Davoren isn't around any more.'

'So why have you come to see me?' But she had already guessed, felt nausea coming on again and fought it.

'Ah well – well –' He licked his thin lips; he had no experience in blackmail. He had investigated cases of it for clients; but that was far different from what he had in mind now. 'I don't think you'd like your father or your husband to know about that affair, would you?'

'No.' Then she had to prompt him: 'Go on.'

'Well – well, I thought some payment would be in order, you know what I mean? Just between you and me.'

'Do you have photos? I understand you people go in for things like that.'

'I've got a photo of you and Mr Davoren coming out of a motel over in Leavaworth. But I got none of you *in flagrante delicto*, as they say. I don't go in for that sort of stuff.'

'I admire your ethics.' She sounded calm and composed again; but she felt that parts of her whole being had been chipped away. 'I take it you and I are to have some sort of business deal. How much?'

'Ah well –' Twenty-five dollars a day and expenses gave him no basis for a blackmail fee. He licked his lips again and took a plunge: 'I was thinking of $5000.'

'Thinking of it as what? A down payment, a retainer or a flat fee?'

He noticed she hadn't even blinked at the sum: he wasn't used to dealing with the really rich, either as an investigator or a blackmailer. 'A flat fee. I won't be back, Mrs Minett, I promise you that.'

'How do I know I can trust you?'

'I've been an honest man up till now . . .'

126

'What made you change your mind?'

He nervously adjusted his glasses. Perhaps he *had* been an honest man, she decided. He looked too uncomfortable for an experienced crook, even a petty one. 'Maybe you won't believe this, but it was your father. I've never worked for anyone in his class before, I mean his sort of money. I had a chance to get into the big money, I mean my idea of big money, in my profession. I wanted the job of tracing Mr Davoren when he disappeared. But your father turned me down flat. I thought he owed me a chance to try, but he didn't give it to me. So . . .'

'So you decided I owed you something? Just so long as you got some Beaufort money?'

'Well, put like that – '

'I can't think of any other way of putting it. All right, I'll pay you. How do you want the money?'

'Cash would be best. I mean, for both of us.'

'Meet me this afternoon where you suggested this morning. The side road the other side of Belton. Three o'clock.'

'I dunno why you didn't come down there this morning – '

'I didn't trust you, Mr Pedemont. To tell you the truth, I thought you might be a kidnapper. Not just a cheap little blackmailer.'

He flushed, adjusted his glasses again, stood up. 'One thing I've never done, Mrs Minett, is cheat on my wife. Don't talk to me about being cheap. I'll see myself out.'

'The door's behind you.'

'That's what your old man said. I wonder what he would have said if I'd told him who was sleeping with his son-in-law?'

She sat on in the living-room after she had heard his rough-engined old car drive away. A maid came in to see if she wanted anything, but she shook her head. The maid, after a curious glance at her, went away. She sat on, unconsciously resting one hand on her belly. She felt locked and frozen into a dark curve that went downwards into the future years. She went to church regularly, but only because her mother insisted; she had never believed in punishment for sin, but now she knew she was being punished. She blinked her eyes, trying to start tears as some relief, but she had never wept easily. Not even now, when she was flooded with self-pity.

She went into Country Club Plaza that afternoon and drew $5000 from her account in the City and Country Bank branch there. If the teller thought anything of such a large withdrawal he did not show it; she was the daughter of the chairman of the bank and, besides that, $5000 was hardly missed from her account.

She went out into the autumn sunlight, crossed the road and sat down on a bench beside the Pool of Four Fauns. Ever since she was a child she had loved the fountains of the city and this had always been her favourite. The fauns spouted water that sparkled in the sun; the fauns themselves looked far too cheerful for her own mood. They mocked her now, reminding her of a time when she had had not a care in the world. She got up hurriedly, avoiding the gaze of two friends she had just seen come out of a store, and walked quickly back to her car. It occurred to her, with sickening irony, that she had been as furtive as this when she had been going to meet Tim.

She drove south to Belton, found Pedemont waiting for her on the side road. She handed him the money and a slip of paper.

'What's this?'

'A receipt, Mr Pedemont. My father taught me never to give money to anyone without getting a receipt.'

'Well, I dunno – ' He looked suspiciously at the slip of paper. 'It doesn't say what it's for.'

'I'll add that, if you like. How do you want me to word it? Just simply, *For Blackmail?*'

'Geez, you're a tough one.' He signed the paper in a crabbed hand, gave it back to her. 'You're not thinking of going to the police, are you?'

She folded the paper, already wondering where she would hide it when she got home. A shot sounded nearby and she jumped; but it was only some hunters after quail. She was nervous, querulous, anything but tough. But Pedemont would never have known it.

'Not now, Mr Pedemont. But if ever I see you again, I might. You'd better start being an honest man again.'

'Sure.' For the first time he smiled, a pleasant smile full of good teeth. 'You stay an honest woman, Mrs Minett.'

She drove home, adjusting her mind to the future. Whether Pedemont re-appeared or not, she would always be vulnerable. In the months ahead she would strengthen her defences, people would come to wonder at how cool and arrogant she had become; but it would only be because she would be preparing for the worst. But being prepared did not mean that she would be successful in handling the worst if it came. The worst being that Nina or her mother should find out about Tim. She could stand to hurt her father and Frank; but not her sister and mother. She drove on through the rain that had begun to fall heavily, the perfect end to a totally imperfect day.

Frank came home almost bouncing like a varsity cheerleader. 'I went in to see your father this afternoon after classes. I'm resigning from the university and joining the Family Trust. Francis B. Minett, vice-president in charge of public relations.'

'What do you know about public relations?' She tried to sound interested.

'Actually, I'm going to be more of a political lobbyist. Over in Jefferson City, maybe even in Washington when I'm more experienced. Don't worry, honey. I'll do all right at it.'

'I'm sure you will.' She kissed him, feeling guilty again; but she wished he wouldn't call her *honey*. Already little things about him were beginning to irritate her, rough edges to him that, perhaps because she had not been too seriously interested in him before, she had not noticed. He was not, to put it bluntly, in Beaufort class.

'You want to go out and celebrate?'

'Not tonight, Frank. I'm a little off – '

He was solicitous at once. 'You do look a bit peaked. I'm sorry, honey. I should've noticed. I was so taken up with myself – '

She put her hand against his cheek, determined to love him. 'Maybe tomorrow night.'

'Sure. We'll ask your mother and father if they'd like to go out with us. They could do with a night out. It's been pretty rough on them, the last couple of months.'

'On us all,' she said.

A week later she got a letter from Nina, written from London.

*I'm at the Savoy again, as you can see – I guess I'm a sentimental traveller,* she wrote with an insouciant unawareness of how elegantly sentimental she was. *I've found no sign of Tim and Michael. I've decided not to come back home yet awhile – perhaps I'll stay over here for a year or two. I have a feeling that Tim won't turn up in K.C. again, that if I hear of or see him again, it will be by chance. And that chance will more likely come on this side of the Atlantic than in America and particularly in K.C. I shan't stay in London for the winter – I have a rather bitter memory of an English winter. I've heard of a place I can rent at Cap Ferrat and I think I'll go down there. Who knows, maybe I'll become one of those expatriate Americans I used to read about in Scott Fitzgerald and used to envy so much. Except . . . Well, never mind except. I miss you all . . .*

Margaret wished she were with Nina, as expatriate as she could possibly be.

# 3

The days slipped by like numbered shadows, disappeared into months that were just as insubstantial: Margaret felt she was in a state of limbo, an un-American state. She did not look forward expectantly to the birth of the baby; it was just *there*, a part of her thickening body. Frank, perhaps out of deference to the loss of her figure and her sexuality, gave up parading around the bedroom in the nude. A couple of months before it was really necessary she told him they had better not have any more intercourse; she was surprised and a little ashamed that he acquiesced so agreeably. She just hoped, for his sake, that the baby would, by some miracle, have some resemblance to him. At the same time she was glad that she did not have to respond to his love-making.

Their social life quietened down. Frank, having left the university, had left all his university friends; Margaret realized with distaste that all his friendships were based on how much his friends could help him. Lucas had not yet sent him to Washington, but he came home talking of the new friends he was making every day in business and over in the State capitol in Jefferson City. Lucas, with Tim seemingly put out of his mind if not entirely forgotten, now had a favourite son, if only by marriage. Margaret had married a man, who, if he didn't entirely please her, certainly pleased her parents.

Beaufort Oil widened its interest in Oklahoma and Texas, where oil was continuing to sprout like liquid weed. Dirt farmers became rich almost overnight: although none of them ever became as rich as the oil companies. But, as economists told anyone who would listen, fortunes were just lying there to be made in America. Up in Boston some masked men made their fortune in a few minutes by robbing Brink's express office; even Lucas, who had the greatest respect for law and order particularly in regard to private property, admitted he admired the robbers' big thinking. Nina wrote from Cap Ferrat that she was well, though France, indeed Europe in general, was not. She still had no clues to Tim's and Michael's whereabouts.

Margaret's baby was born in May 1950 and was named Martha Edith. She was two weeks overdue, but Dr Voss told the father and grandparents that she was two weeks early. That seemed to satisfy everyone that Margaret and Frank had observed the proprieties before marriage. Martha was just a month old when the Korean War broke out. She had colic at the time and neither she, her mother or her grandmother gave a thought to the war.

Lucas and Frank gave a lot of thought to it. Lucas was appalled that, once again and so soon, American young men were to be killed fighting for a lot of foreigners who would never be properly grateful; at the same time he appreciated that the war would be good for business and anything that cranked up the economy couldn't be all bad. President Truman called him to Washington and he went this time without complaint or rhetoric, taking Frank with him. Frank, as a new father, was not yet liable for the draft.

Martha, to Margaret's great relief, was said by everyone to be the spit'n image of her mother; it was a description appreciated by Frank, who possibly thought his own attributes, hirsute or sexual, would have looked out of place on a girl. He came back from Washington in September, full of bounce and ambition, certain now that he was on his way to the top. He took off his clothes in the bedroom and strutted like a pole vaulter warming up. Margaret, hungry for sex again now, didn't laugh at him. She took no precautions, wanting, out of a sense of guilt, to give him his own child. By December she was pregnant again.

'I'm happy about it,' Frank said. 'But I was hoping we could move to Washington. They've asked me to take over a desk in Defence. Your father thinks I should, he says I can build up future contacts for all our companies.'

*Our companies*, she noticed. She had remarked his growing confidence, his easier attitude towards her father: he never over-stepped the mark but he was no longer deferential. 'I'm sorry, darling. I don't think I could cope with the baby and another one on the way, not in Washington. Can't you fly home each week-end?'

'I didn't think it was going to be like this – I mean, being away from you so much. But I can't say no to this job. If I did, they might draft me and I could finish up in Korea. I couldn't fly home from there for the weekend.'

She had not learned to love him, despite her hopes, lukewarm though they had been. She had come to be amused by him, some-times irritated; she had actually begun to feel more mature than he. His enthusiasm for getting to the top seemed almost juvenile to her; born to wealth, she had never been exposed to real ambition. But he was not wicked in his attitude and he had some-thing, she confessed to herself, that Tim had never had: loyalty.

'We'll have no more children after this one.' She patted her belly. 'At least not for a while. We'll just enjoy each other.'

'I love you, honey.'

'And I love you.' She kissed him, thinking how easy it was to lie about love. 'Especially *this*.'

She touched him and he rose to the occasion. He lay on his back and admired himself. She restrained herself from asking him if he thought of it as the biggest weapon in the Defence Department. She ran a hand over the mat of him, wondered what he would say if she tried to Hoover him. She giggled, getting hysterical, and had to start acting playful to cover up. Later, when he was asleep, she wept silently, knowing she had ruined her life.

She had heard no more from Dave Pedemont and she began to feel a little easier. Life settled into a pattern, quieter than she had known when she was single but bearable. Edith, deprived of one grandchild, fussed over Martha; Michael's nursery was redecorated to suit a girl and preparations were begun long in advance for the next grandchild. Margaret had decided that she and Frank would not build their own house just yet; there would be time for that if and when Nina came home. Nina was living in London again, still hoping, still searching.

Frank came home in the middle of July 1951 for the birth of his second daughter, Emma. It was a day of disastrous floods in Kansas City, especially in the stockyards area; the Beaufort Cattle Company alone lost over a million dollars in livestock and property. But Frank might have come in from a shining beautiful day. He was unaware of the elements outside as he beamed down at his new child.

'She's cute, eh? She looks a bit more like me than you. All that hair.'

'Let's hope it just stays on her head.'

He laughed heartily, pleased with her, his children, even the flooded world at large. 'I'm finished in Washington. Did your father tell you I'm coming back as executive vice-president of the bank?' Then he said wistfully, 'But I enjoyed Washington, honey. There's something about that place . . .'

Lucas's relations with President Truman had cooled again when the President had sacked General MacArthur. Feeling a deserter but unable to stay on in Washington any longer, he took the Kansas City floods as an excuse to resign and come home to help organize the city's flood relief and rehabilitation programme.

'I think it's time Nina came home, too,' he said. 'She's on a wild goose chase.'

'I wouldn't suggest it, Daddy,' said Sally. 'She's not exactly enjoying herself over there, but she's not unhappy. Not as much as she was here,' she added undiplomatically.

Sally was eighteen now and due to start at Vassar. She had gone to England to spend the summer with Nina and the two of them had gone on to Paris, the Riviera and Rome; she had come back to Kansas City and confided to Margaret that she could never, *never*, live in this backwater for the rest of her life. She was an attractive girl, not as beautiful as her two older sisters, and there was still a tomboyish quality about her. She was still crazy about cars and Lucas had bought her a new MG as a going-away-to-college present.

'Why don't you take a year off, sweetheart?' Edith said to Lucas. 'We could travel, spend some time with Nina. You don't need to go on making money.'

'I know I don't *need* to.'

'Why do you go on then?' said Margaret: it struck her that it was the first time she had ever asked such a question of her father.

'Satisfaction,' said her father without hesitation, as if he had given the matter a lot of thought. 'That's all there is for people like us. Beyond a certain point, money doesn't mean anything.'

'Let me know when I get there, Lucas,' said Frank Minett.

It was a Sunday afternoon and they were all having tea on the lawn behind the main house. Frank's parents were there, and Magnus McKea. Sun umbrellas had been set up to shade the women; Lucas and Magnus both wore straw panamas. Frank and his father sat bare-headed in the sun, not denying their Sicilian complexion.

'We'll bring Nina home for Christmas,' said Lucas, ignoring Frank Minett's comment. Money might not mean anything beyond a certain point, but you never joked about it.

'If she won't stay, we could all go over there next summer.'

Lucas shook his head. 'Next year is election year. We'll be busy trying to put some respectability back into the White House.'

'Next year's our chance.' Jack Minett was an older version of his son, but he was less energetic. He was a professional politician who had learned to take the long view and conserve one's stamina. 'Did Frank tell you what he's planning?'

'Not now, Pop.' Frank all at once looked uncomfortable.

'Why not now?' said his mother, looking around for her grandchildren, wondering why a nurse should be allowed to take them over. She was a good-looking woman who would have run to fat if her husband, mindful of the fact that he often needed a partner at political functions, had not told her to stay trim. Republican women, he had noticed, did not run to too much fat. Francesca Minett, under her Harzfeld clothes which she had only been able to afford since her elder son had married money, was still basically a peasant woman. If anything was for the good of her husband and sons, she did it without argument. Even if it meant giving up pasta and gelati and having to touch her toes every night Jack was home. 'Tell them what you're going to do, Frank.'

'Yes, do that.' Lucas's voice was a cool note in the afternoon warmth.

'Well, it's only come up in the past week. I was going to discuss it with you, Lucas, but Pop's jumped the gun.'

I was wrong, Margaret thought, he is still as deferential as ever.

'Better late than never,' said Lucas, voice still cool.

'Well, as you know, I've lived over in Johnson County for the last twenty years, except for the time I've lived here. If we, I mean Meg and I, if we moved back there now, I'd still be classed as residentially qualified. I mean, to run.'

'Run for what?' Lucas shook his head at the glass of iced tea which Edith, sensing the stiffening in her husband, had offered him.

'Well, as I said, it's only come up in the last week.' Margaret noticed that Frank hadn't once looked at her. But then he was also having difficulty in looking Lucas in the eye. 'Pop thinks I could get the Republican nomination for Congress and he thinks with my connections I could win the election.'

'They'll be looking for Republicans in Washington next year,' said Jack Minett, who hadn't brought his political nose with him this afternoon or he would have noticed the change in climate. 'Frank could be a shoo-in.'

'What connections were you thinking of?' said Lucas.

For the first time Jack Minett felt the chill on the wind. He had been carried away by the ambience, thinking that this was the life he'd like for himself and Francesca: tea on the lawn, servants, not a demanding voter in sight. But now: 'Well – I mean, I'd been led to believe – ' He looked at his son, wondering how he could have been so dumb as to listen to him.

'I don't think this is a topic for a Sunday afternoon,' said Magnus on a nod from Edith. 'As my English grandmother used to say, tennis anyone?'

'In Dodge City?' Lucas smiled, stood up. Margaret recognized that he was furious about something, but he had always tried his best to be a gentleman. A gentleman did not engage in political argument in front of the ladies: if only because he was convinced that the ladies wouldn't understand the argument anyway. He drank the iced tea that Edith offered him again, then nodded towards the court at the back of the estate. 'Let's knock the ball about. You can lend your father some tennis clothes, Frank.'

'Just a pair of sneakers,' said Jack Minett. 'I'll be okay in these pants.'

'No,' said Lucas. 'I prefer the proper clothes on my court.'

The men went away and Prue, ten now and still the sharpest observer in the family, said, 'Daddy's blowing up a storm.'

'That's enough from you,' said Edith. 'Go see if you can help Nurse look after your nieces.'

'I don't think I like being an aunt at my age,' said Prue. 'It makes me feel so *old*.'

But she went off and Edith sighed. 'That one is going to be a headache when she grows up. You're fortunate, Francesca, that you don't have any daughters to worry about. No offence, darlings,' she added.

'Hah-hah,' said Sally, whose repartee hadn't improved as she grew older.

'Prue was right – Daddy is in one of his moods,' said Margaret. 'I think Frank has sprung some sort of surprise on him. You know how he hates surprises.'

'Leave them be,' said Francesca, still looking for her two grand-children that she might smother them in their right, a grand-mother's affection. 'Men will always sort things out between themselves.'

'Exactly my sentiments,' said Edith, glad to be able to favour Francesca with agreement. She was always uncomfortable with Frank's mother and was glad that Francesca did not expect to be included as part of the Beaufort social circle. Egalitarianism, a newly fashionable word she had seen cropping up lately, was something she felt would work better if kept away from Ward Parkway. 'More iced tea?'

The men played tennis for an hour, then came up from the court and went straight into the house and to Lucas's study. By then Margaret was back in her own house, in the nursery, breast-feeding Emma and watching Francesca fuss over the spoon-feeding of Martha. A car horn tooted outside and Francesca straightened up and put down the spoon and bowl.

'That's Jack. He doesn't like to be kept waiting.' She kissed Margaret and the babies. 'It's been a nice day, Meg. I'm so happy for you and Frank.'

The car horn tooted again. She beamed at the children, then went out, not hurrying but not dawdling, a wife who, as far as Margaret could tell, didn't mind in the least being dutiful.

135

The older Minetts drove away and Frank came upstairs to the nursery. Margaret saw at once that he was dark with anger, the banked Sicilian fires suddenly burning again. She had never seen his temper before and she felt a moment of fear.

'Your father – do you know what he can be *like*?'

'Yes.'

The flat emphasis in her voice seemed to surprise him 'He can be a real son-of-a-bitch – Jesus, I didn't believe anyone could be so – so autocratic in this day and age!'

'Your father is pretty autocratic towards your mother.'

Again he looked at her and all at once she saw his father in him. 'That's the way he is and my mother wouldn't want him any different.'

She made no comment on that, went back to seeing that Emma was properly fed. She had not really wanted to breast-feed either of the babies, but had done so to please her mother. 'What happened with Daddy?'

Frank hadn't yet showered: he smelled of sweat and anger. 'He cut me down – right down! Jesus Christ, you'd have thought I was some goddam office clerk! In front of my own father – '

'What did your father say?'

'That was it – he said nothing!' She could see that it hurt and angered him to admit his father's cowardice. 'He just sat there as if your father was God Almighty.'

'What was Daddy's objection?'

'That I'd even thought of running for office without consulting him. I've got to have a drink.' He rang the service bell.

'You weren't very sensible or diplomatic, if you ask my opinion.'

'I'd expect you to take his side – he's got you all under his thumb.' One of the maids appeared at the door. 'Get me a beer.'

'Please, Ellen,' said Margaret and waited till the girl had gone. 'Don't speak to the maids like that. My father may be autocratic, but he knows how to speak to the servants.'

He made a gesture of apology, but he was still too angry for any conciliatory words. 'He treated me like a goddam servant this afternoon!'

'Did Magnus say anything?'

'He just looked embarrassed. Does your father put him down, too?'

'I think we should have Magnus over for supper. Is he still over with Daddy? I'll call him.'

'Why do we want him?'

'I think he may be able to explain a few things about Daddy

136

that I'd find embarrassing.' She finished feeding the baby, rang for the nurse. 'Take Martha's spoon and plate away from her. She's made enough mess.'

He picked up the food-spattered Martha as both the nurse and the maid came in. He handed Martha to the nurse, took the beer from the maid. 'Thanks, Ellen. Sorry I was a bit grouchy a moment ago.'

'That's all right, Mr Minett.'

But Margaret, watching her closely, saw that the maid had made up her mind who knew how to handle servants and who didn't. Frank had a lot to learn about living with the Beauforts, at both ends of the scale.

Magnus McKea was still over in the main house and said he would be delighted to come over to the Minetts for supper. He arrived half an hour later, looking cool and English: dark blue blazer, cravat at his throat, grey slacks. I couldn't have picked a better spokesman for us, Margaret thought.

After supper, when they were sitting out on the back porch having coffee, she said, 'You were there this afternoon, Magnus, when Daddy let fly. Explain to Frank why he did that.'

No lights had been turned on on the porch and they sat in the evening gloom. Magnus was silent for a while, then he said, 'Am I here as a family friend or the family lawyer?'

'You're here because you're one of *us*,' Margaret said and was sure he would understand whom she meant by *us*.

Magnus wasn't going to be hurried. He took his time about lighting a cigar, then at last he said, 'Frank, I suspect you really don't yet appreciate what you have married into.'

Frank took his own time about replying. 'Maybe not, I just don't know why Meg has asked you to explain it to me.'

'I think I understand. She's part of everything you ran up against this afternoon with Lucas. Tribal customs are often better explained by someone who knows the tribe but isn't a member. I think it would be better, Meg, if you left us for a while.'

Margaret, without a word, got up and went inside. Magnus stubbed out his cigar and looked at the dark shape of Frank. He had felt sorry for the younger man this afternoon: Lucas had been coldly brutal.

'Frank, Lucas is one of a breed that I think is going to die out in this country in my lifetime. He's only two generations removed from a man who had very little money and certainly no position. Now he is one of the richest men in America, but nationally he doesn't really have much position. Not compared to the rich men in the East, the old money. But he likes to behave like an aristocrat. We have an American aristocracy, but again you find most of them in the East. Lucas aspires to be one and he has a code you should have acquainted yourself with. He is interested in making money and always will be – that's not un-aristocratic. Some of the English and French nobility are just as money-minded as Lucas will ever be. But he believes money, or the possession of it, has certain responsibilities. One is that it should not be used to buy political power. Money does buy political power in this country. Some of our so-called better families have done it unashamedly, but Lucas is not like that.'

'I wasn't asking him to buy anything for me.'

'Frank, you were going to use the Beaufort name – and that's synonymous with money. Your father spoke of *connections* – the only connections you have are with the Beauforts. Sooner or later some political columnist would have commented that, supposing you were elected, you were Lucas's man in Washington, that you had been put there with a purpose.'

'I've been lobbying for the Beaufort interests – what's the difference?'

'Frank, that's a dumb question and you know it. Paid lobbyists are a recognized part of our political system. Congressmen with a vested interest are also a part of our system, but they are not officially recognized. Lucas himself has several times been asked to run for office – as Senator, as Governor. I've heard his answer – that he would willingly have done so if he had been someone other than who he is. Of course, then they may not have asked him. But it doesn't alter his point – that when you are rich and powerful as he is, you don't run for office. You work for the government if you are asked, but that's public duty. If you are a Beaufort – and you are one now, by marriage – you serve your country without reward or thought of political prestige. It's what the French call *noblesse oblige*.'

'It's bullshit,' said Frank.

'It may be. You're the professor of political theory, not me. The fact remains that it is the way Lucas thinks. There's something you don't realize – and I don't think Lucas or his family realize it, either. He has an inferiority complex. No, don't laugh. It is a common disease here in the Midwest among the rich. They would never admit it, but they feel inferior towards everyone East of them, the inferiority feeling growing as the distance increases from Kansas City or Tulsa or wherever. There is a reverse complex. The rich in St Louis look down on us, Cincinnati looks down on St Louis and so on and so on. We have one of the most beautiful cities in America right here, but the rest of

138

the country thinks of it as a stockyard full of Wyatt Earps. We'll grow out of our inferiority complex, but it may take another twenty-five years or more.'

'I don't suffer from that.'

Magnus smiled in the dark, but said nothing.

'I've always had political ambitions – I was brought up to have them – '

'Did you explain that to Lucas when you asked for Meg's hand?'

'Asked for – ? Jesus, Magnus, what's with you? *She* asked *me*. Sure, I wanted to marry her, but I never got the chance. We went to her father and she told him we were going to be married and that was that. I've always had it in mind that I'd run for something – Governor, Congressman – '

'Not any more, Frank. You could run for President, a *Republican* President, and Lucas would spend money to see you weren't elected. Anything to prove that you weren't his man.'

'I *am* his man, don't you see that? Or he thinks I am. Telling me what I can and what I can't do – '

'You'd better adjust to it, Frank. You're not the first son-in-law who thought he could be his own man in this family.'

'What about you? Are you his man, too?'

'Only on a professional level. You forget – I'm not married to one of his daughters.'

## 4

Frank had another talk with Lucas, but Margaret never learned what was said. However, there was a change in Frank that soon became apparent; he had suddenly learned he was more alien than he thought in the world of the Beauforts. There was no sullenness or any further outburst of anger; rather, he began to show a cool control that Margaret had never suspected in him. She did not know that he had had talks with his own father and that Jack Minett, who took the long view that no man, not even Lucas, was immortal, had counselled Frank not to make any more waves.

'The only place to shoot your mouth off is when you're at the top,' he had said. 'Politics is full of the corpses of guys who started shouting too soon.'

'Joe McCarthy's doing all right.

'He won't last, that's my bet. He's got his uses now, but he'll be kicked out on his ass when we get into power. The time to be in favour is when your party is in office. You play it cool and bide your time – you're still young. You're gonna need money of your own, so go out and make some. Lucas didn't say anything about not using your connections with the family to make money. Make as much as you can and in ten years' time we'll send you to Washington.'

'Ten years!'

'You'll be – what? Forty, forty-one. You can stay there for thirty years if you play the game properly. By then you'll be your own man and it won't matter a can of piss whether Lucas approves or not. Start learning to be cool and how to make money.'

'That's easy to say. Where do I start making it?'

'Look around you. This part of the country is gonna grow. We're gonna have new highways. They're talking about a major airport. An old Missouri boy once said, Buy land, son, they've stopped making it – that was Mark Twain. It's still good advice.'

'If you know what's going to happen here, why aren't you buying up land?'

Jack Minett smiled. 'When it comes to money, I'm an honest politician. I saw what happened over in Tom Pendergast's territory – greed brought all those guys down. I make a little extra on the side, but not dishonestly. Everybody thinks all Italians belong to the Mafia – I try to prove they're wrong. Some Mafia men have come to offer me money, but I've turned them down. I'm safe here and I'll be here till the day I die, because everyone trusts me.'

'What about me? If I make money on land deals, who's going to elect me?'

'Ten years I said, remember? You make your money soon and by the time you run for office people will have forgotten or won't be interested. All they care about is whether you made it in office or just before you got in. Make your fortune in five years and you can spend the next five years being respectable.'

So Frank made no more waves. He was once more respectful of Lucas, though less deferential; their relationship had cooled a little but Lucas did not seem to mind that. He's brought Frank to heel, Margaret thought, and he's satisfied with that. What worried her was that she had begun to feel no loyalty to either her father or her husband.

The year faded away. In Washington some Puerto Rican revolutionaries tried to assassinate President Truman. Lucas, genuinely horrified that such a thing could still happen in America, buried his animosity and telephoned the President to congratulate him on his escape. 'I thought all that was behind us, Mr President – '

'I wouldn't put money on it, Lucas. There'll always be cranks and fanatics.' The President chuckled. 'We've even had a few back·in Missouri. But thanks for calling. We must get together for a chat when I come home.'

'When will that be, Mr President?' Was Truman hinting that he was not going to run next year?

Again the chuckle. 'Some time, Lucas. I'll be in touch.'

Nina came home in early December, looking much better than when she had gone away over a year before. She was changed in subtle ways that her parents and her sisters did not at once appreciate. Her appearance had altered: she looked older than her twenty-seven years but not in an unflattering way. Her blonde hair was in a chignon, her clothes were French and understated in their chic, her make-up was different and more sophisticated. That was the difference that they all came to recognize very soon: that all round she was much more sophisticated than the Nina they remembered. They had yet to find out whether it was just a shell hiding a still troubled and unhappy woman.

'I've dismissed the private detectives,' she told Margaret. 'They've come up with nothing new in the past twelve months. If ever I find Tim and Michael, it's going to be by accident.'

'Do you think those sort of accidents happen?'

'I have to believe they do. What else have I got to believe in?'

'Are you still in love with Tim?' Margaret managed to keep her voice steady as she asked the question she still often asked herself.

'I don't know. I suppose so. I wouldn't know till I met him – ' She looked at Martha, who sat serene and happy in the middle of the living-room floor. 'It's Michael I miss. Sometimes – ' But she did not break down and weep as Margaret expected her to do. 'You're fortunate.'

'Yes.' Margaret had no difficulty in not sounding smug. She watched as Nina sat down on the floor, played with Martha. She said carefully, 'Do you think she looks like me?'

'Of course. You have to look twice to see anything of Frank in her. But then you have to look twice at Emma to see anything of you in her. I sometimes wonder when I meet Michael again, if I'll recognize anything of me in him.'

Margaret remarked that she had said *when*, not *if*. She suddenly felt a wave of sympathy and affection for her sister and sat down on the floor beside her and took her hand. 'Oh Nin – ' It was years since she had used the childhood name. 'We must get him back for you! Why don't you advertise, offer a reward? Anything that will – '

Nina shook her head, smiled automatically as Martha grabbed at the gold bracelet her aunt wore. 'I thought of that. I even talked it over with Daddy before I went away.'

'What did he say?'

Nina took off her bracelet, gave it to Martha who promptly assayed it by sucking on it. 'You'd better teach your daughter that gold shouldn't be worn in the mouth . . . Daddy left it up to me. He wasn't much help at all. Sometimes at first I thought he was more shattered by their disappearance than I was. In the end I decided I couldn't advertise, not tell the world what had happened. I think I have too much of Mother in me – I make too much pretence of being well bred, as she calls it. But I don't think advertising would have helped anyway – that's what I tell myself. Tim is smart. He has disappeared without trace once already. If someone did get on to him, he could do it again.'

'I still think you should do it. To hell with what people will think.'

'That doesn't sound like you.'

Margaret took the bracelet from Martha, who was trying to swallow it. 'All I care about is you, Nin. You can't go on eating your heart out for the rest of your life – '

'I'll think about it. The trouble is, I keep hoping Tim will come back of his own accord. I don't think I could face it if somehow they tracked him down and he still walked away from me.'

'But you might still get Michael back.'

'Yes. But . . .'

'You still love Tim.'

Nina sighed, took the bracelet, wiped it on a lace handkerchief, put it back on her wrist. 'That's the worst part.'

*Indeed it is.*

'How do you and Frank get on?'

'Fine.' She busied herself again wiping Martha's dribbling mouth. 'Why?'

'Oh, it's nothing. Except – well, he seems *different*. He's not so – outgoing, I guess. Does he still get on well with Daddy?'

She decided she had better be truthful on that fact: 'Not as well as he used to.'

'Is Daddy trying to run him the way he did Tim? You shouldn't let it happen.'

'You tried to stop it happening with Tim, but it didn't get you anywhere – I'm sorry, Nin! God, I didn't mean to say that!'

'It's true. Don't be upset, Meg – *please*. I don't think any of us will ever beat him. He's not an ogre – ' She kissed her finger, put the tip of it on Martha's nose. 'Don't let him spoil your life, darling, when you grow up.'

Nina stayed for a month, over Christmas. Lucas appeared to give her all of his attention and once again Margaret felt the old jealousy. But she knew she could not blame Nina, who did not go out of her way to canvass her father's favouritism. Lucas sounded broken-hearted when Nina announced she was going back to Europe to live.

'But what's the matter with *here*?' he wanted to know. 'Even if you're bored with Kansas City and us, why not New York or San Francisco? There are dozens of places in this country – '

'I know, Daddy. I'm not bored with Kansas City or you or even America. I just want to live in Europe, that's all. I'll come back when . . .'

She didn't finish. Margaret saw her father close his eyes and remain quite still in his chair, as if he had given up hope and was saying goodbye to Nina for the last time. She looked quickly at her mother.

'I think it's time we went home, sweetheart,' said Edith.

Margaret and Frank had had her parents and Nina to dinner and they were in the living-room, coffee and liqueurs finished and the evening dying away as they all realized there would be no more dinners like it for perhaps another year. Frank had sat outside the conversation, being no more than a polite host; at times Margaret had the feeling he was bored by the subject of Nina's return to Europe. Now he stood up, as if silently agreeing with Edith that it was time the evening ended.

Lucas opened his eyes, blinked as if he had dozed off. Or been deep in thoughts that went far beyond this room. 'What? Yes, I suppose so. There's a board meeting tomorrow, Frank.'

'I won't be able to make it, Lucas. I have some business up in Platte County.'

'What have we got going up there?'

'Nothing. This is personal.'

Lucas pursed his lips, but said nothing. He abruptly said goodnight and, stiffly gentlemanly, took Edith by the arm and led her to the door. Then he looked back. 'Aren't you coming, Nina?'

'I'll have a nightcap with Meg. I'll be over in a while.'

Lucas looked disappointed, jealous of every moment his favourite gave to others, even her own sister. But he just nodded and took Edith home to the big house. It would be a long time before he would drop off to sleep, but he would refuse to tell Edith what was keeping him awake. She, worried for him, hurt at being shut out of his confidence, would also take a long time to fall asleep.

When her parents had gone Nina looked at Margaret and Frank. 'I wanted to talk to you about this house. Do you want it?'

'Well, we've been thinking of building our own – '

'Do you want to sell it to us?' Frank said.

'Don't be crazy, Frank. It didn't cost me and Tim a cent, except for the furnishings – Daddy gave it to us. We don't have to make a business deal between *us* . . . You're getting to be worse than Daddy.'

She smiled when she said it, but Frank didn't smile in return. 'We'll take it. We'll have to sign a lease – '

'Frank,' said Margaret quietly but coldly, 'I have a say in this. What if I want our own house?'

'We'll have our own house – when I can buy it for you. And it won't be here on the estate.' He sipped his nightcap, a double whisky; Margaret noticed that lately he had been increasing the size of his drinks. 'How long will you be staying away, Nina?'

Nina looked from one to the other, aware that, unwittingly, she had sparked off some friction between them. 'I don't know. A year, maybe two, three – I don't know. But without Tim and Michael I don't want to come back to this –' She gestured at the house from inside it. Then she looked up at the Hamill painting above the fireplace. 'I'd like to take that with me, that's all.'

Margaret had never liked the painting of the woman and the two small girls: the artist, intentionally or otherwise, had filled it with sadness as well as love, death as well as life. She knew all those things were complementary, but in her present state of mind she did not want to think about them. 'Take it and the others.'

Later, when Nina had gone across to the main house, Margaret said to Frank, 'You might have told me you were planning to buy our own house. I hope it's not up in Platte County.'

'I'm not planning to buy anything for us just yet – you know I don't have that sort of money. Not to buy or build a house that would satisfy your father and mother.'

'Are we still pleasing them?'

She got undressed, put on her night-gown. When they had first married he had liked her to come to bed naked and she had done it to please him; but gradually she had taken to wearing a night-gown, anything to keep even part of her body separated from his hairiness. She no longer enjoyed having sex with him but she knew in her heart that it was not his body that put her off but the fact that she was not in love with him. He still expected to make love three and four times a week and she was finding it more and more difficult even to pretend to like it.

'No. I just want to build a house where I can turn around and thumb my nose at your old man.'

'If you have no money, that may take years. He won't care about any nose-thumbing if he's in his grave.'

'I'll have the money, believe me. You Beauforts aren't the only ones who can make it.'

'Oh, for God's sake!' She was surprised at the petty malice in his voice; then heard herself say with the same pettiness, 'Put some pyjamas on. Stop parading around like an ape!'

He was about to get into bed. Abruptly he swung round, picked up his robe and went out of the bedroom, slamming the door behind him. They never went to bed together again.

## 5

Nina had brought George Biff home with her from Europe, but when she returned to France he declined to go. 'Ain't that I don't like being with you, Miz Nina. Just that I prefers K.C. to Paris and them places on the Riviera. I still got my job here, Mr Lucas?'

'Of course,' said Lucas.

Nina was obviously disappointed that George would not be going with her. 'I thought you liked Paris, George. Some of the men you admire are there. Sidney Bechet, men like that.'

'Ain't the same music there as back here. Same goes for London. All the time I was over there, my ear was listening back home. And I never took to them Frenchmen, somehow.'

'Understandable,' said Lucas, xenophobia showing through like a rash.

So Nina kissed everyone goodbye, vowed she wasn't deserting Kansas City forever and left for Europe again. Sally travelled with her, going back to Vassar. Edith, Margaret and Prue went to the airport to see them off.

'I hope you find Tim and Michael,' said Prue. 'I still miss them.'

'I keep praying,' said Nina soberly.

'I'm giving up prayers,' said Prue, 'for Lent.'

'What on earth is she reading now?' Nina asked.

'*The New Yorker*,' said Edith. 'Some writer called De Freeze or something.'

'I hate to think what she'll be reading when she's twenty-one.'

'The *Kama Sutra*,' said Prue, reading-list prepared well ahead.

Everybody laughed and the farewell was made easier, tears held back. Sally asked her mother, 'When I come home at Easter, may I bring a friend? You'll like her.'

'Of course, darling. Just so long as she's not too radical. For your father's sake.'

Driving back to Beaufort Park, George Biff once more back at his old job as chauffeur and therefore privy to the family affairs, Edith said, 'Did Miss Nina ever get really close to finding Mr Tim and Michael, George?'

He shook his head. 'Not after the first month in England. We tried everywhere, but we got nowheres. She's chasing clouds, Miz Beaufort.'

Edith nodded absently. 'I think so.' And looked at her other two daughters with her, so safe in the proper environment she had provided for them.

She knew nothing of the new sleeping arrangements of Margaret and Frank, though the servants in both houses knew. The Minetts kept up a plausible façade of married harmony in front of their respective parents; in private they did not bicker all the time, though once or twice Frank blew up in anger. He was drinking more, though he never got drunk. Margaret, for her part, kept her composure, though she could feel the private situation and the continual deception in public weighing on her. She knew the problem would have to be solved sooner or later, but she had no idea how.

Then one morning, after Frank had gone to his office downtown, the phone rang. Ellen, the maid, came into the small sitting-room where Margaret was writing a letter to Nina. 'A gentleman on the phone, Mrs Minett.'

'Did he give his name?'

'No, ma'am. He said he wanted to surprise you.'

*Tim!* His name rang in her mind like a gong. She looked down at the letter on her writing table, saw *Darling Nin*; she quickly turned it over, as if the letter might have eyes or ears. 'I'll take it in here, Ellen. Close the door as you go out, please.'

The maid went out, wondering if her mistress was going to take up with some old boy-friend, to get a bit of what she wasn't getting any more from her husband.

But it was neither Tim nor an old boy-friend. 'This is Dave Pedemont, Mrs Minett . . . No, relax. I'm not gonna put the bite on you again. I'm still honest, believe it or not . . . Well, I thought you might like some information.'

'What about, Mr Pedemont?'

'About your husband. I can give you names and places. All I'd want is my regular fee. Say a hundred bucks, two days' work. Prices have gone up since I saw you last.'

'Why have you been following my husband?' She turned the letter over again, guilt gone, read the lies she had written: *Frank is still the same old Frank.* 'Just for practice? Or more blackmail?'

He said nothing for a moment; she could hear the sound of traffic in the background. 'There's no need to be nasty, Mrs Minett. I'm doing you a favour, just like I did last time. It's your father who's had me following your husband. He seems to make a habit of that with his son-in-laws.'

An early spring rain began to spatter the windows. She looked through the distorted glass and, beyond it, through the still-bare maples at her father's house. He had not gone to his office today, was at home with a chill. She was tempted to slam down the phone and hurry across through the rain to confront him; then she thought better of it. Though she raged inside at her father's interference, she saw a dim light at the end of the dark tunnel that was her marriage.

'You still there, Mrs Minett? Don't get me wrong. I don't think your father thought your husband was cheating on you. He had me tailing him for other reasons. Political ones. I got nothing to report there – he hasn't met a politician, not even a hack, in the month I been tailing him.'

'Are you going to tell him about this woman my husband's been meeting?'

'Women, Mrs Minett, not woman. I don't think it's your father's business, do you? But it's yours. If you want it, that is. A hundred bucks.'

'I'll send you the hundred dollars, Mr Pedemont. In cash – to your office. I don't want to meet you. You send me the names and places. Don't keep a copy – unless you're planning to blackmail my husband, too?'

'Easy, Mrs Minett. That's slander.'

She smiled, though on the phone it had no effect. 'Are you planning to take me to court? All right, I'll take your word that there'll be no more blackmail. The money will be in the mail to you today.'

She hung up, gazed at the letter in front of her. Abruptly she put it away unfinished in the drawer of her writing table. She went upstairs, took a hundred dollars from the cash she kept on hand in her dressing-table, and put it in an envelope addressed to Pedemont. She then put on a heavy sweater, a raincoat and rain-hat, left the house and headed down towards the front gates. The security guard came out of the gatehouse.

'You going walking, Mrs Minett? On a day like this?'

'A breath of fresh air, Tom.' How she needed it; and a lot more besides. 'I'll just be walking along the Parkway.'

'You think I better come with you?'

Everyone was so protective towards her, even if this man was paid to be so. 'I'll be all right.'

She posted her letter, almost firing it into the mail-box. Then she walked for an hour under the dripping sky, oblivious of the rain and the traffic swishing by. When she returned home she had decided to ask Frank for a divorce. She was going to make a new start to her life. Somehow.

She spent the rest of the day with Martha and Emma, playing with them, feeding them, watching them as they slept, loving them. She had to protect them against what had happened to her and to Nina; but she knew their future was no more secure and predictable than her own. Emotion built up in her, so that by the time Frank arrived home she could feel the tension making her neck and head ache. He, too, was quiet and edgy, but they had finished dinner before she noticed it. All at once she knew that Pedemont had double-crossed her, had got in touch with Frank.

'There's nobody coming by tonight?' Frank said. 'I want to talk to you.'

'Wait a while. I've given the staff the night off.'

For the first time he became aware that she was tense, so strung-up that she looked pale and ill. He frowned, as if puzzled, but said nothing. At last they were alone in the house but for the sleeping children upstairs. They sat in the living-room, beneath the painting Margaret had bought to replace the Hamill. It was a Grant Wood landscape, calm, soothing, unprovocative.

'All right,' she said. 'Is it Mr Pedemont you want to talk to me about?'

Again he frowned in puzzlement. 'Pedemont. Who the hell's he?'

She faltered, feeling she had lost an advantage. 'I thought – never mind. You said you wanted to talk to me about something.'

He leaned forward, bulky shoulders hunched, a fist clasped in

148

the other hand. She recognized the symptoms: when Frank was unsure of himself he got aggressive. 'Look, I don't know how to put this – No, forget that! Christ, if I can't talk to my wife, who can I talk to?'

She let him argue with himself, just sat quietly, trying to control her own tension.

'I need money, that's what I wanted to talk to you about.' He got up, stood in front of the fireplace. He had lost weight lately and his suit hung limply on him. 'I need a million and a quarter.'

'Dollars?' She knew it was a ridiculous question, but he had caught her off-balance.

'Of course dollars! Jesus, what did you think – fucking potato chips?'

'If you want to talk to me, don't use that language – '

'Okay, okay. No language.' He beat his hands together, drew in his breath in a hissing sigh. 'I'm in trouble, Meg. Real trouble. I need a million and a quarter dollars by the end of the week.'

'Where do you expect to get it?'

'I've tried everywhere – well, not *everywhere*. Not here in Kansas City. I didn't want word getting back to your father . . . You're my only hope, Meg.'

She laughed harshly, but not from amusement: the tension came out of her in a nervous bark. 'You're crazy, Frank. What makes you think I have that much money on hand?'

'You have it in your share of the Trust. You're worth much more than that – Jesus, you must be worth fifty times that! You could realize on your stocks – '

'You've forgotten one thing. None of us can claim any part of what we own in the Trust until we're twenty-five. Nina could claim hers now if she wanted, though she hasn't. But I still have two years to go. Until then all I get is the income from my share of the Trust. And you're wrong about my share being worth fifty million or anything like that. There are two trusts, the Family Trust, which is the holding company, and the Children's Trust. They interlock, but I'm not worth anything near what you think. Some day I will be, when Mother and Daddy die, but not now. You should have checked your facts.'

'I was never allowed to look at the goddam trust deeds! Magnus shut me out as if I didn't belong to the family – '

'If he did, it would be on Daddy's orders. Even we girls don't know everything that's in the deeds. Daddy's just following in his father's footsteps – he didn't know what was in the deeds till Grandfather died.'

He turned away, made a sound that sounded like a whimper. Then he slumped down on the couch opposite her. 'Well, that's it.'

'That's what? You ask me for a million and a quarter dollars and you haven't given me one word of explanation why.'

The anger and the aggression had gone out of him: he looked limper still within the limp suit. 'I've been buying land up in Platte County. I got word there was to be an airport up there – not now, some time in the future. I had to borrow the money, get it where I could. Now I've learned I've bought in the wrong place. It's land that's going to stay zoned for farming and nothing else. The lenders want their money back.'

'Who lent you the money?'

He stared at his outstretched legs; there was a gap between his sock and the trouser-bottom and two or three inches of black-haired leg showed. Then, as if he wanted no comment from her on his hairiness, he reached down and pulled up his sock. He sat up, almost sedately, and said, 'I borrowed the money up in Chicago. Someone here gave me some names.'

'Banks?'

'No.' He laughed, a harsh giggle like hers of a moment ago. 'No, I got the introductions from a man named Scarlatti. The name mean anything to you?'

'No.'

'It would to George Biff. I didn't know myself till the guy himself told me. He was one of Johnny Lazia's men. He shot off George's fingers.'

'You went to a man like *that* for introductions in Chicago? Who did you go to see – gangsters?'

She had meant it flippantly, but he said, 'I guess you'd call them that. They're called other names. But they have the money and they're always looking for places to invest it. It's dirty money, I guess, when they get it. But they're looking for places to launder it. I heard about them and I went to them.'

'Did you use Daddy's name?'

'They knew who I was, so it helped.'

She stood up and got herself a cigarette from a box on a side table. She rarely smoked, but she needed something now to steady her. Her own topic of divorce had gone completely out of her head. 'What will they do if you don't pay back the money?'

'I hate to think about it. Jesus – ' Suddenly he put a hand over his face and laid his head back on the couch.

She felt no pity for him; and was ashamed. 'Why did you do it? Buy up all the land?'

He took his hand away, stared at her. 'I wanted to be rich.'

She remembered a yellowed clipping in the family book kept in her father's library. Her grandfather had been asked why he had worked so hard and Thaddeus had replied simply, *I wanted to be rich.* It was not an admission her father would make, considering himself beyond such vulgar honesty, but she knew he still subscribed to her grandfather's creed.

'Do you want me to go to Daddy?' Not that she intended doing so: she just wanted to know how much he wanted of her.

'It wouldn't be any use.' He stared into the empty fireplace for a while. She stood looking at him and at last he looked up and met her gaze. He frowned, as if he had just remembered something. 'Pedemont? Who's he?'

'A private investigator. He has some names and places concerning you.' She stubbed out her cigarette. 'I was going to ask you for a divorce.'

She had expected him to react in anger; or at least with some show of sarcastic derision. He reached across and poured himself another brandy from the decanter that had been brought in with their coffee. 'It never rains but it pours, eh? How long have you had him following me?' But he didn't wait for her answer: 'What the hell, anyway? If he's got names and places, he's got them. But what the hell did you expect? You kicked me out of bed. You know how I am about that sort of thing – I can't do without it.'

'Will I have to take you to court or do we divorce quietly without any fuss?'

'Do your folks know?'

'No. They don't need to know – I mean about the other women.'

'What grounds do we use, then? The State of Missouri doesn't grant divorces just because the people don't like each other, especially when there are kids to the marriage. You can get me for adultery.' Sarcasm began to roughen his tone. 'And there's cruelty, bigamy, alcoholism – ' He raised his brandy goblet. 'But no one could ever accuse me of being a drunk. I think there's impotency, too – but you couldn't accuse me of that, either, could you? Nobody would believe that, not if I took *this* out in court and slapped it on the table – '

'Don't be vulgar – '

His sarcasm was growing into anger. 'How about pregnancy at marriage? I believe I could get you on that.'

'It was your child – you got me pregnant – ' She was suddenly afraid, felt the tension come back.

But his anger dissolved, he dropped the argument. 'Let's keep the kids out of this. Who gets them if we do divorce?'

'I'd want them with me. But I wouldn't deny you access to them.'

'Access to – Jesus! We're talking about our kids – my kids! No,' he said abruptly and stood up and faced her. 'Divorce is out! I'm not giving up the kids. If anyone's going to have *access* to them, it's got to be you!'

'Then I'll go to court – '

But she knew it was an empty threat and she didn't know whether something in her voice gave her away. For he looked at her, then nodded his head, as if she had just given him an idea. 'Daddy wouldn't like that, would he? Not all our dirty linen washed out in court? About me sleeping around with call girls because you'd kicked me out of bed because you couldn't stand the hair on my belly and the size of my – '

'Stop it!' She shut her eyes, swung away from him. Were all marital rows as degrading as this? Did they all descend to this level when they got to the shouting stage?

'Or maybe – ' He stopped and she looked back at him: afraid for the first time of him, not that he would hit her but for what he might do. 'Maybe your old man will give me the million and a quarter. For that I'll give you – and him – the quiet divorce. No fuss, nothing.' Then he added, because, though he might no longer love her, he still loved the children: 'Just access to the kids, that's all.'

She shook her head, lost for any constructive argument: she only knew that she would not allow him to go to her father. 'I'll get the money – myself.'

'How?' He looked at her suspiciously. Sicilian suspicion, she thought: she had read somewhere that they trusted no one. Not that they could be blamed: nor him, either. 'How?'

'Somehow. I'll – I'll have to talk to Magnus.'

He sneered. 'He's on your father's side.'

'He's a friend – to all of us. I'll see him first thing in the morning.'

He considered and she saw that she had at least won some ground: there was a gleam of desperate hope in his eye. 'Okay. But remember – I've only got till Friday.'

# 6

'It's impossible,' said Magnus McKea.

'I thought nothing was impossible for people like us.'

'Don't give yourself airs, Meg, not with me. Your mother may do it, but you should know better.' He studied her a moment. 'You don't sound too put out by all this.'

She had come to see Magnus in his office in the New York Life building on West 9th Street. Other law firms were moving further uptown as the building boom continued, but Rufus McKea and Son was a firm that did not have to impress any of its clients. Magnus' grandfather had moved into the building when it had been built in 1890 and the law firm had the solidity that the building and the company that owned it enjoyed.

'I am *very* put out, Magnus.' She was dressed as if already on her way to court. A grey suit, white silk blouse, grey gloves: the respectable, wronged wife. 'It wasn't easy for me to come down here and tell you all this . . .'

'I'm sorry, Meg. I didn't mean to be critical. It's just – well, you *are* asking the impossible. I can't break the trust, have money released to you now instead of in two years' time. And there are the other two trustees – they wouldn't even listen to any argument you put up. Is Frank really in such trouble?'

'To people in Chicago, I think they're Syndicate men.'

'Syndicate?'

'Isn't that what Senator Kefauver called them? The Syndicate.'

Magnus had been calm, judge-like, up till now; but all at once he looked perturbed. He came of a family that had known violence and lawlessness, though it had always been on the side of the law. The McKeas were pioneer stock, had been here when John McCoy and thirteen other men, including the first Magnus McKea, had formed the Kansas Town Company. That first Magnus had been a justice of the peace, handing out rough justice to rough men who had expected no less; his son Walter had been a judge who had sentenced a dozen men to be hanged. But the present Magnus had never witnessed any violence, not even in the war, though he had seen its aftermath. He had been on the prosecution team at the greatest of all trials, at Nuremberg, but even there the violence and murder, on an unbelievable scale, had been at a distance. He was appalled at the idea that this girl in front of him, a daughter of one of the city's most respected men, should be touched, no matter how remotely, by mobsters.

'Your only way is to go to your father. But that's advice I can hardly charge you for. I can see you think it's bad advice.'

'I wouldn't have come to you, Magnus, if I thought I could solve everything by going to Daddy.'

He said cautiously, 'How are things between you and Frank? I mean the marriage.'

She owed him honesty: he *was* trying to help. 'It's finished. That's why I want to raise the money. If I give it to him, he'll give me a quiet divorce.'

'And if you don't?'

'A dirty divorce – and there's a lot of dirt. On his side,' she added defensively.

He pondered a moment, running his hand over his crew-cut as if trying to rub up some magical idea. 'Did Frank give you the name of the people in Chicago?'

'No. He was introduced to them by someone here in Kansas City. A man named – I can't remember. All I do remember – ' She shuddered. 'He was one of the men who crippled George Biff's hand.'

'Frank knows some nice characters, doesn't he? If your father knew he'd been in touch with that particular hoodlum . . . Or if George himself knew . . .'

'Would a bank lend me the money?'

'I think you're making a mistake if you're going to bail Frank out. Yes, I think any bank would lend you the money against what you can draw from the Trust in two years' time.'

'Would you go guarantor for me? I can't ask Daddy.'

He hesitated, then nodded. 'All right. Do you want me to arrange it?'

'If you would. Just impress on the bank, whichever one it is, that I don't want Daddy to know.'

'I'll have to ask one of the out-of-State banks. That may well lessen any leak or gossip – banks are discreet, but they're still staffed by human beings. I'll have the money put into my private account. Give me forty-eight hours.'

She came round the desk and kissed him on the cheek. 'Why aren't you married, Magnus?'

He took her hand, kissed the back of it. 'I'm in love with all the Beaufort sisters. If the State of Missouri allowed polygamy, I'd propose to you all.'

'How old are you?'

He smiled. 'Forty. Too old for you.'

'I don't know. I once told someone that I preferred older men.

'What happened to him?'

'He didn't believe me.' She pulled on her gloves. 'Do your best for me with the bank, Magnus.'

'Are you going to tell Frank what you're trying to do?'

'Not yet. Let him sweat a while longer.'

'You have a good deal of your father in you. More so than any of your sisters.'

'Sometimes I wish he'd recognize that,' she said and was gone before she could confess anything more to him.

That evening she told Frank she had had no success so far in raising the money.

'Then it looks as if I'll have to go to your father. He'll think the deal is a good one. Dirty but good.'

She hated him now and all at once she decided not to tell him that she was trying to raise the money herself. She had been going to buy him off, certain that he would accept; he might ask for an extra settlement for himself, but she would give him that out of her income. But what he had just said turned her completely against him: whole lives have been wrecked by a loose tongue and an emotional reaction to what has been said. So she decided on another tack, one that might be dangerous but would give her more satisfaction. *Satisfaction*, her father had said, *that's all there is for people like us.* She was being her father's daughter, though he would never appreciate it.

'Don't go to Daddy yet. I'll talk to him,' she lied.

Instead, next morning, she went to George Biff. He looked at her curiously, then at his maimed hand. 'Why you want to know that feller's name, Miz Meg?'

'It's important, George.'

He shook his head. 'Nothing doing. He was trouble twenty years ago, he still be trouble. You stay away from him. What the heck you want with him, anyway?'

'I could go dig up his name somewhere downtown, George, but I don't have the time. Now please . . .'

'You tell me why you wanna get in touch with him. Otherwise I'm gonna go to your father, tell him the trouble you trying to buy.'

'You wouldn't!'

'I would, Miz Meg.'

She stared at him, knowing that he would indeed go to her father; but knowing, too, that he would do it out of love for her.

155

So she told him why she wanted to find the man who had maimed him and even as she told him she marvelled that her one confidant in the family was this middle-aged black man who was unrelated to any of them and had the least influence . . . 'So there's no time to lose, George.'

'I dunno. You know what you *suggesting*?' He had been outside the stables, polishing her mother's Cadillac, when she had come across to see him. He had already driven Lucas to his office and come back ready to drive Edith to one of her luncheons later in the morning. There was no one within fifty yards of them, but he dropped his voice to a hoarse whisper. 'Jesus God, you can't fool around with people like that! Look what they done to me – ' He held up his hand. 'And I was just a nobody.'

'They aren't going to do anything like that to me. What's the man's name?'

'Pete Scarlatti,' he said reluctantly. 'And I'm gonna come with you.'

'No, George. You shouldn't have to face him again, not after all these years – '

'He ain't gonna worry me. It's the men in Chicago gonna worry me. I'm coming there, too.'

'No. Daddy would kill you if he found out. I remember how he was when you went down to help Mr Tim at the stockyards – '

'I'm more afraid for you than I am of your daddy. When we going?'

She hesitated, then nodded. 'All right. I love you, George, you know that?'

He smiled. 'All the women tell me that. That's why I've never married – can't make up my mind. You come back when you hear from Mr McKea about the money. Then we go and see Scarlatti.'

Magnus called her that afternoon. 'The money is in my account now. You have a five-year loan from our firm's New York bank, at the going interest rate. Do you want me to handle Frank from here on?'

'No, I'll handle it. I'll call you tomorrow night.'

She left the children with their nurse. She was no longer breast-feeding Emma and it would not matter if she was not back for the children's supper. Frank would not be home till 6.30 and she hoped she would be back before then. She would lie to him if she had to, but she would rather not have any questions at all from him as to what had kept her out when the children were being fed. She prided herself on having been a good mother and, if nothing else, she wanted him to retain that image of her.

George had brought Edith back from her luncheon and was free till he had to pick Lucas up at six o'clock. Margaret now ran Nina's Buick, but she let George take the wheel as they drove downtown. He was very quiet, but she made no comment. She had no idea what George's ambitions had been as a musician or a fighter, but he was going to meet the man who had ruined whatever prospects he had had.

She didn't query him as to how he knew where to find Scarlatti. They pulled into a parking lot on West 12th Street; then he led her across the street. It was lined with bars and strip joints; she was in a totally foreign country only five or six miles from home. Out of the corner of her eye she saw a sign: – *In The Flesh Tonite*. Three men came out of a bar and stopped and stared at her: a well-dressed dame in dark glasses and a dinge, going where? George took her up a narrow stairway next to the bar, closing the door into the street in the faces of the gawking trio.

The door at the top of the stairs said: *Peter M. Scarlatti, Theatrical Agent.* It sounded legitimate and somehow she felt less nervous. She did not know what she had been expecting. *Peter M. Scarlatti, Hoodlum?*

The door opened right into Scarlatti's office. There was no need for an outer office; he employed no secretary. The walls of the small room were papered with glossy photos of girls contorting themselves to show as much as possible and still be exhibited in a public place. The walls looked like a gallery of acrobatic *September Morns*, a calendar picture that Margaret remembered from her childhood. But these nymphs had more flesh to them and their virginity looked like something remembered from their own childhood.

'I do something for you?' Scarlatti was one of the fattest men she had ever seen; he looked obscene even dressed and by contrast the girls on the wall behind him suddenly looked innocent. He looked Margaret up and down and recognized class: she was no hooker or stripper looking for a job. 'You looking to buy some entertainment, lady? I got all sorts.'

'I'm here to buy some names,' said Margaret.

Scarlatti had too much flesh on his face to furrow into a frown; but he succeeded somehow in looking puzzled. He peered at them out of slits of eyes; then he leaned forward, staring at George. He looked at George's hand, then he let out a loud hiss and put his own huge hands, which reminded Margaret vaguely of udders, on the worn desk in front of him.

'Jesus Christ – George Biff!'

George said nothing, but took some girlie magazines from a

chair, dropped them on the floor and offered the chair to Margaret. His whole air was that of ignoring Scarlatti and Margaret saw at once that it was unsettling the fat man. She sat down.

'My name is Minett, Mrs Frank Minett. You gave my husband the names of some men to see in Chicago, some businessmen. I'd like their names. I want to go up to see them. Tomorrow.'

Scarlatti seemed to drag his eyes away from George. He let out another hiss, softer this time, took a tablet from his pocket and popped it into his mouth. 'Mrs Minett? Well, I dunno, Mrs Minett. I give your husband them names in confidence, you know what I mean? I don't know if the – the businessmen up in Chicago would want me handing out their names to everyone – ' His voice was the only pleasant thing about him, a deep bass. 'What you want to see them for?'

'Business. Call them and see if they will see me at ten o'clock tomorrow morning. Call them now, Mr Scarlatti. I don't have much time.'

Scarlatti looked at George again, then sank his head into the thick fat of his neck and shoulders, the reverse of a shrug. He dialled a number, got long distance and asked for a second number. Margaret picked up a pencil and wrote it down on the back of a photo of a fan dancer that was one of a pile on the desk. But Scarlatti reached across and the photo was crumpled in one of the huge hands and tossed into a drawer of the desk.

'No numbers, Mrs Minett. You forget you heard that number, okay? . . . Hello, this is Pete Scarlatti . . . No, *Scarlatti*. Down in KC. *Kansas City*, for Crissake. I give a guy an intro to you people some months ago . . . Well, I'm sorry about that. How was I to know? He couldn't of had better connections, could he? . . . Well, I got someone else here. The guy's wife. She wants to see you tomorrow, ten o'clock a.m. in the morning . . . Hold it – *please*. This is the guy's *wife* – she's got even better connections than he's got, you know what I mean? What?' He looked at Margaret. 'He wants to know what you want to see them for?'

'Tell him I want to give them some money.' She was an innocent in this world: the girls behind Scarlatti sneered at her, looked at her over their shoulders with swindlers' eyes. Yet she felt confident: as Scarlatti had said, she had connections. The Beaufort name meant something even here among the cheap display of flesh, the tatty end of show business. 'A business deal. But they are not to contact my husband until after I have seen them.'

Scarlatti relayed the message, listened, nodded and hung up. 'They'll see you. Here's the address – no names, they said, till you get there.' He scrawled an address on a slip of paper, pushed it across the desk. Then he turned the paper over, saw a name on the back of it and scratched it out. 'She's a bubble dancer. You won't be wanting her name.'

Margaret stood up, took some money from her pocketbook and laid it on the desk: she did not want to touch one of those repulsive hands. 'A hundred dollars, Mr Scarlatti, for your trouble. And don't *you* get in touch with my husband.'

He flicked the money with a teat-like finger. 'That's pin money, Mrs Minett. I'm worth more than that.'

She looked around her, at a wall of bottoms and breasts. 'None of your clients would make that much in a night, Mr Scarlatti, let alone in a few minutes as you have done. That's your commission – take it.'

'Shove it,' he said, but didn't shove the money towards her. 'I tell you, I'm worth more than that – '

George Biff came round the desk, stood over him. 'Mr Scarlatti, you twice the size you were when you done me over – you wouldn't be able to move too fast now. Also, you ain't got that other feller with you, the one held me while you shot off my fingers. You better take the money or I'm gonna send Mrs Minett downstairs and I'm gonna beat the hell outa you. I can do it, even with one hand.'

Scarlatti glanced from one to the other without moving his head. He hissed again, then picked up the money and put it in his pocket. Without another word George opened the door and ushered Margaret out. When she got downstairs and out into the street she felt her legs trembling and she began to perspire. She was relieved to see that the three inquisitive drinkers from the bar next door had gone.

'George, I was afraid you were going to kill him!'

He grinned, took her arm and escorted her across the street. 'I ain't a killer, Miz Meg. I might of roughed him up a bit, but not in front of you. But there wasn't no real worry. He used to be tough when he was Johnny Lazia's man. But not any more. He just small stuff now. Well, not exactly small – he damned fat!' And he began to laugh, was still laughing when he handed her into the Buick.

She also began to laugh, with relief. She looked at the piece of paper with the address on it. 'Do you know Chicago?'

'I played a gig there once. Three weeks. Then the joint was shot up by some guys and it went outa business. I come back to KC.'

'George, what a life you've led!'

'Everybody got his own living to do. You got a long way to go yet.'

Margaret would never know how she got through dinner that evening without giving herself away to Frank. But, without her realizing it, she was already establishing her character, or at least her public personality, for the future. So we lay bricks in the building of ourselves and never know the blueprint.

'You see your old man?' Frank said.

'No. Magnus is helping me. Your problem should be over by tomorrow night.'

He gazed at her across the table, absent-mindedly picked a tooth with his little finger: a habit she thought she had cured him of. 'It had better be, Meg. I'm sick to my stomach –.' His plate, the food only picked over, had been pushed away. 'I'm getting desperate.'

She felt no sympathy, no feeling at all for him. 'I'm doing all I can.'

'What worries me is the kids are going to be the pawns in this game.'

'I'm not the one who's using them. If we keep the divorce quiet, it'll just be between you and me.' Then, because she was curious, she asked, 'When you pay off these men, what happens?'

'I dunno. I'll own the land, I guess. But it'll only be worth half, maybe less, what I paid for it.'

'Half a million? You'll still be better off than when you married me. Rich, almost.' She couldn't help herself: she was driving the needle in deeper.

He uttered a half-laugh. 'I was aiming higher.'

Then he got up and left the room and a few minutes later she heard him go out of the house and drive away. She was glad and relieved: if the conversation had gone on she might have given herself away. Her satisfaction, revenge perhaps, had to wait till tomorrow night.

Frank left at 7.30 next morning for his office, as he always did. Five minutes later she and George drove out the gates. 'How did you manage to get away from Daddy for the day?'

'I told him I got a sick sister over in Independence. That one good thing about a big family – you can always have a sick brother or sister.'

'Has he left for his office yet?'

'He went out same time as Mr Frank. He driving himself. One thing about your daddy, he ain't a proud rich man. Not like some of them I seen over in Europe. They go nowheres without their sho-fers.'

'Oh, Daddy's proud all right. You know that as well as I do. Now get a move on or we're going to miss the plane to Chicago.'

'Wouldn't mind if we did just that.'

'I didn't ask you to come, remember?' Then she said, 'I'm sorry, George. That was mean. I'm grateful to you, truly.'

'You girls,' was all he said and she wasn't sure whether he was condemning all women or just the Beaufort sisters.

They made the plane to Chicago with just minutes to spare. They flew through a shining morning that turned to wind and cloud as they landed. Lake Michigan was like chipped green marble and the occasional flags on the city's buildings stood stiff as metal pennants. It was not a day for feeling confident about meeting strangers.

Margaret rented a car, asked the clerk for directions and she and George drove north. She had expected to finish up in a business district; she had never been in Chicago before and knew nothing of its layout. But they drove through a residential district, then they were in what she recognized as country club territory; she was getting her first lesson in the geography of America's cities. The houses continued to improve, the grounds got larger; they were on a street that reminded her of Ward Parkway. Then George pulled the car in before high wooden gates set in a high stone wall that stood back from the roadway. A man, who must have been waiting for them, came out of a small side gate and approached the car.

'You Mrs Minett?' He was dressed as if for business: suit, collar and tie, polished shoes. Margaret was too inexperienced to notice, but George saw the bulge of the gun under the man's armpit. 'The boss is expecting you. Who's this?'

'My adviser,' said Margaret.

The man looked suspiciously at George, then went back inside the wall and a moment later the gates opened. George drove the car in and up a long curving drive to a Tudor mansion, circa 1948. Margaret, who knew her history, hoped she was not going to be subjected to the same sort of double-dealing as there was in that long-ago reign.

Two men, business-suited, came out of the front door of the house, stood waiting at the top of the steps. 'Just like home,' said George. 'Only they got more security fellers than your daddy got.'

He got out of the car with Margaret and one of the men came

down the steps. 'This way, Mrs Minett. You stay in the car, boy.'

'No,' said Margaret. 'He comes inside with me.'

'I'm sorry, Mrs Minett.' The man, young and burly, was roughly polite. 'Mr Gentleman don't allow Negroes in his front door.'

'Who?'

'Mr Gentleman, the boss. Tony Gentleman.'

'Mr Biff works for my father and he has been coming in and out of our front door for as long as I can remember. He comes in with me now or you'd better ask Mr Gentleman – ' the name was a joke: she wanted to laugh ' – to come out here and talk to me.'

The young man looked up at the other, older man at the top of the steps. The latter went back inside and returned in a moment. 'The boss says okay.' He shook his head as George followed Margaret into the house, as if he didn't know what the world was coming to, a spade going in the front door of a house like this.

The house was beautifully furnished: Margaret saw that at a glance. There was as much evidence of wealth here as there was in the big house back in Kansas City. There were perhaps too many paintings on the walls for her taste, but all the paintings were good: she thought she recognized a Titian, though it might have been just an excellent copy. All the paintings were of the Italian school: it struck her that perhaps Mr Gentleman was laundering his money by investing in the art of his homeland.

There were five men waiting for her in the huge living-room. Four of them were elderly and dressed as soberly as any of her father's banker friends back home; the fifth was a young man in a tweed jacket, a button-down shirt and silk repp tie. One of the old men came forward, a silver-haired slight man who walked with a limp.

'Please sit down, Mrs Minett.' He looked at George a moment, then nodded to him to take a chair. 'You know my name. This is my son Philip. The other gentlemen are my partners. They're no relation,' he added and she saw that he enjoyed the humour in his own name.

The unnamed, unrelated gentlemen smiled and nodded their heads. They did not look at George at all, but they were obviously pleased that they were going to be dealing with a beautiful young woman. They all sat down, arranging the creases of their trousers as they crossed their legs. It occurred to her then that they were all *too* well-dressed, that they were uncomfortable inside their expensive suits and custom-made shirts. She saw that the soles of the brilliantly-shined black shoes were almost unmarked and she wondered, irrelevantly, if they had all gone out and bought new outfits to meet her. She wanted to smile at their determined respectability, but this was no time to be snobbish.

She got down to business at once, not wanting to stay in this company longer than was necessary. 'I understand my husband owes you a million and a quarter dollars, part of the collateral being land he has purchased in Platte County, Missouri.'

'He owes us a million, one hundred thousand, Mrs Minett.' Tony Gentleman had a soft high voice that instantly made a mockery of everything that surrounded him: the banker's suit, the elegant furniture, the art collection. There in his throat was everything he was trying to leave behind: the Maxwell Street ghetto, the battle for survival against the Irish mick kids, the hoodlum youth. 'That includes the interest.'

They were being honest: the double-dealing was back home in her own house, where Frank had hoped to make $150,000 out of her or her father. 'May I see the note?'

Philip Gentleman took a legal-looking document from a brief-case and handed it to one of the old men who passed it on to Tony Gentleman. Margaret noticed that all the old men moved stiffly, awkward with arthritis and old age and (she wondered) old wounds. She took the paper and read it.

'If I pay you the money, the one million one hundred thousand, this makes me the owner of the land?'

'In effect, yes. But we don't want to get into no argument between a man and his wife. Your husband looked like he was gonna renege on our deal, but he's still got a husband's rights.' The other three old men nodded; but Margaret thought she saw a slight smile from Philip Gentleman. Somewhere in this house, she thought, there are women who know their proper place. 'You gotta talk it over with him.'

'Oh, I'll talk it over with him, be sure of that. May I take this with me?'

'You got the money with you, Mrs Minett?' Gentleman smiled, a surprisingly kindly smile, grandfatherly. 'A cheque, I mean. Not cash.'

'A cheque for the full amount will be deposited this afternoon. Do you have a bank in Kansas City?'

Gentleman smiled again and nodded. 'We have banks all over, Mrs Minett. Who's gonna write the cheque – you?'

'My attorney Magnus McKea will draw the cheque on his private account. Give me the name of your bank and I'll phone him now.'

Gentleman gestured to a phone on a secretaire against the wall. Magnus came on the phone as soon as Margaret asked for

him, asked at once about her safety. 'I'm all *right*, Magnus . . .
Yes, everything is all right. Now listen . . .' As she spoke she ran
her hand idly over the porcelain plaques that decorated the top
of the secretaire; she recognized them as Sèvres and knew this was
a piece of furniture her mother would love to possess. Tony
Gentleman, advised by someone, had surrounded himself with
what a gentleman would appreciate. She wondered if he did
appreciate it or if this was just another way of laundering dirty
money. But she could not afford to be contemptuous: she was
about to launder some more money for him: 'Can you have the
cheque deposited in the next hour and then have the bank call Mr
Gentleman to let him know? . . . What?' She looked at the old
Italian. 'Whom do we make the cheque out to?'

'The Christopher Columbus Trust. It's an exploration fund.'

Then he laughed, a high croaking laugh, and so did his partners: old men enjoying a joke that had taken them years to
achieve. Even George Biff smiled and the old men looked at him
and accepted his sharing of the joke, because he did it with the
proper respect that a nigger should.

Margaret gave the instructions to Magnus, assured him again
that she was all right, then hung up. 'May I keep this note?'

Tony Gentleman looked at his partners. As far as Margaret
could see none of them nodded his head, but Gentleman knew his
colleagues. He smiled at Margaret. 'If we can't trust a Beaufort,
whom can we trust?'

She acknowledged the compliment, said goodbye. The old men
stood up, stiffly gallant. They smiled at her, said how pleased
they were to have met her. None of them so much as looked at
George; that way they didn't have to say goodbye to him. Philip
Gentleman escorted Margaret and George out of the room and
down the panelled hall.

'Is that a Titian?'

'Yes. My father bought it as an investment, but now he loves it
for itself.'

'He has some beautiful things here.'

'I'll tell him.' He had a better voice than his father, soft and
educated. He was good-looking, too, in a quiet, unobtrusive way.
'He likes his possessions to be appreciated.'

'Possessions?'

He smiled as he opened the front door. 'He is jealously proud
of them, Mrs Minett. How else do people like us make an impression on people like you?'

He walked down the steps with her, handed her into the car.
Then he nodded at George. 'Goodbye, Mr Biff. You must for-

give my father his prejudices. He was brought up in a district where every ethnic group hated each other.'

George had never heard the word *ethnic*, but he knew all about prejudice. 'Don't worry me, Mr Gentleman. Down South us niggers never had any time for wops.'

He got into the car and Margaret looked out at the still smiling Philip Gentleman. 'I shan't apologize for George. He's been ticking our family off for years. Where did you go to school?'

'London School of Economics.' He continued to smile, but now it was fixed. 'None of our better colleges wanted me. I was never sure whether it was because I was a wop or a Gentleman. Good-bye, Mrs Minett.'

# 7

'Your goddam father put you up to this!'

'My father knows nothing about it. The only help I got was from Magnus – he helped me raise the money. I understand that all the collateral you had in the land deal was $25,000 of your own money. You did very well to raise a million on a stake like that. You must have waved your Beaufort connections pretty high.'

They were in her bedroom, the door shut. She had waited until the children were asleep in the nursery and the nurse had gone downstairs to her supper in the servants' wing on the far side of the house. Rich though the Beauforts were, Edith had taught her daughters middle-class values: never give the servants something to talk about if it could be avoided. They would be talking now if they could hear Frank.

'What else was I getting out of my fucking Beaufort connections? No fucking, that's for sure – '

She hated that sort of language: it insulted her as much as if he had spat in her face. And he knew it: he kept on at her until she suddenly shouted at him. 'Stop it, for God's sake! Try and talk like a civilized person – '

'Oh Jesus!' He sat down on the bed in which he had not been welcome for so many months. 'You cut a man's balls out and you talk about being civilized!'

'If I cut them out, you deserved it. You were playing even more dirty than I thought – you were trying to take either me or Daddy

165

for an extra $150,000. What were you going to do with it?'

'Buy us another house.'

She didn't know whether to believe him or not; for a moment she was nonplussed. She didn't want expressions of love, any attempt at reconciliation: she had gone too far from him ever to want to go back. Then the comedy of his remark hit her: he was going to buy a house for them with *her*, or her father's, money. So she ignored his answer and waved the legal note at him.

'I'm your creditor. I'll give you the land and you can sell it for whatever you can get for it. In return you give me the quiet, no-fuss divorce I asked for. And you get out of Kansas City, right out of Missouri. Even if you have to sell the land at a loss, you should get something over half a million for it. That's more money than you would have made without your Beaufort connections.'

He stared at her, hating her: the worst of it is, she thought, I deserve it. 'What about the kids?' he asked finally.

'They stay with me. They're young – they won't even miss you after a year or two.'

'Not even access, eh?'

'No.'

'I could do a Tim Davoren – take them with me. Disappear.'

Fear stabbed her; but it did not show. 'Not two of them, especially so young. You'd be found. Sell the land, Frank, take the money and go.'

'It might take time.'

She shook her head, determined to be rid of him: hating herself as much as hating him. But he had to go. 'Turn it over to a real estate broker. But I want you gone within twenty-four hours. I don't care where you go, just so long as you are miles away and out of Missouri. I've looked up the divorce laws for this State. If you are absent for longer than a year. I can sue you.'

'No,' he said, shaking his head with slow, continuous emphasis. 'I'm not giving up the kids.'

'Then I'll stop the cheque and you can take your chances with Mr Gentleman and his partners.'

He attempted a last show of defiance: 'Then we'll go to court and you'll get all the dirt you're asking for.'

'That's where I'll have to take *my* chances,' she said. 'But you'll still have to face the men from Chicago.'

He sat staring at her, shoulders hunched, hands spread out on the bed on either side of him. At last he stood up, sighed heavily. 'I really loved you. Once.'

He went out, closing the door quietly behind him. She heard

him go down the hall and into the nursery, but she didn't follow him. She knew she could trust him with the children.

## 8

The body of Frank Minett was found next morning in his car beside the thirteenth tee on the golf course of the Kansas City Country Club. Death was by a gunshot wound to the right temple; the gun, still clutched in his hand, had been stolen from a drawer in the security gatehouse on his father-in-law's estate. He left no suicide note and the reason for his death was known only to a select few. And of those all but one, his wife, had only educated guesses.

# Chapter Six

♦

# Margaret

I

Frank was buried quietly with no fuss; his funeral got much less space than a Minett-Beaufort divorce would have done. Margaret wept beside the grave. They were not crocodile tears but genuine: now that he was dead, and because of the manner of his death, she at last felt sorry for Frank. She had not meant to drive him so far; indeed, it had never occurred to her that he would even contemplate suicide. She was burdened with guilt, but there was also genuine sorrow. She made a beautifully sad figure beside the grave, but she was unaware of it.

Next day Jack Minett came to see her. He looked suddenly aged: the pain of grief and shock crippled the broad dark face. 'Why did he do it, Meg? His mother will never get over it. She thinks his soul is damned forever.'

'I don't know why he did it, Mr Minett. Things weren't too happy between us – '

'He never said anything.'

'We kept it to ourselves. My parents didn't know. There were other things troubling him – he was in debt – '

'Couldn't you have helped him there?'

'He wanted more money than I could raise without going to my father. I couldn't do that.'

'You should've gone to him, your father, I mean. If it meant saving Frank's life – '

Faintly, from the back of the house, came the sound of a

168

radio: Kay Starr was spinning the *Wheel of Fortune*. Margaret reached for the bell to call one of the servants, have them turn down the radio. Then she changed her mind, turned a deaf ear to the song. There would be a lot in the future to which she would have to turn a deaf ear.

'Mr Minett, I didn't know he was going to commit suicide. Don't you think I'd have gone to my father if I'd known that?' She told herself she would have done just that; but there would always be the nagging doubt. She had felt differently towards him that last night from what she felt now. Guilt was a breath blowing on some dead ashes. 'If only he'd left a note, we'd have known . . .'

'Well, don't blame yourself. Things go wrong.' He looked around the living-room; he had never felt at home in this house when he visited it. 'Maybe he should never have asked you to marry him.'

'Perhaps.'

Once a month after that she took the children over to the Minett home in Johnson County. Jack and Francesca Minett showed no desire to visit her at Beaufort Park and she never encouraged them. The children were still too young to form any attachment to their Minett grandparents and Margaret knew the Minetts would never become possessive towards them. The least she could do was give them access to the children.

Nina had not come home for the funeral, but she wrote a long letter of condolence to Margaret. Then she suggested that Margaret should bring the children to Europe: *Come over here and live with me for a year. You need a break from that atmosphere at home. I'm moving on to Rome and taking a villa there . . .*

Margaret wrote back and said she would think about it; but she would not come immediately: *Mother is still reeling from the shock of Frank's death. First, Tim's and Michael's disappearance; then this tragedy. I don't think it ever entered her head that you and I would be anything but gloriously, blissfully happy. I must stay here, at least for a few more months . . .*

'I think we should wear mourning for three months,' Edith said.

'Mother, you don't have to – Frank wouldn't have expected it.'

'Darling, I'm doing it for you. And for him, too, of course.' But the last sounded like an afterthought, a polite bow to custom. Edith would never understand why her son-in-law had visited such grief and shock on her daughter and grandchildren. And on herself. She had begun to wonder if there was some forgotten sin in her past life that merited all the punishment God was giving her. 'Your father has his business to attend to. And there will be the election campaign. Thank God he has that to take his mind off what has happened to you.'

'I'm glad for him,' said Margaret and managed not to sound sarcastic.

Sally had flown home for the funeral, then returned to Vassar the next day. Now she came home for Easter, bringing a friend with her. Cindy Drake was a small, pretty girl, quiet and almost too feminine, the very opposite of the bouncing Sally.

'We have nothing in common except a crush on our English prof,' said Sally as Margaret drove them home from the airport. And we both love Europe. Cindy's father is with the State Department. He's one of Dean Acheson's pet diplomats.'

'I shouldn't mention that to Daddy. Has she warned you about our father, Cindy?'

Cindy smiled shyly. 'My mother is a Republican, too. When we were at the embassy in Paris she had to clear everything with Dad before she spoke.'

'Fortunately we don't have to do that with Daddy,' said Sally. 'Though he wishes we would.'

Another rebel, thought Margaret. And wondered what problems Sally was going to raise for herself and their father.

Lucas was still stiff-necked in his attitudes; he knew what was best for himself, his family and America. He was not very concerned with what was best for the world, just so long as America was pre-eminent in it and could set the standards. The Beaufort empire within the United States was doing well; the Cattle Company had already almost recovered from the devastation of last year's flood. Beaufort Oil was now well established in Abu Sadar, had outlets in Britain and was in partnership with local companies in France, Germany and Holland. Beaufort Trust money was being invested overseas in Australia, South Africa and certain South American countries which were governed by the more reliable dictators. Lucas still indulged his xenophobia, but one didn't have to carry it to ridiculous lengths.

Despite his obstinate attitudes, he had softened; or anyway was quieter in expounding them. He still blamed himself for what had happened to Nina; he would never forgive himself but he could never confess it to her. He had a recurring nightmare that, when he was dead, Tim would return and tell only half the story, that he had been paid to disappear by Lucas. Now he had a further worry: he knew that, in some way, he had helped ruin Margaret's life. He had never been close enough to her to ask her to confide in him; and he blamed himself for having failed, too, in that direction. But it was too late for him to change. He could only hope to avoid mistakes with his two younger daughters.

'You girls have a wonderful life ahead of you. When we elect General Eisenhower President in November, there will be a whole new America opening up. Is your father a career officer, Cindy?'

'Yes, Mr Beaufort.'

'Then he'll appreciate working under a President who knows how to run things properly. He must have been a very disturbed man these past few years.'

It was Easter Sunday and they had all come back from the morning service at St Andrew's Episcopal Church. They were sitting out on the wide back porch while George Biff and two of the maids served morning coffee. No one had yet changed into casual clothes and, with the servants hovering around, the table set with a lace cloth, a passing stranger might have been forgiven for thinking that time had slipped back into a more gracious era. The same stranger might have also been forgiven for wondering, if such a scene could take place in President Truman's day, what elegant graciousness must lie ahead under President Eisenhower.

'I liked Reverend Luckson's sermon on idealism.' Edith, like Margaret, was dressed in dark clothes; though she had been relieved when Margaret had vetoed any idea that they should go as far as wearing plain black. 'We should have more of that.'

'Idealism is what you talk about on Sundays,' said Lucas, who had thought the Reverend Luckson could have done with a course in common sense. 'Practicality is what gets you through the other six days of the week. Would your father agree with that, Cindy?'

'Her father probably doesn't have time to be idealistic,' said Sally. 'He has to be watching out for Senator McCarthy.'

'Your father isn't on the Senator's list, is he?' Lucas looked startled, wondering what Vassar had sent home this time.

'I don't think so,' said Cindy. 'Mother wouldn't have married him if he was even remotely sympathetic to Communism. Mother is a staunch Republican, though I'm afraid she is more for Senator Taft than for General Eisenhower.'

Lucas relaxed. 'Either is better than what we have. As I said, you're very fortunate girls. It's a pity you aren't old enough to vote, so that you could claim some credit for putting America on the right road.'

'I think I'll vote for Henry Miller when I grow up,' said Prue, all dressed up but for her shoes, which she had kicked off.

'What party does he stand for?' asked her father.

'The Capricornia Party,' said Margaret.

'Capri – ? You don't mean the *Tropic of Capricorn* Miller?' Lucas looked in horror at his youngest daughter. Vassar was bad enough but the Barstow School seemed worse, far worse. 'Are you reading that at school?'

'Of course not, Daddy.' Prue had never been afraid of her father; she might not be his favourite but she had her own way of handling him. 'I've been reading it here at home.'

'Where on earth did you get it?' her mother demanded.

'In the mail. In a plain brown wrapper. It was advertised in *Esquire* and I wrote off for it.'

'What was she doing reading *Esquire*?' Lucas turned on Edith, who evidently couldn't run a clean house.

'How on earth do I know? Darling – ' Edith looked at her youngest. 'You had better give me Mr Miller's book.'

'Oh, let her keep it,' said Sally. 'You're not corrupted by it, are you, Prue?'

'I don't know,' said Prue. 'I hope so.'

During this Margaret had been observing Cindy Drake. The girl, demure as a convent novice, hardly took her eyes off Sally except when someone spoke directly to her. Occasionally Sally would look towards her and smile, but Cindy's answer would only be in her eyes, a secret smile that one had to watch closely to catch. Margaret, disturbed at the thought that suddenly entered her mind, mentally shook her head. She had to be wrong in what she was thinking.

'Time I was getting back to the children.' She stood up. 'What are you doing the rest of the day, Sally?'

'Oh, we have plans,' said Sally lightly, after a glance at Cindy.

'May I come over and see the kids?' said Prue.

'Children,' said Edith. 'Kids are what goats have. Go and get me Mr Miller's book first.'

'I lent it to Sue Harrap.'

'Oh good heavens, what will Helen Harrap think of me!'

'You'd better call her,' said Lucas. 'Tell her our youngest daughter is disseminating obscene literature.'

'Am I?' said Prue, unworried, beaming with braced teeth at her father. 'That sounds really *criminal*.'

'Come on,' said Margaret and took her youngest sister off towards the other house.

As they crossed the lawns Prue said, 'Do you like Cindy?'

Her tone was too innocent, even for an eleven-year-old: Margaret looked at her warily. 'She seems nice enough.'

'She never says much. Unless you ask her.'

'You could take some lessons from her.'

'Don't start talking like a mother, even if you are one. I caught them kissing last night.'

'Who?' But she knew.

'Who do you think? Sally and Cindy. Real kissing, too. Do you think they're lesbians?'

'For God's sake!' She stopped suddenly beside the spaced line of shrubs that curved round the house. Azaleas bloomed red and pink, syringa was a creamy-white hoar frost; early spring hung in the air like an innocence itself. *You're not corrupted, are you?* Sally had said. 'You don't know what you're talking about. That's a dreadful thing to say about Sally.'

Prue looked unrepentant. 'I think it might be true. I don't miss much, you said that yourself.'

'Well, you should! Miss things, I mean. You're too damned watchful. Don't you dare mention this – '

'I'm not *stupid*. Mother would have a fit. What are you going to do?'

'What am *I*? What the heck do you think I'm going to do? I don't believe it, for one thing. And even if it were true, which I doubt very much – ' *Am I arguing too hard?* ' – it's none of my business. It may be just a phase she's passing through.'

'Did you go through a phase like that when you were her age?'

'No, I didn't. But I had crushes – '

'Not on girls, I'll bet. You had a crush on Tim – ' Prue looked up at her, an angel with braces on her teeth. She's too artless, Margaret thought. And looked for horns among the blonde curls. 'But then we all did. Even Sally.'

'Well – ' She was at a loss. She did not want to interfere with Sally; that would be too much like their father's attitude. Yet she had to protect her parents from discovering Sally's . . . Sally's what? Indiscretion, aberration, perversion? She couldn't bring herself to put a name to it. 'Well, I'll have a talk with Sally. But you stop spying on her.'

Prue was indignant. 'I wasn't spying! It was an accident I saw them. Sally's bedroom door was open – '

'All right, all right! Just let's keep it quiet. You could be all wrong about what you saw – I hope you are. Now let's go in and feed the children.'

After lunch Margaret saw Sally and Cindy driving out of the park in Sally's MG. They looked exactly as she had thought of them up till a couple of hours ago: two attractive girls in whom any boy would have been interested. But it occurred to her now that since Sally and Cindy had arrived home on Thursday night, no boys had come near the place. She wondered if the same thought had occurred to her mother.

She spent the afternoon with the children. She loved being with them, a fact that sometimes surprised her; till she had become pregnant with Martha she had never shown the slightest interest in children, had, indeed, been bored by them. Now she was fascinated by them, even the baby Emma; and she loved them both. She did not have to pretend to herself on that: she loved Frank's child as much as she did Tim's. She still thought of Frank, sometimes with regret, more often with guilt, never with love. She also thought of Tim, less frequently but still with yearning.

That evening Lucas and Edith went to the Kansas City Country Club for supper. Prue had gone to spend the night with her friend Sue Harrap, her co-admirer of Henry Miller. Margaret knew that Sue's mother, Helen, would not make a big thing of her daughter's reading *Tropic of Capricorn*; Helen was one of the new breed of progressive-minded mothers, a philosophy that Edith thought was only a synonym for dereliction of a mother's duty. Margaret would not be surprised if Helen Harrap, her daughter and Prue were right now sitting grouped together discussing Mr Miller.

It was nine o'clock in the evening when Margaret decided she was bored. The children had been asleep two hours, she had had her supper, she had watched television: she *had* to get out of the house. She went out, crossed the lawns, was entering the back door of the main house before she admitted to herself that she was not bored, that all day she had been trying to put her mind against talking with Sally. Yet now she came into the house slyly, like a spy.

She heard the soft laughter in Sally's room as she came quietly up the stairs. Faintly from the servants' quarters there came the sound of other laughter, canned: someone was making a fool of himself on television. Sweating a little, afraid of what she was going to find, she knocked gently on Sally's door. She knocked gently because she knew she did not want to be heard. Then she opened the door.

Sally and Cindy, both nude, were in bed together, arms round each other. Margaret stood unable to move; all at once she wanted to retreat but couldn't. She had wanted to spy on them, and now she was shocked and ashamed. Sally turned her face away from Cindy's and looked at her. Later Margaret would recall that there was no defiance in Sally's expression. She looked surprisingly and incongruously sad.

Margaret started to close the door, backing out. 'Don't go, Meg,' said Sally.

She sat up, reached for a robe and slipped into it as she got out of bed. She didn't look at Cindy, who had rolled on to her back, pulled the sheets up to her chin and lay staring at the ceiling. Margaret, suddenly wishing she had stayed in her own house, came into the room and closed the door.

'Now you know.' This was a Sally Margaret had never known: quiet, adult, nothing of the hoyden she had always been. 'I'm sorry you had to find out, Meg.'

'You haven't made much effort to hide it.' She did not mean to sound sharp, but she was ill at ease. All day she had been thinking of talking with Sally, putting it off but knowing she would eventually have to do it. And now she had no reasoned argument to put and consequently was awkward and abrupt. 'Even Prue knows. Or suspects.'

Sally sighed worriedly, looked at Cindy. 'Better go back to your own room, Cindy.'

Cindy slid out of bed, pulled on a robe and looked at Margaret. 'I don't know how Sally feels, but I'm not ashamed. I love her.'

Margaret had had no experience in this sort of love, not even as an observer. There had been girls who had been suspected lovers at college, but the girls and the subject had always been avoided. Lesbianism was something that only girls who couldn't get a man went in for, a last resort for love.

Margaret said nothing and her silence seemed to upset Cindy, who looked at Sally, then put her hand to her face and ran out of the room. Margaret waited for Sally to say something, since for the moment she had nothing herself to say.

'I suppose you think I'm a pervert?'

Margaret went to sit down on the bed, the side where Cindy had lain; then she changed her mind and sat in a chair. She had the feeling she was backing off from everything and was annoyed at her cowardice. Nobody had pressed her to come here, she had come of her own accord to interfere. But with the best of intentions, she told herself.

'I'm shocked, Sally – I admit that. But I've never thought of what you've been doing as a perversion – maybe it is with some girls, but not all. It's not with you, is it? I mean, you're not doing it for the thrill?'

Sally looked for a moment as if she was going to be angry; then she sat down on the bed and once more looked sadly at her sister. 'I'm not like that, Meg. I mean the thrill bit. I saw you looking at the bed – what were you looking for? A dildo, something like that? You're like a man – they all think we have to use those things.'

'I wasn't looking for anything,' Margaret said. 'How did you get – involved like this?'

'I don't know why I got into it, if that's what you're asking. It just sort of happened.'

'Is Cindy the first?'

Sally nodded. 'She started it. Made the first advances, is that how they say it? I'm not blaming her. I didn't hold off. I think I welcomed it. Not the sex bit, but just someone loving me for myself.'

'Oh God – how can you say that? We've always loved you!'

Sally shook her head almost fiercely. 'You all thought you did. But I was always the odd one out. Daddy was always only concerned for Nina. Mother was always fussing over you.'

'What about Prue?'

'She's self-contained, even at her age. I'm not – ' Suddenly she began to cry, tears streaming down her face.

Margaret got up, went quickly round the bed and took her in her arms. She held Sally to her, stroking her hair and back while Sally drained herself of tears. Part of her mind wondered if Cindy had done this, and she began to understand. Whatever else they had done did not matter. It could not have been any worse than the deceitful sex she had given Frank.

At last Sally sat back and dried her eyes on the sheet. 'Thanks. I mean for being so understanding – '

'Cindy has to go home. I'm afraid that Mother and Daddy will catch on if she doesn't.'

'You won't tell them? No, I shouldn't have said that. I can see you won't. What about Prue? You said she suspected – '

'She's a shrewd little devil. But she's not a mischief-maker. Don't discuss it with her, just let it ride. If she brings it up with me again, I'll say we, she and I, were mistaken. You and Cindy just liked each other.' She looked carefully at her sister. 'Cindy says she loves you. Do you love her?'

Sally didn't reply at once, then she said, 'No. I could never tell her, but there are times when I get bored with her. I still like boys . . . Do you think I'm – what do they call it? – double-gaited?'

Margaret suddenly laughed: she had never heard the expression. 'You sound like a trotting horse!'

Sally also laughed; or rather, smiled. She was still quiet, nothing like the girl who in the past would have let out a gust of laughter. Margaret wondered how much of that laughter had been forced. 'You know what I mean. Maybe there's some hope . . .'

'Of course there is! For God's sake – ' Margaret squeezed her sister's hand; it was hard to believe that Sally thought no one had loved her. 'Look, tell Cindy to go home. She can tell Mother that she got a phone call tonight about some crisis at home. Then when she's gone, you can start working things out for yourself.'

'She's still going to be there – at Vassar, I mean.'

'Yes, that won't help. But it will only be for another semester. You can't leave Vassar now – that would cause too many complications with Mother and Daddy. And Prue might start asking questions. You never were a very good liar . . . Look, I'm going to Rome in the summer to stay with Nina. Come with me and the children.'

It was a moment or two before Sally said, 'You're not doing this because you're sorry for me?'

Margaret leaned forward and kissed her on the cheek. 'I'm doing it because I love you.'


## 2

Cindy Drake went home next morning without any fuss, but to the regret of Edith. 'She's such a nice girl. You must have her again.'

'Of course,' said Sally.

At the end of June, when Sally came home from Vassar, Margaret asked her, 'How did it work out with Cindy?'

'She left. She's transferring to Bennington next semester.'

'Are you glad it's over?'

'I'm glad it's over. But I'm not sorry it happened. At least it brought you and me closer together.'

Prue had proved no problem. Margaret had told her that she had been mistaken, that there was no lesbian relationship between Sally and Cindy. 'I suppose they were just fooling around when you saw them kissing.'

'Some fooling! Any girl kisses me like that she's going to get kicked in her what's-it.'

Margaret was afraid to ask what a what's-it was. 'Well, we have nothing to worry about with Sally. So forget it.'

'I wasn't making a big thing of it,' said Prue airily. 'It's life, isn't it?'

'Oh God. What are you reading *now*?'

When Margaret announced that she was going to Rome and taking the children with her, Lucas erupted with some of his old bombast. 'You don't appreciate what you have here! Nina's over there, lonely and unhappy among all those foreigners – '

'How do you know she's lonely and unhappy?'

'I *know*.'

'Then I'm doing the right thing going over there. I'll help relieve her loneliness and unhappiness. You should be glad. If you were a loving father, you'd be coming over, too – '

'I *am* a loving father! But there are things to do here – '

'Like electing General Eisenhower,' said Sally, but only Margaret noticed the acid note in her voice. 'I'm going to Rome, too. For the summer, anyway.'

'Darling,' said Edith, 'you sound as if you're thinking of staying over there.'

'I may,' said Sally with polite defiance: she did not want to fight with her mother. 'I just think it will be nice for the three of us to be together.'

'What about me?' said Prue.

'You be the sensible one and stay with us,' said Lucas, as if he had to reason with an eleven-year-old daughter who wanted to go tearing off to Europe.

'For the life of me I can't see why you all want to run away from home,' said Edith, trying not to sound hurt.

'You'll all be glad to come back some day,' said Lucas. 'This is the heart of America. The country's crumbling all around the edges, but not here. We've got stability here. Standards and principles. Some day you and all the ones like you will appreciate that the Middle West is the heart and soul of this country. You'll come back.'

'We're not going *forever*,' said Margaret in exasperation. 'We are just – just broadening our horizons, I suppose. Broadening our perspective,' she said, looking at her mother.

'There are limits,' said Edith, who had become like her husband, more isolationist. The broader world had not treated her or her two eldest daughters kindly at all. They might still be happy if they had married their own kind. 'Just be careful in Rome, that's all I ask. Those Italians – sorry, darling.'

'It's all right, Mother,' said Margaret. 'I don't think Frank ever thought of himself as an Italian Italian.'

The day before she left for Italy Margaret went to dinner with

Magnus McKea. He took her to a small French restaurant where the proprietor, a French-Canadian, had hopes that the natives might consider something besides a T-bone or rib roast. He was also aberrant enough to refuse to serve any pre-dinner drink but an aperitif, contending that diners at his establishment should not shrivel their taste buds before eating his food. He was the spiritual descendant of those traders who had passed through here over a hundred years before hoping to sell soap to the buffalo hunters. Magnus was one of his favourite customers, a man of enlightened tastes.

'Henri has hopes for us,' Magnus said. 'Having you dine here will give him a boost. Your name will be in next week's *Independent*.'

'It won't be much of a boost for him when they also read that I've just left town. Will you look after things for me while I'm gone, Magnus?'

'I'm taking care of Nina, why not you? Did you hear from your friends up in Chicago after Frank's death?'

'Just a condolence card from Philip Gentleman – that's the old man's son. Perhaps his father got him to send it.'

'Did you write and thank him? No? Good girl. Write all of that off to experience. I mean meeting them. I don't mean Frank.'

'I've written him off to experience, too. Does that sound callous?'

'Yes. I know you don't mean it that way, but I shouldn't repeat it to anyone else.'

'If you proposed to me, Magnus, I think I might marry you.'

Henri came to the table, a dark-haired plump advertisement for his own food. He showed Magnus a bottle of wine. 'A Pommard 1947, m'sieu. A very, *very* good year.'

'The lady is suggesting champagne.' Margaret was surprised at Magnus's light touch.

Henri shook his head. 'Too soon, madame. Later.'

He poured the red wine and went away. Magnus said. 'There's your answer. Too soon. You'd be marrying me on the rebound or out of gratitude, Meg. You should never do that.'

*Don't tell me*: *I know*. 'I think you're afraid of marriage. What do you do – I mean, for *women*?'

'You mean for sex, don't you? I'm a gentleman – or I try to be. I have my little affairs. Not here, but in other places. I don't go to St Louis and Tulsa and Omaha just on business. There are plenty of women of my age, widows and divorcees, who are willing to share their bed with a gentleman. A discreet one, such as I am.'

She laughed softly, shaking her head at him. 'You make it sound like a legal service. The lawyer with the bedside manner.'

'None of the women has complained.'

They had champagne with their dessert and by the time they left the restaurant they were both merry. And Margaret was also a little sad.

'I'm going to miss you, Magnus.'

'Don't stay away too long. For your own sake.'

'I'm going to miss Kansas City, too.'

'I don't think so. You don't really know KC. All you know is the country club district and that's not this town. You haven't a clue about how the people live out on Wornall Road or down in Little Italy or the Mexicans over on the West Side. Or the blue-collar workers over in the North East. You're an over-protected rich girl whose family made a fortune out of this town. When did you ever go down to the pit at the Board of Trade and watch the bidding for wheat or corn or barley? Or down to the stockyards? The only time you ever see beef on the hoof is at the American Royal show every November and I doubt very much if you pay much attention to it even then.'

'Magnus, you are starting to sound like Daddy.'

'Sorry. But I'm sold on this town and you annoy me when you say you're going to miss it, because I know you're not. All you're going to miss is Beaufort Park and what lies between it and Country Club Plaza. I guess I'd feel the same way about the café-society lot who say the same thing about New York City but never move off Park or Madison Avenues. Kansas City is in my blood, but I don't think it's in yours. But that's probably more your parents' fault.'

'Well, it's a little late now. But when I come back . . .'

'That's the important thing. To keep coming back.'

He drove her home, in past the security guard (where did the guard live? she wondered. Out on Wornall Road?) and pulled the car up outside her house. He switched off the engine, reached across and kissed her on the mouth, no lawyer's kiss.

'You should have taken me back to your place,' she said. 'Showed me how the other half lives.'

'I know that. It took a great deal of willpower to get the car on to the Ward Parkway. One of us might have regretted it to-morrow morning if I hadn't brought you home.'

'Which one of us? You or me?'

He didn't answer, just kissed her again and squeezed her breast. She kissed him in return, putting her arms round his neck and pulling him into her. She felt a cheat: she wanted to be made

180

love to, but she knew he was right. One of them in the morning would regret it.

'Goodnight, Magnus. Keep in touch.'

He touched her breast lightly, smiled in the darkness. 'Like that? Some day when I'm even merrier than I am now, I'll tell you why I've never married. Take care of yourself.'

She went into the house wondering what secret *he* had.

Her goodbye to George Biff was shorter and less complicated. They had had no discussion since Frank's death; she had taken him enough into her confidence *before* that unexpected tragedy. She knew he would respect that confidence and she hoped he would ask no further questions of her. At least his attitude towards her had not changed: she still seemed to be in his favour.

'You can have the Buick, George.' He had never had a car of his own. 'I'm sure Miss Nina would like you to have it.'

He was carrying bags out to pack them into the two cars that were taking Margaret, Sally, the nurse Ruth and the two children to the railroad station. Margaret had decided, for the children's sake, that they should go by train and ship to Italy. Miss Stafford had, with her usual efficiency, arranged all the tickets, but she had hinted in her manner that she agreed with Edith, that Margaret and Sally were doing the wrong thing.

George shoved the bags into the trunk. 'Your daddy always loans me a car when I want it. Dunno how he gonna feel, me having a car of my own.'

'George, sometimes you sound like Uncle Tom when you talk about my father. He's not nineteenth-century.'

He grinned. 'I hear you girls sometimes, you talk like you think he just that.' Then he sobered. 'You take care over there, Miz Meg. You got all that other trouble behind you now. Don't buy yourself any more.'

'Thanks, George. For everything.'

The farewell to her parents *was* complicated. It was a quiet whirlpool of love and resentment; Edith and Lucas did not hide their hurt at this desertion. Francesca Minett, still in black, came to the station to say goodbye to her grandchildren; her farewell kiss to Margaret was perfunctory, as if the latter no longer meant anything in her life. Margaret, for her part, was suddenly glad to be leaving. Relationships in Italy should be much simpler than here.

'We'll come to see you after the elections,' said Edith. 'Your father will want a vacation.'

'The country will be in good hands then,' said Lucas. 'You're foolish to be leaving now. You should have gone when that feller Truman was re-elected back in '48.'

A bell rang, a whistle blew, a voice cried *All Abo-o-a-a-rd!* They were sounds that were dying out, already echoes, but none of the travellers knew it then. The train rolled out of the station and Margaret looked back at the city that Magnus had told her she did not know and wondered whether she would be back in six weeks, six months or six years. She felt she was throwing off a corset that, though it had constrained her, had had its feeling of security. A corset: there's a nineteenth-century thought.

'I feel like starting a new life,' said Sally, who had been told by her parents that she must return to Vassar in the new school year.

'I wonder how people do that?' And Margaret, going to live with his wife, wondered once again about Tim.

## 3

That year was a momentous one, at least for Republicans. For the first time in twenty years they at last had one of their own in the White House; God, who could have voted in a Republican primary any time He wished, was in His Heaven and all was right with the world again. President Eisenhower, who was not God and very soon began to look as if he wished he were not President, sent for Lucas and offered him a Cabinet post. Lucas, to everyone's surprise, declined the offer. He had begun to feel that doors were closing on rooms in his life. He did not want to be in Washington when his daughters came home to Kansas City; and he was certain that eventually, if not soon, they would do that. He had to believe that they would or his whole life would collapse like a house of cards.

In the meantime his errant daughters had fallen in love with Italy and the Italians. By September Sally had decided that she was not going back to college and that brought Edith flying across the Atlantic with Miss Stafford; Lucas had to remain at home, caught up in the efforts to have General Eisenhower elected. There were arguments and tears between Edith and Sally, but the latter was adamant. Finally Edith flew back home, comforted by Miss Stafford, having extracted a promise from Nina and Margaret that they would never, never let Sally out of their sight.

Edith had been impressed by the villa Nina had leased on the Appia Antica. It was an old house that had belonged to a rich Fascist before the war, had been the headquarters of a German general during the war, and since the war had been the home of a successful black marketeer: it could not have picked a better set of owners for keeping it in the best of condition. The black marketeer had made his money and fled to Switzerland, where respectability could be bought at the border with a resident's permit. He had recognized that de Gasperi's Christian Democrats, frightened by the growing support for Togliatti's Communists, were about to embark on a campaign against such corruption as his. Campaigns against corruption, in Italy, were almost as seasonal as the pasta harvest; but some were more serious than others. The black marketeer recognized that the government, pressed by the Americans who seemed to think that any country which accepted their aid had to be less corrupt than themselves, might even go so far as to throw him into the Regina di Coeli prison and forget all about him. Blaming the Americans for the pious influence, he set about finding an American tenant for his villa, extracted a ransom rent from her and left for Lugano and respectability.

'It's beautiful. Much better than that place you had in England.' Edith had not meant to be tactless, but her thought processes of late had started to become muddled. 'It must be full of history.'

'The partisans shot seven Nazis out there in the garden,' said Nina.

'I wasn't thinking of *that* sort of history.' Edith was selective in her view of history; there were enough good things in the centuries past without paying attention to the bad. 'Look at that furniture! I'd love to take some of it back with me. I wonder where your landlord got it?'

'Probably stole it.' Nina had no illusions about her landlord.

'I love you all so much,' said Edith and wept all the way back across the Atlantic, an emotional reaction that worried Pan American Airways, who thought there was something wrong with their service until assured by Miss Stafford that everything was all right.

The three Beaufort sisters settled down to enjoy Rome. Sally bought a car, an apple-green Maserati, and once more began to look and act like the old Sally, though there was a sheen of sophistication on the hoyden now. Nina had already become slightly Europeanized, helped by the fact that she had a better ear for languages than her sisters. Margaret was the one who found it hardest to adapt.

She was still troubled by guilt. At what had happened to Frank; at running away from her parents; but most of all, at having stolen Tim from Nina. He and Michael were still part of Nina's life: a large silver-framed photo of the two of them stood on her dressing-table. She never mentioned them unless Margaret or Sally did, but she still had the private investigators on retainer in case they came across a clue to Tim's and Michael's whereabouts. And Margaret occasionally saw her stop in a crowd and look, with a mixed expression of pain and delight, at some passing man who would resemble Tim. The pain would be reflected in Margaret's own face and she would pray that night that Nina would never learn of her and Tim's deception of her.

In the spring of 1953 Sally announced that she was going to enter the Mille Miglia. That brought Lucas and Edith across the Atlantic faster than Sally would drive the 1000 kilometres around Italy.

'You were supposed to be looking after her!' Lucas thundered at his two elder daughters.

'She'll be killed!' Edith would have preferred to have fainted instead of being as angry as she was; that might have brought her daughters to their senses, showed what they were doing to her. 'I've seen how those Italians drive!'

'Mother, they are not going to run her off the road. She'll be safer in this race than just driving around Rome day to day. They'll all be going in the same direction. That's something for Italians.'

Margaret had been angry and upset when Sally had told her and Nina what she intended doing. Both of them had tried to talk Sally out of it, but she had been wilful and stubborn and in the end they had given in. They knew she was an excellent driver and they knew, too, that she was not reckless. She drove fast but always within the outer limits of safety.

'I think one of you should go with her,' said Edith.

'Mother – how illogical can you get?'

'Then it must be dangerous!' Logic, in Edith's view, had nothing to do with mother love.

Margaret looked at her father. 'Daddy, will you reason with her? She's getting more dithery every day.'

'Don't add insult to injury,' said Lucas. 'Come outside.'

They went out into the garden, walked round the marble-faced swimming pool. It had been a cold winter and the air still had a chill to it. A gardener was trimming some frost-damaged shrubs and a houseman was pulling in leaves from the cold-looking water of the pool. Lucas shivered and put his hands in the pockets of his tweed jacket.

'Your mother hasn't been the same since you all left home.'

'Daddy, it had to happen sooner or later. She still has Prue.'

'Prue isn't enough. She's not old enough yet. Your mother was looking forward to all of you growing up, being old enough to talk to, to take her into your confidence.' He made his own confidence: 'I was looking forward to it myself.'

'Daddy,' she said gently, 'it's always been hard to talk to you.'

He nodded, not looking at her. 'I think it was all of you being girls – it would have been easier for me if I'd had sons. I tried with Tim and Frank – '

'You weren't very successful.' She still spoke gently, having no desire to hurt him further.

'I was never close enough to them. I'm never comfortable with outsiders. I'm like that when I go to Washington. Perhaps it was my father's fault. He and Mother, your grandmother, sheltered me too much.'

*Oh Daddy, how can you be so blind?* But it would be useless to point it out to him: he would forever go on trying to shelter his own children. It was too deeply engrained in his nature: they were Beauforts, a different species, and they had to be protected. Yet she knew, despite Magnus's criticism of her lack of knowledge of what made Kansas City and by extension the rest of America tick, that she and her sisters were not so much different. Except, of course, in their wealth. The rich are different, someone (Fitzgerald? Hemingway?) had said. But whoever had said it had not been rich and really did not know.

The gardener went by, touched his cap, said *Buongiorno, signore*; and Lucas nodded acknowledgement and approval. Perhaps the Italians were not so bad after all: they had the proper respect for class. They knew nothing about democracy, of course, and that probably gave them an advantage. He had heard that President Eisenhower had been upset to learn that Washington could not be run like the Army. America could do with a dose of respect and discipline. It was a pleasure to see some proper respect here in this walled garden, even if he was not quite sure what the attitudes were outside it.

'Don't worry about us, Daddy. We'll all come back some day, perhaps sooner than you expect. Why don't you stay on with us for a while? Sally would love to know she had your moral support.'

'She'll get none from your mother, you know that. But all right. Can we stay here?'

'It has twelve bedrooms and six bathrooms – why not?'

'Can't understand why they don't build a bathroom to each bedroom. These Europeans seem afraid of plumbing.'

*He knows no more than I do.* 'Have you been in Appalachia lately?'

He suddenly smiled and just as suddenly put his arm round her. She hid her surprise, not wanting to hurt him; but she had to thrust the stiffness from her body and relax within his embrace. She felt for his hand and held it.

'You see?' he said. 'We *can* talk.'

'Of course we can,' she said and wanted to weep, knowing that it was too late.

Lucas and Edith stayed for a month. Sally, accompanied by a mechanic from the garage that serviced her car, went off to Brescia to practise for the Mille Miglia. Unlike most of the private starters in the annual race, she was not handicapped by lack of finance. The works teams drove round the 1000-kilometre route at least once, sometimes twice; most private drivers could not afford to do that, but Sally and her mechanic did it twice. She ran the car off the road once, but confided this only to Margaret and Nina.

'I'm all right, so there's no need to scare the pants off Mother. I'm having the dents hammered out and we'll be there at the start tomorrow morning.'

Margaret, Nina and their parents had come up to Brescia the night before the race was to start. Sally was quartered in the town, but the rest of the Beauforts had had to stay in a hotel at the northern end of Lake Garda. Lucas, who never went to a sporting event of any kind in Kansas City, was not happy about travelling fifty miles to see the start and finish of a race, the greater part of which would be run well beyond the sight of him and everyone else in Brescia.

'Ridiculous,' he said. 'At least at Indianapolis you can see them going round and round.'

'I'd rather not see it,' said Edith. 'My heart would be in my mouth for the whole time – how long will it take you, darling?'

'I don't know,' said Sally. 'Thirteen or fourteen hours, if I'm lucky. Maybe longer. I don't expect to win. All I want to do is finish.'

'I've always believed winning is important,' said Lucas, forgetting himself.

'It is not!' said Edith. 'You just finish, darling, that's all I ask.'

Lucas was not happy when he learned he would have to stay up half the night to see his daughter start off down the Viale Rebuffone; even in his youth he would not have stayed up half the night to see Babe Ruth go to bat or Man O' War run, supposing those two sports figures had competed at night. He had stayed up *all* night to hear Julia Lee and Count Basie and others, but that had been different. He was also not happy when he saw the size of the crowd in the Piazza Vittoria and the Viale Rebuffone and heard the noise of revving cars, brass bands, firecrackers and what seemed to be a million shouting, gesticulating Italians. His third daughter must be a lunatic to want to belong to such an atmosphere.

Sally, using money, had managed to get her parents and sisters a vantage point on a balcony overlooking the start. The first cars went off at nine o'clock, tiny family cars taking their drivers on their one day of glory in the year; at half-minute intervals up to ten o'clock and then at minute intervals after that, the cars continued to roll down the ramp and start the long journey. The noise was deafening and Margaret knew that her mother and father would be suffering headaches long before Sally got away. She persuaded them to go and lie down and the owner of the apartment, a motherly woman older than either Edith or Lucas, pushed them into a bedroom, chattering at them in Italian and oblivious of the fact that neither of them understood a word she was saying. She closed the bedroom door on them and shooed Margaret and Nina out for a breath of fresh air.

They went out for a breath of gasoline-and-oil-filled air. They fought their way through the crowd, several times having their bottoms pinched by men whose interest was not solely in the cars thumping down off the starting ramp. They found Sally and her mechanic standing beside the apple-green Maserati, both of them in driving overalls. With them was another driver whose back was to Margaret as she and Nina were squeezed out of the crowd into the tiny space beside the car.

'Here's another American driver,' said Sally. 'So I shan't feel so isolated. My sisters Nina and Meg. Philip Mann.'

The driver turned and smiled at the arrivals. 'Hello,' said Philip Gentleman.

'Mr Mann?' said Margaret. 'No longer gentle?'

'What is this?' said Sally and Nina.

'A joke,' said Margaret, suddenly afraid of giving herself away. 'Mr Mann and I once met at a party.'

'You know Kansas City then, Mr Mann?' said Nina.

'I was there only once. Your sister and I met only fleetingly.'

Then he excused himself and went away to his own car, a red Ferrari. Margaret said, 'Is he here just for the Mille Miglia?'

'In Italy you mean? No, he lives in Milan. He represents some

Chicago investment firm. He's attractive, don't you think?'

'I was thinking that,' said Nina. 'What a pity he doesn't live in Rome.'

'Maybe it's just as well,' said Margaret, for reasons of her own.

'What's the joke about *gentle*?' said Sally. 'Oh, I get it. Gentle Mann.'

'Something like that,' said Margaret. 'Let's go and have a drink.'

The three of them had no difficulty in getting a table in a bar. Three beautiful American girls, one of them about to drive in the Mille Miglia, brought every man in the bar to his feet. They ordered Camparis and the bar owner brought them free, on the house, *con molto fortuna*. The bar throbbed with excitement and passion; a car thummed its engine out in the street and men moaned as if they were hearing the sound of love-making. There were no other women in the bar, but the Beaufort sisters did not feel and the men did not let them feel that they were breaking some rule of propriety. Sally, in her driver's overalls, her helmet hanging by its strap from her arm like an outsize handbag, brought them all together in, as far as it was possible in an Italian bar, a sexless paean to the race.

Then it was time for Sally to leave. The entire bar stood and raised their glasses, blew her kisses, came to the door and cheered her. Flushed, laughing, eyes glistening, she went out with her sisters and across to her car, slipped into the driver's seat beside the mechanic who was already waiting for her.

'Oh God, aren't they marvellous!'

She's all right, thought Margaret. While she responds like that to men cheering her, she's not going to look at any girls. She bent and kissed Sally. 'Good luck, darling. Come back safely.'

'Holy Jesus, I wish I were coming with you!' Nina shouted above the noise of the crowd. 'Tell Angelo to get out and I'll take his place!'

'Drunk on two Camparis,' said Margaret, dragging her away.

'No,' Nina waltzed along the edge of the crowd. Margaret had not seen her so gay since ... Since Tim had gone away. 'Drunk on Italy!'

They went up to the apartment, went out on to the balcony with their parents, saw Sally bring the green Maserati up under the glare of lights on the starting ramp. Sally looked across towards them, but they knew she couldn't see them. They saw a gloved hand wave, then the car rolled down the ramp, there was a screech of tyres as it accelerated, then it was heading down the Viale Rebuffone between the creek-banks of people. It disappeared into the dark morning and Margaret turned away to follow Nina and her parents back into the apartment.

Then she saw the red Ferrari already on the ramp, crouched there like an animal of prey. Then it slid down the ramp and went in a thunder of exhaust down the long road to Rome after Sally.

4

Sally was unplaced in her class in the Mille Miglia but she did finish. Philip Gentleman, or Mann, was not so fortunate. He went off the road coming down out of the Radicofani Pass north of Viterbo and was taken to hospital. Margaret read about his crash in the newspapers and wondered if she should send him a sympathy note; then decided against it and put him out of her mind. Sally sent him fruit and magazines, but did not go to see him in hospital.

Lucas and Edith, satisfied now that Sally was safe, satisfied also with their three daughters now they had spent a happy month with them, went home to Kansas City. As soon as her parents were on the plane for home Sally announced she was entering the Le Mans Twenty-Four-Hours race in France.

'Like hell you are,' said Nina and Margaret agreed with her. 'We promised Mother we'd keep an eye on you and we're going to.'

'You can come to Le Mans and keep an eye on me for the whole twenty-four hours.'

'No,' said Margaret flatly. 'I don't know anything about motor racing, but I'm sure you're not experienced enough for that one. Anyhow, I don't think they'd accept you. Try something else, if you must keep racing.'

Sally argued, but her sisters were adamant. In the end she accepted their decision and did not seem to resent it. The argument, which went on for several days, never got heated; indeed, it seemed to deepen the relationship among the three girls. Without actually being able to put her finger on it, Margaret became aware of a growing interdependence among the three of them. Never stated openly, it was as if each of them was coming to realize that she needed the other two, that there was a link binding them which, back home, they had never noticed because they had taken it for granted.

So Sally went in for rallies, travelling all over Europe to compete in them. Margaret and Nina became part of the social life of Rome. The Italian film industry was now off its knees, having given up making films about partisans and bicycle thieves; it was standing up and looking around before heading off in the same direction as American and British films. It had discovered the box-office value of bosoms, and film posters now looked like advertisements for over-developed glands. Audiences flocked to see Silvano Mangano, Elena Drago Rossi and the new girl Gina Lollobrigida; and the young men stamped their feet and whistled just as the youths in Tulsa or Leeds or Melbourne did when Jane Russell or Marilyn Monroe swung their personalities across the screen. Rome had at last shoved the late war to the back of its mind and, aided by its growing film industry, started to become a social centre to rival Paris and London. It would not reach its peak till the Sixties, but the Beaufort sisters would always be remembered as among the foundation members.

The sisters did not go home for the summer; instead they promised their parents faithfully to go home for Christmas. One night in late summer they threw a party for two hundred guests at the villa. It was an extravaganza, the sort of social event that made good anti-capitalist propaganda in *L'Unita*, but was run as a spread in *Life* magazine as an example of how Europe was at last beginning to enjoy itself. The guest list ranged over expatriate Americans, impoverished Italian aristocrats, homosexual English aristocrats, a go-getting Hungarian aristocrat, assorted diplomats, film stars, racing drivers and such clergy from the Vatican as could persuade themselves that staying up late would not merit purgatory, excommunication or being featured in tomorrow's *L'Unita*. The garden was hung with coloured lights, a board floor was put down for dancing, a toga-dressed band played in a scaled-down model of the Forum. Everyone except the clergy came in fancy dress. Some of the women's dress was so fancy that one or two of the clergymen, years ahead of the anti-celibacy movement, wondered why sin was so bad.

Margaret thought it was all vulgar and in dreadful taste and loved every moment and spangle of it. She was dressed as Dolley Madison, Nina was Nell Gwynne and Sally was Annie Oakley, an unlikely trio of sisters. Half-way through the evening a slim Nero appeared beside Dolley Madison.

'I can't remember you being on the guest list,' she said.

'I came with a friend,' said Philip Gentleman. 'That's her over there. The Venetian Doge who's trying to get the monsignor to reverse his collar.'

'I thought Doges were male.'

'That wouldn't worry Michele. She's a very versatile actress. No talent but versatile.'

Margaret looked across at the actress with feigned interest, while she wondered if she was glad to see him or not. 'Are you down from Milan just for the night?'

'I'm living in Rome now. We're putting money into the Italian film business.'

'Who's we?'

'My father and his partners.'

'Do the locals know who they are?'

'No. I don't think they'd care even if they did know. In the film industry money is money, Mrs Minett. It is in any business, if you really cared to look into it. Your husband understood that. I was sorry to hear about his death.'

She changed the subject quickly. 'I'm glad to see you recovered from your accident. Are you still racing?'

'No. I'm afraid my father doesn't like the idea of his only son taking too many risks.'

*Another protected one.* 'Do I go on calling you Mr Mann?'

'If you have to be formal, yes. But I'd prefer Philip.'

'Do you want me to tell my sisters who you really are?'

'That's up to you.' He seemed unworried, a Nero who would turn his back on Rome burning. 'But it might be awkward for you.'

Then Sally, in fringed buckskin, swept up to them. 'I *thought* it was you! Who are you supposed to be?'

Nero looked at his fiddle. 'Jack Benny?'

'Are you still racing?'

Margaret left them and moved on through the crowd. The Venetian Doge had forsaken the Vatican monsignor and was talking to Nina, the two of them sitting in a small rose bower.

'Meg, this is Michele Mauriac.'

If there was a more beautiful woman at the party Margaret had not seen her. Michele Mauriac was a mulatto and the two races, black and white, had combined to give her the best of each. Her skin was slightly darker than *café-au-lait*, but she was very little darker than some of the Italians just back from summer at the seaside. She had taken off her Doge's pointed cap and her black hair, cut very short, lay close to a perfectly shaped skull. Her dark, heavily-lidded eyes were coolly amused and there was the hint of a smile on the full, very red lips. Margaret was fascinated by such beauty.

'French? In Italian films?'

'I haven't got as far as Paris yet. Rome was my first stop north from Ougadougou and I don't seem to have got past it,' Her English was good, though heavily accented.

Margaret had no idea where Ougadougou was, but she wasn't going to show her ignorance. This French-African girl looked ready to be amused by the ignorance and weaknesses of everyone she might meet. She had the arrogance of someone who was not only intelligent but truly beautiful; there was a sophistication to her that hinted of decadence that she had survived without scars. Margaret felt suddenly provincial.

Nina said, 'Michele was telling me she'd really like to go to Hollywood, but she's afraid she would come up against the colour bar there.'

'Not only there,' said Margaret, thinking of Kansas City, wondering what effect this girl would have on the men at the country clubs. Probably give them hernias while they sorted out their lust from their prejudices. 'Don't you run into it here?'

'Only outside Rome,' said Michele. 'And I'd run into it here, too, if I weren't a woman. Being a woman helps, don't you think?'

Nina and Margaret looked at each other. 'Sometimes,' said Margaret, replying for both of them. 'Not always.'

A ravaged elderly woman, dressed as a houri, went by on the arm of a handsome young hussar. 'Principessa,' he was saying, 'you must introduce me to – '

'How tragic.' Nina looked after the odd couple.

'More so than you think,' said Michele, but there was no pity in her voice. 'All she has is her title and all he has are his looks and no brains. It's not enough these days.'

Margaret said, 'Who looks after you when you're not working?'

'Philip does, don't you, *caro*?' She put out a long slim arm, lithe as a snake, and took Philip Gentleman's hand as he and Sally came up. 'He has a very generous nature. Like all Americans.'

'Thank you,' said Nina. 'For all us Americans.'

Michele smiled at them all, then took Philip away. She did not snatch or pull him away; she just seemed to glide off and he went with her like her shadow. Margaret was surprised: she had not expected him to be so pliable and obedient. At least not to a woman, though perhaps to his father.

'My God,' said Sally, 'what a beautiful couple they are!'

'Who invited her?'

'I did,' said Nina. 'I met her the other evening at the Orbanis'. She's on everybody's guest list, because she's so unusual. The story is that her father was a French diplomat and her mother a chieftain's daughter. Whether it's true or not doesn't matter. She *looks* as if it could be true.'

'We must have them again,' said Sally.

'Who are you interested in?' Margaret said.

'Both of them,' Sally looked at her innocently, Annie Oakley straight as a gun-barrel. 'Aren't you?'

Then an Arabian sheik grabbed her arm and swept her away to dance. Nina and Margaret moved on slowly through the gardens and their guests. 'I think,' said Nina, 'I'd like a man to spend the night with.'

'Take your pick. There must be more gigolos here tonight than you could shake a cheque at.'

'I wouldn't know how to begin. I haven't had an affair since – ' Nina smiled a hostess' smile at Snow White who looked as if she was about to be slushed by an outsize Dwarf. 'I wonder what Mother would say if she could hear us talking?'

She's lost, Margaret thought. And all at once felt an aimlessness of her own. 'Do you think we should go home?' she said abruptly.

Nina did not attempt to confuse the villa where they lived with the house where they had been brought up: Kansas City would always be home. But she had to keep looking for Tim and Michael and she knew she would never find them in Kansas City. Her memories of Tim were still as fresh as if they were yesterday's: the desire for a man to go to bed with tonight grew out of memories of the flesh that she had had so long ago. 'It would be no better there. Do you want to go back?'

The party, like so many Roman parties, was winding down. Margaret did not know how parties progressed in the rest of Italy; or even in the rest of Rome. But these guests seemed to bring their own *ennui*, like a social disease that had infected every-one above a certain social status. The band was playing listlessly and a few dancers still lingered on the open-air floor like the survivors of a marathon contest. Margaret wondered if these people, even the diplomats from other countries, still suffered from war fatigue. Only some of the expatriate Americans and English were making a noise, but even their efforts had a forced heartiness about them. They had the embarrassing gaiety of Anglo-Saxons trying to be Mediterranean.

*Do I want to go back? To what?* 'Not yet,' she said at last. 'I'll give Europe another chance.'

'The Europeans will be flattered. Shall I make an announce-ment?'

'Not while I'm around. I'm going to bed.'

'Alone?'

'How else?'

So they both went to bed, watched regretfully by an assorted pack of harlequins, hussars, condottieri, Grenadier Guards, sheiks, cowboys and a lone Tarzan, all of whom would have deserted their partners to spend the night with either or both of the beautiful American heiresses. The third heiress had disappeared.

She re-appeared next afternoon, still in her Annie Oakley outfit, as Nina and Margaret, covered in sun-tan oil and eye-shades, lay beside the pool. With her were Philip Gentleman and Michele Mauriac, no longer Nero and Doge.

'We had the most marvellous night. We've only just woken up.' Sally stripped off her buckskins and in her panties and brassiere dived into the pool.

*Whom did she spend the night with?* Margaret, disturbed, looked at Philip and Michele. They were both in slacks and silk shirts, sleek and beautiful. But Margaret hardly noticed Philip. Her eyes were drawn to Michele. She had been fascinated by the mulatto's beauty last night, but the Doge's cloak had hidden her body. Now Margaret found herself staring at the body that the shirt and slacks seemed to expose rather than clothe. She shivered, suddenly aware that she was falling in love with the beauty of this coffee-skinned, lazily-smiling girl. There was nothing sexual to it: it was as if she were moved by something so incredibly beautiful: a piece of statuary, a sunlit sky, anything that suddenly made the eye, the mind and the soul helpless before its perfection. At the same time she knew, only too fearfully, that Michele had her sexual appeal, though not for her.

Nina, behind her dark glasses, had also been studying the French-African girl. But now she spoke to Philip. 'Would you do me and Meg a favour? Try and persuade Sally to give up motor-racing. You've had a bad accident, you know the dangers of it.'

'I never try to persuade a woman to do anything.'

'Not even make love?' said Margaret, one eye on Michele.

'Not even that.' Philip smiled. 'I've never been a hunter.'

'Is that true, Michele?' said Nina.

'If he is, he disguises it well. I've never noticed it.'

'That's because you're a hunter yourself,' said Philip.

He said it off-handedly: if it was meant to be an insult Michele ignored it. 'You do what you can with what you have. All I have is this.' She ran a graceful hand down the outline of her face and body. It was done without conceit: just as a hunter might gesture at a favourite gun, Margaret thought. 'I don't have the advantages that you have.'

She included them all in her smile: a good-natured smile but mocking, too. Then Sally lifted herself out of the pool, wiped water from herself with her hands. Her brief underwear clung to her wet, tanned body: in a different, more innocent way she was almost as beautiful as Michele. But there was a healthiness to her that made her looks almost commonplace beside those of the indolent, more sensual mulatto.

'Ask Michele to persuade Sally,' said Philip. 'They are going north tomorrow to compete in some rally in France.'

'You might have told us,' said Margaret.

Sally had picked up a towel and was drying her long hair. Head down, avoiding Margaret's gaze, she said, 'I've had my entry in for some time. I just needed a partner.'

'Do you drive?' Nina asked Michele.

'A little.'

'Is that good enough?'

Sally came out from under her towel. 'We're not trying to win. It's just the fun of it. Right, Michele?'

'It fills in time.'

'Between what?' said Margaret.

'Come inside, Michele.'

Sally stalked off into the villa, leaving her buckskins lying beside the pool like last night's skin, an identity she no longer wanted. Without a word Michele got lazily to her feet and followed her. She was smiling her arrogantly mocking smile and that too, thought Margaret, is a weapon.

'Don't depend on Michele to do anything for you,' said Philip.

'I don't like her,' said Nina.

'That wouldn't worry her in the least. She's not looking for love or affection. She'll marry some rich guy and be entirely self-contained even then.'

'Some rich guy like you?' said Margaret.

'You flatter me, Meg.' But he did not explain whether he meant she was flattering his financial status or his chances with Michele.

'May I take you two out to dinner tonight?'

'What about Michele?'

'I think she and Sally have something arranged.'

He took them to dinner at the Grand Hotel and Nina remarked upon his choice. 'Why here? Why not the Excelsior or George's or even Doney's?'

'I'm not trying to impress you. But this is one hotel in Rome where our American disease, café society, hasn't been allowed to penetrate. They are very discreet here and anyone who wants his name or picture spread across the newspapers isn't welcome. I like anonymity and I get it here. Even the Shah of Persia can be anonymous here if he wants it that way.'

'I don't mean to sound rude, Philip, but why do you want to be anonymous?'

He smiled. 'Meaning you think I'm anonymous anyway? You're right. I just thought you'd prefer it for yourselves. I thought Meg was very keen on anonymity.'

Touché, thought Margaret.

Later they drove home through the soft Italian night. Philip no longer had his Ferrari, had replaced it with a dark blue Fiat, a good anonymous car. They drove past the stone latticework of the Colosseum, past the long-dry Caracalla's Baths, through Porta San Sebastiano that was no longer a gateway to anything. Whores stood by the roadside, the only living relics of history: Vespas were no substitutes for chariots, white-gloved policemen were pale stand-ins for centurions. The moon came up over the Tomb of Cecilia Metella and in the Catacombs of San Sebastian shadows moved among the bones, though no light reached there. The past brushed Margaret like a bat's wing and she felt the humility of being totally anonymous.

'Rome is a humbling experience,' said Philip, and Margaret, with a start, wondered if she had spoken aloud. 'Especially to empire builders.'

'Perhaps we should bring Daddy back here again,' said Nina. 'What does your father do?'

'He's an empire builder, too.' Sitting beside him in the front seat, Margaret saw the profile of Philip's smile. 'In a smaller way than your father.'

'Has he ever been to Rome?'

'No. He saw Naples, on his way to America. He was not impressed.'

'So your name isn't really Mann?' said Nina shrewdly.

'It's good enough.' He did not sound awkward or uncomfortable. Perhaps after all he is not ashamed of his father, Margaret thought. 'America is full of families who have changed their name. Some day there may be a Beaufort who will wish they had another name.'

Neither of the sisters said anything. He turned his head, looked first at Margaret, then at Nina in the back seat. But he, too, said nothing. He drove the car in at the gates of the villa. There was no security guard, something that had worried Lucas when he had been here. But kidnappers and bandits were only to be feared in Sicily and Sardinia; Rome was still safe, kidnapping on the mainland still lay in the future. And if a security guard were needed,

Margaret thought now, what better one than the son of a Mafia don?

He kissed them both goodnight, in a most gentlemanly way. 'I'm going to France tomorrow.'

'With Sally and Michele?'

'No, I'm flying to Paris.'

'I wonder if Sally is home yet?'

'She's probably spending the night with Michele. I told you, Michele is versatile. Goodnight.'

'Does he mean what I think he meant?' Nina watched the car go down the long drive.

'Sally can look after herself,' said Margaret, lying bravely, feeling sick.


# 5


Sally, Michele and Philip left next morning for France. Margaret, Nina and the children and the nurse went down to Amalfi for a month, each sister driving down in her own car. Villas were being renovated and re-decorated and, with the season coming to an end, it was not difficult to rent a place. Other Americans were living in nearby villas; a small colony of writers, most of whom seemed to be homosexual, lived just round the coast. That section of the coast had become fashionable and Nina seemed to take pride in the fact that she and Margaret were in the front line of the foreign invasion.

'It will all be overrun in a couple of years. The Germans are being allowed to spend money outside Germany now – they'll be down here soon. And when the English have some money to spend . . . I can remember once in Hamburg – the day I met Tim – ' there was just a faint pause – 'I remember looking at a queue of people and feeling sorry for them, wondering if they had any future at all. And now – '

'I don't think the Germans would be too welcome here.'

'They'll be welcome if they have money to spend.'

*She sounds just like Philip.* 'Nin, are you trying to be a Scott Fitzgerald heroine?'

They were sitting out on the terrace of the villa they had rented, shaded from the noon sun by a grape arbour. The sea glittered like a field of diamonds below them; far out it faded into a mountain range of white-topped clouds. A ferry boat had come round the point from Salerno, heading for Capri, another hedonist retreat.

Nina did not turn her head, just continued to stare out through her dark glasses at the smudged horizon. 'What makes you say that?'

'You mentioned it in one of your letters. We're just wasting time here.' She had taken off her own dark glasses, but now she put them back on. 'You'll never bump into Tim down here.'

'Jesus, you can be cruel!'

'If I am, it's with the best of intentions. You know the sort of reputation we're getting? Easy touches for all the bums who want a free party or a free meal.'

'Who told you that?'

'I don't need to be told. I can see it. So could you, if you wanted to. We hadn't been here two days before the first of those writers came up and introduced themselves – they knew all about us. They've been in our hair ever since, bringing their friends – '

'They're interesting. A damn sight better than most of those we've been entertaining in Rome.'

'Rome was no criterion. Nin, can't you see what a lazy, decadent lot they are? Oh, I know one or two of them may have some talent. But the majority of them – '

'They keep us entertained, don't they? How much wit did you ever hear back home to compare with what we hear every night? They're so much livelier – '

'I wasn't thinking specifically of Kansas City.'

'Where, then?'

'I don't know. Just somewhere where you might, *might*, hear something about Tim and Michael.'

She knew that was cruel and she intended it to be. She got up and went along to the far end of the terrace where Martha and Emma were playing under the supervision of the nurse. Sometimes she felt guilty about the children. She loved them, but too often, as now, she felt she retreated to them as a defence rather than approached them out of sheer love and the desire to be with them. They had become the nurse's responsibility, not her own.

'Let's take them in and feed them, Ruth. We'll take them for a drive this afternoon.'

Ruth was a thin pleasant girl from a farm in Nebraska; some day she would finish up back on a farm with children of her own.

On the surface she did not appear to have a critical thought in her head, but Margaret sometimes wondered what she thought of this life the Beaufort sisters lived.

'They're both very tired, Mrs Minett. They didn't sleep very well last night.' She picked up Emma, her face hidden behind the child. 'The noise of the party – '

'Do you think we should take them back to Rome?'

'It's not for me to suggest it, Mrs Minett – ' Last night she had seen two of the men guests kissing each other, something that did not happen on the farms around Chappell, Nebraska.

'We'll do it. Pack the things and we'll leave right after lunch.'

From the other end of the terrace Nina watched her sister and the children. There were times when she envied Margaret her good fortune; today she hated her for that cruel remark about Tim and Michael. Margaret could not guess at the emptiness that was still there within her, that was not helped when she saw Martha and Emma or heard their pealing laughter. Sometimes she wanted to sweep them up in her arms, smother them with the love that she could not expend on her own missing child.

She reacted quietly but coldly when Margaret told her she was returning to Rome. 'If that's the way you feel – '

'I think it's better. I might enjoy all this more with you if it were not for the children – ' Margaret had softened her attitude; she was ashamed of her moment of cruelty.

'Are you going back home?'

'I don't know. I was going home at Christmas anyway. I'll think about it when I get back to Rome. You'll stay on for the month here?'

'Yes.' Coolly. 'Perhaps even longer.'

Margaret drove back to Rome, arriving after dark. The children were put to bed as soon as they were bathed and fed. Margaret herself had a bath, put on a robe and made herself comfortable in bed with the air-mailed copies of the *New York Times* and the *Kansas City Star* which arrived each week. Then the phone rang.

'Meg,' said Sally, voice strained and crackling from a bad connection, 'I'm not coming back to Rome.'

'Where are you?'

'Antibes.'

'I thought you were supposed to be in a rally around Rheims or somewhere. How did you do?'

'That was last week. We won the women drivers' section.'

'Congratulations. What's the rally at Antibes?'

'Meg, I don't think you've got the drift of what I'm trying to tell you. I'm not coming back to Rome. At all. Michele and I are taking a place here in Antibes for the winter. Then we're going up to Paris in the spring. Michele thinks it's time she tried her luck in French films.'

'And what are you going to do? Try your luck in French films, too?'

'I'll keep driving. I'm going to enter the Monte Carlo rally next January.'

'With Michele as your co-driver?'

'Maybe.'

'Sally – ' It was as if she were stumbling with a new language. 'Sally, is Michele taking Cindy's place?'

There was silence at the other end of the line, but on the line itself there were cracklings, whistling, something that even sounded like a truck changing gears. Mountains, valleys, rivers, a border separated them on the line: but something else also separated them. At last Sally said, 'I'm afraid so, Meg. We're in love.'

'Oh Sal – ' She cried aloud in anguish. 'God Almighty, can't you see she couldn't be in love with anyone but herself?'

The line went dead. Margaret sat with the phone still held to her ear. Then a man's nasal voice said, '*Fini, madame?*'

'I think so.' Margaret looked at the phone. '*Si. Oui.*'

She lay back against the headboard, staring at the newspapers scattered in a debris of headlines: Ike Veto . . . Train Wreck . . . Earthquake . . . The world was falling apart here in her bed. Then she sat up, reached for the small address book on the side table. She flipped through it, thinking, even as she did so, that she had never believed she would be calling on him for help. Then she dialled a number.

'Philip? I've just been talking to Sally. We – we were cut off. Do you know where she and Michele are staying in Antibes?'

She could sense his hesitation. 'Yes. I don't think you can do much about it, Meg.'

'I can try.'

'I think I better come and see you.'

'Not tonight.' She wanted time to think. 'Tomorrow morning?'

'I'll be out at Cinecittà all morning. May I come for lunch?'

She hung up, debated whether she should call Nina, decided against it. Perhaps Sally would come to her senses; there was no need to broadcast the disaster just yet. She swept the newspapers off the bed: a headline slid out of sight: Dow Jones Climbs . . .

There was hope for some, even if they were only the money-makers. She put out the light and slipped into a dream that gave her no hope at all. Tim and Michele, hand in hand, smiled their mocking smiles as they retreated into the distance . . .

Philip came for lunch, which they had out on the terrace over-looking the pool. The weather had cooled, clouds coming in over the Alban Hills. She wore a cashmere twin set, he a tweed jacket and a silk club tie with a button-down shirt. He thought she looked Junior League and she thought he looked Ivy League, but neither made any comment. They did not look like a pair who should be discussing what to do about a couple of lesbians.

'You'll have to let it run its course,' he said over the *vitello tonnato*. 'Sally, as you know, is a pretty stubborn girl.'

'What about Michele? Is she stubborn, too? Or can she be bought?'

'Oh, she can be bought, all right. Everyone has their price, my father says.'

She did not want his father brought into the conversation. 'I should think Michele would think of nothing else but her price. I'm just surprised you let her attach herself to you.'

He smiled. 'Don't be hypocritical, Meg. I saw you looking at her that Sunday we were here. She's the most gorgeous thing either of us has ever seen. She knew she wasn't going to be any-thing permanent with me – I told her that the first night we met. For one thing, you know what my father thinks about blacks. Even half-niggers.'

'Does she know you call her that?'

'I don't call her that at all. I'm quoting what my father would call her if ever he met her. What will your father call her if ever he meets her?'

'He won't, I'll see to that. But my father is not anti-Negro. He would be prejudiced against Michele for other reasons.'

He waited till the young houseman took away their plates and came back with the fruit and cheese. 'I like the white gloves on your servants. Sometimes I wish I could settle here, have a place and a staff like this, be a Roman gentleman.'

'Why don't you? You can't be short of money.'

'My father would cut me off without a cent if I mentioned it. I don't have any money of my own. It's all in the family.'

A long time later she would realize that he had meant The Family: but she was ignorant then of Mafia society. 'Ours is family money, too. But we're allowed a certain amount for ourselves.'

'I should get your father to talk to mine.'

She ignored that, instead said, 'I think I'll go to Antibes anyway. Just for a couple of days.'

'Leave them be, Meg.'

'She's my sister – I have to do *something*! That Michele is – she's evil. God knows what she'll do to Sally.'

'She'll grow tired of her eventually, look around for another buyer. Michele isn't a natural lesbian. She's almost asexual, if you like.'

'Like hell she is.'

He shrugged. 'I've been to bed with her. You haven't. It's like making love to a machine. She doesn't care whether you're male or female. All you have to do is meet the price.'

'Oh God – ' All at once she broke down, began to weep.

He gave her a handkerchief, sat and watched till she had recovered and dried her eyes. 'Don't go to Antibes. I'll give you their phone number and you can call them. Every day, if you like. But don't go to see them. It would only be ugly and you might lose Sally forever.'

'How do you know so much about women? Did they teach you that at the London School of Economics?'

'I just try to be the opposite of my father. He's an old-style Sicilian, the sort who never made any attempt to understand a woman. My mother told me that on her death-bed.'

'You should talk to Nina. She says she's never felt so womanly since she's been in Italy.'

'That's Italy, not Sicily. Didn't any of you feel – *womanly* in Kansas City?'

*I did, with Tim. And I suppose Nina did, too, if she were truthful.* 'Occasionally.'

That night she called Sally in Antibes. She made an effort to sound friendly, even helpful. 'Do you want me to send your things over to you?'

'I'll send you a list. And Meg – thanks for calling.'

'It was a bad line last night.'

'Meg – have you told Nina yet? No? Well, shall I write her or will you explain?'

'Sally – ' She tried not to sound like a mother; or even like an older sister, one who thought she knew too much. She was skating on virgin ice: which was not a good metaphor in the circumstances. 'Sal, let's keep it between us for the time being.'

'Meg, I'm not ashamed of what I'm – '

'Don't let's argue again – please. I'm not making any moral judgement. All I'm trying to do is not have Mother and Daddy

202

find out. You may not be ashamed of what you're doing, but it would wreck them both. You know what they're like. You don't want that, do you, if it can be avoided?'

'No, of course not – '

'All right, then. I'll just tell Nina you've decided to set up house in Antibes because you want to start preparing for – what was it? The Monte Carlo rally? Let her find out in her own time what's going on. I don't for a moment think she would tell Mother and Daddy if she knew, but the less lines we have to Kansas City the better. All I ask, Sally, is – please be discreet.'

Margaret thought she heard what could have been a sob. Then Sally said in a strained voice, 'I do love you, Meg. All of you. But I can't help this . . .'

'Goodnight, darling. Give – ' But she could not send any love to Michele. 'Remember me to Michele.'

# 6

Nina came back from Amalfi at the end of the month with two American writers in tow, both homosexual. They kissed Margaret as if they were long-lost maiden aunts, admired the shirt she was wearing, flicked fingers at the children and went off to one of the guest rooms for a nap. One of them was short and fat and the other tall and thin and they reminded Margaret of an illustration she had seen.

'They look like Don Quixote and Sancho Panza, less a few hormones. Do they attack windmills in their writing?'

'I don't know. I've never read anything they've written. Have you heard from Sally?'

'She's staying on in France, at Antibes. She and Michele are going to drive in the Monte Carlo rally at the end of January.'

'With Michele, eh?' Nina seemed unconcerned, even uninterested.

'I'm going home, Nin. I don't think Rome suits the children. You don't mind, do you? I mean my going home?'

A faint shadow crossed Nina's face, but it was gone in the flicker of an eyelid. 'Of course not. You have to think of the children. I may come home for Christmas.'

'Do come, please. For Mother's sake. I spoke to Daddy a couple of nights ago. He says she isn't as well as she used to be.'

'I'll come, then.' The shadow crossed her face again, lingering this time. 'Have we been cruel to them, Meg?'

'I think so,' said Margaret after a moment.

She left for home at the end of the week. Philip, Nina and the two writers came to the airport to see her, the nurse and the children safely aboard the plane. The writers were as compulsively witty as they had been for the past five days and Margaret noticed that even Nina seemed tired of them. Impulsively she wanted to ask Nina to walk on to the plane with her, come home at once; but she held back. Nina and Sally had to go their own ways, she could not take on the responsibility of both of them.

'I have to go over to France regularly on business,' Philip said. 'I'll drop in on Sally if I'm down her way.'

She kissed him goodbye. Then the two writers fluttered around her, pecking at her, each giving a witticism as a farewell present, one trying to out-do the other. Finally she had a moment alone with Nina.

'I'm fed up with them,' said Nina, nodding towards the writers clucking like peahens above the children. 'I heard Philip say he was going to France and would drop in on Sally. I think I'll go with him.'

Should she warn her or not? Then again she took the line of least resistance, least interference. 'Try and bring Sally home for Christmas with you. Without Michele, if possible.'

'You mean because Michele is black?'

Margaret nodded, glad of any excuse. 'You never know how Daddy will react.'

'How would it be if I brought Michele and Tony and Freddie?' She nodded at the two writers who, limp-wristed, were doing a soft-shoe shuffle that was entertaining the children, the porters, the airport police and the rest of the passengers about to board the aircraft.

'Daddy would generate his own tornado. Goodbye, Nin. Take care. And keep looking.'

Nina knew what she meant. 'I never stop. Not even when you think I'm wasting my time.'

The plane took off and Rome fell away like a cracked ceramic plaque. Goodbye Italy, Margaret thought. It had been an experience but she had had enough of it. Unexpectedly, she found she was looking forward to Kansas City, where the stones were younger by centuries, the philosophies simpler, the hopes less jaded. She had tossed coins in the fountains of Rome, but none of her wishes had been granted. There were more fountains in Kansas City than in Rome: she would try her luck with them.

Though, unlike Nina, she was not exactly sure what she was wishing for.

The welcome home was so warm that Margaret wondered why she had gone away. Edith was thinner and paler, but she said nothing about not feeling well and seemed to take on vigour and colour as she fussed over her granddaughters. Martha and Emma had forgotten her, but Edith was a grandmother not to be denied and before they reached the estate the children had once more taken to her. Lucas, for his part, just sat back in the car and beamed as if he had been guaranteed personally that henceforth everything would be right in his world. The return of his children and grandchildren had begun, the Dow Jones index would do nothing but continue to rise, the Republicans would be granted a perpetual lease on the White House.

Margaret moved back into the second house in the park, felt at home at once, almost as if she had never been away. But there was a difference: the ghost of Frank had, somehow, been exorcized. She no longer felt any guilt about him.

Prue came across to stay with her that first night home. 'What books are you reading now?'.

'*Sexual Behaviour in the Human Female.*' Prue had already been divested of her braces and had a smile that enthralled Margaret. *She's going to be a knock-out, make the rest of us look plain and homely.* 'Golly, Meg, we Beauforts live a simple life, don't we?'

Margaret smiled. 'Not so simple. Your turn will come. How has Mother been?'

Prue made a face, shook her head. 'Rather poorly, as Jane Austen would say. You see? I do read other books besides sex ones. I think she's just been pining for you and Nina and Sally. Which is very crappy for my ego.'

'You still reading Henry Miller? Watch your language in front of my kids, kiddo. Oh Prue!' She grabbed her, held her tight. 'I'm so glad to be home!'

Two night later she went to dinner with Magnus McKea at Henri's. 'We're surviving,' said Magnus. 'But only just. The country's going backwards under Ike.'

'How can you say that, a true-blue Republican? I thought everything was just fine.'

'There's no spirit of adventure left. Everyone's settling for security. He's moved the White House to the Burning Tree Country Club. That's the national aim now, lower your golf handicap. I'm beginning to wish I'd voted for Adlai Stevenson.'

'Does Daddy know?'

'Even he's disappointed in Ike. He has hopes for Nixon.'

'I don't know anything about him except that he talked about his dog on television. I thought only the English voted for pets.'

'Where have you been the past year? For a girl who was married to a professor of political history, you sound dumb.'

'I just turned off, Magnus. I suppose it was a way of getting Frank off my conscience. It worked.'

'He's all past history now?'

She nodded, then reached across the table for his hand. 'You didn't keep in touch, you know. Just those quarterly statements and a scrawled *Hope you are well* on the bottom of them. Is that how you keep in touch with your ladies in St Louis and Tulsa and Omaha?'

'I don't even send them statements.'

'Do you still live in that big house of your father's?'

'No, I sold it. To a heart surgeon whose fees guarantee him a clientele for life – all his patients keep having relapses when they see his bill. No, I'm now living in The Chestnuts, preparing for retirement with the blue-rinsed old ladies and the whisky-soaked old codgers.'

'You're far too young for there!' The Chestnuts was the most exclusive block of apartments in town, populated mainly by elderly retired people who had found their own mansions too empty and lonely as their families had grown up and moved out.

'I don't spend all my time cooped up in my apartment. There's still St Louis and Tulsa and Omaha.'

'Is it a nice apartment?'

'Do you want to see it?'

'I thought you'd never ask.'

An hour later they were in bed, as naturally as if they had done it many times before. He was an experienced lover: St Louis, Tulsa and Omaha could have nothing to complain about. She felt no inhibition: she had gone too long without sex. Observe, Dr Kinsey: no kinkiness, just hunger. The sexual behaviour of the human female who, if she had lost love, had not lost the desire for love-making. She surprised him with her passion, as she had surprised Tim and Frank; but he was too experienced to show it. But St Louis, Tulsa and Omaha would have to raise their standards from now on.

When they had at last exhausted themselves, he got up, went into the bathroom, had a quick shower, came back, put on a robe and sat in a chair facing her.

'Do you always have a shower right after it?' she said.

'You scratched hell out of me. I wanted to put some mercurochrome on the marks.'

'I'll wear gloves next time.'

'There's not going to be a next time. You know that as well as I do.'

She agreed with him. There was always a cold clear mind after making love without love: she had discovered that with Frank. But she was grateful to Magnus for the release, no matter how temporary, that he had given her. 'I shouldn't want it to stop us being friends. And that's probably what would happen if we went on going to bed. Are you friends with those women in those other places?'

'Not the way you and I have been. I think you'd better look around for another husband. Someone you really love this time.'

'It's not easy. Finding someone you love, I mean.' *I know whom I really love, but I can't go looking for him.*

When she was dressed and leaving she said, 'You said once that you would tell me why you never married. Are you still going to keep it a secret?'

He smiled, kissed her. 'I have several secrets. Tonight is another one.'

'You're a good lawyer. You're also a terrific lover.'

'Sh-h-h. I'd be thrown out of The Chestnuts if that got around.'

'You're kidding. The ladies here would never let you get to St Louis or Tulsa or Omaha again.'

She did not go looking for someone to fall in love with. She settled back into the routine she had left. She rejoined the Society of Fellows of the Nelson Gallery. She was co-opted as a late member of the social committee of the American Royal, the annual saddle horse and livestock show; she had not ridden a horse in three years and all breeds of cattle were the same to her, but she was a Beaufort and that made *her* prime livestock. She accepted an invitation to join the board of the Kansas City Philharmonic, replacing Edith who confessed she no longer had the energy to fulfil all her engagements.

'There's nothing seriously wrong with me, darling. I think I've just been worn out by worry.' She managed not to sound as if she were complaining.

'I'm sorry about all that, Mother.' She tried to joke: 'You shouldn't have brought us up with so much respect for perspective. That's why we all rushed off – to get perspective.'

'I'm beginning to think your father is right. Security is better than perspective.'

Perhaps you're right, Margaret thought. And felt the first

beginnings of change in herself.

Nina and Sally, as promised, came home for Christmas. It was a warm wonderful two weeks for all the family, only spoiled by the knowledge that Nina and Sally would be returning to Europe. But Lucas and Edith had given up trying to persuade their daughters; it seemed that they now settled for whatever the girls were prepared to give them. But Margaret, the new stay-at-home, saw the pain that sometimes marked her father's face as he sat gazing at Nina and Sally.

Margaret waited till after Christmas itself had gone before she asked Sally about Michele. 'How is it working out with her?'

'Great. No, really, Meg – ' As she saw the still-questioning look on Margaret's face. Then, after a moment, she shrugged. 'I don't know, that's the truth. Sometimes she's marvellous. Other times . . .'

'Have you seen Philip?'

'He's dropped in a couple of times. He's nice.'

'Don't get involved with him,' she said carefully. 'He has a father something like ours. He runs Philip's life.'

'He told you that? Well, don't worry. I'm still hoping things will work out permanently with Michele. She's not driving with me, though, in the Monte Carlo rally. She has a part in a film they're shooting in Paris. Do Mother and Daddy know about her? I mean, you haven't told . . .?'

'They don't know. Does Nina?'

'I think she suspects, but I'm not sure. She came up to Antibes once with Philip, but she didn't stay with us. They stayed the night in Nice.'

'You mean she stayed with Philip?'

'I don't know. Don't worry so much, Meg. You're developing into a real mother hen. If Nina wants to sleep with Philip, that's her business. No matter what his father's like. What does his father *do*?'

'I don't know, exactly. He's something in investments.'

'Then Daddy would probably know something about him.'

Margaret felt on the verge of panic, but she still sounded cool and casual. 'I don't think he wants to know about our European friends. He has a mental block about Europe. Sal – ' She looked with tender love at her sister. Sally, the most resourceful of them all, the most adventurous, was really the most vulnerable of them. 'If anything happens with Michele, call me at once. You'll need someone to talk to.'

Sally blinked back tears. 'You'll be the first I'll call on.'

She and Nina went back to Europe the first week in January.

208

At the end of January she drove in the Monte Carlo rally with an English girl she had met, crashed her car in the mountain section above Grasse but was unhurt, though the car was a write-off. She told all this by letters to Margaret, who told none of it to her parents, just saying that Sally had been unplaced in the rally and was thinking of buying a new car.

Nina wrote from Rome that she had grown tired of that city, that Meg had been right about the hangers-on, that she was now moving to London, where she had leased an apartment in Eaton Square.

*I'll be there for Wimbledon, if you feel like coming over. Who knows, I may be sitting in the stands and catch a glimpse of Tim on the other side of the Centre Court? He always loved Wimbledon, though we never went there together. Michael will be seven, going on eight, old enough to enjoy the game with his father. Or his mother . . .*

Time went by, like a careless, endless river, like the Missouri itself. The country settled into an era that, even only a decade later, people would remember with nostalgia and a certain disbelief, as if they were not quite sure that everything had been as it seemed. Youth had not yet discovered it was a separate species; even the market survey scientists had not yet stumbled on that fact. The kids of America still listened to the same music as their parents; mothers and daughters alike wished they could go to Rome and toss coins in the fountains and they swooned together as Eddie Fisher crooned to them about his papa. Fathers and sons went to boo Yogi Berra or Willie Mays and, if the son was old enough, maybe shared a cigarette but never a joint. If there were any demonstrations they never got any coverage in the media, a word that, like youth, had not yet been discovered; the loudest shouts still came from high school cheer-leaders, who all looked alike, as if they had been shipped out by Sears Roebuck. Sloppy joes were the nearest thing to rebellion in fashion; boys were short on hair and long on cleanliness; girls wore brassieres that turned their breasts skywards like searchlights. Ike was still sinking two-putts from the edge of the green and everything was right with the Burning Tree Country Club if not with the world at large.

True to Jack Minett's prediction, Joe McCarthy was shoved overboard: not by his fellow politicians but by the Army and a Boston lawyer. Politicians are always reluctant to kill off one of their own, as they would once again prove in another twenty years in the future; they will wrap up the body if only someone else will first pull the trigger. The Army scored one of its greatest and most honourable successes when it took on Senator McCarthy.

but its victory would never be marked by a battle star on any of its flags. In Vietnam ('Where the hell's that, for crissake?') the French were defeated at Dien-Bien-Phu; and Ike, coming in from the greens, substituting one game metaphor for another, warned about the domino effect. But soon a treaty was signed in Vietnam and Washington said it was satisfied and Ike went back to the golf course. There was still the Cold War with the Russians to worry about and that was enough worry for anyone. There was no dividend in getting mixed up with a lot of Asians you couldn't sell anything to.

In September 1955 President Eisenhower had a heart attack while vacationing in Denver. Everything plunged: Republican hopes for next year's election, the stock market, the sale of golf clubs. 'I hope he retires,' said Lucas. 'I've never been so disappointed in a man. He's no better than Ulysses S. Grant, except he's sober. It only goes to prove that running an army is no training for running a country.'

'I thought you'd said General Franco was doing a great job in Spain?' said Margaret. 'The only stable country in Europe, wasn't that what you said?'

'How did you hear that? The only time I've mentioned Franco was last week over lunch at the River Club. Did you tell her, Magnus?'

'Yes,' said Magnus. 'Was it supposed to be confidential?'

'Why did you mention it to Meg?'

Margaret answered. 'I asked him if he knew anything about Spain. Nina is leaving London and going down to a place called Torremolinos to live.'

Lucas shook his head in quiet despair. 'Why doesn't she come home? Always running from place to place . . . Does your mother know?'

'I haven't told her yet. I only got Nina's letter yesterday.'

'Well, keep it to yourself for a few days. Till we find out what's wrong with Mother.'

Edith had had a mild collapse two days before and had been put to bed to rest. She insisted that it was only exhaustion from trying to do too much, but the doctors had insisted on her submitting to some tests. Margaret, her father and Magnus were now waiting for one of the doctors, Dr Kenning, to come out to the house with the results of the tests.

'If it is just exhaustion, I think you should take Mother away on a long vacation. Take her on a cruise and then perhaps go across and join Nina at Torremolinos. Forget work and give yourself up to Mother for a whole year. Don't you agree, Magnus?'

'It would be a good idea, Lucas.'

'I'll think about it. You're probably right. It'll take some adjustment – a whole year doing nothing.'

'Not a whole year *doing nothing*. A whole year looking after Mother. Something you haven't done all the years you've been married to her.'

'You know how to poison your arrows, don't you?' But he did not seem to mind her accusation; and once again she remarked the lessening of spirit in him. He was no longer the Lucas Beaufort who was always right. 'I'll try. I promise I'll try.'

Dr Kenning arrived at six o'clock. He was a tall thin man with a booming voice not designed for imparting bad news; but he did his best to keep it down to a whispered shout. 'It's not good, I'm afraid. In fact it's the worst. She has leukemia. Acute.'

Lucas remained silent and after a moment Margaret said, 'What can be done for her?'

'Nothing, I'm afraid. It's too late. I don't want to sound facetious, but she has a galloping case of it. The leucocytes, the white blood cells, are multiplying while we look at her.'

'How long?' Lucas said at last.

'A month. Two at the outside.'

'Should she be told?'

'That's up to you. I think she already knows it's more than just exhaustion, as she's been telling you.'

'I'll tell her.' Lucas raised himself slowly out of his chair; he looked gaunt and suddenly aged. 'Leave me alone with her for half an hour, Meg.'

'I'll phone Nina and Sally to come home at once.'

Lucas just nodded and went out of the room, walking stiff-legged as if willing his legs not to collapse beneath him. Margaret called Nina and Sally, only to find that neither phone answered; she felt the unreasonable annoyance the distraught feel, as if everyone should be on call at all times for bad news. She hung up and went back into her father's study where Magnus sat in one of the big leather chairs weeping quietly.

'Magnus – ' She went down on her knees in front of him. 'What's the matter?'

He wiped his eyes with a handkerchief, blew his nose, leant his head back against the chair and drew a deep sigh. He stared at the opposite wall, composing himself, then he looked down at her still kneeling in front of him.

'That's the secret. I've been in love with your mother.'

She at once hated herself for the stupid remark:

'But she's so much older than you!'

'Nine years, that's all. There's much more difference between you and me and we might have married in other circumstances.'

'I'm sorry, I shouldn't have said that. How long has it been?'

'Years. I was sixteen when I first fell in love with her. She was already married and she'd already had you and Nina. But it made no difference.'

'Does she know?'

'No. I've never given so much as a hint. And you must never mention it to anyone, promise? You owe me that.'

'Whether I owed it to you or not, Magnus, I'd never tell anyone.' She got to her feet, leaned down and kissed his cheek. 'How did you stand it all these years? Why didn't you move away?'

'I thought of that while I was in Germany. But in the end I knew I had to be near her. So I settled for being her friend and legal adviser.'

*Could I have settled for something like that if Tim had not gone away?* But she knew that she could not have. 'Do you want to come up with me to see her?'

He shook his head. 'I'll go home. I'll see her tomorrow.'

He seemed to move as stiffly and slowly as her father when he got up to leave. Margaret went with him to the door, then went up to Prue's room. Prue, her radio playing softly, was preparing work for tomorrow's classes at Barstow.

'It's a real drag, all this study. I've been reading about a school in England where they let the kids do what they like – ' Then, sharp-eyed as ever, she stopped. 'What's the matter, Meg?'

'It's Mother.' She sat down on the bed, determined to remain dry-eyed. She realized even then that she was going to have to take her mother's place, not only with Prue but with Nina and Sally. She turned down the radio: Lena Horne faded away into silence. 'She has leukemia. The doctors say she has only a couple of months to live at the most.'

Prue blinked and for several moments remained expressionless, as if she were thinking about what she had been told. Then she slowly bent forward, laid her head in Margaret's lap and began to cry silently but with her shoulders shuddering as if she were in some dreadful fever. Later Margaret would recall that it was not a child's weeping but a terrible adult grief. She held Prue to her, saying nothing, her mind utterly empty of words.

At last she lifted Prue, wiped her eyes and cheeks with the edge of a bed-sheet. 'Go and wash your face. Then we'll go in and see Mother.'

They went along the hall and into their parents' huge bedroom. Edith sat propped up in the big four-poster bed and Lucas sat in a chair beside it. Margaret and Prue kissed their mother without saying anything. Edith looked at each of them, bit her lip, then smiled weakly.

'Well, it's disappointing, isn't it?'

'Edith – ' Lucas's protest was weak, hoarse.

'No, sweetheart, I'm not going to use stronger words. I was looking forward to so many things and now I'm not going to be able to do them. So I'm disappointed. My biggest disappointment will be if I don't see Nina and Sally.'

'They'll be here,' said Margaret. 'I tried to call them, but I'll also send off cables.'

'If they reach them,' said Lucas. 'You can never be sure where they are. Always gallivanting – '

'Sweetheart – don't. They'll be here.'

Nina and Sally, reached at last by phone, arrived within forty-eight hours. They were shocked by the change in their mother since they had seen her in January; to Margaret she seemed to be dying by the hour. Lucas never left the house, was just a silent grey man already hollowed out by grief. Magnus came by the house every day, but never stayed longer than five minutes. The four girls took it in turns to be always with their mother, aided by Miss Stafford, who moved into the house to stay till the vigil was over.

Late one afternoon, a week after Nina and Sally had come home, Margaret was sitting with Edith. Fall dusk had darkened the room, but so far Margaret had put on no lights. A wind blew from the north-east out of Kansas and Nebraska, bringing the bitter promises of winter; leaves flattened themselves against the windows like the dismembered wings of dead birds. It was weather for secrets, for confidences.

'Meg – '

'I'll put on a light.'

'No.' Edith's voice was little more than a whisper, a sighing of soft words in the darkness. 'Meg, take care of them all – '

'Of course. Don't tire yourself – '

A fragile claw found her hand, rested on it rather than held it. 'Don't leave your father alone again . . .'

'No, Mother. But please rest – '

'Is Magnus coming by this evening?' The shrunken skeletal face turned on the pillow. 'Give him my love, Meg . . .'

The voice died away suddenly, was no longer even a whisper. Margaret reached behind her, fumbled for a switch, turned on a

213

lamp. When she looked back Edith was at the last threshold, at the moment when secrets no longer have any meaning. Margaret looked into her mother's eyes, saw that Magnus's love had never been as secret as he had thought. Then the eyes were just marbles, reflecting the light without recognition. The lids slipped down over them, sealing Edith Beaufort's life.

# Chapter Seven

◆

# Margaret

I

Edith's burial brought together all the people she would have loved to see at the wedding of any of her daughters. Aunts, uncles, cousins, friends came from all over the United States; ex-President and Mrs Truman attended, the Governors of Missouri and Kansas and a dozen Senators and Congressmen.

When her will was read Miss Stafford, faithful secretary of twenty-five years, was given a pension that made her more than comfortable for the rest of her life. George Biff was remembered with a lump sum that brought a lump to his throat; and the cook and the maids and the gardeners and the security guards were also remembered. Edith had forgotten no one and she was shrewd though not cynical: she knew that the poor remember better if their memories are not diverted by money worries. To each of her daughters, whose memories would never be diverted from her, she left five million dollars; twenty million dollars went to a trust fund for her grandchildren, born and still-to-be-born. The residue of her personal estate, some ten million dollars, went to various charities and institutions, all of them based in Kansas City. Her perspective had narrowed, she knew where her money belonged.

Nina and Sally stayed for a month after their mother's death, then they went back to Europe. Nina took Lucas with her and he went without protest, as if now one place was no different from another. He did not like the expatriates, American and

British, living in Torremolinos and Nina took him back to London and booked passage for herself and him on a Union Castle liner going to Capetown. The sea cruise seemed to do him some good and at Capetown he suggested they should book on a P & O liner and go on to Australia, then back across the Pacific from Sydney by a Matson ship. Nina, who had grown bored of shipboard life on the Union Castle liner before they were half-way to Capetown, agreed that it was a good idea and made the onward bookings. By the time they got to Sydney Lucas, too, was bored, but he was touched by and appreciative of Nina's care for him and he did not like to suggest they find a quicker way than by sea of getting back to America. So they crossed the Pacific in twin boredom that they both managed to hide. On arrival back in Kansas City Nina said she would stay on for a while.

'I think you need some help with Daddy.'

Sally had gone back to France, this time to Paris, where she continued to live with Michele in an on-and-off relationship at which she only hinted in her letters to Margaret. She gave up car racing and bought herself a light plane, getting her pilot's licence with a minimum of effort; she was as natural-born a flier as she had been a driver. The plane revived Michele's interest and the two of them flew about Europe, causing comment and admiration wherever they landed. *I'm happy, Meg,* she wrote in May 1956, *so don't worry about me. We flew down to Rome to spend a weekend with Philip. His father wants him to go back to Chicago, but Philip is doing everything he can to stay over here. Michele sends her love . . .* Which Margaret knew had to be a lie.

Eisenhower had been re-elected, a result only accepted by Lucas because the alternative, the election of Adlai Stevenson, would have been in his eyes far, far worse. He resigned from the Missouri Republican committee, giving no reasons and being asked for none; but everyone knew he did not like Ike. For months he had been unable to maintain any continuous enthusiasm for anything; he would go to his office for a week, then stay at home for two weeks. He would potter around in the garden with the gardeners, take his two granddaughters for walks round the park, play listless tennis with his daughters or even George Biff. Once on the spur of the moment he flew with Nina to Paris to see Sally, but they were back two weeks later. He complained that the French were no better than they had ever been and he could not see why Sally was wasting her time there. He made no mention of Michele, but he said he'd met a nice young feller, Philip Someone-or-Other, who had taken him and Nina and

216

Sally to dinner at La Tour d'Argent, where, if nothing else, the food was good.

'Mother would have liked it.' Only occasionally did he mention Edith; though he was not entirely successful, he tried not to wear his grief as a badge. But each night he went to bed with her ghost and, still, sometimes cried himself to sleep. 'She always said the French could cook.'

'You should write General de Gaulle,' said Margaret.

'A fine leader. Just what the French need. They should ask him to take over France again.'

'Another general,' said Magnus. 'There must be some similarity between running a country and an army, after all.'

'It's escaped our feller,' said Lucas sourly.

Then he started going to his office again regularly, began to pick up and look and sound more like the old Lucas. As if to prove to his executives that he had not lost his old touch, he drove down one day with George Biff to Springfield and came back the next day with the news that he had bought the city's largest bank to add to the Beaufort empire. It was not a large purchase in terms of the empire's wealth and holdings. It was just a rich man's way of slapping his desk to let everyone know that he was back in business and running the show again.

The purchase of the bank brought Bruce Alburn to Kansas City. Margaret's first impression of him was that he was a dull man: in looks, demeanour and intellect. With the exception of a week's vacation to Mexico City and a week at a banker's conference in Montreal, he had never been out of the United States. His only other language besides English was Osage, a linguistic achievement that failed to impress Margaret.

'It was a hobby of mine,' he said in his soft dry voice. 'But now it's an asset.'

'Oh?' she said politely, wondering what sort of skirmishes with the Indians still went on down in Springfield.

'I also have a bank over in Oklahoma. When they discovered oil on the Osage reservation over there, the Indians were happy to talk to a banker who spoke to them in their own language.'

'You're not a banker who speaks with forked tongue, I take it.'

'You're pulling my leg, Mrs Minett. People have been doing that all my life. Somehow I've managed not to become lop-sided.'

She looked at him again, though still not with a great deal of interest. She was playing hostess for her father, who had arranged this dinner party to introduce Bruce Alburn to the Beaufort executives and their wives. Alburn was unmarried and Margaret

217

had asked Nina to be his dinner partner.

'I'm sorry,' Nina had said. 'I'm Magnus's girl for the evening. Try Prue.'

'You don't get sixteen-year-old dinner partners for bankers, not in this country.'

'He comes originally from Arkansas, doesn't he? Down there the age of consent is seven or eight. On second thoughts, Prue would probably be a bit advanced for him.'

In the end Margaret nominated herself as Alburn's dinner partner and invited a widow friend of Lucas's to make up the even number. Now she was beginning to wish she had pushed the widow on to Mr Alburn.

'Are you moving up here to Kansas City permanently?' she asked, hoping she would not have to include him too often on their guest list.

'Not till I see how things work out. I've managed a short-term lease of an apartment in The Chestnuts and I'll use that as a *pied-à-terre*.' He pronounced it as pyed-a-ter; he paused and looked at her. 'My French isn't very good, is it?'

'I don't think they go in very much for French at The Chestnuts.'

'I'd heard you were a cold bitch, Mrs Minett.' His voice was still soft and dry, his smile polite and attentive. 'What have you got against me? Or are you just against everyone who isn't a Beaufort?'

She was surprised that someone should think she was cold. Rude, she admitted to; but not cold. 'Is that really my reputation, Mr Alburn? That I'm cold?'

'Snooty was the actual word I think I heard. But down south where us peasants hang out, it means the same thing.'

'What do they think of my father down there among the peasants?'

'He's respected. That's the most anyone from KC or St Louis can expect.'

'Will they respect you now you've joined the major leaguers?'

'Oh, they're rooting for me. I'm their fifth column.'

'Does my father know?'

'I told him as soon as we'd signed the deal. He's delighted. He said something about the satisfaction of a challenge. How do you get your satisfaction, Mrs Minett? Cutting people down to your estimate of their proper size?'

'Mr Alburn,' she said on the spur of the moment; she was bored, had been for months, and looked for her own challenge, 'would you care to take me out to dinner tomorrow night?'

She had surprised him, as she had hoped; but he recovered. 'My pleasure, Mrs Minett. What will it be? Pistols or daggers?'

She gave him her first genuine smile of the evening. 'Pick me up at eight-thirty, Mr Alburn. I like to dine a little later than the locals. It's a habit I picked up living in Rome.'

'I'm a six-thirty man myself, but I'll try and hold out.'

Then George Biff came to the table, leaned close to Margaret. 'Miz Sally on the phone. She calling from Paris.'

Margaret excused herself, got up and went out to her father's study. The trans-Atlantic phone cable had been put in last year and normally the connections now were good. But not tonight: Sally's voice came and went as in the old days, as if a wind were blowing across the line.

'Meg — I'm — ' Her voice faded and there was nothing for a moment. 'Michele has left me.'

'Sally, this isn't the first time — '

'No, it's for good this time. She's married — she's been seeing him all this time and she didn't tell me — '

'Who? Philip?'

'Philip?' Again her voice faded; then came back in what sounded like a laugh. 'No, of course not. Not Philip. A man named Onza, Gaston Onza. He's an African politician or something. Meg, I don't know what I'm going to do — '

'Come home. Get on a plane right now and come home.'

'No. No, I don't want to do that. Daddy might start asking me questions — I don't think I could lie well enough to cover up. Meg — what am I going to do? We were breaking up, but I didn't think it would happen like this . . .'

'Would it help if Nina or I came over?'

'Oh, would you? Could you come? I can talk to you better than I can to Nina — '

'I'll come as soon as I can. I'll phone again as soon as I know what plane I'm on. And Sally — please don't do anything foolish.'

'I shan't, I promise. Philip is here for the week — he'll keep an eye on me.'

It was Philip who had introduced Sally to Michele: but this was not the moment for bringing *that* up. 'I'll be there as soon as I can.'

She went back to the dinner, sat down beside Bruce Alburn. 'I'll have to postpone our date. I have to go to Paris.'

He raised an eyebrow. 'I'm impressed.'

'How's that?'

'I'm comparing you with my sister, my only close relative. If she has to leave Springfield to go to Joplin to visit my cousins, that's only an hour's drive, you'd think she was setting out on the Santa Fé Trail. But just like that, you're going to Paris. I'm certainly in another league, Mrs Minett.'

'I'm beginning to think you'll survive, Mr Alburn.'

## 2

It was another three days before, for various reasons mainly connected with the children, she could get away. Lucas wanted to go with her, but she told him she was going with the object of bringing Sally back with her – 'She wants a girls' talk with me, Daddy. She has a problem.'

'With some feller? Not a Frenchman, I hope.'

'I shan't know till I get there.'

Nina had not volunteered to go with her. 'I'll stay with Ruth and help her look after the children. The trouble's with Michele, isn't it? I never did like that bitch. I'm afraid if I came with you I'd upset Sally by saying too much. Try and bring her home, if only for a while. Anything to get her away from Michele.'

A storm delayed the take-off of her plane from Kansas City and she arrived in New York too late to make her connection for Paris. She stayed the night in New York and caught a plane out of Idlewild next day. Crossing Ireland the plane developed engine trouble and the pilot changed course and headed for London instead of Paris. They landed there without mishap, but there were no seats on any planes for Paris leaving that evening. She finally got away next day at noon and landed in Paris exactly a day later than she had planned.

Sally and Philip were waiting for her at the airport. She only recognized Sally because of Philip. Sally, the girl with the long untidy blonde hair and the utter disregard for clothes, looked like another person. Her hair was cut short, exposing the back of her neck; she was wearing a tailored suit that Margaret knew at once had come from one of the best houses; she was even wearing a string of small pearls. She looked so elegant, so French. And she certainly did not look heart-broken.

'Congratulate us,' Sally said, her arm linked with Philip's. 'We were married this morning.'

## Chapter Eight

◆

# Sally

### I

Sally would often wonder in later years what would have happened if Margaret's plane had not been delayed. Did airlines know or care what they did to people's lives when their aircraft did not run to schedule? All the tragedies were not caused by crashes.

There had been time for Sally to change her mind about marrying Philip. Michele had been gone for a week with her new husband before Sally had called Margaret. In that time Philip had arrived unexpectedly from Rome. Michele had called him to ask him to wish her luck and would he please go up to Paris and console poor darling Sally who must be desolate. Sally had fallen into his arms because they were the only ones available; and too, she did love him, in a kind of way. He did not ask her to go to bed with him, but he did ask her to marry him. Impetuous as ever, as desolate as Michele had said she would be, loving Philip for just being there, she had said yes. He had gone out at once and got a licence; only to come back and say they would have to wait ten days before they could be married. He still did not ask her to go to bed with him and she had appreciated that; it showed how considerate he was and properly loving. In the intervening days she had had time to consider if she was doing the right thing; but she had not been able to bring herself to discuss it with Margaret over the phone. In the end, when the arranged date for the wedding arrived and Margaret had not, she went ahead and married Philip. And, as always when she had committed herself, was happy, as if the decision itself and not the consequences was the most difficult to bear.

'But don't you know who he is?' Margaret said.

'I know his real name is Philip Gentleman, not Mann. I'm going to have to get used to that, being called Mrs Gentleman. It's kind of funny.'

'It's not funny at all, it's the unfunniest part of all.'

They were alone together in Sally's apartment just off the Avenue Matignon. Philip had gone out on business, but promised he would be back to take them to dinner. Sally was closing up the apartment and she and Philip were going back to Rome at the end of the week. She had been aware of Margaret's agitation ever since they had met at the airport, but she had put it down to travel exhaustion and the delays en route. But now she saw that something deeper was worrying her sister. 'What are you trying to say, Meg?'

'His father is Tony Gentleman. He's a Mafia don, a gangster. Philip is the one who invests their money, all that they make out of their rackets. He launders it, as they call it. Making dirty money clean, putting it into legitimate businesses.'

Sally sat very still. 'I won't say I don't believe you. You haven't come all the way over here to lie to me. But how do you know what you're saying is true?'

Margaret leaned back in the couch where she sat. The room was ultra-modern in its furnishings, a contrast to the building that housed it. White walls were enlivened by paintings splashed with vivid colours; black leather-and-chrome chairs and glass-and-chrome tables looked like artefacts sent back from the future; bright rugs, matching the colours in the paintings, were strewn on the thick white carpet. Sally had no interest in furnishings and she had allowed Michele to do the apartment to her own taste. She had never felt comfortable in it; it was an edgy room, one that rubbed against her nerve ends. Margaret looked around it now and looked just as nervous and edgy. Then Sally realized that the room had nothing to do with Meg's nervousness.

'I thought I'd never have to tell this to anyone . . .'

Sally listened, feeling herself going blind while her hearing increased to an acuteness where every word was like a sharp pain. She did not know that Margaret was not telling her everything about Frank and herself; but what she was told was more than she really wanted to hear. She was a turmoil of feeling: anger, shame, pity. Anger at how fate had treated her; shame at some of the things she had thought about Meg in the past; pity for all Meg had had to go through. At last her senses reversed themselves: she no longer heard what Meg was saying, her eyes cleared and took in the pain in her sister's face. Abruptly she stood up, no longer able to sit still.

'God, we get ourselves into messes, don't we? What are we going to do?'

Margaret looked at her; she smiled wryly, but she was not really amused. '*I'm* not married to him. I'll help you, but I really can't interfere. I've interfered enough – Oh God, why weren't those damned planes on time!' She looked for something in her handbag, couldn't find it, snapped the bag shut angrily. 'Would you have still married him? I mean if I'd got here in time. *On* time.'

Sally stood at the window. Down in the street a man and a girl met, kissed as if they were alone in a room, went off hand-in-hand. She had always loved the lovers of Paris; they were probably no different from lovers anywhere else, but Paris itself had always had its romance for her. But no longer.

'I don't know . . . God, listen to me! I've been married exactly – ' she looked at her watch – 'Exactly seven hours. I haven't even had my wedding night yet. And now I'm saying I don't know if . . .' Her voice trailed off in a dry, stifled sob.

Margaret got up, put her arms round her. 'Perhaps Philip will never go back to Chicago. Things may work out – '

'You don't really believe that. I should have come home when things started to break up with Michele – '

'What made her marry? An African, too, isn't he? I thought she was running away from the black side of her.'

'He's like her, he has white blood in him, Belgian. He's also like her in that he's ambitious – though I don't know what hopes there are for ambitious politicians in Africa. Especially in the Congo. But he has money and he's charming and she went and married him and that's that.' She couldn't help the bitterness in her voice; self-pity swamped her like a fever.

Margaret began to gather up her things. 'I'd better go. I can't stay here. I'll call the Crillon.'

'Can't you wait till Philip gets back? No. No, I suppose not. I don't know how I'm going to face him. I mean, ask him those questions – '

'You've never been lacking in courage before.'

'Racing cars, flying a plane – that's different. I *enjoy* that – I don't think of those sort of things needing courage. But I've always been a moral coward. If I hadn't been I'd never have got myself into the messes I have. Cindy, Michele, Philip. Yes, even him, I guess. I always took the easy way out.'

223

'Call me if you need me. Otherwise, I'll see you tomorrow.'

'How long are you going to stay?'

'Just a few days. I have to go back – I can't leave the children too long.'

'Are you a good mother? No, I shouldn't ask that. You *are*. You've been more understanding towards me than I think Mother would have been.'

'You don't know how Mother would have been. She might have surprised us all.'

'What about Daddy? How is he going to react when he finds out who his new son-in-law is? He doesn't even know he has a son-in-law yet.'

'I think you'd better have your talk with Philip first.' Margaret kissed her. 'Nina and I have survived our troubles. I don't think we're any stronger than you are.'

Sally did not know how strong she was, but she knew how weak she could be. 'I'll call you tonight. Will you have dinner with us?'

'See how it works out with Philip first.'

Sally felt that the next hour was the most agonizing she had ever spent. She waited for Philip's key in the front door; it seemed that she walked miles and miles round the apartment. When he eventually opened the door and came in he was smiling, the happy bridegroom.

'Where's Meg – lying down?'

He kissed her before she could stop him; but she wondered even as he did so why she should not want him to kiss her. 'Philip – she's gone to stay at the Crillon. She told me something about you – '

He took off his topcoat, put it on a hanger and hung it in the closet. She had noticed before that he had a habit of deliberately pacing himself when he was careful about what he was going to say next: he had proposed to her in the same careful way.

'I know what she's told you. I knew it was going to happen – I could see it in her face at the airport when you told her we were married.'

'Why didn't *you* tell me?' She tried to keep her voice level; but she wanted to cry out. 'Good Christ – the Mafia!'

'Sit down, darling. *Sit down!*'

She had taken a step away from him, turning to keep moving about the room. But the tone of his voice cut the legs from under her; she sat down with a thud in the nearest chair. He drew up another chair, sat down with his knees almost touching hers.

'*Mafia* is a word we don't use back home. My father, if he ever

224

calls our organization anything and he rarely does, calls it The Honoured Society. Which is what it was called in Sicily when he left there. So don't use that word again.'

'All right. But semantics aren't going to change what you represent.'

'I don't represent anything. Not the way you mean it. Everything I do is legitimate, as perfectly legal and decent as anything your father does. You may think the money I handle isn't as clean as your father's, but it all only comes out of providing something that people want.'

She couldn't argue with him: he seemed so cool and – self-righteous? 'Philip, please don't talk to me as if I'm a child. Your – Honoured Society makes its money out of *crime*. I don't know what sort of crime – '

'Prostitution. Betting – the numbers game. And back in Prohibition days, before I was born, my father made a living bootlegging.'

'I suppose he worked for Al Capone?'

'No, he didn't. He worked in New York in those days. All those things I mentioned are, or were, against the law. But the man who bought a bottle of bootleg whisky or the one who pays a girl to go to bed with him – you ask him, he doesn't think of himself as a criminal.'

'Oh, for God's sake stop it! You're *gangsters* – that's the only word to describe you! You kill people – you're all covered with blood – '

He reached across deliberately, almost slowly, and slapped her across the face. 'I'm sorry to do that. But you're getting hysterical. I'm not trying to excuse anything the Society – even my father – has done. We have our own way of doing things. By and large, we kill only our own. And I've never been even remotely connected with a killing. I don't own a gun and I don't intend to. I'm the respectable son of my father and my father wants me to be nothing else. That's why they chose me to handle their investments.'

'*They?* You see – you belong to the – the Society!'

He was silent for a moment, as if she had just pointed something out to him that he had not wanted to admit to himself. 'Okay, I belong to it. But it is never going to ask me to do any more than I'm doing now – it's in its own interests for me to stay the way I am. As for you and me – there's no reason in the world why you should be involved in the Society. It is always only the men who are involved.'

She shook her head dumbly, pulled herself back as he reached

225

out a hand for her.

'Sally – I didn't marry you out of pity. I married you because I love you.'

That was a lie, but, said in his quiet voice, it had the ring of truth. He had married her because he liked her and because she was a Beaufort: principally for the latter reason. He had not married her for her money but for the respectability of her name. Some day soon he would retire from what he was doing now, would turn his back on the Society, be Philip Mann, gentleman.

'I should have been honest with you – I would have been if there'd been more time. But I was afraid you'd say no – You would have, wouldn't you?'

She nodded, looking at him cautiously, afraid of his sincerity.

'I've been worried by it. I knew I'd have to tell you – sooner rather than later. I think I was relieved in a way when Meg turned up today.'

'Why can't you just turn your back on – on the whole thing? Tell your father you want nothing to do with it.'

'I'm my father's only child.' There was a certain formality to the way he said it. 'I love him – as much as I love you, I suppose, but in a different way. I mentioned your father's money a while ago. It wasn't all that clean to begin with. Not the way your grandfather made it. But it doesn't seem to worry you.'

At least her grandfather had never killed: not even his own. Or had he? Heads had been busted by strike-breakers in plants owned by her grandfather; maybe men had died. She had just never wanted to know: a moral coward again.

'What makes you run away from your father?' he said.

It was an unfair question in the context; but she had no answer to it. She got up from her chair, waiting for him to tell her to sit down again; but he said nothing, just watched her as she moved aimlessly about the room. She passed the windows, looked out into the dark night, then drew the drapes.

At last she said, 'What are we going to do, then?'

'I think we should give our marriage a chance. We'll go back to Rome and settle there. It's a good city and it's getting better all the time. I think I can persuade my father that I should stay in Europe – it's a good area for investment now. There's no reason why we should ever have to go back to Chicago, except on business.'

'I'd never go.'

She couldn't see his face clearly; he was against the light. But he sat very still and she sensed the anger and hurt in him. But he controlled it, said quietly, 'Then you can't expect me to go to Kansas City.'

It took her a few moments to make the concession: she could not put her father on the same level as Tony Gentleman. 'All right. But it's not a very good start for us, is it?'

'We'll work it out somehow. I love you, Sally, and I'm not going to give you up without giving ourselves a chance to make a go of it.'

So Sally, who was weak and knew it, gave in. They took Margaret to dinner at Le Grand Véfour. It was Sally who suggested the restaurant and Philip wondered aloud if the Beaufort sisters ever dined at small intimate places.

'In small intimate places you can be overheard,' said Sally. 'I don't want strangers listening in to us tonight.'

So there in the restaurant where Napoleon and Josephine had exchanged confidences, Margaret was told what Sally and Philip decided.

'I'll give you my blessing, if that's what you want, but it isn't easy. You should have told her the truth before you were married, Philip.'

He nodded, toying with his food. They should not have come to this restaurant; none of them had an appetite. The waiters hovered in the background, contemptuous of the three Americans who obviously did not appreciate good food, who would have been more at home with hamburgers. Philip, his eye sharpened by prejudice against himself all his life, had begun to suspect that the biggest snobs in the world were those who worked in expensive establishments rather than those who paid the bills. He took a mouthful of the *entrecôte à la bordelaise*, nodded appreciatively just to prove himself to the waiters. One of them nodded in acknowledgement and Philip decided he had done his bit for American taste. Then he thought, the hell with them; and wondered why he had such an inferiority complex. None of these waiters knew he was the son of Tony Gentleman. But even as he wondered, he knew the answer: he would never be truly respectable, no matter how much he wished for it or how much his father encouraged him. He would never be a gentleman with a small *g*.

'I think you had better call home tonight,' Margaret said, 'and break the news. Tell Nina first, so that she can break it gently to Daddy. Though he should be getting used to his daughters springing weddings on him. Well – ' She raised her glass, looked at the wine in it, then shook her head. 'No, I'll be traditional. I'll drink to you both in champagne.'

The *sommelier* was impressed when Margaret named the champagne she wanted: these Americans were not so uncivilized after all. He brought it and Margaret toasted her sister and her new brother-in-law. 'Be happy, that's the best I can wish you. It hasn't been a tradition so far with the Beaufort sisters. You try and break the run of bad luck.'

'We'll try,' said Sally, and wanted to weep, wondering how much good luck she had had so far. She and Michele had sometimes come to this restaurant together; she looked about, hoping she might see her now, even if with her husband. She thought of something Lamartine, another diner here, had once written: *Sometimes, when one person is missing, the whole world seems depopulated.* Guiltily, she pressed Philip's arm: he, for all his faults, was trying to take Michele's place, make the world less depopulated.

## 2

Margaret flew back to Kansas City two days later. Sally closed up the apartment and she and Philip flew back to Rome in her own plane. The news of her marriage had surprised Nina, who had called to congratulate her and Philip but had not said much else. Lucas also was surprised, but predictably wondered why all his daughters had to rush their weddings as if their husbands were going off to war.

'Your mother and I were engaged for twelve months before we were married. A decent long engagement we had in my day.'

Sally had not tried to explain: because she had no explanation that would satisfy him and she was not a good liar. 'We'll be happy, Daddy. That's all that matters.'

And she fervently hoped so. Having committed herself to the marriage, she was determined to make the best of it. Except for his family background she really did not have anything to complain about in Philip. Having told herself that, she then, because she was always so honest with herself, admitted it was not much of a basis for marriage. She loved him, but she knew it was not the sort of love that – well, that Nina had felt for Tim. She had loved Michele, but that had brought her only intermittent happiness; and she could not imagine Philip's being as cruel and callous as Michele had sometimes been. So she tried for happiness

228

as she might have tried to win the Mille Miglia, determinedly and with a certain physical recklessness.

She had had little experience of men in bed. She had been made love to by a Yale man when she had been at Vassar. He was studying law and he had seduced her as if he were trying to win a case before a jury; he had advanced point by point and climaxed his argument with a pounding that would have had him charged with assault had he actually been in court. Her only other encounter with a male lover had been a French racing driver at Le Mans, where she had gone to watch the running of the Twenty-Four-Hours race. He had had none of the finesse she had expected and she had emerged from the bed feeling she had been driven round it in lap record time. After those two experiences she had shied away from men in bed.

Philip made love to her gently the first night. Any man, taking the place of a former lover, knows there must be a comparison, even if only subconsciously. To take the place of a woman as lover was a handicap that might have made him brutal or impotent. Instead of which he was compassionate, if also passionate when the moment was right. She fell asleep in his arms, convinced she was going to be happy.

They set up house in Philip's apartment in an old palazzo on The Corso. Sally had had no experience of housekeeping, having always employed a woman to look after her and Michele. So Philip's housekeeper was kept on. Lucia Giuffre was a plump plain woman who knew who her new mistress was and decided that the apartment was not sufficiently grand for such a rich girl.

'There is an apartment above us, signora. It is much bigger, it is where the family lived in Mussolini's day. You and I could make it into something beautiful for Signor Mann.'

It troubled Sally that, though she had married Philip under his real name, they were still known in Rome as Signor and Signora Mann. 'That would take a lot of money, Lucia.'

Lucia spread her hands: if Signora Mann didn't have money, who did? 'What is money for, signora?'

Sally had always been the most indifferent of the sisters towards the family wealth. She had indulged herself with her cars and her plane, signing cheques without ever giving a thought as to what her bank balance might be. Yet her extravagances were intermittent and over a year she probably spent no more than Nina or Margaret. She was not a determined, or even a conscious, profligate. But as Lucia had just said, what was money for if not to spend?

So the Manns moved up into the larger apartment, but it never became one of the salons of Rome. Sally did not have the skills of Nina or Margaret as a hostess; she was glad that Philip liked to keep a low profile in both business and social life. They never became part of the growing American colony in Rome and she began to enjoy their comparative anonymity. Then she found she was pregnant.

'Are you glad, Philip?' She was happy with him, happier than she had expected to be. She loved him, though not in the passionate, fascinated way she had loved Michele.

He lifted her hand, kissed the inside of her wrist: such gentle intimacies endeared him to her. He did nothing with a flourish, being always quiet and restrained; but he was not a dull husband and lover and there were always quiet gestures and expressions to tell her how much he loved her. For his part he now did love her; or more so than he had expected. He patted her belly.

'He's the best thing that's happened to us.'

'You're sure it's going to be a he?'

He smiled. 'I don't really care. Maybe a girl would be better.'

*Because a girl could escape from the Mafia.* She did not say it, because she did not want to hurt him. She still was not able to accept his background, but she kept pushing the problem to the back of her mind. If any emissaries from Chicago came to Rome, she never met them or even knew of them. Philip saw them at his office out at EUR, where he had taken a suite because, he said, he could not work in the dingy offices available in the centre of the city. She sometimes wondered if his going out to EUR was to keep his Chicago connections completely separate from his life with her. She had noticed that at their occasional small dinner parties very few Americans were on the guest list.

They had been married six months before Tony Gentleman came to Rome to see his daughter-in-law for the first time. Lucas had flown over the first week after they had returned from Paris. He had got on well with Philip, asked him about his business, seemed satisfied with whatever answers Philip had given him, then returned home. Once a week he phoned Sally, shouting and grumbling at the bad connections, always ending with the same question: when was she coming home for a visit? To which Sally, always with the thought that Chicago was only a few hundred miles north of Kansas City, said soon, Daddy, soon.

Tony Gentleman never used the phone unless he had to, though his daughter-in-law did not know that. He knew the dangers of a wire-tap, a hazard that never entered her head. Tony Gentleman was a rare *capo*: in all his life he had been

230

arrested only twice but never indicted. His record was clean, but he knew the FBI did not regard him as a model citizen and J. Edgar Hoover was once known to have kicked one of his pet dogs in a fit of temper when Tony Gentleman's name was mentioned. So he never committed anything important to the United States mail, figuring that neither snow, nor rain, nor heat, nor gloom of night was as hazardous as the FBI; and for the past year he never made any business phone calls unless unavoidable and no overseas calls at all. All his communications to his son in Rome were delivered by hand by a courier who flew the Atlantic once a week.

He arrived in Rome seemingly without company; but two of his security guards had travelled separately in economy class. He had travelled a roundabou troute: Chicago, Pittsburgh, Buffalo, Montreal, Paris, Rome: along the way he had lost any tail the FBI might have had on him. He travelled on a passport that said he was Carlo Borzello, a native of Palermo, Sicily, but an American citizen. He told no one that the main reason for the hiding of his real identity was not to escape the attentions of the law but to avoid embarrassing his son. He wanted nothing so much in life now as respectability for Philip. It did not occur to him that he would have given him more chance of respectability if he had disowned him.

Sally was cautiously friendly in her welcome of the old man. He did not *look* dangerous; though she was not sure what she had expected. Philip had had no photos of his father; because Tony Gentleman, if it could be avoided, did not stand in front of cameras, no matter who was operating them. This extremely well-dressed, silver-haired man looked every bit as distinguished as her own father, perhaps even more so. The rough, uneducated voice was the letdown: he *sounded* just as she had expected. She read her own sense of menace into the soft hoarse voice.

He shook her hand, awkwardly: he had none of his son's social graces. 'You're a lovely girl. Philip is very lucky. Right?'

'I told you that, Dad.' Philip was hiding his shock at how old his father had become in the year since he had seen him last. 'Let's get out to the car. You look tired.'

'A little. It's a long way to come.' His limp seemed to have increased; he leaned on a silver-topped stick. 'I think I oughta retire, go to Florida to live. Chicago ain't the right climate, a man my age.'

Driving into Rome Sally, for want of something better to say, said, 'Are you going to visit Sicily too?'

The old man looked at Philip, then back at Sally. 'You know

anything about Sicily? It ain't a place to go back to.'

He said no more and Sally, still trying, for Philip's sake, to do her bit, plunged on: 'I believe you've met my sister Margaret.' He looked at her again: not blankly, yet with no expression. 'Mrs Minett.'

'Just a little business. For her husband.' She had the feeling that he was speaking carefully, one eye on Philip. 'A nice girl.'

That night the three of them dined in the apartment. Lucia, dressed in her best black, supervised the meal; her nephew, in black livery and white gloves, served the meal. Tony Gentleman was impressed.

'You got a nice place. Very grand.' He waited till Lucia and her nephew had retired from the dining room. 'When I was a little kid, I work in a big house in Palermo. Cleaning the pots and pans. I never see the inside of the house, nothing but the kitchen. But I remember the servants used to come into the kitchen dressed like that feller. The white gloves and all.'

'You've come a long way,' said Philip. 'Enjoy it all, Dad.'

'Oh, I'm gonna do that. You live like this back in Kansas City, Sally?'

'No white gloves.' She knew Philip would not want her to call his father Mr Gentleman; but she could not bring herself to call him Dad. 'Philip loves the life style here. I think he's an old Roman senator at heart.'

'You wanna stay on here?' The old man looked at his son.

'We're making a good life here. Neither of us wants to go home to America.'

The old man looked at his daughter-in-law. 'You too? You don't wanna go home to your father some time?'

'I don't think so.' She wasn't quite sure whether it was a lie or not; she still occasionally thought of Kansas City with nostalgia, still missed her father and her sisters. 'Not to live there, I mean.'

Tony Gentleman nodded to himself. 'I can't complain, I guess. I run away from Sicily, I don't never wanna go back. I just can't understand people running away from America, that's all. I mean, people who ain't gotta run away.'

He stayed in Rome a week, enjoying the company of his son and daughter-in-law. But it was obvious that he was uncomfortable, insecure; he missed the security of the house where he had lived for the past ten years on the North Side of Chicago. He could not imagine anyone's wanting to run away from America; but he had settled for the smallest piece of territory, a house behind a high wall that shut out what America stood for. He was dying and he wanted to die in the only place where he could be certain of being honoured as a 'man of respect', in his own house.

He kissed them both at the airport, holding his son tighter and longer than he did Sally. But he did not ignore her. 'God bless you with the baby. How soon will it be?'

'Just over two months. We'll call you the minute he arrives.'

'He? You want a son?'

It had been a slip of the tongue. 'A boy, a girl, it doesn't matter. Just so long as it's healthy.'

'You can't ask for more,' he said, who had no health left.

He left them and limped away through the gate and out to the plane. Sally saw two men pause and wait for him and help him up the steps and thought how considerate it was of them. Then she looked at Philip and saw the tears running down his cheeks.

A month later the phone rang in the apartment: it was Chicago, the first time ever. The caller told Philip his father was dying.

'I'll catch tonight's plane. Will you be all right?'

She was glad that he did not ask her to go with him. 'Don't *worry*, darling. I'm as healthy as a horse. I'll call you every night. What's your father's number?'

It was only later that she noticed he had not given her the number. 'No, I'll call you. Every night.'

He rang her twenty-four hours later and even through the bad connection she could hear the grief in his voice. 'Dad died an hour after I got here. He was consicous when I saw him, so at least I got to say goodbye to him.'

'I'm sorry, darling. How long will you be staying?'

'The funeral is the day after tomorrow. Then there'll be the estate to be looked into. Sally – ' There was a long pause and she thought they had lost their connection. Then: 'You wouldn't come over here? Just for a month or two, have the baby here? There's a lot I have to attend to – '

'I'm sorry.' She put her hand on her stomach, glad of the baby therein. 'I just couldn't face all that travelling, not now.'

Again the silence; then: 'Sure. I shouldn't have asked.'

He called every night during the next week, promising each time to be on his way home in a day or two – 'There's so much to be done. I'm trying to wrap it up as quickly as I can. Be patient, darling. Another day or two, that's all.'

On the Saturday the phone rang at noon. But it wasn't Philip: it was Michele. '*Darling* – ' The sweet husky voice had not changed. 'I'm in Rome just for the weekend, on my way to Paris. Can you and Philip have dinner or something?'

Sally shivered with panic, looked down at her swollen belly.

She could not let Michele see her like this. Michele had never liked children nor even the sight of pregnant women – 'They look disgustingly ugly. Filling up the world with too many people.' To meet Michele looking like this would be disastrous, humiliating. And yet she could not resist the lure of the dark-toned voice.

'Michele – ' She wanted to be firm, to tell her to go to hell; but she could not. 'I wouldn't be good company. Philip is in Chicago – his father's just died. And I'm – I'm pregnant. Eight months gone.'

'Oh, my love – no! Poor you.'

That angered her, gave her strength. 'No, not poor me. I'm looking forward to being a mother.'

'Well – ' There was no apology; but Michele was incapable of apology for anything. 'Well, I'll call you next time I'm in Rome.'

She relented, not wanting to lose contact. 'How are you? Are you – are you happy with Gaston?'

'Are you happy with Philip?'

'Yes,' she said emphatically: to make the point to herself as well as to her ex-lover.

'I'm glad. He's a beautiful man – as men go.' She chuckled; and Sally was surprised that it sounded dirty to her. 'Oh, Gaston and I get along. I just don't like Leopoldville, that's all. But Gaston's business keeps him there now. But he indulges me. This trip to Paris, for instance. Goodbye, darling. I'll call you next time I come through.'

She hung up and Sally sat there with the dead phone in her hand, feeling the trembling in her limbs and the nausea welling up in her throat. She longed for Philip's comforting embrace. She wanted to call him, but she had no number. *I'll get his father's number through directory enquiries in Chicago*; but suddenly it was all too much effort. Instead she called Kansas City, the number that came so readily to mind.

'Meg?'

'Sally! What's the matter! It's only five-thirty in the morning here. Is something wrong with the baby?'

'No-o.' All at once she felt foolish. 'I just – just wanted someone to talk to. Philip's still in Chicago. You know his father died?'

'I know. It was in the papers. There was a huge funeral.'

'Philip wouldn't have wanted that.'

'I know. I've tried to call you twice, but couldn't get through. Perhaps Philip wasn't the one who decided about the funeral. I hate to say it, but every Mafia chief in the country was there. It was spread all over the newspapers and television.'

234

'Did – were there any pictures of Philip?'

'I'm afraid so. But he wore dark glasses and a moustache. You didn't tell us he'd grown a moustache.'

It had to be a false one: but she was not going to confess that, not even to Meg. 'It's recent. Did Daddy recognize him?'

'I don't know. You know what he's like – he rarely watches television. And you wouldn't have recognized Philip from the newspaper photos. Don't let it worry you, Sal – please. How's the baby?'

'Kicking.' She felt ready to give birth right at this moment. Suddenly she broke: 'Oh Meg, I wish I were home!'

'Why don't you come, then? No. No, if you feel like I felt with Martha you won't want to get on a plane and come all this way. Look – I can't come over, Emma is down with the measles and Martha looks as if she's getting them. But I'll ask Nina – '

'No, please don't – I'll be all right – '

But Margaret would take no arguments. Nina arrived two days later with Lucas and Prue. 'You need all the moral support you can get,' said Lucas. 'What are these Italian doctors like?'

'He was going to bring over the Mayo Clinic,' said Prue. 'Fly it over holus-bolus.'

'The Mayo Clinic is not an obstetrical hospital,' said Lucas.

'You're getting old, Daddy. Your sense of humour isn't too sharp.'

He smiled, accepting the joke against himself. 'You're right. Well, I must say you look beautiful, Mrs Mann. Nothing like a racing driver, thank God. You're not still flying your damned airplane, I hope?'

Sally was thrilled to see them all, though at first she had had misgivings about the arrival of her father. He looked well, though older. Nina looked elegant and composed, as if she had at last come to terms with her loss of Tim and Michael. Prue was gay and beautiful, already hinting at dangers ahead for men if not for herself. Sally once again felt a sense of security, only now aware of how much she had missed it. For now at least she did not feel adventurous.

The apartment was big enough to accommodate them all: Lucia was a jelly of delight at having the signora's family to look after. She had been worried for Signora Mann, not understanding how Signor Mann could remain away in America, even though his father had died, at a time like this. Then Philip came home two days later, minus moustache and dark glasses.

But he was changed, different from the Philip who had gone away only two weeks before. Sally noticed it as soon as they

235

were in the car on the way back to the city. Wishing to be with him before his meeting with her family, she had had Lucia's nephew Enrico drive her out to the airport. Philip sat holding her to him in the back of the car, though now with the baby so big in her she found it difficult to lean into his encircling arms. At last she straightened up and sat back in the seat.

'I'm too big for cuddling – we'll have to wait a few more weeks. How was it? I mean – ' She wasn't exactly sure what she meant. 'You look worried.'

'I've just lost my father.' He sounded defensive.

'I know that. But it's not just grief – Did something happen in Chicago?'

He nodded almost imperceptibly at the back of Enrico's head. 'No. I'm just worn out, that's all.'

Perhaps so: but she knew there was more to it than that. She felt for his hand, held it all the rest of the way into the city. The meeting with her father and sisters was warm and friendly, restrained only by the awareness of his bereavement. Then he excused himself, saying he wanted a bath. Prue pulled Sally into one of the guest bedrooms.

'He's divine! God, he's got that absolutely tragic look – ' Prue had not previously met Philip.

'Don't be so extravagant. What's got into you? You used to be so down-to-earth.'

Prue grinned: the kid Sally remembered peeped through the façade of the beautiful young woman. 'I guess I'm trying to be European. I want to come back here and live, as soon as I get through college.'

'Another three years. By then you'll learn that the only Europeans who use extravagant adjectives are the English girls from expensive schools. What are you reading now? Barbara Cartland?'

'Who's she? No, I think I know everything I need to know now. About sex, I mean. It's a dull subject, actually. To read about, I mean.'

'It's taken you a long time to find that out.' Then, seriously: 'Prue, don't start *practising* it. I mean, not until you're sure about the boy, whoever he is.'

'I've already started. I went all the way when I was fourteen.'

Sally felt the baby jump. 'For God's sake – !'

'I've shocked you, haven't I? I didn't mean to. I just can't be hypocritical about it. I wouldn't tell Daddy, but I thought I could tell you without you acting like some Mother Superior in a convent.'

'Who was it?'

Prue shook her head. 'I'm not telling his name. He was a track star at Rockhurst. When he found out I was only fourteen, he broke the marathon record getting out of the State. But he's past history – ' She waved an airy hand, putting a used lover down the waste disposal. 'Don't *worry*. I'm careful.'

'Do Nina and Meg know about your – your lost virginity?'

'It's not lost. I know where it went.'

Sally stared at her sister, then she started to laugh. Prue also began to laugh and they lay side by side on the bed shaking with merriment. Then Sally felt the first pain and she froze with her mouth open, the laugh turning to a sob.

# 3

The baby was born at midnight on 20 August 1958 and died two minutes later before the doctors could save it. It was the ninth anniversary of the disappearance of Tim and Michael; Sally did not remark the coincidence, but Nina did. And so did Lucas, who had the date burned in his mind, the brand of his own guilt.

Independent of Nina and unbeknown to her, Lucas had never given up the search for his son-in-law and grandson. He would not have been at all upset if he had learned that Tim Davoren was dead and would have said so to Edith had she still been alive; he was no hypocrite, he told himself, and spoke ill of the dead if they deserved it. But Edith *was* dead and he had no one to confide in any more; so he said nothing to anyone about Tim. He knew that he and Tim had not been hypocrites when they had expressed their opinions of each other. Enemies are often closer confidants than friends.

He went to the hospital on the morning after the birth and death of his fourth grandchild. He asked to be alone with Sally; and Philip, Nina and Prue went out into the corridor. He sat down beside the bed and took Sally's hand.

'What is there to say? They tell me there was a malfunction in the heart. It would have been an invalid if it had lived.'

'I wanted it so much, Daddy.' She was wan with grief and exhaustion. 'It was a boy, too. That would have pleased you.'

He nodded, keeping his thoughts to himself on that fact. 'You're still young.' He continued to hold her hand; as he had not done since she was a child. 'I'd like you to come home.'

Her hand contracted in his. 'Daddy – not now. *Please*. I have to stay with Philip. We need to be together right now – '

Lucas sighed, put her hand carefully back on the bed as if it were a fragile token. 'I wish you'd think about it.'

'Later, Daddy. In a few months.'

He kissed her, wanting to weep for her; and for himself. Then he went out into the corridor and jerked his head at Philip. 'Could we go somewhere for a walk and a talk?'

'The Borghese Gardens?' The hospital was not far from the gardens. 'I could do with some fresh air after sitting here in the hospital all night.'

The two men went out into the breathless summer morning. Two Vespas went by, coughing fumes; the girls on the pillion seats looked back, arrogant as circus bareback riders. A water truck laid a small rain on yesterday's dust; two priests skipped aside, laying down a curse on the truck driver's head. Overhead the sky was a bleached blue: it had been a long hot summer.

It was early but the tourists were already appearing, stretching the day as far as it would go. The two men walked past them, oblivious of them. 'Well, I suppose it's time we had our talk,' said Lucas. Philip looked sideways at his father-in-law, a man he did not know. 'What talk is that?'

'About you. I'm sorry the baby was born dead – that's a shock that both of you should have been spared. But in a way I'm glad. I'm sorry to be so blunt and, I guess, callous.'

'Callous sounds about right. But go on, Mr Beaufort.'

Sun filtered through the trees, reviving yesterday's heat which had not really died; ducks, their jewelled heads shining, glided lazily on the artificial lake. A gardener swept up yesterday's leaves and discarded candy wrappers; he longed for winter when he and the ducks would have the gardens to themselves. Across the river the dome of St Peter's caught the sun, God's morning blessing for the One True Church; Protestant churches in Rome got the sun a little later in the day. On the Spanish Steps the artists and flower-sellers set up their competing colours and the tourists flowed down the steps to them like lemmings. But Philip, watching his father-in-law closely, was aware of none of it.

'What are you going to do now your father is dead?'

'I'd like to go on living here in Rome. But I don't know if it will be possible.'

'Have they asked you to take over your father's position?'

'They?'

'When Sally married you, Philip, I had you looked into. Investigated, if you like. The only time I'd met you, that night we had dinner in Paris with Sally and Nina, you hedged too much when I asked you what you did. I didn't worry then, because I didn't think Sally was serious about you. But when she married you and neither you nor she was forthcoming in telling me any more about you, I had you looked into. It seemed strange to me that I was never invited to meet your father. I only understood it when I found out he was Tony Gentleman.'

The gravel crunched beneath their feet as they walked, the sound of tiny bones being ground to dust. From a nearby church there came the sound of a bell tolling: a requiem Mass was being said. An attendant went by carrying a dead duck that he had fished from the lake. Philip suddenly had a premonition of death: the sun cooled, though there was no cloud.

'Do you belong to the Mafia?'

'Yes.' He said it fatalistically and made no attempt to correct Lucas on the terminology.

'Does Sally know?'

Philip hesitated, then said, 'Yes. I don't think she knows to what extent I'm involved.'

'How involved are you?'

'More than I wanted to be. Much more.'

He had worked for the Society but had never thought he had *belonged* to it. That, he knew, had been self-delusion. His father had protected him, always keeping him dealing only with the *clean* business side; the other *capos* besides his father had seemed in agreement to the arrangement. He had worked in a situation that had had its own slow-burning fuse; he was intelligent enough to know it but too sentimental to escape it. He had loved his father with a devotion that he had never attempted to explain to Sally; even the long separation while he had lived here in Italy had not lessened the love. He had stayed with his father, working for him and the Society, because there had always been the hope at the back of his mind that some day they could both retire honourably from the Honoured Society. He knew now that that hope had been futile and stupid.

'Then I am going to take my daughter away from you.'

A nun came towards them, held out some holy cards. Each of them gave her some notes, Philip giving his with a silent prayer. The nun shoved a holy card on them and moved on like a dark spirit. Again Philip felt cold.

'You can't do that, Mr Beaufort,' he said evenly. 'There's such a thing as the law.'

'Don't quote the law to me. Not you.'

'Then we'll leave it to Sally to decide.'

Lucas nodded after a moment. 'All right. But I'll tell her everything she should know.'

*You don't know even the half of it.* 'I'll tell her. I promise.'

'Can I trust you?' Lucas looked at him, at first quizzically, then confidently. He had had confrontations with all three of his sons-in-law; he wondered if other fathers had had so much bad luck in the draw. Philip had the worst handicap of all of them; yet he liked him the most. He felt sorry for Sally, though he wondered why she had risked so much for love. 'All right, you tell her. Everything. But you and I will still have something to talk about even then.'

They walked back to the apartment on The Corso. The city, invaded over the centuries by Gauls, Goths, Arabs, French and Germans, was just about to be invaded by the motor car, the worst of all because every citizen wanted to be a collaborator. Horns bugled arrogantly; the older, poorer natives fled before the charges; traffic cops became field-marshals. The decline and fall of Rome had just begun again, but Lucas and Philip, brought up to be wheel-borne, saw it only as progress. It was the one thought they had in common as they walked back through the seething traffic.

That afternoon Philip went to the hospital alone. As soon as he was beside her Sally reached for him and held him to her. 'Darling – '

He had no words for the moment, yet he knew that the next few minutes would bring from him the most important, the most difficult words he had ever had to speak. He laid his head on her breast, still full of the milk that would not be needed.

'Are you terribly disappointed?' she whispered. 'God, I just wanted to die when they told me – '

Now was not the time to tell her; but he had to. He lifted his head, held her hands cupped in his 'We'll try again. But first – Darling, we have to go back to Chicago.'

She looked at him in puzzlement, her lips murmuring some vague word of query. This was not what she had expected them to be talking about: not *now*.

'They killed my father.'

'They?'

He was aware of the echo of his own voice that morning with Lucas. The world was full of echoes, he guessed: time and history were made up of them. 'My father's – ' He searched for the word, let it fall as if it were phlegm: 'Friends. The pall-bearers at his funeral.'

'How did they kill him? You said it was cancer.'

'He had cancer. But he might've lived another year, two, even three. But they weren't prepared to wait for him to die, they wanted him out of the way. They poisoned him.'

'Poisoned?' She thought all Mafia murders were by the gun. 'How do you know?'

'The doctor told me. He'd been my father's friend for years. He signed the death certificate as death from cancer, but he told me the truth.'

'Why didn't he tell the police?'

He wanted to smile, but couldn't. 'We never tell the police anything. He didn't belong to the Society, but he was a Sicilian. He came from the same town as my father. If he had gone to the police they'd have killed him, too.'

All the time she had been married to him words like these had been in her mind, whispers that had been like a migraine. But she had hoped, with the desperate hope of the helpless, that if she turned a deaf ear the whispers would go away. But they hadn't; and she had known they never would. She lay back on the pillow, less from shock than from resignation. Her life was doomed: the dead baby had been only another proof of that.

'Why do we have to go to Chicago?'

'There are some men in the Society, younger guys, who want me to take over. They are tired of the old men – '

'No!'

He could not tell her the real reason why he had to return to Chicago. She would never understand the need – no, the *command* to avenge. His father had asked for it with his last breath: he had known, somehow, that he was dying of more than cancer. Tony Gentleman, eyes dimmed by approaching death, acting on instinct out of tradition, had forgotten that he wanted his son to be respectable. A true man of honour had to be avenged. And Philip, honour inherited in his blood, bound by love to his father, had given his promise.

'All right,' he said reluctantly. 'I'll say no to them. But I have to go back – just for a while. There are things to do.'

'What things?'

But he had already told her too much. More, he knew, than his father would ever have told his mother. He was becoming secretive, as his father had been: silence was the best defence, the old proverb said. 'Just business.'

'Will we go on living here then?'

Ah, he thought sadly, that's another matter. There were three old men to be killed. If the deed were done, then he himself would already be dead: the premonition this morning had really been precognition. They could not change their name and disappear: she, being who she was, would always mark him, like a flare above a target. A Beaufort son-in-law might disappear (he knew about Nina's husband), but Lucas Beaufort would never allow one of his daughters to disappear without trace. He realized sardonically that he would have been safer, just as respectable, if he had married someone other than a Beaufort.

The only way to survive would be to take over as *capo* in Chicago, as the younger men wanted. And that would always be a fragile survival; the vendetta did not wither away with the victory of one side or the other. He had talked with the doctor in Chicago, the man from the Sicilian mountain town, and he knew now things his father had never told him. The vendetta had started fifty years ago; there had been truces but it had never died. One of the old men, posing as a friend, had been his father's enemy all those years. Just waiting, as only a *mafioso* could wait.

Sally held his hand tightly. 'Darling – don't go back. Let them have whatever's there.'

'I don't have any money.' He used the first excuse that came to mind. 'Not enough.'

His father had left him money but he had no idea how much. Most of it was in a bank in Zurich and he had not yet had time to go there.

'Philip – if the baby had lived, would you still go back to Chicago?'

She had no right to ask such a question. She was like a surgeon who had blundered on to a nerve. He had wanted a son, even though that would have increased the risk against a safe future. There had been a mixture of grief and relief last night when they had told him the baby was dead; but the former had outweighed the latter. He believed in a son succeeding his father: that was why he had to go back to Chicago now.

'How would I know?'

But Sally knew: the answer was there in every expression in his eyes, every nuance in his voice. She let his hand go, put her own hand on her empty belly. There was still pain there, despite the drugs they had given her; and between her legs. The doctors had had difficulty in taking the baby from her; they had wanted to perform a Caesarean, but she had objected strongly to that. She had gone through all the agony for nothing.

He kissed her, not with love but with tenderness. He had tried to love her, if for no other reason than to repay her for her love for him. He had had doubts at first that she really loved him, but the doubts had soon evaporated. He felt ashamed for what he had done to her. There was no way of repaying her. What a pity she wasn't poor: the money in Zurich, however much it was, might have been some compensation.

She returned his kiss, trying to hide the fact that she did not love him. She had tried, so hard at times that it had been almost like a physical pain. He was kind and considerate and he had rescued her from despair after Michele had left her. But always there had been something in him that she had not been able to reach and she had not succeeded in loving him. But she would never let him know. She owed him that.

'I'll be back tonight. I'll take your father and Nina and Prue to dinner afterwards.'

'Don't tell them you're going back to Chicago. They'll be going home in a few days.'

'I don't want you left alone. Maybe you'd better ask Nina to stay on.'

'I'll think about it.'


# 4

He came down into the street from the apartment, glad to escape from Lucas Beaufort. At last night's dinner nothing had been said between the two men. It had just been a family gathering, subdued but pleasant. Nina and Prue had looked elegant and beautiful and, despite the sadness they felt at Sally's losing her baby, they had been good company. Philip had found himself looking at Prue, attracted by her as he had been by none of the other Beaufort sisters, but he had been careful not to give himself away. He had wondered if, in other circumstances, he might have fallen in love with her. But then, a man of honour, as he now saw himself, he had chided himself for being untrue, even if only in his mind, to Sally.

This morning he had had his talk with Lucas. Nina and Prue were still asleep and the two men had breakfasted together in the dining room of the apartment. Both men ate American breakfasts: cereal, ham and eggs, toast, coffee. Lucia, who otherwise admired Americans, had never become accustomed to such barbarism and served them with ill grace.

'I told Sally everything last night.'

'What did she say?'

'We're going to work things out when I come back from Chicago. I have to settle the estate.' He would not be coming back; but he had not even told that to Sally. He would be leaving here at the end of the week, saying goodbye not only to her but to Philip Mann. He was going back to being a Gentleman: he smiled at the bitter joke.

'You'd do better not to come back,' said Lucas.

Philip let that pass. 'You have a great deal of power. Does it ever go to your head?'

'Is that meant to be personal?'

'No. It's a question I've always wanted to ask someone like you. Ever since I was at the LSE. The London School of Economics.' He explained as he saw Lucas's eyebrow go up.

'I know what it stands for. I'd forgotten you'd gone there. I've got used to thinking of you only in your other context. Power? No, it doesn't go to my head. You use it if you have it, that's what it's for. But once you let it get the better of you, you're finished.'

'Lord Acton was right then?'

Lucas chewed on some toast. 'Of course. But why didn't you ever ask your father that question? He had power. The wrong sort, but he had it.'

'I never thought of it.' But he thought of it now, felt heavy, as if the coffee in his mouth were a potion. If he should become *capo* . . .

After breakfast he put on his jacket, picked up the Gucci brief-case Sally had given him on his birthday, said goodbye to Lucas and went down in the creaking cage of the elevator. He went out through the echoing entrance hall of the palazzo, his heels clacking hollowly on the terrazzo floor. Men of power had passed through this hall on visits to the family who had owned the palazzo: the Orsinis, Mazzini, Mussolini. Power had corrupted some of them, but he would see that it did not happen to him. He would study Lucas Beaufort, use him as a model.

He stepped out into the street, felt the heat at once even though the morning was young. He walked along The Corso, then turned into the side street where he garaged his car. He did not see the two men until they came up, one on either side of him, as he got to the short tunnel that led into the garage.

'Don't make any fuss,' said one of the men, a big man in a seersucker suit and dark glasses. 'Just keep walking. Where's your car?'

His step faltered, but the man on the other side of him poked something hard into his waist. He was a thin young man, this

244

one, dark-suited, dark-glassed and Italian. He said nothing, but he did not need to: the gun in his pocket spoke for him.

Philip walked down the slight slope of the tunnel into the dimly-lit garage. A car came in behind them, engine growling, and for one crazy moment he thought of breaking away and trying to run to the other side of the car. But he knew he would be dead before he had moved three feet.

'Where are we going?'

'Someone wants to talk to you,' said the big man. He had a Texan accent and Philip wondered why Chicago had sent some-one from Texas all the way here to Rome. 'This your car?'

The dark blue Fiat stood at the end of a line of cars, but he could hardly see it. All his senses had stopped working.

'Get in,' said the Texan.

'You – do you want me to drive?' His voice sounded like his father's: high, dry and soft.

'It don't matter.'

He slid into the driver's seat, looked up as the big man took the pistol fitted with a silencer from his pocket.

'Don Carlo said to say goodbye.' Don Carlo Belgini had been his father's friend and pall-bearer, the enemy who had killed him.

*Jesus, Mary and . . .* Philip died before he could finish the prayer.

# Chapter Nine

◆

# Sally

I

Philip was buried two days later, quietly and without any notice in the newspapers. Lucas went through his papers in the apartment and the office out at EUR and found two passports, one in the name of Philip Gentleman, the other for Philip Mann. He was buried under the latter name and his murder was filed under that name. The police came to see Sally, but Lucas told them she was still in hospital, suffering from the shock of losing both her baby and her husband; but no one at the hospital was told of Philip's death and Lucas made arrangements to get her out of there as soon as possible. He told the police he could think of no reason for the killing of his son-in-law except that of robbery. His son-in-law had left the apartment with a brief-case and no brief-case had been found at the scene of the crime. He had no idea what might have been in the case, but he presumed it must have interested the murderer or murderers; there had been no witnesses to the crime, the attendant at the garage saying that he had been away delivering a car at the time the murder was assumed to have taken place. Lucas told the police his son-in-law was a quiet-living businessman, happy in his marriage, doing his best, in his own quiet way, to increase American investment in the Italian economy.

The lieutenant in charge of the investigation knew with whom he was dealing. 'Are you yourself investing in our economy, signore?'

Nina, sitting in on the interview, translated for her father. He shook his head. 'Not at present. My son-in-law had his own interests, mostly in motion pictures. I never invest in motion pictures.'

'Forgive my asking, signore, but what were your relations with Signor Mann?'

Lucas took his time about answering that after Nina had translated it. 'We respected each other. And he was a good husband to my daughter.'

The lieutenant nodded, but it was impossible to tell how he accepted that argument. He was a gaunt untidy man with a face grey from pessimism and bad diet. 'It may be difficult to keep the matter out of the newspapers – '

Lucas said, through Nina, 'I understand that, lieutenant. All I ask is that my daughter be left alone. If her name were not mentioned – '

Nina said, not bothering to translate her own remarks for her father's benefit, 'If our name could be kept out of it, lieutenant, I think a substantial donation could be made to any police charity you care to name.'

'Are you trying to bribe us, Signorina Beaufort?' The lieutenant looked sideways at the sergeant who had come with him. They were both middle-aged men who knew they would probably climb no higher up the promotion ladder before retirement.

Nina looked at both of them in turn. 'Yes, I think I am. There is no scandal involved in this. All I'm asking for is privacy, especially for my sister. Wouldn't you wish the same for your wife or sister in the same circumstances?'

'The circumstances could never be the same, signorina,' said the lieutenant, eye running round the grand apartment, then winking at the sergeant, finally settling back on Nina. 'But the sergeant and I appreciate your position.'

'What's going on?' demanded Lucas.

'I'm offering them some inducement to keep our name out of the matter.'

'No! I'm against any sort of bribery.' But Lucas did not look squarely at her as he said it. He had bribed her husband, which was worse than bribing any policeman.

Nina turned back to the two policemen. For the first time in God knew how long she had acted positively for someone else's benefit. What she was suggesting was both immoral and illegal, but ethics did not worry her if it meant Sally could be protected. 'My father dissociates himself from what I've just offered you. He is sometimes more honest than pragmatic.'

The lieutenant raised an eyebrow. He believed that an honest

247

rich man had to be a contradiction in terms, pragmatic or otherwise. 'We all have our standards, signorina,' he said tongue in cheek. 'Will you pay in cash or by cheque?'

'Cash,' said Nina. 'A cheque would have our name on it. Ours and yours.'

The lieutenant did not miss the point: he smiled at the acumen of this beautiful American woman. No wonder the Americans were successful in business, when even their womenfolk knew how to make the dollar work. 'The sergeant and I will leave the amount to your discretion, signorina. Americans are noted for their generosity.'

The police went away and Lucas made a show of being angry at the bribery. He was surprised that Nina had taken such a course. It would have been more likely coming from Margaret or Prue; or himself. But he was afraid to offer a bribe any more: the last one had bounced back at him too hard.

'I hope you don't make a practice of that,' he said.

'I thought I was doing the right thing. You were actually asking them to keep our name out of it, yet you wanted them to do it for nothing. I didn't think you were that mean with money.'

'I'm not.' He tried to sound indignant but it came out more like petulance. Which made Nina look at him, for he had never been petulant, either. 'It was the principle.'

'Well, it's money under the bridge now. We'll bury Philip and leave for home as soon as we can. You'd better leave before the funeral, just in case. If Sally feels up to it, Prue and I will go to the church and cemetery with her.'

'Is he being buried as a Catholic?'

'I suppose we'd better. I don't know what he was, but his father was a Sicilian and I guess all Sicilians are Catholics of some sort.'

'Did you know who his father was?'

'Yes.'

'And you introduced your sister to a man like that? The son of a Mafia gangster.'

'I only found out when it was too late. We seem to have a talent for that – us girls, I mean. Finding out things too late.'

That hurt him, but she did not know it. 'Well, while we're bribing people, there's the housekeeper and her nephew to be kept quiet. Though I doubt if Italians can keep secrets, they're so damned talkative.'

'You haven't read any Italian history. Lucia and her nephew will be all right, they have a lot of affection for Sally. Italians protect the people they love. Unlike Americans.'

248

'What do you mean by that?'

'Don't be so touchy, Daddy. It was only a general observation.'

As Lucas had said, Sally was indeed in a state of shock. But she was brought home from the hospital and put to bed in the apartment, where Nina, Prue and Lucia took turns in nursing her. Margaret was telephoned and said she would fly over immediately but was dissuaded from it by Prue, who all at once had the chance to prove she was as adult as she claimed.

'It won't help, Meg. The fewer Beauforts around, the better. We're going to get Daddy out of here as soon as we can. We'll bring Sally home as soon as she's fit to put on a plane. We're chartering a Constellation and we'll get away quietly. Will you ask Magnus to fly over as soon as possible? Daddy says there is not much of Philip's estate here in Italy, but some things may need to be cleaned up.'

Lucas left for home on the morning of the funeral. Only Nina went to the funeral, Prue remaining with Sally. The priest looked askance at the small crowd of mourners: Nina, Lucia, Enrico and Philip's secretary from the EUR office. The secretary had wondered if some of Signor Mann's business acquaintances should be invited, but Nina had vetoed the idea. Signor Mann's unexpected heart attack had made Signora Mann very ill and she did not want to have to face the condolences of strangers. Signor Mann had been a quiet man, as the secretary must have noticed, and it would be a mark of respect for him to be buried as he had lived. The secretary, wreathed in black and with a much larger severance cheque than she had expected, had agreed wholeheartedly that Signor Mann deserved what he would have wanted. The news of the manner of his death might eventually leak out, Nina thought, but the Beaufort sisters would be gone by then.

They left Rome in the chartered Constellation two days after the funeral, a nurse, brought in by Magnus from Kansas City, travelling back with them. Magnus himself stayed on in Rome to dispose of the lease on the apartment, all the furnishings, Sally's plane which she had not flown for six months, their two cars and the odds and ends of Philip's life. It was Lucia who came to him and told him she had witnessed a will for Signor Mann only the day before he had died.

'Almost as if he had a premonition, signore.'

'Where is it, signora?'

Lucia's English was not good, but it was good enough for Magnus to understand her. She had taken an envelope to Signor Mann's bank. It would be there in his safe deposit box.

It was, along with other papers. Magnus did not find it easy to get access to the box; he had to bring someone from the US Embassy to confirm that he was acting for the widow of Philip Mann and that, since Mr Mann had been a United States citizen, his papers were the property of his wife, a United States citizen. The bank spread its hands and gave over the contents of the box; it also reluctantly revealed that it held a considerable balance in Signor Mann's account. Several billion lire, to be inexact. Magnus, accustomed though he was to zero numbers, still blinked. He wondered what astronomical figures Lucas's wealth would add up to in lire.

Besides Philip's will, a six-line document that left everything to Sally, there was a letter from a Chicago firm of lawyers and a photostat copy of Antonio Gentleman's will, leaving everything to Philip. The letter stated that it was understood where certain bequests by the said Mr Gentleman could be found. In the safe deposit box, among the other papers, was the address of a bank in Zurich and the number of an account held there.

Magnus tidied up everything that he could for the moment in Rome, then flew to Zurich. He checked into the Baur au Lac, treating himself to the best at Lucas's expense. Next morning he went to Tony Gentleman's bank, introduced himself to the Director. The Director had not heard of Philip's death, but Magnus produced the death certificate and gave a short verbal account of how Philip had been shot by some unknown robbers.

'So many of our foreign clients seem to die violently,' said the Director. 'We Swiss only die violently by breaking our necks on the ski slopes.'

Magnus sympathized with the risks the Swiss took on their mountains and asked if he might see a statement of Mr Gentleman's secret account. 'There will be no withdrawal, of course, until my client has decided what she wants done with it.'

The Director had not missed the significance of the middle name, Sarah Beaufort Gentleman, in the will. Magnus had said he was from Kansas City and the Director had put several facts together in his mind, though he had been surprised that Beaufort money should be linked with Mafia money. The Swiss prided themselves on knowing where all the substantial money in the world was located. It meant that no *faux pas* as to identity were made when the substantial money came to Switzerland looking for a haven.

'Mr Gentleman had a substantial amount in his account.' *Substantial* was a favourite word with the Director; men of substance were his gods. 'Shall I quote it to you in Swiss francs or US dollars?'

'Dollars,' said Magnus, afraid of more zeros.

'Seven million three hundred and forty two thousand eight hundred and sixteen dollars. And some cents, which we normally do not bother about in such sums. You look surprised, Herr McKea. I thought you would have been accustomed to such substantial amounts.'

'I am,' said Magnus. 'Only not from those sources.'

'We make no moral judgements, Herr McKea. All money is clean once it enters our doors.'

Magnus was impressed by such piousness but said nothing. He went back to the Baur au Lac. By chance he met an English-woman in the bar, took her to dinner, spent the night with her and caught a plane out next morning for New York and Kansas City. He could not remember having had a more interesting and enjoyable trip since he had entered his father's firm.

On the way back he debated whom he should see first, Sally or Lucas. It was Lucas who was paying his fee and expenses, but Sally was the beneficiary of the will. In the end he decided he would see them together.

Lucas and Sally waited for him in the drawing-room. Though summer was almost over, the weather was still hot. Lucas wore a seersucker suit and Sally was in a simple black dress that accentuated her thinness and the lack of colour in her face. Her blonde hair, still cut short in the French style, was as lustreless as an elderly woman's.

'Your husband has left you – ' Magnus looked at his notebook and quoted from it. 'All of it, I'm assured by the Director of the bank, perfectly clean respectable money.'

'Ridiculous,' said Lucas.

'I don't want the money,' said Sally.

'Of course you don't!' Lucas was the Lucas of old; he strode about the room stiff with fury and authority. 'It's some sort of sick joke! You can't touch it!'

'You can't leave it there,' said Magnus.

'Why not?' said Sally.

But Lucas suddenly looked dubious. 'It *is* criminally wasteful. One shouldn't leave money lying around doing nothing.'

'Could we give it away to some charity?' Sally was too wan and listless to care about the money: it was another burden she did not want.

'We could, I suppose. But it's an awful lot of money to unload without giving away the source.' Magnus saw that Sally could dismiss the money, turn her back on it. But Lucas, a money man all his life, could not do the same without a great deal of heartburn. It would be like turning his back on the flag. 'Unless we spread it over a number of years. You could give it to one of the international charities based in Europe.'

Sally waved an indifferent hand. 'Do that, then. You choose the charity, Magnus. I really don't care.'

Magnus looked at Lucas. 'Well?'

'It's her money. But if it ever got out where it came from . . . That's what worries me. When you are dealing in sums like that, there is always the possibility of a leak. I – ' It was almost a physical effort for him to say it: 'I think it should be left there for a while. A year, maybe two. Until we are sure that Sally's name won't be connected with the Gentlemans.' He frowned, the word not sounding right in his ear. 'Philip and his father.'

Sally shrugged: we could be talking about some petty cash, Magnus thought. 'Anything. I said I don't really care.'

So the money was left in the bank in Zurich on an interest-drawing basis. Lucas could not accept the thought of the money just lying there doing *nothing*.

2

Sally did not recover quickly from the events of that late summer of 1958. It was six months before she began to act and sound like the girl her sisters remembered. Then she bought herself another Maserati and another plane, this time a ten-year-old British Tiger Moth, and began to look for freedom on the back roads and in the skies of Missouri and Kansas. She drove fast and flew high, working herself out of her depression as if it were a physical thing that could be blown away by the winds.

It was Prue, the youngest and least experienced in misfortune, who put her on the road to recovery. 'You're dosing yourself up with self-pity.'

Sally would not accept that, if only out of pride. 'You just don't know what I've been through – '

'Nuts. You and Nina and Meg have all been through hell – I just hope it never happens to me. But sometimes you sound as if you're trying to act like a poor little rich girl. Other people go through what you've all been through, but they don't do it in such comfort. You wouldn't get much sympathy from some poor girl who's lost her husband and her baby and is living in some slum in New York or Chicago or somewhere.'

'What are you, a Communist or something?'

'That would make some of the boys I know laugh. They say I cost them twice as much as any other girl they know. No, I'm a dedicated hedonist and I think our money is lovely. But if anything bad ever happens I'm not going to mope about and think there's nobody worse off than me.'

'You just wait till it happens.'

But Sally had to concede to herself that there was a lot of truth in what Prue had said. She liked being back home in Kansas City; there were indeed far worse places to be unhappy. She thought of herself as an uncomplicated girl whose adult life had been a series of bruising complications; she was not aware of the full measure of herself, that within her lay the seeds of the complications that had struck her. It did not occur to her that she might have gone to an analyst for help; that would only have antagonized her father if he learned of it. She had been brought up on the unspoken principle that one did not go to an outsider for help, did not confide in a stranger. Comfort and advice was there in the family for the asking; the very extreme any of them might do would be to consult Magnus. So far no one in the family, for all their sympathy, had helped her understand herself.

So over the next year she went seeking the girl she had been before she had left to go to Vassar. At first she seemed to be succeeding; she began to fit easily into the pattern of the family. Nina and Margaret, she noticed, were no longer girls: Nina was thirty-seven, Margaret thirty-two: they were old enough now for her to see shades of their mother in them. Nina still lived in the main house with their father, engaged herself in a full social life but had no steady man. Margaret lived in the second house with Martha and Emma, was devoted to them but managed to live an even busier social life than Nina. Her constant escort was Bruce Alburn.

'He's no Marlon Brando, but he's steady and reliable. And that's a change for any of us.'

'Are you going to marry him?' Sally asked.

'He hasn't asked me yet. Bruce likes to take his time. I don't think he'd even clean his teeth on the spur of the moment.'

'God, you make him sound dull!'

'He has his moments.' But Margaret did not elaborate and

Sally could only surmise that Bruce, having given a great deal of thought to it, had at some time got Meg into bed.

In June of 1960 she read that Belgium was giving the Congo its independence and she wondered if Michele and her husband were still in Leopoldville. The thought of Michele brought back an ache she thought she had cured.

In the late summer of that year Margaret and Bruce began working for Richard Nixon in the coming election against John F. Kennedy. Lucas had seemingly lost all interest in politics, but Margaret was turning into Kansas City's Perle Mesta. She had to scratch for talent to come even remotely close to a comparison; unlike Perle Mesta she restricted herself to Midwest Republicans and the faithful of that year were not rich in salon wit. But they were shrewd and what they lacked in wit they made up for in common sense. At one of Margaret's parties Sally met Charlie Luman.

A visiting British professor, on exchange to the University of Missouri, was holding forth on his impressions of America. It was a time when Americans, succumbing to a national streak of masochism, were paying foreign lecturers and writers to come and tell them what was wrong with them.

'Take American football,' said the visiting professor, who had not played sport since he had won the egg-and-spoon race at his prep school. 'It is designed solely for the pleasure and ego-gratification of men who have already stopped playing the game, namely the coaches. There is none of the creative imagination one finds in rugby, where the players are encouraged to have initiative. If any player on the field in the American game had a spontaneous thought, it would be as sinful as sodomy in the huddle.'

'I think I'll crash-tackle that English faggot,' said a tall, heavily-built man standing beside Sally. 'He's talking sacrilege.'

'Do you play football?' Sally asked.

'For the Los Angeles Rams,' he said with some quiet pride.

'You're a long way from home.'

'This is home. KC. My old man is Senator Luman, Walter Luman. I'm Charlie Luman. Hi.' He put out a hand that looked as if it could have cupped a football lengthways. 'You're one of the Beaufort sisters. Which one?'

She told him, after extricating her hand from his paw. 'Do you live out in California?'

'Laguna Beach.' He had one of the friendliest smiles she had seen, simple, innocent and trusting. He had been smiling ever

254

since he had first spoken to her and she wondered if he went into crash-tackles with the same broad flash of teeth. 'You're the one who drives and flies, right? I've got a licence myself, a commercial one. I've been working for two years with Pan Am part-time. I'm retiring from football the end of this season.'

'I thought all football players wanted to be coaches?'

'I'm too kind-hearted. I'd pat the guys on the back after losing, instead of kicking them in the ass. Pardon the language.'

He was too clean to be true, like someone out of a comic book. He had that sort of look: crew-cut blond hair, strong jaw, bright blue eyes, a physique like that of Superman. She looked a little closer, wondering if his smile was painted on.

'Are you always kind-hearted? With girls too?'

'Always.' The smile seemed to widen, if that were possible.

Then Jack Minett was beside them, appearing with that sleight-of-hand skill, like a modest genie, of the best behind-the-scenes political worker.

'Nice to see you again, Sally.' He had not been on the estate since the death of his son. Once a month Margaret took her and Frank's children over to the house in Johnson County and he respected her for that; but until tonight neither he nor Francesca had been invited here. And Francesca, not that he could blame her, had pleaded a headache and not come with him. 'You've met our hero.'

'Hero?'

'Last year he was voted Most Valuable Player. He's worth 20,000 votes to his old man in this year's election.'

'Not with rugby players,' said Charlie Luman, but Jack Minett just looked blank.

'Meg's the one who should be running for office. It's time we had some women in it. There aren't enough of them in Washington.'

'There are one or two,' said Sally, 'and my father thinks that's one or two too many. He'd never let Meg run for office. You should know that,' she said, not meaning to be unkind but realizing at once that that was how she sounded.

Jack Minett was used to unkind words, unwitting or otherwise. 'I once told Frank that your father isn't immortal. When your father dies I hope I'm still around to see what happens to you girls.'

'Jack,' she said, surprised, 'you sound malicious.'

'No,' he said, 'just expectant.'

He disappeared with the same cloud-of-smoke effect as he had appeared and Charlie Luman said, 'Who's he?'

'A nice man in a dirty game. Are you going to follow your father into politics?'

He shook his head, the smile still there like a pleasant birthmark. 'I told you, I'm too kind. Who was the last kindly politician you heard of?'

'Jesus Christ,' said Prue, coming up to them. 'And look what happened to him.'

'Don't listen to her profanities,' said Sally.

'I've had you pointed out to me,' Prue said to Charlie. 'They say you're a killer on the field. You be kind to my sister or I'll kick you in your protector.'

For a moment Charlie's smile seemed entirely without humour or kindness. Then he said, 'I've just been telling her, I'm always kind to women.'

'Then you'll be a change.' Then she looked at Magnus as he joined them. 'Except you, of course, Magnus.'

'What have I done now?' he said.

'Take me out on the terrace for a dance. They're playing our number.'

Magnus cocked an ear. '*The Missouri Waltz?* How did President Truman get in here?'

The two of them drifted off and Sally said to Charlie, 'Would you like to go for a flight?'

'Now?'

'Why not? There's a full moon.'

On the way out they passed a painting hanging in the entrance hall. 'Is that a Titian?'

She stopped in surprise. 'How did you know?'

'I went to college on a football scholarship – my old man doesn't have any money despite the fact he's a senator. I had to study *something*, so out of the blue I picked art history. And I got interested in it. Where'd you get that? Is it your father's?'

'No, it's mine. It was left to me. I've lent it to Meg till I have a place of my own.'

'Boy, were you in luck! I suppose you've got to be someone like you Beauforts to be left something like that.'

She put a firm hand on his arm. looked up at him. 'Charlie, before we go out that door, let's get something straight. You make another remark about *you Beauforts* and I'll loop the loop and do my best to toss you out of the plane. You understand?'

He had stopped smiling. 'Sure. You're just Sally Smith from now on.'

'It's as good a name as any.'

She had not even looked at the Titian. Magnus had been contacted by the Chicago lawyers and he had gone up there and returned with the news that there was much more of value in the Gentleman home than he had expected. Sally had refused to go back with him and in the end Margaret, for a reason she did not name, had said she would go with Magnus. The house had been sold and all its contents but the Titian and a secretaire with Sèvres porcelain plaques. Margaret had brought those two items back with her.

'The Titian is too valuable to give away to some museum just now,' Margaret had said. 'Someone might start trying to track it down and your name could come out.'

Sally was tired of trying to hide; she was beginning to feel like a criminal on the run. Someone from the Mafia . . . 'Won't the dealer who sold it to Philip's father wonder what's happened to it? He'll know that Tony Gentleman is dead.'

'The lawyers are going to say, if anyone asks, that it has gone back to relatives in Italy who wish to remain anonymous. The funny thing is, the lawyers are not the crooks I expected. They're every bit as respectable as Magnus, only stuffier. Tony Gentleman was doing his darnedest to look respectable.'

'What about the secretaire?'

'I just liked the look of that. It made me think Mother would have liked it.'

'Not from *him*, I'll bet. All right, you can have it. But I wish you hadn't brought home that painting.'

'You don't have to think of its being Philip's or his father's – it doesn't have any sentimental value like that painting of Nina's. It's a Titian and the last value you'd put on it would be sentimental.'

'Oh God, how mercenary can you get!'

'I said that to you once as a kid, remember? Keep it, Sally – you'll get used to it. You don't just go throwing away treasures like that to museums as if it was an old suit of Philip's. That's profligacy and Grandfather would spin in his grave if he knew of it. I think even Daddy might go a bit light-headed, too.'

'He wanted to give away the money in Switzerland.'

'You can always make more money. You can't make another Titian. A good fake one, maybe, but not a real one.'

So Sally had kept the painting, but put it out of mind by giving it to Margaret to hang in her home. She went out of the house now without another look at it. Charlie paused a moment

257

to look at it again, then he followed her.

They drove in to the Municipal Airport and he walked around the open two-seater Tiger Moth admiring it as much as he had the Titian.

'The only way to fly,' he said, and she warmed to him for that; he was a man after her own heart. 'Pretty soon flying like this is going to be dead. Another fifteen, twenty years and nobody's going to know what it's like to fly with the wind in your face.'

'Make sure of your seat-belt. I feel like some aerobatics tonight.'

She was pleased that he accepted without question that she could fly well enough to indulge in some stunt flying. They took off and climbed straight into the face of a full moon that threw the countryside below into bright relief. She always felt a sense of escape, of freedom, as soon as her plane was airborne. She wore no helmet and she let the wind tear at her hair. She turned west and flew out over Kansas. The farmlands stretched away beneath the moon like a vast quilt: America was in bed. She picked up the Union Pacific railroad tracks heading for Topeka: steel lightning frozen and laid on the countryside. A freight train crawled west: she could imagine the hoarse cry of its whistle; the sound of the heart of America at night. What sounds had Du Tisne, Bourgmond, Pike heard in the night as they had headed out across the plains? All at once she wished for the long ago; but she knew at the same time that nostalgia was only another form of escape. She pulled the Tiger Moth up into a loop, spun out of it and went down in a series of long fluttering sweeps, waltzing the plane down till she was only 1000 feet above the ground. Then she turned east and headed back towards Kansas City. She flew over the city, swung back along the river and at last touched down at the airport.

Charlie was out of his cockpit at once, stood beside the plane waiting to lift her down. But she sat for a few moments, feeling like a prisoner who had been recaptured. Then, reluctantly, she clambered out of the cockpit and let Charlie lift her down.

They drove back home. The party was still going on in Margaret's house, but she had lost the mood for any sort of gathering. She got out of the car, waited till Charlie came round and stood beside her.

'Goodnight, Charlie. Don't get hurt in any tackles.'

She put her face up for the expected goodnight kiss, but he just squeezed her arm. 'I'm going to be busy huckstering for Dad, but I'll be back here the end of the week, before I go back to California. How about dinner Saturday night?'

She went inside to bed. She thought about him for a few minutes, without excitement or much interest. Then she fell asleep and dreamed of Michele and woke in the morning depressed and inexplicably, terribly lonely.

To throw off her depression she went flying again that day, taking George Biff with her. But storm clouds came up out of the south; far away to the south-west she saw the dark cone of a tornado. For one awful moment, that brought a shiver to her immediately afterwards, she wanted to fly towards the storm, right into the heart of the twister, to have the plane and herself disintegrate into pieces too small ever to be found. Then she thought of George and she turned the plane round and sped back towards the airport.

Driving home in the Maserati George said, 'You ain't happy. You still miserable about your lost baby?'

'That's part of it, George. But don't go playing the wise old black retainer with me. Sometimes you sound like Uncle Tom.'

'I wasn't black, sometimes I'd whip the ass off of the lot of you.'

She jerked her head in surprise. He had often chastised her and her sisters when they were young, but she had never heard him as angry as he sounded now.

'That was your daddy's biggest fault – he never carried a whip with him.' She had allowed him to take the wheel of the car and he was staring straight ahead, concentrating on the road. 'He give you all a belt or two once in a while, you'd of bounced back quicker from all the things've happened to you. My sister, the second one, she just lost her third baby. She ain't sitting around waiting for Judgement Day.'

'George, what's got into you? And slow *down*. You don't usually drive as fast as his. You want to get us a ticket?'

He eased his foot off the pedal, sat further back in his seat, continued to stare straight ahead. 'Sorry, Miz Sally.'

'All right, don't start sounding like Uncle Tom again. Sound like George Biff. What's the matter?'

He took the car along the Ward Parkway at a sedate pace, past the mansions that looked as impregnable as castles. But he was indifferent to them: after all he lived in the grandest castle of them all. But he knew that stone walls could be conquered from the inside. 'I been to a coupla meetings with my brother, the youngest one. Things is changing for us blacks. I'm too old to care, but I guess the meeting last night infected me. Affected?'

'Either way, I know what you mean.'

259

'You better get used to it. Us folk ain't gonna be the same from now on. Not the young 'uns.'

'Have you let Daddy know how you feel?'

'It ain't the way *I* feel. Not all the time, that is. You just got me worked up back there, was all. But your daddy knows what's happening. He's knowed it ever since Little Rock three years ago. Him and me, we talk about it. Miz Meg, she knows what's happening. But you and Miz Nina and Prue, you never give a mind to it. All you mind is yourself. That was what got me spitting a while ago.' He turned the car in through the gates, drove it down to the stables, pulled up and got out. 'Thanks for the ride.'

'Don't you dismiss me like that, George. I do mind what happens to other people. I know someone in Europe who's mulatto, and she's told me what it's like to be snubbed because she's not all-white.'

He grinned, shook his head. 'Miz Sal, you trying to tell me some coloured friend of yours in Europe, she gets snubbed in one of them fancy places you always going to, you think that's the same as Jim Crow back here in Mississippi or Alabama, someplace like that? You ain't that dumb. You just ain't thinking right.'

He turned and walked away to his quarters above the stables, not hurrying, back straight, unafraid of anything she might say or do. She was furious with him; at the same time she wished she had his dignity. She was almost back to the main house before she realized she was half-running. She slowed down. Suddenly she wanted to write to Michele, but had no idea where to address the letter. She remembered with bitterness that Michele had not written to offer condolences on the death of Philip.

Saturday night Charlie took her to dinner in a restaurant in Country Club Plaza. It was a modest restaurant and it occurred to Sally that, though she had eaten in such places in Rome, Paris, Nice, she had never done so in Kansas City. Occasionally, in such small inconsequential revelations, she realized how rigidly protected she had been in her home town.

'You hungry?' Charlie picked up the menu.

'You order for me.' Food had never concerned her; she had a goat's palate. 'Do you have a girl out in Los Angeles?'

'I play the field.' For a moment he was sober as he looked at her over the top of the big menu card; then there was that wide bright smile again. 'That sounds big-headed. I just don't want to get tied down, that's all. Not yet anyway. How about a nice juicy sirloin?'

'Great,' she said, comparing him with Philip who had said no to steak every time it had been presented to him. Charlie Luman, she decided, was a nice uncomplicated man with simple tastes, someone restful and nice to have around. She wished he was not going back to California tomorrow.

He told her about himself, a simple uncomplicated biography; she supposed it was the life of thousands of boys, though not all of them finished up playing for the Los Angeles Rams. He did not ask her about herself and she proffered nothing; he would never understand about Cindy and Michele and nothing must be revealed about Philip. People stopped by the table and patted him on the back, proud of him and proud to be seen talking to him; he accepted all the compliments with a modesty that she saw was as natural as his smile. All the passers-by asked was that he stay whole until Old KC had a football team of its own and he could come home so that they could cheer him every week of the fall. He smiled and promised to try and do that.

He introduced Sally and everyone smiled politely and their pride in Charlie increased: he was in the right company, sure enough. When they left the restaurant everyone nodded and waved and smiled again: they went out on a surf of goodwill.

'They love you!'

'They liked you, too.'

'Only because I was with you.'

He took her to a night-club downtown, where again everyone seemed to recognize him; his size, if nothing else, made people look at him twice. At, she guessed, six feet four and 230 pounds, he was not inconspicuous. They listened to jazz that was her father's sort of music; she was tone deaf but she enjoyed looking at Charlie's obvious enjoyment of the band. Idly, almost with detachment, she thought he would be the sort of beau for her whom her father would approve.

'Charlie Parker, Bird, used to play here,' he said. 'I was too young to have heard him. Do you ever regret you came too late to meet some of your heroes?'

Though romantic, she could not remember ever having had any heroes. And it was too late now. 'Sometimes,' she said.

He drove her home through the soft summer night. She had expected him to ask her to go somewhere with him and she had been undecided whether she would say yes or no. But the question did not come up, they drove straight home. He pulled in before the main house, but made no attempt to get out of the car.

'Would you like to come in for a while?'

He had been quiet and sober all the way home, no hint of a smile. 'I think we better call it quits.'

'Quits?' She had enough sensitivity to see that something was worrying him; she did not attempt any sarcasm when she said, 'Have we started anything?'

'Maybe not you. But me –' He put his huge hand gently on the back of her neck, stroked the short hair there. 'I like you more than any girl I've met. But you're – *sad*. What makes you that way, I don't know. But you are. And I wouldn't want to add to that sadness.'

Some day, she knew, the whole story of Philip and her marriage to him would come out. Lucas had seen that no announcement had ever been made, but it had been known in their own circle in Kansas City that Sally Beaufort had been Mrs Philip Mann. When she had come home the word had quietly been put out that her husband had died of a heart attack and that at the same time she had lost her baby; the double tragedy had seemed to silence any gossip that anyone might have wanted to voice. The two policemen in Rome had done their job well, better than any police could have done in the same circumstances in an American city; nothing had appeared in any newspapers and the Manns had quietly disappeared from the scene. The American correspondents in Rome had been more concerned with more important things; by the time the Manns were missed, Pope John had just been elected and everyone was busy thrusting their heads into the windows in the Vatican that he had thrown open. The Beauforts, none of them believers, should have been properly grateful to the Catholic Church. But Sally, pessimistically, was convinced that some day, somehow, the fact of her marriage to Philip and the circumstances of his death would emerge.

So Charlie knew nothing of what made her sad; but it had been perceptive of him to notice it. More perceptive of him than she had expected: she thought she had at last managed to hide her depression from outsiders.

'You knew I'd lost my husband?' She did not want to pile it on by mentioning the baby.

'Sure. But it's more than that makes you sad.'

*Indeed it is.* 'Why do you think you would make me unhappy?'

'I'll tell you some other time.'

He leaned across and kissed her; not roughly or passionately but almost like a brother. God, she suddenly thought, he's queer! Then was both amused and angry at herself: why shouldn' he be a homosexual? It was just that he was so different from the ones she had known in Europe. After all, wasn't she one herself?

'Are you homosexual, Charlie?' Maybe he would understand about Michele after all.

He leaned away from her, started to laugh. But she noticed that he laughed silently; then the laughter subsided into great sighs. She leaned forward and saw that he was crying. She reached for his hand, held it.

'Charlie – I *understand*. I know what it's like – '

He shook his head, took out a handkerchief and wiped his eyes. 'You *don't* understand! Jesus, I'm not a faggot. I just can't get it up, that's all. I'm impotent!'

She had not expected that he had anger like this in him. She let go his hand, suddenly afraid of the physical force throbbing in him; he seemed to fill the front seat of the car, threatening to explode.

'It happened my first year in pro football. I got kicked in the balls. I was wearing a faulty protector and it just cracked and sliced into me like it was glass. At school I read that book of Hemingway's, *The Sun Also Rises*, and I used to think about that guy, Jake whatever-his-name-was, and how terrible it would be to be like him. I was a stud at school. I'm not boasting. You played football, the girls were always available. And then?' He put his hand down to his crotch, let it lie there a moment. 'The doctors did everything they could, but the damage was too great. It was just one of those once-in-a-lifetime things, one of 'em said. Who'd want it to happen to him twice? How could it happen more than once?'

'Who else knows?'

'My mother and dad. And the head coach of the Rams.'

'No girl knows?'

'Only one, a girl out in California. The first one I went to bed with after I got out of hospital. I wouldn't believe what the doctors had told me. Maybe she's told other people about it. Girls talk about things like that, I guess.'

'Not all of them. This one wouldn't.'

He reached for the back of her neck again, gently stroked her hair. 'Come out to LA some time, see me play. I'm still 100 per cent out there on the field.'

'No, Charlie. I think I prefer the man you are here. Out there on the football field I think you might be another man altogether.'

'You're right,' he said slowly. 'I hate every son-of-a-bitch who pulls on a helmet. I'm better now than when they first

263

signed me on. They had to ruin my balls to make me Most Valuable Player.'

'Don't be so bitter.'

His hand stopped: for one awful moment she thought he was going to snap her neck. 'Don't be stupid, Sally. What do you expect me to be?'

'I'm sorry. It slipped out.' And it should not have: if anyone should have understood his feelings, it should have been her.

His hand resumed its stroking. 'Okay, you're forgiven. The funny thing is, if anyone could make me forget being bitter I think it'd be you. There's something between you and me that clicks. I don't know what it is, but it's there. For me, anyway.'

'For me, too,' she said and tried for his and her own sake to be truthful; but couldn't be certain. She leaned across and kissed him on the lips. It was not a passionate open-mouth kiss; but it had love in it. 'Write me occasionally, Charlie. When you're feeling bitter.'

## 3

So Charlie Luman went back to California and she did not see him again till November, when John F. Kennedy was elected President; a political disaster that convinced Lucas that God was not only a Roman Catholic Democrat but un-American as well. But he had not made the mistake this time of throwing an Election Night party to honour Richard Nixon as the new President. Remembering a previous lost wager, he had not been game enough to bet against his worst fears.

'Money has always run this country, there's nothing wrong with that,' he said. 'But it should not be used to buy the White House.'

'Well,' said Prue, home from Vassar for a few days, 'I voted for Jack Kennedy and I think he's the best thing that could have happened to the country. At least you should be happy we have a politician as President instead of a golfing general.'

'Richard Nixon is a politician. And if he'd been elected he'd have got in on his merits, not his father's money. And I'll thank you not to go around boasting that you voted for Kennedy. I was sorry, Charlie, that your father lost out. I thought he was bound to be returned. The country's going to the dogs.'

'Dad's philosophical,' said Charlie. 'He's always said you shouldn't go in for politics unless you expect to lose.'

'How are you taking *your* retirement? I understand you had to give up football before you intended.'

'It was going to be my last season anyway. But my knee has gone, so they let me go early. I'm full-time now with Pan Am. I do a couple of years on piston-engined aircraft, then I start a training course for jets. We're getting into a whole new era.'

'The prospect doesn't excite me,' said Lucas.

As if to forget the defeat of their Republican candidate, Margaret and Bruce Alburn announced that they were to be married. Lucas suggested that Inauguration Day might be a suitable date; all their friends, being Republicans, would not be interested in what was going on on that day in Washington. But Margaret, who had a sense of occasion and an eye to the future, vetoed that.

'No. Some of our friends may turn out to be Kennedy-lovers. Even some of our business friends.'

'God forbid,' said Lucas, but he had no real faith in the Almighty any more.

Margaret and Bruce were married a week after Inauguration Day and went off to Rio de Janeiro for their honeymoon. Lucas had formed a new bank, Missouri International, and several branches had been set up in South American countries. Bruce thought the honeymoon trip would be a good opportunity to look in on the Brazilian office.

'I swear that their foreplay consists of profit and loss figures,' said Prue. 'Meg's getting as bad as Bruce. I'll bet right now on their wedding night she's sitting up in bed checking the cost of the reception.'

'Did you hear what the city government gave her for a wedding present?' Nina said. 'Not that they meant it as a present. They have re-zoned that land up in Platte County, the land she got from Frank. Magnus tells me it's now worth about five million dollars.'

'Poor Frank,' said Sally.

The three sisters, still in their wedding reception gowns, shoes off, were lolling about in Nina's bedroom. It had been a long happy day and Sally was once again aware of how content she could be in her sisters' company. But she had begun to grow restless again, though she had not yet said anything.

'You were marvellous, Prue, with Martha and Emma,' she said. 'You're the last one I'd expect to be a child-lover.'

'I hope you haven't turned over your old library to them,' said Nina.

'I love their innocence,' said Prue, smiling warmly at the

thought of Margaret's two children. They were now nine and ten, both pretty, both quiet, sometimes seeming like strangers among the more outgoing Beaufort sisters who were their mother and their aunts. 'I shouldn't want to spoil that. It'll happen, nothing's more certain, but I shouldn't want to be the one who does it. It's hard to believe we were once as innocent as that.'

'Are you kidding?' said Nina. 'You stopped being innocent when Mother took you off her breast.'

'Was it as late as that?' said Prue innocently.

'Let's hope Bruce proves a good stepfather. How's Charlie coming along, Sally?'

Sally shrugged, determined to keep Charlie's secret. 'I don't think he's the settling down kind.'

'I'd have thought he was just that kind,' said Prue. 'I saw him this afternoon, he never took his eyes off you. You haven't turned him down, have you?'

'You're an idiot if you have,' said Nina.

Over the next few months Charlie stopped in at Kansas City on his way across country and each time Nina and Prue asked Sally what was happening between her and Charlie. The pressure began to tell on her; yet she could not bring herself to tell Charlie that she did not want to see him any more. She liked his company, felt a deep aching sympathy for him. But he never mentioned marriage and she knew as well as he that any sort of permanent relationship between them was hopeless.

The world spun on, seemingly moving a little quicker now. The Russians shot a man into space, which pet-lovers all over the world thought was more humane than the Russians' previous missile, a dog. Cuban exiles, aided and abetted by Washington, landed at a place called the Bay of Pigs; Lucas suggested it should have been re-named the Bay of Scapegoats, since over the next few weeks everyone but Mary Pickford was blamed for the fiasco. Then the Americans shot a man into space and President Kennedy talked of landing a man on the moon before the end of the decade. Word came out of New Guinea that men there were still killing each other with bows and arrows. Perspective, as Edith would have said, was always there if you looked for it.

At the end of summer Sally announced that she was going back to Europe for an extended stay.

'I'll come with you,' said Prue, who had finished at Vassar.

'Dammit!' said Lucas. 'Why can't you girls stay put?'

Though he had had responsibilities as both a father and a

266

businessman, Lucas had never really been subjected to great personal pressures. He had married a girl who had been his own and his parents' choice and his marriage had been ideally happy. But sometimes he wondered if he had failed his daughters, though he could not find enough evidence to convict himself. He did not believe in too harsh self-prosecution, except for what he had done to Nina. And time, he sometimes thought, was healing that.

'We'll go to London,' said Prue, 'and live a quiet simple life.'

'You can live that here.' But he knew now that he could never win an argument with any of his daughters. His favourite was turning out to be Margaret, who seemed to think more and more like him as she grew older.

Charlie Luman came by Kansas City a couple of days before Sally and Prue left for England. He came to dinner at the main house and Lucas spent the evening beaming at him as if he were the answer to a father's prayer. Charlie, bemused by such approval, was not the brightest and wittiest of dinner guests. Afterwards he and Sally went for a walk in the grounds.

'Why was your father all over me tonight? I was waiting for him to ask me to join the Beaufort Oil football team.'

'He's looking for another son-in-law.' They had reached a level in their relationship where they could talk without embarrassment.

He held her hand as they walked along the path: from a distance they looked in love. Which they were, but not in a way that Lucas wanted. 'Sally, I'm never going to risk it. Marriage, I mean. If I married you, or anyone else for that matter, and you got tired of never getting any proper sex and you went off and had it with some other guy, I'd go out of my mind. I'm not capable of an erection, but I sure as hell could get jealous.'

'Maybe in our old age we'll get together.'

She had not been able to bring herself to tell him about Michele. He was terribly straight about sex; she could not imagine his being tolerant about any deviation. Though they did not preoccupy him, he talked of fags and dykes as if they were the worst result of Original Sin: what they got up to was too original for him. He would probably back off from Michele if he met her with more fear than if he were faced with the entire offensive line-up of the Green Bay Packers.

'Maybe by then they'll have solved my problem.' He kissed her on the lips, holding her to him; his hands never touched her

267

breasts, he was always as chaste in his embrace as a Victorian parson. One of the better ones. 'Then, as they say, we'll have a ball.'

'Two,' she said, and back in the house Lucas heard their loud laughter and wondered why such a happy pair would not announce their engagement.

# Chapter Ten

◆

# Sally

I

Sally and Prue left for London.

The British capital had finally put the war years behind it; a new generation was emerging who thought the biggest battles to be fought were to make a quick quid or get a bird into bed. A photographer married into the Royal Family, putting the royal seal on yet another profession. Hordes of young men rushed out of the East End and the provinces to buy cameras and be professional photographers; the glossy magazines were deluged with self-portraits of Cockney cameramen who appeared too busy to button up their shirt fronts; Britain had never seen so much chest hair since the Celts took off their pelts at their summer solstice wingdings. Later on it was to see the eye-level lowered as pubic hair, never before thought an adornment, was paraded on stage and in voguish magazines; pharmaceutical companies found a new market area for their shampoos. The country began to prosper, though only the sharpest made fortunes; Prime Minister Macmillan had campaigned at the last election on the slogan *You've never had it so good*, but a few still had it better than most. The term had not yet been coined, but the Swinging Sixties was beginning and London seemed to be the place to be.

Sally and Prue rented a house in Wilton Crescent and settled in to lead a simple rich life, with Harrods as their corner grocery store and a cook-housekeeper and a manservant to take the load off their shoulders if the burden of living simply became too much. Sally bought herself an Aston Martin and once more took up racing, while Prue took up men. Again.

'I led a virtuous life back in Kansas City.'

'I noticed that,' said Sally. 'What sort of life did you lead with those men from Yale and the rest of the Ivy League?'

'Interesting. I think I'm a controlled nympho.'

'I never know when you're kidding and when you're not.'

'Neither do the men. I don't think I'm as basically honest as you and Nina. That's been the downfall of both of you.'

*You don't know me as well as you think you do.* 'You don't think Meg is honest? I mean with men.'

'I don't know,' Prue confessed. 'She plays things much closer to her chest than the rest of us. I still don't know what she ever saw in Frank Minett. Something went wrong there and I don't think it was all Frank's fault. I never liked him, he was a bit too pushy, but he never deserved to have his brains blown out. Not even by himself.'

In November 1961 the two sisters went to Hamburg where Sally had entered in a rally. She was partnered by the English girl who had raced with her previously in French rallies when Michele had made herself unavailable. Mary Venneker was a tall gangling girl who just missed being beautiful and finished up being handsome rather than pretty. She had a bosom rather too large for the slenderness of her body and expressive hands that were continually moving about as if looking for a place to rest.

They stayed at the Atlantic and the first night at dinner Mary said, 'I have someone coming by afterwards. Would you like to meet him? He's *years* older than me and he's too short, but he's absolutely adorable and if I can get a hammerlock on him I'll get him to marry me.'

'Sounds an ideal match,' said Prue. 'Is this him coming across now?'

He was in his late 40s but looked younger, except for his eyes. His hair was blond enough to hide any grey in it and under his beautifully cut suit his figure looked like that of a man who spent a lot of time on the tennis court or in the gymnasium or in the bed of a loving masseuse. But his eyes, Prue, the observer of eyes, decided, were too old to be rejuvenated by any health exercises.

'Rudi darling!' Mary rose up like a high-jumper; for a moment Sally thought that Rudi was going to disappear under Mary. She hugged him, kissed him, then introduced him. 'Rudi Schnatz. Baron Rudolph von Schnatz. He is one of the burghers of Hamburg, but that's only when he wants to become stuffy.'

Rudi Schnatz bowed, but did not click his heels as Sally and Prue expected. 'I once met your sister – I've forgotten her name. The one who was kidnapped down in Frankfurt. How is she? Is she still married to my English friend Tim Davoren?'

Tim's name was rarely mentioned now in the Beaufort family. 'No,' said Prue coolly. 'They separated a long time ago.'

'Oh? He didn't say so.'

Both sisters sat up as Schnatz sat down. 'When was that?'

Schnatz took the wine Mary poured for him, raised his glass to the three of them. 'Ladies . . .' He drank, wiped his mouth with a silk handkerchief. Then for the first time he noticed that Sally and Prue were leaning forward impatiently. 'When was it I met my friend Tim? Oh, two – no, three years ago. In Beirut.'

'Beirut? Is he living there?' Sally could feel herself pulsing with excitement. She'd be on the phone to Nina tonight, as soon as they found out where Tim could be found.

Schnatz shook his head. 'I don't think so. We met by accident, in the casino there. He was there on business, as I was.'

'What sort of business?' Prue asked.

'His or mine?' He smiled. 'No, you wouldn't ask a rude question like that of me.'

'I told you,' said Mary Venneker, suddenly sounding defensive of her loved one. 'He's one of the pillars of this town. You are, aren't you, Rudi?'

'Every centimetre of me, *Liebling*. But I'll answer Miss Beaufort's question. I was there selling arms. A perfectly proper business these days, now we are no longer at war.'

'Who do you sell to, then?' said Sally.

'Other people who want to go to war. Sounds cynical? It is,' he said disarmingly. 'But it is perfectly legitimate and governments recognize us. They don't like to sell their obsolete equipment themselves, so they have people like me do it. Well, not exactly *me*. One of my companies. That was why my friend Tim was in Beirut. He was buying guns for someone. He was a very good soldier in the war, y'know. He would know all about guns.'

'Did he tell you whom he was buying for?'

'No. To tell you the truth, he did not seem very pleased to see me. We chatted for only a few minutes, then he was gone. I wanted to have dinner with him, chat over old times, but I couldn't find him. He wasn't at any of the best hotels.' That must have sounded snobbish in his own ears because he said, 'I mean, he looked as if that was where he would stay. Most successful looking.'

Sally glanced at Prue, then both stood up. 'Excuse us. We're sure you don't want us cluttering up your night together. Just don't tire yourself out, Mary. We have to be on the starting line at eight o'clock.'

Mary had her long arm round Schnatz's shoulder. They looked an incongruous pair, she long, gangling and untidy, he short, trim and impeccably smart. What seemed even more incongruous to Sally was that Schnatz seemed genuinely fond of the awkward English girl. She had the abrupt, unexpected image of him in the company of someone more like Michele.

Upstairs in their suite looking out on the Altersee Prue said, 'Well? Do we tell Nina?'

'What's to tell?' Coming up in the elevator Sally had been thoughtful, trying to put herself in Nina's place at the other end of the phone in Kansas City. 'That he was alive and successful in Beirut two or three years ago?'

'She could get those investigators of hers to go there and see if they could pick up his trail.'

'And what if they pick up nothing? All her heartache starts all over again. She's at last adjusted herself – well, as adjusted as she probably ever will be. I don't know that she wants to see Tim again, not after all this time.'

'There's Michael. She wants to see him. He'd be – what? Fifteen now. She'll still be wanting to see him when he's fifty. I think we should tell her.'

'Let's sleep on it.'

Prue, for all her sophisticated talk and her experience with college boys, had had no experience in heartache. Sally knew she could not explain to Prue how she understood what Nina might go through again if the ghosts of Tim and Michael were raised, only to disappear once more without trace. She knew how much she treasured the quiet interior she had achieved within herself; it might be as fragile as gelatine, but it was a haven after what she had gone through in the past eighteen months. She had the feeling that Nina had tried for and achieved the same repose; but it would be equally fragile, unable to bear the weight of further disappointment. Unless there was a certainty that Tim and Michael could be found, it was better that things were left as they were.

In the morning Prue said, 'I lay awake for a long time last night. In the end I decided you were right. You'd know more about unhappiness than I do.'

'Maybe some day she'll find them. But I'd rather she found them herself than us do it for her.'

272

Sally and Mary spent the next two days touring in the rally, doing well but not well enough to gain a place. Sally did not mind; she was not competitive enough to think only of winning; the mere taking part gave her enough enjoyment. It filled in time, kept intact the vacuum of the quiet interior. It was selfish and self-indulgent, she knew; to have done charity work would also have filled in time, been more contributory than driving an expensive car around the back roads of Schleswig-Holstein. But charity work would have meant involvement in other people's lives and she had not the strength to suffer other people's suffering.

When she and Mary returned to the hotel after the rally Prue and Rudi Schnatz were waiting for them. 'Rudi wants us all to go out to his place in the country for the weekend. He's having a shoot.'

'There'll be others there,' said Schnatz. 'Some business associates and their wives. And some unattached men.'

Mary went off with Schnatz at once and Sally said, 'I wish he'd marry her. She moons over him instead of navigating for me.'

'Then we'll work on them over the weekend. We'll have them engaged by Sunday evening.'

But Sally forgot all about Mary Venneker and Rudi Schnatz's romance as soon as she arrived at the Schnatz country home. It was south-east of Ratzeburg, not far from the East German border, in flat rolling country that was losing its green under the winds of autumn. A manor house standing in the midst of its own farmlands, it had been in the Schnatz family for over a century, had been lost in the post-World War Two depression and now regained and restored by the last survivor of the family, Rudi. It was not an attractive house, but it had a solidity to it that suggested security, an ability to survive the tempests of men, their politics and their wars. Rudi, standing on the broad front steps to greet them, looked another man from the one they had met in Hamburg, one to whom tradition meant as much as, if not more than, business profits. His one unpatriotic note was that he was dressed in English tweed and looked more like an English squire than a German Junker.

The other guests were waiting inside the house to meet the newcomers. As soon as she walked into the big, high-ceilinged drawing-room Sally saw Michele. She felt faint, as if the floor had suddenly opened up beneath her. It seemed to her that Michele floated forward, took both her hands so lightly and kissed her so softly on the cheek that she felt she was dreaming. But she could smell that scent that was Michele's alone, the combination of skin and perfume that was as much a memory as the sight of the beautiful face, the sound of the husky voice and the touch of the experienced hands. She clutched Michele's fingers in hers and returned the kiss. And was aware that Prue, eyes alert as ever, was watching them.

'Darling, how marvellous!' Michele said. 'I couldn't believe it when Rudi said who was coming.'

Sally introduced her to Prue, then was gently pulled across to meet Michele's husband. She was shocked at the jealousy she felt as she approached the tall slender man with the skin slightly darker than Michele's and the close-cropped black hair that looked as if it had been straightened. He had had a Belgian mother but his African father had prevailed in him. He looked to be about forty and Sally wondered what sort of white woman his mother had been that she had married a black man right after World War I. She was putting bad marks against him before she had even shaken hands with him, jealousy making her malicious.

'Miss Beaufort.' Gaston Onza's English was more accented than his wife's; he did not shake Sally's hand but bent his head to brush it with his lips. The Belgian in him was not entirely submerged. 'Michele has told me so much about you.'

They exchanged the usual banalities, but they were observing each other closely. Michele, their mutual lover, stood off from them, watching them with cool, barely concealed amusement. Sally could feel everything breaking up inside her; the quiet interior was now a shattered glass ball that pierced her every time she looked at Michele. She knew now she had done the right thing in not calling Nina last night.

'Rudi said you were here on business. You're a long way from Leopoldville, M. Onza.'

'Business and religion, they spread like the plague. My father could never get accustomed to the thought that men came all the way from Brussels to buy ivory from him. Then the missionaries came and tried to sell us Jesus Christ. My father never saw it as an even trade. He tried eating the missionaries but they were indigestible.'

'Stop exaggerating, Gaston,' said Michele.

He smiled at her: lovingly? Sally wondered. But it was impossible to tell. 'Since the Congo got its independence, Michele thinks we should act in more civilized ways. Don't worry, *cherie*. I'm sure Miss Beaufort appreciates how civilized I am.'

Later, in the bedroom the two sisters were sharing, Prue said, 'So that's *the* Michele.'

274

'Who told you about her?' Sally wondered why she was so much on the defensive.

'Nina. I think she thought she was teaching me some of the facts of life. She did it in the nicest possible way – she wasn't criticizing you.

'Were you – well, shocked?'

'Of course not. I suspected you were a bit that way years ago. With that Cindy whatever-her-name-was.'

'Oh God! I should have known. Well?' She waited on judgement.

'Sal – *please*. Don't look so – so vulnerable. It's your life, it's the way you are.'

'You're not shocked. But you're – puzzled?'

'We-ell. I suppose it's because it's the way *I* am. I mean, all I want is to be made love to by a man. Sometimes *any* man. Why do you do it? I mean, why a woman?'

'I – I feel *safer*, I suppose. It's hard to explain. Love-making with a girl isn't all tenderness – you can get carried away, the same as with a man. When I'm with a man – ' she was busy unpacking her suitcase, trying hard to make her words sound part of a natural everyday conversation – 'I don't hate what we're doing. But I'm – I'm frightened. There's more violence in a man's love-making – don't they call it the small death?'

'I don't know if it's for that reason. Sometimes after I've been with a really good man I feel just like dying. But I think it's more from ecstatic exhaustion than anything else.' Prue, as if to keep up the sham of an ordinary dialogue, began to unpack her own suitcase. 'You're sure – I mean you're not suffering some sort of complex about Mother or Daddy?'

Sally hung up a dress, not bothering to see if the creases fell out. Since Philip's death she had once again lost interest in clothes; but she would have laughed if Prue had suggested that it in itself was another manifestation of her homosexuality. She laughed, too, at the suggestion that she was suffering from some fixation about her mother or father. She turned away from the closet and faced Prue squarely.

'I never had any fantasy about Mother, if that's what you mean. I loved her, but I never wanted to see myself in her image. And you know what she was like – she never tried to make us ashamed of our bodies. I've read that that can sometimes drive girls round the bend.' She smiled, feeling more at ease now. 'Though I don't think I'm round the bend. I'm just, well, different from you and Nina and Meg, that's all.' '

'You never resented Daddy for anything?'

275

'Never. Except sometimes he favoured Nina more than the rest of us. But he'd have been a sainted marvel if he could have split himself equally four ways amongst us. No, I don't think I have any complex about Daddy. But sometimes – ' She paused. 'Sometimes when I was with Michele, I was conscious of an anti-male prejudice. I didn't hate all men, but I – resented them. For what they have, I suppose. It's their world. And I'd resent Daddy along with the rest of them. Then I'd look at Michele and I could see that she would hold her own in any man's world.'

'I can see how you could fall for her – she's the most gorgeous thing I've ever seen. But I don't think she could love anyone but herself. And if that's the only way you can keep your place in a man's world, I don't think it's for me.'

Sally went to the window and looked out on the farmlands stretching away under the greenish-blue sky. Some of the men, led by Rudi, were already going out to shoot, moving in groups of two or three, guns over their shoulders, the rich Maquis of the post-war world. They strode across the fields with certainty, as if any living creature, bird, hare, woman, was fair game for them. Ducks scribbled a black line across the sky, heading south, refusing to be the enemy. Gaston Onza, walking alone, turned and looked back at the house and raised his gun in salute. Sally waved in reply, an automatic gesture. Then she realized that he was not saluting her but Michele at another window. He turned and walked on, as arrogantly sure of himself as all the men in front of him.

'But what a coincidence,' Prue said. 'Meeting her here – of all places!'

'Not really.' She turned back from the window, began to undress. 'I remember Magnus once telling me – above a certain level in business or politics or diplomacy or whatever, he said the world was divided up into parishes just like everything else. The boundaries, he said, are just money or status. So the coincidence is pretty small. I don't know what gets Michele's husband into this parish, but he obviously belongs. I noticed it when I lived in Europe before. After a while you keep meeting the same people.'

'We must find out what he does. He's smooth, I'll say that for him.'

'I remember Michele telling me something about him, just before she left me to go off with him. She said there were only thirteen black college graduates in the whole of the Belgian Congo and he was one of them. One graduate for every million

276

blacks, something like that. The Belgians didn't believe in educating the natives.'

'Well, now the natives are independent maybe he's a big shot. That would suit your friend Michele. Big shot would be her line, I think.'

'You don't have to be so nasty.'

'I'm being nasty to protect you. Can't you see the danger there? I don't mean the lesbian bit – fall in love with any girl you like, if that's how you are. But Michele – ' Prue shook her head. 'She'd never bring you happiness. Please be careful this weekend.'

Sally was both annoyed and moved by Prue's concern for her. 'You watch out yourself. Some of those unattached shooters were eyeing you.'

'I'm no sitting duck. But there was a Frenchman there, Guy someone-or-other . . .'

In the afternoon the women went out with the men. The wind had dropped and the sun laid long shadows across the heath. Estate workers beat their way towards a long line of trees; birds exploded out of the long grass and guns went off in a quick battery of fire. Beyond the line of trees was East Germany: Sally wondered what the border patrols there thought of all the shooting. Prue had been taken in tow by her Frenchman who at lunch had given her more attention than he was now giving to his gun. Sally lingered behind with Michele. She was a good shot and would have liked the offer of a gun, but she could not resist the lure of Michele's company.

Sitting on their shooting-sticks, wrapped in their fleece-lined suede coats, they watched the line of guns disappear towards the trees. A jet went by high overhead, sketching a chalk mark of contrail in the cold sky; Sally looked up at it and suddenly felt the urge to be up there, flying her own plane. Escaping again.

'I've often thought of you.' Michele put a cigarette into a holder, lit it, then blew out smoke in a thin stream. 'The times we had.'

Sally turned up the collar of her coat. 'It's all finished, Michele. I've gone through too much.'

'I heard Philip was dead only months afterwards. I came to Rome again and telephoned your apartment. The housekeeper said Philip had died in an accident.'

'I'd rather not talk about it. I lost my baby at the same time.'

'Oh, my darling!' Michele put out a sympathetic hand;

277

Sally, against her will, felt her own hand clasped. 'Why didn't you write me?'

Sally carefully drew her hand away. 'Michele, what's the use? You're tied to Gaston.' She changed the subject, afraid of it. 'What are you doing here, anyway?'

Michele gazed towards the distant trees; the hunters were almost invisible against the dark frieze. 'The Congo is full of men who want to run it. Gaston is one of them.'

'You mean he wants to be President or whatever it is you have out there?'

'Yes.'

'Do you want to be the President's wife?'

Michele turned her head slowly: regally: or presidentially. The modest house in Ouagadougou, the drunken French engineer who had been her father, the Mandingo woman from Guinea who had been her mother: they were all a long way behind her. She had come a long way and the road was not yet finished.

'Yes. Why not?'

'Is Rudi going to help your husband?'

'Gaston needs certain things. Money, too,' she added, looking sideways at Sally, who pretended to miss the hint. 'It's a rich country, especially Katanga province. The right backers would find it a profitable investment.'

'If you're suggesting I should talk to my father – *no*.'

Michele stared at her, face set, eyes hard; then she relaxed, smiled. 'Darling, I still love you. You try so hard to remain innocent – '

Sally interrupted. 'Don't patronize me. You people always sneer at us Americans. But you know where to come when you want a hand-out.'

Michele smiled again: you could not insult her, she had become inured to abuse. 'Darling, you shouldn't be so sensitive. If Gaston wanted money from Americans, he would not go to Kansas City. He wouldn't have to go further west than Wall Street. As it happens, we don't think we'll have to cross the Atlantic at all.' She looked towards the trees again; the hunters were lost among them now. 'If this weekend turns out as we hope – '

'Who else knows why you're here?'

'Only Rudi and the Belgian, M. Luc.' Sally had sat next to the Belgian at lunch, a large fat man who looked as if he would have trouble getting a gun to his shoulder. 'I think you'd better not mention to anyone what I've told you. Gaston would kill me if he knew – ' She looked at Sally. 'I mean it. He doesn't place much value on life. Except his own.'

'Why do you stay with him?'

There was another burst of fire, this time from beyond the trees; the hunters must now be within sight of the border patrols. The wind began to rise again, coming down from the Baltic, bringing messages of winter: coldness against the cheek, the last birds fleeing south, the skeletons of trees appearing even as one watched them. The first of the hunters came back through the copse, guns still warm, laughing and calling to each other, happy with the kill.

'I've just told you,' Michele said. 'He can take me further than anyone else. Further, darling, than I could ever have gone with you.'

That night, when they were undressed, Prue said, 'I'm spending the night with Guy.'

Guy de Belfrage had hardly left Prue's side during the afternoon and evening. He was a man of medium height, young and handsome and with Gallic charm that he kept on a rein; Rudi Schnatz, as if feeling it was the proper reference in the circumstances, had mentioned to Sally that Guy was also wealthy and not a fortune-hunter. Sally had liked what she had seen and was not surprised when Prue made her announcement.

'Good luck. And be careful.'

Prue looked at her bed, the covers turned down. 'I wish you'd picked out someone at dinner to keep you company. That nice boy Hans had his eye on you.'

'Don't worry about me. I'm still getting over the effects of driving in that rally. I'll sleep better alone.'

Prue pulled on a robe over her night-gown, opened the door and stood stockstill. Then she looked back over her shoulder and said coldly, 'There's someone here to say goodnight.'

She went out and Michele came in, closing the door behind her. She wore a scarlet silk robe that made her look like a dark cardinal. She sat down on Prue's bed, gazed at Sally propped against the pillows in the other bed.

'Gaston is in conference with Rudi and M. Luc. I thought I'd come and say goodnight.'

Sally watched her carefully, afraid of temptation. She suddenly wished Prue had not deserted her; but maybe the temptation of Guy was as strong as that she felt herself. 'What's the point of starting again, Michele?'

'Darling, why do you always think in the long term? Love is never permanent anyway.'

279

She stood up, let the red silk slip from her: the dark incomparable body was as perfect as ever. Unhurriedly she pulled back the covers of Sally's bed and slid in beside her.

## 2

In the morning Mary Venneker said she would not be coming back to London. 'Rudi has asked me to stay on in Hamburg. I think marriage is in the air.'

Sally and Prue kissed her, delighted at the happiness in her long handsome face. 'If it's a big wedding, ask us,' said Prue. 'My three sisters have been married, one of them twice, and I've never yet been to a white wedding. Though – ' She paused and looked at Sally. 'I think I could wangle one for myself.'

'With Guy? Not so soon?'

'I'm going to have another look at him in his home territory. I'm not coming back to London, either – not right away. Guy is taking me home to meet his mother – his father's dead. They live in the Loire, near Saumur. He's actually a count, Comte de Belfrage. How would that sound back home in the *Independent*?'

'You, a title-hunter. I never thought I'd live to see the day.'

Prue looked at Mary, soon to be a baroness. 'These peasants really don't know about love at our level, do they?'

Mary, in love with Rudi at any and all levels, waved her arms ecstatically, like a semaphorist gone mad. 'Oh, everyone should be as lucky as we are! Find yourself someone, Sally, and join the club!'

'I may do that,' said Sally, but avoided Prue's eyes which were once again shrewd and alert.

They drove back to Hamburg that afternoon. But first Sally said goodbye to Michele and Gaston Onza, shaking hands with each of them, careful to give nothing away to Gaston, who also had a shrewd and alert eye. And a cold one: Sally could imagine his killing someone. She shivered, but she had already turned away and if Gaston noticed it she hoped he had put it down to the cold wind that was bringing rain in from the north.

'Goodbye, darling,' said Michele. 'Come and visit us in Katanga some day.'

Sally saw Onza's quick look at Michele when she said the word *Katanga*. But Sally protected her lover: she did her best to look innocent. 'Katanga? Wherever it is, I may do that some day.'

She dropped Prue and Guy off in Hamburg to catch a plane for Paris, then drove on alone to London. Three days later Prue returned to the house in Wilton Crescent, bringing Guy with her.

'We're going to be married. I'm taking Guy home to meet the family. He'd better know what he's marrying into.'

'Where will you be married?'

'Guy's mother has the most marvellous chateau – a girl could have a dream wedding there. But we think we owe it to Daddy to see if he wants me married at home.'

Sally, as always, was amused at the mixture in Prue. She was a romantic who could sometimes sound as cold-blooded as a prostitute about sex; she was selfish about what she wanted to do with her own life but she would have her wedding, the most important event in her life up till now, wherever her father wanted it. Sally wondered what Guy would make of the mixture.

Right now he obviously thought the mixture was wonderful. But he was not gauche in his devotion; she was not the first girl in his life. Sally, not a good judge of men, gave him the benefit of her doubt and decided that at worst he would be a one-woman-at-a-time man. *Love is never permanent* . . . She hated herself for being infected by Michele's cynicism.

'We'll be married in May or June,' said Guy.

'Just in time for the tornado season back home.' It was obvious that Prue wanted to be married at the chateau in the Loire. 'We'll point that out to Daddy.'

'Kansas City has been hit only about once in the past fifty years,' said Sally. 'That one four years ago. Don't try to influence Daddy. Let him make up his own mind.'

While Prue was out of the room Guy said, 'Your father – Prue tells me he is not enthusiastic about foreigners.'

Sally smiled. 'Especially the French. But he hasn't exactly been lucky all round, so I shouldn't let it worry you. He's due for a change of prejudice.'

Prue and Guy left two days later for America. Sally debated whether she should go with them, not wanting to be alone in London; but decided she would be surplus cargo. If Prue needed support against Lucas, there would be Nina and Meg on hand. So Sally stayed on in London, feeling more lost and lonely each morning as she got up and looked out at the grey November skies. She had to get away to some sunshine. But where?

Then one noon the phone rang. 'I'm in London, darling. Can

I come and see you?'

Anyone was welcome, even Michele. Particularly her . . . 'Is Gaston with you?'

'No. How soon can I see you? It's urgent.'

She could not remember anything ever being urgent with Michele. 'Come round now. We'll have lunch.' She had never been able to bring herself to say *luncheon*: but that, probably, would be the least of her sins now in Edith's eyes.

Michele arrived swathed in mink against the cold day. Hislop, the manservant, took the coat and gave her a discreetly admiring glance. So far all the visitors to his new employer had had style and looks, but this darkie was something out of the box; he had the usual English prejudice about colour, but if they all looked like this one he wouldn't mind England being taken over by the blackies. But Michele did not see him or his admiring look. Below a certain level she was socially blind: there were no dividends from servants unless they were one's own. Hislop's and her prejudices matched each other, the one thing they had in common.

Sally had not even enquired of the cook what was for lunch: Prue would have done better. It was brown Windsor soup, a cutlet, potatoes and peas, a trifle. The cook had once worked at Eton: what was good anough for schoolboy gentry was good enough for Americans. Michele looked at each course as if it were a plate of African mealies; but she made no comment. Food, good or bad, can sometimes bring men closer together; but not women. Michele had other things on her mind besides her palate.

Over coffee she said, 'We need money desperately, darling. Everything with Rudi and M. Luc has fallen through. The other side got to M. Luc and now he doesn't want to know us.'

'Who's us? Just you and Gaston?'

'And some others. The Congo is there for grabs, as you Americans say. Any one of a dozen men could come out on top. Tshombé, Kasavubu, Mulele. And Gaston. But we need money – in a hurry.'

Sally knew she should close the subject at once; but boredom with her life, loneliness, plain curiosity, made her ask, 'Why?'

'We have arms and men waiting just over the border in Angola. The Portuguese would like to see Gaston take over, but they don't want to upset their own apple-cart by appearing to take sides. So they turn a blind eye and let us keep our men and equipment there. But now payment is due – for the men and the equipment. Planes, tanks, things like that. All second-hand but still good.'

'How much do you need?'

'Four million dollars. Almost.'

'Four milli – ?' She laughed, suddenly seeing how farcical it all was. She had expected Michele to be more intelligent and practical-minded; ambition **had** got the better of her. 'Are you wanting me to ask my father for that much? He'd just shut the door in my face.'

'I told you in Germany – our country is *rich*. Any investment there would be returned tenfold in five years. Gaston will sign options – he's a man who honours his business deals. Your father could check with Union Minière in Brussels – '

Sally shook her head. 'No, Michele. I know Daddy too well. It would be useless asking him.'

Michele pushed her coffee away from her, making a face: the whole lunch had been a total failure, she had wasted her time coming here. 'I thought you might help. You're bored – you told me that at Rudi's place – '

She couldn't remember what she had said in bed that night. She sat silent, staring out through the lace curtains at the grey rain falling out of the grey sky into the grey street.

'Darling – Have you any money of your own?'

She turned her head slowly, away from the grey unpromising day. 'Yes. But what would I get for it?'

'What do you want?' The black eyes glistened with diamonds of hope: all wasn't yet lost.

'Not a tenfold return on my investment. I'm not interested in money.'

*Ah, how easily the rich can say that.* 'I wouldn't leave Gaston – not if he becomes President. But I could come to Europe three or four times a year – Is that what you want?'

*Oh God, why can't I say no to her?* 'I'd like more . . . I can lend you the four million dollars.'

Michele leaned forward: Sally had never seen her so excited, except in bed. 'Do you have to go back to Kansas City for it? We don't have much time – '

'It's in Zurich. I'll have to go there – '

Michele rose, took Sally's face in her hands and kissed her on the lips. Her musky scent was strong: she was as excited as if by sex. 'Darling, we'll have such times together – '

They left that afternoon for Switzerland. On the way over they discussed how the money was to be got to Katanga. To transfer it to a bank in the Congo would only result in its being confiscated by the present government; a strict watch was kept on all money coming into and going out of the country. To lodge it in a bank in Angola would only result in delay and a possible leakage of the news that it was there. Most of the money *could* be lodged in a bank in Switzerland: three million dollars, the price of the equipment. But the other million was needed in the Congo, to pay the troops and provide for all the ancillary needs of a small army.

'How much do you pay these troops?'

'The blacks? Almost nothing. They wouldn't know what to do with more money.' Gaston Onza had better turn out to be a dictator; his wife did not sound like the concept of a democratic President. 'The white mercenaries are the expensive ones. They are asking $1000 a month each. They are up for auction. They know there are other people who want to buy them, too.'

'How can you trust men like that?'

'They seem to have a peculiar code of honour. Once they're signed, they fight for the man who pays them.' But Michele was too cynical to believe that any man had a code of honour: 'Maybe it's because they know that if they desert on one job, they won't get another.'

'So how do we take the money to these men?'

'Do you still have your pilot's licence? Good. Then we can hire a plane and fly it out to Katanga. The money can always be hidden in the plane and the Customs people along the way are never that conscientious anyway. They won't be with two good-looking women like us.'

Sally had felt her own excitement growing from the moment she had stepped aboard the Swissair plane at Heathrow. During the drive out to the airport she had been torn between wanting to go on and turning back; but as if sensing her indecision, Michele had taken her hand and held it gently but firmly. Again the old weakness had taken hold of her; she told herself that being with Michele was better than being alone; but she knew that being with Michele was better than anything at all. Then as the plane had climbed into the traffic lanes and headed for Zurich, as the whispered talk about the planned revolution had progressed, there had been no longer any thought of turning back. And now that she might fly a plane all the way down through Africa to the Congo, she sat waiting impatiently for them to land at Zurich.

They checked into the Baur au Lac: Sally remembered Magnus's recommendation of the hotel. They made love that night and everything was as it had been when they had first met. Sally went to sleep exhausted and happy; all the tension had gone out of her and she looked young and ready for any adventure. Almost like the carefree tomboy of ten years ago: but Michele had never known that girl.

In the morning they went to the bank, met the Director and arranged for the money to be handled as Sally directed. As she signed the various forms she wondered what Philip, or more especially old Tony Gentleman, would think of what she was doing with the money. It was not going to be used for respectable purposes: it was being turned back into the dirty money it had once been.

The Director was disappointed that so much money was being moved out of a single account at the one time, but he did not ask questions. There was still a deposit of almost another four million dollars, including the interest that had been earned over the past two years.

'You will be retaining the balance, Madame Mann?'

'Indefinitely,' said Sally, hiding her reaction to being called Madame Mann; she had long ago given up thinking of herself as such. 'I shall be back tomorrow morning for the cash. I take it that this will go no further than it has to in the bank?'

The Director knew she did not mean to be insulting. 'Discretion is the other interest we pay on your account, Madame Mann.'

They left the bank, went to the airport and caught a plane for Marseilles. The man they wanted to see in Marseilles had an office at the end of the airport. He was short, muscular, had a black beard and dark suspicious eyes. But he smiled, showing tobacco-stained teeth, when Michele mentioned who had given her his name.

'Him? Sure, I went out to Libya and serviced those planes for him. So your husband bought them, did he? They're good. A bit old but good. You want to buy some more?'

'No, we just want to hire a plane.'

'A two-engined job,' said Sally. 'One with a good range.'

'How long will you want it?'

'Two weeks.'

'Two *weeks*? Where are you going? No, don't tell me. You get your own papers if you're going to fly it out of France. But the price is going to be high. I'll have to treble the insurance – '

'The price doesn't matter,' said Sally; her father would have chided her for such a reckless business approach. 'Will it be ready to go in two hours?'

'It'll be ready,' said the man. 'Just make sure you bring it back. Don't go fighting any wars in it,' he said, looking at Michele. 'It's a Beechcraft, not a B-52.'

They flew back to Zurich in the Beechcraft in the late afternoon. Next morning they went to five consulates in the city.

Michele already had visas for the countries the consulates represented. She stayed outside in the rented car; she did not want any of the consulate officials to know that she would be accompanying Sally; news can fly faster than planes. Sally, paying extra in cash without a receipt, got the quick service she asked for at each consulate. She told the consular officers that she was flying out to Kenya, delivering the Beechcraft to a friend in Nairobi. She could not be sure that all, or any, of them believed her. But her money and her looks were good and the necessary papers were passed over without too many enquiries. She had given up thinking of herself as Sarah Mann, relinquishing her passport in that name to prove it to herself; now she had to produce her new passport in her maiden name. A couple of the consulate officers looked at her carefully, but no comment was made. Beaufort was not a common name, but it was not as uncommon as Rockefeller: that name would be a real handicap.

After the visits to the consulates she and Michele went to the bank and collected the million dollars in Swiss francs, packing them into the two suitcases they had brought with them. Michele had bought the suitcases while Sally had been in one of the consulates. Sally remarked that Michele had a proper sense of the fitness of things: the cases were Vuitton bags, you didn't carry a million dollars in any old carry-all.

They drove out to the airport and spent some time stowing the money away behind panels in the cabin. It was an obvious hiding place but again they were relying on their femaleness; women smugglers were not as common then as they were later to become. There was no reason why Customs officers along the way should suspect two good-looking women, obviously wealthy, of any nefarious business in Nairobi, the stated destination on their papers. By the time they had finished hiding the money it was too late to take off.

'Which of us stays with the plane?' said Michele.

'Why?'

Michele sighed with exasperation and wonder; gradually her hard shell was cracking under the pressure of the excitement growing within her. 'The money, for God's sake! Someone could steal it.'

Sally did not argue: she knew she had been stupidly careless in thinking that the money should be left unguarded. Certain people at the bank, if no one else, knew that she had taken the money away in cash. But: 'All right, we both sleep out here. We can say we want to get off first thing in the morning. But are we going to sleep with the money all the way to the Congo?'

Michele swallowed the exasperation that threatened to grow into anger. Sally just didn't know what people had to go through on their way to the top. 'It's not too much, is it? If you want to sleep in a hotel, all right. But I'm staying with the plane.'

Sally could see she had upset Michele. All at once she did not want the journey spoiled by a lovers' quarrel. 'We'll sleep with the money all the way. I just hope some randy ground mechanic doesn't think we're easy meat and tries to attack us.'

'There's a gun under the passenger's seat. A Luger 7.65. Gaston tells me it's very effective.'

'For God's sake! Who put it there?'

'I did.' She leaned back against the plane, pulling the collar of her coat up against the cold wind blowing off the lake. She was not wearing the mink: that in itself would invite a thief somewhere along the trip. This coat was black leather, expensive but not blatantly so. 'Darling, this isn't going to be like some of those jaunts we used to take here in Europe. We're not flying to Rheims or Monza to watch some Grand Prix motor race. Africa, north, south or in the middle, is nothing like what you've been used to. And once we get down to the Congo it is going to be dangerous.'

'I've never been afraid of danger before.' Which was true. 'You said that yourself when we were driving in the rallies.'

'This is different. It's not a game, Sally, not any more.'

Sally pulled her own coat tightly about her. It was an old camel-hair coat of Nina's that she had found ideal for driving or flying; it was worn on the cuffs and there were stains on it but she never noticed those blemishes. She did not know that it had already been worn through one terrible ordeal, that Nina had been wearing it when she had been kidnapped and had never worn it since.

'I know that, Michele. I don't think of anything between you and me any more as a game. Least of all this. But I still have to get used to the idea of what we're doing. I'm not as ambitious as you. I don't want to be the President's wife.'

She had not meant to say the last words. But they were part of the jealousy she still felt towards Gaston Onza and it would always be there just below the surface.

Michele straightened up, chin out. 'It's not too late for you to change your mind!'

Later Sally knew that was the moment when she should have said she was not going, that the whole adventure was foolish and couldn't possibly succeed. But she was not here because of faith in an adventure, not even for the sake of adventure itself. She was here because of Michele.

'I'll go back to the hotel and collect our bags. We'll leave first thing in the morning.'

## 3

Because Sally had not been able to learn for certain where fuel could be bought along the way, she took the longest route. They flew from Zurich to Rome, then to Tunis, then to Casablanca. From there they went on down the west coast of Africa. They met storms, officious Customs officers, mechanical trouble; but nothing delayed them unduly. They did not stay longer than one night at any place, except at Conakry where they had to wait two days while Sally went seeking a replacement for a damaged piston. The man in Marseilles who had rented them the plane had provided a kit of spares, but he had forgotten to include a spare set of pistons.

'My mother came from here,' said Michele. 'She was born up-country but she met my father in Conakry.'

'Is she still alive?' Sally knew so little about Michele's life.

Michele shrugged: with her the umbilical cord had never been more than a thin frayed string. 'I don't know. We never got on.'

Sally was appalled at such lack of feeling: one should love one's mother, even if one sometimes also hated her. She had always loved her own mother, more perhaps than Edith had ever realized. 'If you – if Gaston succeeds in what he's trying to do, won't she try and get in touch with you?'

'I doubt if she'd hear about me. My father's dead and if she's still alive she could have gone back to her village. They often do.' *They:* the blacks. She said it as if their blood was completely alien to her own. 'I changed my name when I ran away from home. She wouldn't know who Michele Mauriac is.'

'What is your real name then?' Somehow she felt a sense of betrayal, as if she were in love with a stranger. Even her own husband had not used his true name.

Michele smiled, put a long slim finger against Sally's lips. 'Darling, names don't matter. We're not in love with each other's names.'

They stayed with the plane that night and the next, as they had done all through the trip. Sometimes they had felt it wise to bribe the airport security men, being careful to pay just so much and not too much. Sally, who had all her life been so indifferent to money, was now acutely aware of the Swiss francs stowed away behind the panelling in the aircraft. She slept only fitfully in the locked cabin of the plane; but Michele slept as if she were in bed at the Baur au Lac. Only once, at Dakar, had someone come trying to open the cabin door: Michele had sat up at once, the Luger pistol in her hand, and whoever it was had scuttled off into the darkness. Sally was finding that being on the ground was the most wearing and nerve-wracking part of the trip. She began to wish she had chosen a more direct route, down through Egypt and the Sudan. But Michele had told her things were just as unsettled in the Sudan as they were in the Congo. The long way round had its disadvantages, but it was best. The coast, said Michele, the white in her speaking, at least was civilized.

So two days in Conakry, then they took off for Abidjan, then Lagos, Douala, Libreville and Brazzaville. From there they had to fly direct across the Congo to an airstrip in the mountains north-west of Elisabethville.

'Gaston won't be there to meet us. He is going to run things from the inside, in Elisabethville. We'll be met by the mercenaries and they'll take us in in their convoy.'

Sally had had moments of apprehension throughout the trip, but they had been outweighed by the exhilaration she had felt. She was once again *doing* something; and for love of someone. But now she felt a sudden sense of danger; she looked out across the Congo River. It was more than just a border between two countries; it was the boundary between neutrality and commitment. Once across there, in the company of Michele and with all that money hidden in the aircraft, she would be a rebel, part of the enemy of the government.

They had landed at Brazzaville at dusk, coming in when the airport was almost deserted. The air was heavily humid, making them both sweat; Michele glistened like polished brown marble. It seemed to Sally that she looked darker, as if, chameleon-like, she were taking on the colouring of their environment, letting her mother's blood come out in her. Sally all at once felt conspicuous, whiter than white: the detergent commercial didn't know the dangers in its slogan in certain parts of the world. She wiped the sweat from her face, not all of it due to the humidity, and looked at the man in the white drill suit appearing like a ghost out of the dusk.

'Madame Onza! They told me two ladies had just arrived in their own plane. I had no idea it was you.' He was black and heavily-built and spoke French fluently in a soft bass voice.

'Inspector Luba!' Sally detected the edgy note in Michele's voice, she who normally was never put out by anyone. 'On duty at this hour?'

'A policeman's job is a twenty-four-hour one.' He looked at Sally. 'A friend?'

'Mlle Beaufort, a very old friend. Inspector Luba is an old friend of my husband's. Their fathers were cousins.'

'On opposite sides of the river,' said Luba, smiling broadly, but did not explain how the family had been separated. 'Where are you staying, Madame Onza?'

'We haven't checked in at any hotel. We're concerned for our plane.'

'You have nothing to fear here.' Luba waved a big graceful hand; it seemed that he was trying to be more Gallic than de Gaulle. Sally had heard about the British colonials who did their best to sound more British than their masters. She wondered who in time would want to be more American than the Americans. Possibly only pop singers. 'I personally shall see that your plane is guarded. How long are you staying? Just tonight? I shall take you personally to the best hotel we have and see personally that you are accommodated. Perhaps you will be my guests at dinner?'

'Inspector Luba, you are too kind – '

Luba waved a deprecating hand; it was dark now and all that showed was the gentle wave of the white-clad arm. 'So few people say that about a policeman. We are here to help – '

'But we are exhausted, Inspector. Perhaps next time?'

Luba took the refusal graciously. He conjured up two policemen out of the darkness, summoning them with a whistle. detailed them to guard the aircraft, then insisted on driving Michele and Sally into town.

'I shall take you to the Hotel Independence.' He banged his fist on the horn button; two cyclists fell away in front of the speeding car as if they had been mowed down by gunfire. 'Africa is full of Hotels Independence these days. Soon they will rival the Hilton chain.'

'Is there an Independence chain?' Sally asked.

'What a droll sense of humour your friend has, Madame Onza.' He laughed suddenly. 'No, Mlle Beaufort, they are all owned by Europeans trying to prove they are in favour of independence. And we know how much they were in favour of it, don't we, Madame Onza?'

'Yes.'

In the back seat Sally could see the stiffness in Michele's body, felt the tension tighten within herself. Beyond the yellow swath of the headlamps the blackness of Africa suddenly threatened her. She wanted to turn back, but knew it was already too late.

Luba left them at the hotel, personally telling the manager that Madame Onza and Mlle Beaufort had to be given the best room and the best attention. Then he kissed the hand of each woman and retired, a black *boulevardier* who could sweep everyone off the boulevards if he wished.

Sally and Michele had dinner in their room, a service they might not have received had it not been that the manager wished to please Inspector Luba. Later, when it was time for bed, Sally switched off the light and pushed open the shutters of the window.

'Close them,' said Michele sharply. 'Anything might fly in during the night.'

Sally closed the shutters, pausing for a moment to look out at the yellow moon shedding its fleece of cloud. A lamp hung from a tree in the back garden of the hotel; a living shade of moths and insects shrouded it. Vampire-bats flew stiff-winged above the trees and a cat crept along a path like a mangy leopard. A gramophone was playing in one of the other rooms: Edith Piaf consoled some expatriate who couldn't go home. She closed the shutters, groped her way through the darkness into the single bed. The manager had shown them to a room with twin beds; Sally had noticed that Michele had not stated a preference for a room with a double bed. Perhaps she felt the night would be too warm, for the room had no air-conditioning; perhaps she felt that two women sleeping together was something frowned upon in the new Africa, that independence was only for men. In any case she made no comment to Sally, who now suddenly longed for the comfort of Michele's arms but was afraid to ask.

At seven in the morning they caught a taxi out to the airport. 'We want to get away before Luba comes to see us.'

But Luba, in a khaki uniform this morning, peaked cap set rakishly on his head, was waiting for them. 'As I told you, our job is a twenty-four-hour one. We never rest. I came to wish you bon voyage, I'll send a radio message to Gaston that you have left and are on your way.'

'No, don't do that!' This was a Michele Sally had never seen before: nervous, edgy almost to the point of panic. 'I – I want to surprise him. He doesn't expect me back for another week. And he doesn't know about Mlle Beaufort.'

Which was true. Michele had explained to Sally that she could not communicate with her husband openly. A cable had been sent from Zurich but all it had said was: *Medical report satisfactory. Arriving as arranged.* Gaston Onza would know that Michele had obtained the money and would be bringing it in at the appointed meeting place with the mercenaries. He would not know that Sally would also be coming.

Luba smiled, winked a big dark eye. 'Just as well Gaston is the faithful type. I don't think I'd want my wife arriving back from somewhere to surprise me. Well, bon voyage. May he be surprised. He is a very fortunate man. Doubly so,' he added, smiling at Sally.

They took off into a pink morning. Sally had not slept well because of the heat and humidity and she opened a window of the plane; even so, the wind that blew in was hardly a tonic. The Congo did not seem to flow but stood still beneath them, a silver-green border touched with pink reflections, between two jungles that looked exactly alike. A small paddle-wheeler came downstream, trailing a peacock's tail of wake behind it; a canoe, a single man standing up in it, floated on the water like a stick insect. A cloud of flamingos rose up, got above the sun's rays and turned into white herons; rocks moved at the river's edge, as at an earth tremor, became hippos on the move. The cloud-cover enveloped the plane for a minute, then they were above it and heading south-east. I'm committed, Sally thought.

Their range was going to be stretched to the limit to make the rendezvous that Michele had marked on their map. Sally kept the cruising speed down to a minimum, conserving fuel; but knowing at the same time that she was not at all eager to put down at the rendezvous. She was afraid, no longer excited by the thought of adventure. She wondered how all those women adventurers she had read about as a girl had felt when they had set out on their first passage. Jane Digby, Isabelle Eberhardt, Amelia Earhart: had they all wanted to turn back once they had taken the first step? She looked at Michele for some sort of answer, but the latter was resting her head against the window, eyes closed, dreaming . . . Of what? Of being the President's wife? All at once Sally knew her own journey had been futile. Once they had landed Michele would no longer need her. Or would be dead.

But there was no turning back: they had reached the point of no return. They flew on, each of them silent for her own reasons. The clouds evaporated and Africa burned bright beneath them. Then it was time to start looking at the map, comparing it with the contours of the land below. Hills came up ahead of them and beyond them a low range of mountains. Sally checked her bearing, saw the landmarks Michele had told her to expect, knew she was on course. Whatever else she might be, she knew she was a good pilot and a good navigator. She put the plane's nose down, looking for the landing strip between the river and the road. There it was, exactly as Michele had described it.

She did a circuit, looking for the trucks that were supposed to be there waiting for them. Then she saw them, a dozen or so, parked like elephants beneath a screen of thin acacias. She straightened up, put down her wheels and went in for the descent. Then she saw the Land-Rover swing out from under the trees and speed down the strip towards her. She saw the driver frantically waving a hand at her, but there was nothing she could do. She was out of fuel and she had to land here.

'Take it up!' Michele shouted. 'There's something wrong!'

Sally was about to argue, then changed her mind as the window behind her suddenly cracked as a bullet hit it. She gunned the engine, lifted the nose and took the plane up in a steep climb only feet before the plane would have touched down. She banked steeply, climbing away from the strip. She was trembling with shock, but she was still in control of the plane. She looked down past Michele and saw the Land-Rover swing off the edge of the strip and disappear again into the trees and scrub.

'What do we do?' She tried not to panic, but she was staring at the fuel gauge. 'We're out of gas!'

'How much do you have?' Michele looked and sounded less frightened than angry.

'Five, ten minutes' more flying. No more. I've got to put down soon. What's happened down there?'

She had taken the plane up to what she guessed was a safe height but she had no idea how far a rifle or machine-gun could shoot. The strip was down to their starboard side, seemingly deserted; they could see nothing, not even the trucks now. Then Michele suddenly pointed. A train of dust was belting its way through the scrub, coming in their direction. Sally, no longer watching the gauge because it now stood at *Empty*, cautiously took the plane down lower. Then they recognized the Land-Rover at the head of the train of dust. She swung the plane round in a wide circle, came in above the Land-Rover. The driver now had another man with him, who was looking up at the plane and pointing ahead. Sally waggled the wings, went in above the Land-Rover, climbed and saw the flat stretch of ground up ahead and the straight strip of dirt road running through it.

'Hang on!'

She put the nose down, heard the engine cough but ignored it:

they were going to make it. They were less than a hundred feet above the ground when she saw the three trucks coming down the road a mile or two ahead of them. But she could not gun the engine this time, could not lift the nose again. She put the wheels down, felt them bounce in the ruts, fought to hold the aircraft steady as they went down the rough bumpy road that had looked so smooth from the air. Then the plane slewed sideways, tilted and out of the corner of her eye she saw the port wing fold like a piece of cardboard. The seat-belt cut into her and she banged her head against the window. There was a crumpling sound, then a roaring as the engine gunned itself on the last of the fuel; the plane stood on its nose, turned turtle, then everything seemed to be falling apart around her. She felt a dreadful pain in her right leg and she thought she screamed, but didn't hear herself. Then she smelled the fuel and saw the first tongue of flame.

She undid her belt, flung herself against the door and it fell open. She dropped out into the thick dust, dimly aware of Michele tumbling out after her. She began to crawl away as there was a sudden *whoosh!* and the plane was engulfed in flames. Black smoke shot up, blotting out the sun, and she crawled desperately away, like a broken-legged crab, through choking darkness. She could feel the heat of the flames, felt them reach out for her; then she was out in sunlight again, scrabbling her way through the dust, whimpering like a madwoman. Then abruptly she stopped, remembering Michele.

She looked back, saw Michele lying beneath the black volcano of smoke, just beyond the reach of the flames but not beyond their heat. Michele stared at her out of a mangled face, one hand outstretched; then the hand dropped and the face fell into the dust. Sally swung round, screaming as the pain of her leg bit into her again, and crawled back. She grabbed Michele, tried to pull her away from the fire. She could feel the heat threatening to crack her skin apart; she shut her eyes, afraid that they would boil in their sockets. She was screaming and yelling at Michele, but could not hear herself. Unable to get leverage from her right leg, she had to put all the strain on her left as she dragged Michele away through the smoke.

Then she felt the strong arms lift her by the shoulders, saw the two dim figures through the swirling smoke, then everything went black. But not before she had looked up into the face of Tim Davoren.

# 4

Before she opened her eyes she could feel the terrible pain in her leg, right at the knee-cap. Her nose and mouth were choked with dust and smoke and, from the *inside*, like some fantasy feeling, she could feel the brittleness of her scorched skin. She could hear loud cracks quite close to her and a man's voice was cursing. Cautiously she slid back her lids, shut them again instantly as she looked straight up into the sun.

'Put them in the truck!' The voice was familiar, but she knew she was dreaming. 'We'll make a run for it!'

'Where are those other bastards?' That voice was guttural, not familiar at all.

Then the man, smelling of sweat and tobacco, picked her up and almost threw her into the back of the truck. She cried out with pain, but he paid her no heed, had turned round and picked up Michele. Sally, eyes wide open now, saw Michele, blood running from a gaping wound in her face, dumped in beside her. Then the Land-Rover took off with a jerk. Only then did Sally become aware of the bullets hitting the small truck.

She cowered down, putting her arms about Michele, pulling the other woman into her. The Land-Rover bumped over the ground, swerving and swaying as the driver hurtled it through the scrub. Dust swirled in on Sally and Michele, but, tossed and buffeted as they were, being bruised with every bump they hit, they hardly remarked it. Sally held her lover tightly and prayed that they could make their escape from whoever was pursuing them.

Then the Land-Rover was climbing a steep slope, the driver slowing it as he slammed it into four-wheel drive. Sally felt herself sliding towards the back, put out her left leg and propped herself and Michele against the tailboard. The truck kept climbing, then flattened out and soon they were travelling over what seemed a relatively smooth track. No more bullets were hitting the Land-Rover and Sally wondered what had happened to their pursuers.

Then at last the truck slowed, came to a stop in a thick stand of trees. The shade itself was like a balm; just to be out of the glare and heat of the sun was a relief. Dark waves kept flowing through Sally, threatening to engulf her; but somehow, through will-power and nothing else, she retained consciousness. She could feel nothing now in her right leg so long as she kept it still. But she was acutely conscious of the still-inert Michele in her arms, of the gashed and bleeding face, no longer recognizable, that was held against her own breast.

The driver and the other man came round to the back of the truck. They swung down the tailboard and she stared at the driver. He was dressed in camouflaged battle fatigues, wore a battered old British officer's cap with no insignia and had a sub-machinegun slung over one shoulder. His face was caked with the mud of dust and sweat and he no longer wore a moustache. But she knew she was not dreaming: it was Tim Davoren.

'Sorry about the rough ride, ladies – ' Then he looked at the unconscious Michele. 'Get the dark one, Kurt. She looks in a bad way.'

The other man, young and lean, looking not much more than a boy, gently took Michele and lifted her out and laid her on the ground. Then Tim picked up Sally. She cried out in a stifled scream as he lifted her right leg and he instantly shifted his grip.

'Sorry.' He carefully laid her on the ground, pulled a pack from the back of the Land-Rover and put it under her head. 'Kurt, go up to the top of the rise there and see what's happening.'

The young soldier went off at a run and Tim looked first at Michele, then came back to Sally and gave her a drink of water from his flask. He took out a knife and ripped the leg of her trousers. She glanced down, saw the mess of flesh and bone and almost fainted.

'Steady, old girl. Don't look at it. Shut your eyes. Or even try looking at me.'

She shut her eyes, then opened them and stared at him. She recognized the old smile, though his teeth were dust-stained and the black moustache was no longer there as a contrast. The nausea settled in her and her brain began to clear. All at once she realized that he did not recognize her.

'I'm afraid Madame Onza is in a pretty bad way. Incidentally, I'm Nigel Burgess, the chap you were supposed to meet.'

'Hello, Tim,' she said quietly. 'I'm Sally. Sally Beaufort.'

Even beneath the mask of dust and sweat she saw the pained shock in his face. He sat back on his haunches and returned her stare. 'Jesus Christ – '

'You haven't changed. Except for your moustache – '

He was not interested in small talk. 'How are you involved in this?'

'I supplied the money. A million dollars in Swiss francs.'

'*You?* Where is it?' Then he sat down abruptly as the realization hit him like a blow. 'Oh Christ – no! Back there in the plane?'

'All of it. It was packed behind the panelling.'

'Then it's gone up in smoke, every bloody franc of it.' He stood up, went to the front of the Land-Rover and looked up towards the top of the rise where Kurt was crouched behind some rocks. Then he came back, stood over her. 'Nobody but me and Onza knew that money was coming in. I trust my boys, but I'm afraid he didn't – he thought some of them might decide to give up his little war and take off with the money instead. I don't think they would have, but we'll never know now. But I think you and I had better keep our little secret for a while. If they knew their pay had gone up in the fire, some of them might decide they'd had enough and move on. I can't afford that. I need them for another week or two.'

'Does your friend Kurt know?'

'No. And he doesn't need to know. He's a splendid soldier, but he can get awfully bad-tempered about small things.' He squatted down beside her. 'I can't get you two to a decent hospital just yet. The best I can hope to do is get you to some sympathetic doctor at one of the missions.'

'What went wrong? Who were those men firing at us?'

'Government troops. Someone spilled the beans back in Elisabethville. Onza is already dead – we got the word on our radio about half an hour before you put in an appearance. I tried to get in touch with you, but you must have been on a different frequency – I couldn't raise you. Where did you stop last night?'

'Brazzaville.'

'Did you meet an Inspector Luba there?' She nodded, and he spread a hand. 'There's the leak. That chap hated Onza's guts – ' He remained squatting beside her, gazing at her as if he did not believe she was who she claimed to be. 'You and I will have to have a talk. Not now, but later. In the meantime I think it would be a good idea if we didn't say who you were. What can we call you?'

She thought a moment. 'Sarah Mann. Sarah is my given name, anyway.'

'What about Mann?'

'It was my married name, but I never use it now.'

'Another one that went wrong?' he said cryptically. Then he stood up as Kurt came running down the slope. 'Don't forget *my* name. It's Nigel Burgess.'

297

'Our chaps have gone back.' Kurt was a young German. He was no more than twenty and Sally wondered what had brought him here to fight small unsuccessful wars in Africa. Was it adventure or money or idealism? Whatever it was, he seemed to see this as just another day in the life he had chosen. A crashed plane, wounded women, a gun battle with government troops: they were all just part of his young way of life. 'They're probably trying to push those government bastards back over the river. What are we going to do?'

'We'll head for Simka. Father Lebrun should be there.' Tim looked down at Sally. 'That's a medical mission station. Father Lebrun is the priest in charge. He's also a doctor.'

He and Kurt lifted the two women into the back of the truck. Michele was still unconscious and Sally looked worriedly at her. 'Is she going to be all right?'

'I don't know, Mrs Mann. I'll get there as quickly as I can, without bumping you around.'

None the less it was a bumpy, uncomfortable ride. It took them two hours to reach Simka, a collection of huts, two of them with wide verandas, on the banks of a narrow, swift-flowing river. Dusk was turning into night as they pulled up on the outskirts of the mission. Sally heard a bell tolling as Tim switched off the engine.

'The Angelus. Just in time for a few prayers from you, Kurt. You're a Catholic.'

The boy laughed as he got out of the truck. 'Don't tell Father Lebrun – he's got more on his mind than trying to re-convert me. I'll go in and see if there's anyone around.'

As Kurt went off Tim said, 'We don't want to get Father Lebrun into any trouble.'

'Whose side is he on?'

'Nobody's. He's a true Christian, I guess. How is she?' He nodded at the still unconscious Michele.

Sally stroked the head lying in her lap. 'I'm worried for her – ' She felt the tears running down her cheeks, but could do nothing to stop them.

'Sally – how did you get into this, for God's sake?'

Sally touched the once-perfect face, marred now by the ugly wound; but she could not see Michele any longer, the face was shadowed and indistinguishable in the sudden darkness as night came down. She knew that Michele was dead and it no longer mattered if anyone was aware of what they had been to each other.

'We used to live together. We were lovers.'

'Oh Jesus, Sally – ' She could not see his face, either; he sounded as if he had sighed deeply, almost like a sob. 'We joked about it once – the lesbians in the pits at Indianapolis. Did you know about it then?'

'No-o . . .' But it was difficult to remember. 'I'm glad you don't act shocked. A lot of men would.'

He felt for her shoulder, touched it. 'Sally, I don't judge people any more. We all love in our own way.'

Then Kurt came back with Father Lebrun. The priest was dressed in a ragged white soutane; he wore a piece of rope instead of a cord round his middle. He was middle-sized and middle-aged but in tomorrow's light Sally would be surprised at how old he looked.

'No government troops,' said Kurt. 'They came through here this morning, but Father Lebrun told them he hadn't seen any of us in weeks.'

'What have we here?' said Father Lebrun in French and looked in at Sally and the dead Michele.

'One dead and one with a badly shattered knee.' Tim also spoke in French. 'I don't think you need to know the name of the dead woman, Father. Kurt and I will take her off into the bush and bury her – '

'No!' Sally said fiercely.

Tim put a comforting hand on her arm. 'I'm afraid that's the way it's got to be – for Father Lebrun's sake, if for no one else's. He can't afford to take sides, not even with the dead. Oh, this is Madame Mann, Father. I'll move her on as soon as you can fix up her knee.'

Father Lebrun looked at Sally; they were barely distinguishable shapes to each other. He had a smell of incense about him and she wondered if he had been at a service when Kurt had called him away. As if reading her thoughts he said, 'I say Benediction once a week. It helps one's faith – '

Sally went to say something: about faith, love, something like that. But the whole day, exhaustion, pain and grief, abruptly caught up with her. She lost consciousness, slipped into merciful blackness.

When she woke she had a moment of panic trying to establish where she was. She was in a bed beneath a mosquito net; something was wrong with her right leg. She clutched at the net, tried to pull herself up. Then the net was lifted and Tim was soothing her. She stared at him: the sight of him only made her more disoriented. Then memory flooded back. She put a hand down to her leg, felt the splints starting at the middle of her thigh and running down below her knee.

'Father Lebrun operated on you.'

'What time is it?'

'One-thirty in the morning. Here.' He handed her a drink that tasted of limes. She noticed that he was in a white soutane even more ragged than the priest's had been. 'I'm supposed to be another priest, just in case any of the patients notice me. You're in Father Lebrun's house. He thought it safer than putting you out in the ward with the other patients.'

'How's my leg?'

He hesitated a moment. 'Not good, I'm afraid. Unless the doctors back in the States can perform a miracle, he thinks you're going to have a gammy leg from now on. I guess you're lucky at that. Compared to Madame Onza.'

'Did you bury her? Out in the bush, like some native? She wouldn't have liked that.' She wept quietly for the dead Michele: Africa had reclaimed her after all.

Tim sat with his hand resting on hers: he could have been a priest comforting a sinner. But the image would not have pleased him: he had never been hypocritical about his own sins. 'Sally, we're going to have to move you from here very soon. Father Lebrun hasn't said you have to go, but he's in a hell of a situation. He's here to care for the blacks, not people like us.'

*People like us*: a phrase from home. 'Tim – why did you run away? And take Michael with you? That was the cruellest thing. For Nina, I mean.'

He let the net drop back between them as mosquitoes came humming in. She could just see him beyond the thin pale screen, his face half-lit by a small oil lamp on a side table. 'I had my reasons for going.'

'Nina never knew them. Or so she said.'

'No, I don't believe she did.' He was silent for a while and she waited, hoping for some revelation. But there was none: 'I took Michael with me because I wanted him to be *my* son, not your father's grandson. You probably won't understand that – you were too young to realize what it was like then. Perhaps he's changed – your father, I mean. Has he?'

She didn't reply at once, looking for a truthful answer. 'Maybe not all that much. Where is Michael now?'

He shook his head. 'He's safe.'

'Won't you come back? Now I've found you – '

'You didn't find me. We stumbled on each other. I've been afraid of something like this all these years, though I never dreamed I'd meet one of you out here. But coincidence never surprises me. It only surprises people who never get off their arses, who never expose themselves to chance.' He looked at her. 'You and I seem to be two of a kind.'

'Are you coming back with me? Nina still loves you.'

'It wouldn't work, not after all this time. There'd be too many recriminations. And there's still your father. Nina might forgive me. But he never would.'

'Where have you been all these years? Have you been doing – *this* all the time?'

He chuckled, a little sourly, she thought. 'No. There's just so much demand for mercenaries. The market may pick up, especially here in Africa, but up till now it hasn't been much of a living.'

'Do you call it a living, killing other men for money?'

'Oh, come on, Sally!' He laughed. 'Weren't you bringing the money to pay us?'

She had never been good at argument, mainly because she never thought matters out beforehand. She saw something crawling up the net and she reached up to brush it away, but Tim's hand flicked it away first.

'Cockroach. Don't get out of bed without your shoes – you'll have jiggers under your toenails before you know where you are. This isn't Beaufort Park.' He was only gently sarcastic. 'I'm not coming back with you, Sally. And you have to promise me you won't tell Nina or anyone else that we met.'

'I can't do that! How can you ask me to do that to her?'

'It'll be kinder – she's probably got over it all by now.'

'She hasn't – '

Again he was silent: *nor have you*, she thought. 'It'll still be for the best. Don't tell her.'

'I can't promise that – '

'You'll have to. You owe me something, Sally. If it gets out why you were here – flying in with your lesbian girl-friend, bringing a million dollars of Beaufort money to pay some cheap mercenaries in a cheap little rebellion – '

'Stop it!' She felt sick; she had not expected him to be as cruel and unprincipled as this. But why not? Hadn't he been cruel to Nina? 'You're blackmailing me – '

'I know. But only to protect Michael. I've made a new life for him. He's happy – '

'Where is he? How can a boy be happy when he doesn't know who his mother is?'

'He's happy,' he said doggedly. He stood up: she saw that the soutane was much too short for him, looked more like a dress. 'Go back to sleep. I'll see you in the morning.'

It was not easy to go back to sleep, despite her weariness. Her mind ached as much as her leg; she was crippled in more ways than one. She lay there, watching the cockroaches climb up the snowy hill of the net above her. She could hear the grunting chorus of frogs down by the river and from the hospital ward there came the sound of someone crying in a thin ululating wail, like an incantation against pain. She fell asleep just before daylight and did not waken when Father Lebrun looked in on her before he went across to his chapel to say morning Mass. He wondered what had brought her all this way to the Congo, but he had given up asking such questions years ago. He went across to the tiny chapel and, as he did every morning, prayed for an answer to the biggest question of all.

Sally woke at noon when the priest and a black nurse brought her lunch. 'It's not much,' he said. 'Do you speak French?'

'Yes, Father. Thank you for what you have done for me.'

He dismissed the nurse and sat down beside the bed. 'Major Burgess has gone away.' He put out a reassuring hand as he saw the look, a mixture of fear and surprise, on her face. 'He'll be back. He has to do something about his men. They aren't going to be needed any more, I gather.'

'How long will he be?'

'A couple of days at least. But we couldn't move you before then in any case. When he comes back, he's going to take you over the border to Angola. It will be a long hard journey and I hope your leg stands up to it. It would be much easier for you to go over into Northern Rhodesia, but I understand you have reasons for not wanting any questions asked. The Portuguese tend to ask fewer questions than the British, at least out here. I think you should go into a hospital in Luanda for a few days when you get there, so that they can check on your leg. Then go home to America as soon as you can and have the American doctors look at it. They have everything available to help you.' He said it wistfully rather than enviously.

'Father, make out a list of what you need here. No, not what you *need*. Everything you'd *like*.'

'Ah – ' He smiled at her innocence. 'I'd like the Mayo Clinic. No, Mrs Mann, a small donation would be welcome. But it isn't necessary.'

'You work here alone? I mean, are you the only white?'

'There were two other priests here with me, but they were killed earlier this year. The government won't allow our Order to send anyone out to replace them. So there's only me and four black girls I've trained as nurses. We get by,' he said, but it sounded more like a prayer than a statement.

'What do you know about – Major Burgess?' She almost tripped on Tim's alias.

Father Lebrun shrugged. 'Just that he seems a nice man in a job I don't admire. He's been in this part of the country about six months, off and on. He seems to come and go.'

'Where does he go to?'

'I don't know. And I've never asked.' His tone was unexpectedly curt.

'I'm sorry, Father. I was just curious, that's all. He's been so kind and helpful, for a stranger.'

'That's funny. I had the feeling you two knew each other.'

'No.' She hoped her lie didn't show. 'He's just an attractive man, that's all.'

He smiled, showing teeth ruined by bad diet. 'I'd forgotten how men and women react to each other out there – ' He nodded vaguely. 'Would you really care to send us some things for the mission? I could make out a small list.'

'As large a list as you like, Father.'

'Not too large. Otherwise the government would confiscate everything.'

Over the next two days Sally had time to think. She found the heat uncomfortable and she struggled out of the Mother Hubbard night-gown and lay naked under the single rough sheet, only putting the gown back on when Father Lebrun came to examine her leg. She lay propped up in the bed gazing out the window. Natives came and went across the river in canoes that seemed to have no freeboard at all; on one occasion there was a hullabaloo as four men in two canoes chased away a large crocodile. In the early morning birds rose in a vari-coloured cacophony, drowning out the tinny sound of the chapel bell. During the day the heat lay like a depressing mood on the mission; people drifted in slow motion through the harsh green glare. It was a tiny world in which Sally knew, to her shame, that she could never play a part. Such sacrifice was beyond her.

She thought of her talk with George Biff and what was happening with the blacks in America. The same was happening here in

303

Africa, only the spectrum of hate and violence and revolution was going to be so much wider. George had accused her of not knowing what was happening in her own country; he could accuse her of the same thing here. She was here solely because of her love for Michele; she had not even wanted to ask the background to Gaston Onza's planned coup. She wondered how selfish other people were: worlds fell apart but unless it was one's own small world, how much did one care? She looked down at her leg under the hoops holding the sheet off it. She had been crippled in a cause that meant nothing to her.

Tim came back late in the evening of the second day. He was alone, still driving the Land-Rover but no longer dressed in battle fatigues. He wore a bush jacket, slacks, desert boots and a battered slouch hat with a puggaree. She had seen pictures in magazines of professional hunters who looked exactly like him and she wondered if that was what he was when he was not a mercenary soldier. But she did not question him.

'It's going to take us at least three days to get to Luanda. You can go into hospital for a couple of days while they look at your leg. Then you can catch a plane for Lisbon. I think it'd be a good idea if you had someone meet you there.'

'I don't have any money – '

He grinned. 'Never thought I'd hear a Beaufort say that. Never mind, I have enough to get you home.'

They left at first light next morning. Sally was put on a mattress in the back of the Land-Rover; a canvas top had been rigged up, leaving the sides open. Tim had brought tinned food with him from wherever he had been; he said nothing about what had happened to his men and again Sally did not question him. She only wanted to go home, to break and forget all involvement with Africa. But she knew that was not going to be easy.

She said goodbye to Father Lebrun. 'You could do with so much more than what you have on your list – '

'I'm afraid if I asked for more it wouldn't reach me. Perhaps you could give something to our Order?' He was a man of charity, but to ask for it was difficult.

She promised to do that. 'Thank you, Father. And pray for me.'

'Of course. And for you too, Major Burgess?'

'There are more deserving cases, Father. Good luck.'

They drove off, watched by natives standing like shadows among the morning shadows. Sally, propped up in the back of the truck, looked back at the diminishing white figure of the priest fading into nothingness as the sun came up over the trees and swallowed him.

Several miles along the narrow road Tim pulled up. 'I buried your friend over in there.'

On an impulse she said, 'May I see her grave?'

'No.' He was blunt but not unkind. 'It's just a heap of rocks. It wouldn't do you any good, Sally.'

She shook her head, but stopped herself from weeping. 'She was so ambitious. She wanted to be the President's wife, did you know that? I mean she wanted it, well, like a title or something.'

'I'd heard people talk about her. What made you love her?'

'I don't know.' One couldn't explain love; or anyway she could not. If it had been love: but it was too late now to examine that. As Tim had said, it wouldn't do her any good. 'I don't think it was the sort of love you had for Nina.'

'Hardly.'

'I didn't mean it that way – '

'Don't let's talk about it.'

They drove on and Michele, under a cairn of stones, beautiful no longer and beyond the spur of ambition, dropped away into memory. Where love is at its least vulnerable.

They camped that night on the border, though Sally would not have known had Tim not told her. 'Lines on a map, that's all. Nobody ever asked the blacks what they thought about who owned them. The joke is, the new black governments are jealous about the borders the whites gave them. I think Africa might be the original home of black comedy.'

'Why do you never take anything seriously, Tim?'

'Your father used to accuse me of being whimsical. He was wrong – and so are you. I take a great many things seriously. Including what's happening out here.'

'Then you're going to stay on here?'

He smiled at her across the camp fire. 'Ah, you don't get me that way. I told you – you drop a word to Nina or anyone that you met me and I'll spill the beans about why you were here.'

'Right now I don't think I'd care.'

'Care about someone but yourself, old girl.'

'That sounds good coming from you!'

'You'd be surprised how much I did care – still do. I left Kansas City because I cared for other people, not just for myself.' Over the years he had come to believe that: self-justification is necessary in self-exile. He hadn't the faith of Father Lebrun, another self-exile.

He picked her up, put her back in the truck. 'I'll sleep in here, too, if you don't mind. Just in case.'

'In case what?'

He grinned. 'Beasties and things that go bump in the night.'

He lay down beside her on the floor of the truck. He had given his Schmeisser machine pistol to Kurt, who had gone looking for another war that needed mercenaries; now he carried a Springfield .30 rifle, a gun that either a soldier or a hunter might use. He loaded it and put it down between him and Sally.

'Goodnight. I'm glad your father can't see us.'

'What do you mean?'

'He had some idea that I slept with other women than Nina.'

'Did you?'

'No.' Margaret was only a dim memory now compared to Nina.

Nothing came into the camp during the night; or if it did Sally did not hear it. They drove on again next morning, picking up a graded road that led through tiny settlements where Tim took on petrol and where natives congregated at the back of the Land-Rover and stared in silently at the white woman lying on the mattress. They came to a town slightly larger than those they had passed through and Tim pulled up outside a general store and post office run by a portly Portuguese who spent all his time picking at his teeth with an ivory toothpick.

'We can send a cable from here – it will save time. By the time you get to Lisbon perhaps someone can be waiting there for you. Do you know Lisbon?'

'I was there once for the Portuguese Grand Prix.'

'Still mad on cars, eh? Where did you stay?'

'The Ritz.'

'Of course. Where else?'

He wrote out the cable: *Please meet me urgently in Lisbon Hotel Ritz. Explanations later. Sally.* Then he came out to the truck. 'Whom do I send it to?'

'Nina. She goes under her maiden name now.'

He looked at her steadily, eyes narrowed against the glare bouncing up from the red earth of the roadway. 'Are you trying to score a point off me?'

'No. I just think she's the only one who could leave at a moment's notice. And she's reliable.'

'She always was,' he said and went back into the store and paid extra to make sure the storekeeper sent the cable off immediately. He addressed it to Miss Nina Beaufort. He felt a pang, that of the middle-aged man for the lost love of his younger days. There was an almost irresistible urge to add his own name to that of Sally. *Explanations later.* But no amount of explanation would

306

alleviate the complications that would follow later.

The storekeeper spelled out the name. 'B-e-a-u-f-o-r-t.' It meant nothing to him, nor did Kansas City: his world stopped at the end of the dusty street, he was another self-exile. 'It will go today, senor. Promptly.'

They drove on, stopped the second night in a small town with a single hotel. Tim found a doctor, an elderly man with straggly yellow-grey hair and the smell of cheap cigars about him. He looked at Sally's leg and pronounced it all right.

'But you could save yourself a lot of discomfort if you got them to fly a plane out from Luanda. They're not cheap, but you're not short of money, are you?' Tim had told him they had been on a safari when Sally had had her accident. Women safari-hunters, especially Americans, were never short of money. 'How much is my fee, did you say? What do American doctors charge?'

When the doctor had gone Sally said, 'Do you have enough money to hire a plane to take us in? I'll pay you back.'

He shook his head, smiling. 'Where would you send it? You'd know where I was and, once you're back with Nina, you might feel tempted . . . I don't have enough to hire a plane and then put you on the one for Lisbon. You'll just have to put up with another day in the Land-Rover.'

She had loved him when she had been a schoolgirl, but she had never really known him. She realized now that she would probably never really know him. She wondered if she still loved him, in a schoolgirl way, but she could not tell. But she felt certain that, if he ever returned to Kansas City, Nina would still love him.

They reached Luanda the next day, driving in past the trappings of colonialism: the solid white buildings that reminded the colonists of home, the statues of past governors, the flags fluttering from white-painted flagstaffs like imperialist totems.

'The Portuguese were the first Europeans into Africa,' said Tim, 'and they may be the last out.'

'Would you fight for them or the blacks if a war broke out here?'

'I think I'm finished as a mercenary.' She wondered if other mercenaries used the term to describe themselves; he did not appear embarrassed by or ashamed of it. 'I took it up because, really, it seemed to be the only thing I was good at. Soldiering, I mean.'

'Were you doing it when you met Rudi Schnatz in Beirut?'

'Yes.'

'Did you need the money?'

'That depends whose standards we're using.' The $250,000 Lucas had given him was in a bank in Switzerland, drawing six and a half per cent on American commercial bonds. Tax-free though it was, it did not allow him to live lavishly; but it was comforting to know that he and Michael would never be on the bread-line. 'No, I took it up because it gave me something to do.'

'Does Michael know what you do?'

'No. He thinks I'm a part-time Big White Hunter. It fits his image of me.'

'Does he love you?'

He thought of the boy in boarding-school in Nairobi: fair-haired like his mother, athletic, extraverted and easy-going. Who accepted that his mother was dead; but sometimes, memories of his babyhood stirring in him like a deep current, would ask questions that Tim had difficulty in answering. 'Yes, I think so. We get on well together. That's not something every father and son does.'

'I'm glad,' she said. 'For your sake. But you shouldn't deny Nina the same joy.'

He said nothing to that. He found the hospital and, without too much fuss, Sally was admitted. The doctors looked at her knee, shook their heads at the long-term prospects for it but said it was doing well enough for her to travel. Tim came back in the evening and said he had booked her out on a plane for Lisbon the following day. He handed her a hundred dollars in single bills.

'I went to a *bureau de change* and got you dollars – you can use those anywhere. I can remember when the pound had the same usefulness,' he added sardonically. He longed to go home to England, but he might be too easily found there. 'I wish I could give you more, but that's all I can spare at the moment. I have to get home myself.'

'Where's home?' But she smiled when he smiled and shook his head. 'I thought I might trap you.'

'No. You and I have a bargain. I hope you're a woman of honour.'

'I'll keep my part of the bargain, Tim. I owe you too much.'

He leaned over, kissed her on the cheek. 'I loved all you Beaufort sisters.'

'Do you have a new wife? Or a girl-friend?'

'No new wife. But I get by. If you know where to look, there is always a pretty woman waiting to be consoled.'

'Will you come to the airport tomorrow?'

'Yes. I want to make sure you leave Africa. For your sake.'

'And yours,' she said and he didn't deny it.

The plane took off early the next morning. She was carried on board on a stretcher and Tim went with her to say his final farewell. He kissed her again, on the lips this time. He felt an emotion he had not felt in years; he hoped that his eyes were not glistening. Again he felt the temptation to see Nina once more; all he had to do was sit back in the seat and buckle on the seat-belt. But reason, the bane of love and lovers, held him back. There had been aching periods of loneliness in the years past and there would be another one tonight. But he could never go back till Lucas and Margaret were dead. And by then it would be too late for what he and Nina had once had.

'Goodbye, Sally. Take care. And don't shed too many tears over Michele. It would never have worked out.'

From the plane's window she saw him standing on the tarmac. He had put on dark glasses against the glare and under the slouch hat he could have been anyone, a stranger growing smaller and smaller as Africa grew larger about him. The plane climbed, the continent fell away under a wing, slipped into the past: a scribble of surf breaking on a palm-fringed shore, a stone-marked grave, the taste of lost love upon the lips.

# 5

Nina arrived in Lisbon the day after Sally checked into the Ritz. The flight up from Luanda had not been too uncomfortable. The hotel called a doctor who looked at the smashed knee and said that, if Senorita Beaufort insisted, there was no reason why she should not fly on in a day or two to America. Sally thanked him, then asked him to add his bill to the hotel's. Next she cabled Magnus to send her money, sank back into the bed in the best suite in the hotel and slept till noon the next day. When she woke she phoned the man in Marseilles and told him she had crashed his plane and it was a total write-off. Because she did not want any enquiries by the insurance company, she asked him to send her a bill for the plane. She would pay for it out of the money in the bank in Zurich.

Then Nina arrived. 'Where the hell have you been? A cable from some place called – ' She looked at the cable she had taken from her handbag. 'Vila Teixiera de Sousa. Where's that, for God's sake?'

'Sit down. *Please.* I'll tell you all about it.' Which she did, leaving out only the most important item: Tim.

'How did you get out of there?'

'Some mercenaries brought me out. Professional soldiers. They were fighting for Michele's husband. Oh Nin!' She began to weep, more for Nina than for herself.

But Nina was not to know the reason. 'Sal – it was for the best. You had no future with her. Prue told me you had met her again in Germany.'

They caught a Pan American plane out next day for New York. A day later they were home in Kansas City. She was admitted to hospital and a team of doctors looked at her knee. One look at their faces told her the worst.

'You'll be able to walk,' said the senior surgeon, 'but I'm afraid you're always going to have a limp.'

'The damage wasn't done by the doctor who originally fixed me up?' She did not want to think the worst of Father Lebrun.

'No, we think he did as well as he possibly could have in the circumstances. I understand you were in a car accident somewhere in Africa, that right? Whoever he was, he did a good job. I doubt if any of us could have done a better one, not the way the knee was shattered. I'm sorry, Miss Beaufort – '

'It's all right.' She had reached a stage of resignation that hovered on the thin edge between acceptance of the impending handicap and total depression. She would buy a silver-topped cane . . . She thought of Tony Gentleman, whose money she had used for a most unrespectable venture. He had got his revenge. 'Do what you can for me, doctor.'

After the operation Lucas came alone to see her. He was still as straight-backed as ever but his face had aged and he no longer had the energy that used to fire him. He had lost interest in politics and had taken to having an occasional lunch with Harry Truman at the Kansas City Club, two old men who had buried their differences in the recognition that their respective worlds no longer belonged to them. President Truman's place in history was safe and Lucas Beaufort's fortune was still secure, but younger men were making their mark. Camelot had come to Washington and conglomerates, a word that brought shudders to Lucas, had come to the business world. Without admitting it to himself he was half-way to surrender, another word that would have brought a shudder to him if anyone should have suggested it.

'Do I ask what you were doing in Africa or isn't it any of my business?'

'It was an adventure, Daddy.' She had known he would ask the question and she had worked out her answer. 'I was invited down there to see a friend and I thought it would be fun to fly all the way. It just didn't work out as I'd planned, that was all.'

'Did you get to see your friend?'

'Yes. She was the one who arranged my passage back.'

There were other questions he wanted to ask, but he refrained. He and Edith had never had any secrets from each other – except the secret about Tim's pay-off and disappearance. But he realized that there would always be secrets between his daughters and him. 'Charlie Luman called the house last night.'

'Good old Charlie.'

She was discharged from hospital a week later and went home to the big house. Margaret and Bruce were living in what had been Nina's house and it was now legally theirs. Nina, Prue and Sally were now back in their old rooms in their father's house. Sally had a feeling that life was turning backwards, but she had never indulged her imagination and she put the thought out of her mind.

Prue told her about Guy. 'We're going to be married in June. At his mother's place in the Loire. A white wedding in the family at last. Do people really still believe that white signifies virginity?'

'If they do, you should be the final disillusionment. How does Daddy feel about the marriage taking place in France?'

'He didn't argue.' Prue was abruptly sober. 'He seems to have given up on all of us. Poor Daddy.'

Magnus came to see Sally and she asked him to do her two favours. 'There's a list of things. Would you arrange for them to be sent to this mission in Katanga? Addressed to Father Lebrun.'

'Katanga, eh?'

'No questions, Magnus, please. The second thing is, arrange for the bank in Switzerland to send $250,000 to this mission Order in Belgium. The gift has to be anonymous.'

'And I'm not allowed to ask any questions at all?'

'None.'

A week later he came back to the house. 'I asked a question of the bank in Zurich. I'm told the Gentleman account has been

311

reduced by some four million dollars on your signature.'

'That's right.'

Magnus was surprised at her calm control: this was a new Sally. 'I hope it was for a good cause.'

'I thought it was at the time.'

'Some day I hope you'll tell me what happened out there in Africa. Tell it to me as your friend, not your lawyer.'

'Never, Magnus.'

# Chapter Eleven

♦

# Prue

I

Prudence Mary Beaufort was married to Guy Antoine, Comte de Belfrage, in June 1962, a quiet month in an otherwise eventful year. The marriage took place at the Belfrage chateau at St Cast near Saumur in the Loire valley. It was a Catholic ceremony, a fact that upset Lucas; he had done a little research and learned that Saumur was one of the old Protestant strongholds of France and he had expected the Belfrages to be Protestant. Though no true believer in religion, he preferred to be entangled with only one faith. Prue, for her part, had no qualms at all, since her belief or even interest in any religion was almost non-existent. It was Nina, the only one who had not done so, who remarked that the Beaufort sisters seemed to make a habit of marrying Catholics. Privately she wished Prue more luck than Margaret and Sally had had.

Lucas chartered a Boeing 707, filled it with the family, relatives and friends and flew them across the Atlantic for the wedding. Guy's mother, Stephane, was filled with horror at the prospect of being invaded by such a horde of Americans, particularly a group coming out of the primitive Middle West, wherever that was. Guy had told her that Kansas City was actually a beautiful city and she had looked it up on a map, only to discover that it was over a thousand miles west of New York. She was an educated intelligent woman, but she was French provincial: her world was France. All else was *Ultima Thule*, including America.

313

The Middle Westerners turned out to be much less barbaric than she had expected. True, the women did have their hair done in a style that she thought had gone out with Marie Antoinette's head, but their dressing was relatively smart, when one took into consideration how far they were from Paris.

Prue and Guy had consummated their union virtually every night they had been together for six months prior to the wedding ceremony; but Prue still managed to look unsullied and expectant, if not pregnant, in her traditional white wedding gown. Nina and Margaret and Sally added to the beauty close to the altar, and Martha and Emma were very pretty flower girls. Lucas, in tail-coat and grey silk cravat, looked handsome and dignified and younger than he had looked for years. Magnus, Bruce Alburn, Charlie Luman and all the other American male guests looked equally impressive. Stephane de Belfrage had to admit that, for cowboys, they were surprisingly civilized.

The guests were all accommodated in various hotels and inns in the Loire valley, Margaret, with her usual efficiency, making the arrangements and Lucas footing the bill. George Biff had been sent over in advance to Paris and he brought down Sidney Bechet and a full band to play real American music at the reception. Lucas took Stephane on to the dance floor, where everyone commented on what a handsome couple they made and politely made no comment on them at all regarding their dancing; Lucas had rhythm and kept beaming at Sidney Bechet every time he passed the band, but Stephane's dancing seemed not to have advanced from the *polonaise* and she had never been very good even at that. Lucas's Francophobia was not lessened while Stephane was in his arms, beautiful though she was.

After the wedding the Beauforts, their friends and relatives all went home; perhaps it was only coincidence that over the next twelve months construction was begun on two French-style chateaux in Mission Hills. Prue and Guy came back to St Cast from their honeymoon in Martinique, tanned, sated and still happy in each other's company. The only cloud in their heaven was Guy's mother.

Stephane insisted that Guy, as master of the de Belfrage estate, should live in the chateau: it was more than large enough for her and the newly-weds. Indeed it was: she had a large suite in one wing and Prue and Guy had an even larger suite in the opposite wing. The only dimension that was not taken into consideration was the one to accommodate temperaments. From the first day of her return it was evident to Prue who was still mistress of the chateau.

'Guy darling,' she said at the end of the first month, speaking in English because she did not trust her French in argument, 'why can't we live in Paris?'

'My darling,' he said in French; he had come to recognize Prue's ploys, 'it is impossible. I cannot run the estate from Paris. Especially now with the grape harvest coming in. We'll go up to Paris for a few weeks just before Christmas.'

'Then I think we'd better come to an understanding with your mother,' said Prue, still sticking to English. 'I'm your wife, not the daughter of the house.'

He changed to English to placate her. 'She will change. Give her time to adjust to the idea that I'm no longer hers but yours. Didn't you tell me that your father could be too possessive? Mothers can be the same.'

Ah, but there was a difference, she thought. Lucas's daughters had all shown their independence of him; but Guy would never rebel against his mother. There had been hints of Stephane's dominance over Guy, but Prue, too much in love to care about minor problems, had ignored them. But now, part of the family, locked into the way of life in the chateau, she saw that the problems were going to be a long way from minor. Stephane would continue to run Guy's life and, by projection, that of Guy's wife.

'Your mother is, I don't know, *different*. I mean from what she was before we married. If I'd known – '

Guy did not take that up: he wanted no doubts about their marriage so early in the piece. Things *were* different with his mother; and she had explained why. But he could not pass on the explanation to Prue. 'Give her time, darling – please. She has had only me ever since my father died – '

'What was your father like? You've never told me anything about him.'

They were driving back from Saumur where they had been to lunch with some of Guy's officer friends at the cavalry school. He had resigned his commission in the army three years before, but he had kept up certain friendships and each time he visited the cavalry school he regretted that his army life was behind him forever.

'He was a man of honour,' he said, speaking in French again. Prue, who had an ear almost as sharp as her eye, appreciated that the non-Parisian French sometimes spoke in an almost literary way, without embarrassment and as naturally as if they were speaking colloquially. 'He was the acting-commander at the cavalry school in 1940. Americans would not have heard of it, but the students at the school, my father's students, performed a *beau geste* that we still treasure. They left their classes and went north to fight the Germans. They were wiped out almost to a man, or rather a boy, for that was what most of them were. My father went with them, but he was not killed or even wounded. He looked around at his dead boys, he cursed the politicians who had given France away, then he shot himself. I was eight years old then and I remember standing by my mother's side when one of my father's students came home and told her what had happened. My mother did not cry, or at least not in front of me. All she said was that she understood why my father had done what he did and she hoped I would undertsand, too.'

'And do you?'

'Yes. One does not leave one's friends, even when they are dead.'

Prue turned her head away, looked out the car window. She tried to remember her history: Americans, she was sure, had died with the same sense of honour. But America had never known the disgrace that had overwhelmed France in 1940; the French could not be blamed if they set a certain quiet grandeur to the small *beaux gestes* such as those of Colonel le Comte de Belfrage and his young cavalry students. She was moved by what Guy had told her and she had no words, English or French, with which to reply

The day was hot and the Loire, glinting like a broken wine glass, looked inviting. Impulsively she grabbed Guy's arm. 'Let's stop for a swim!'

'No. We have no bathing suits. One doesn't swim nude in the river, not here. Not us.'

'We could swim in our underwear. Don't be so stuffy, Guy – '

'No.' He increased the speed of the car. 'We have to get home.'

She settled back, hot and irritated. The Citroën had no air-conditioning; the chateau had neither air-conditioning nor central heating. Stephane de Belfrage, though she did not live a Spartan life, was set against comforts that she considered were coddling. It suddenly struck Prue, her irritation from the heat and the revelation of the manner of Guy's father's death coming together in her mind, that Stephane, after all these years, still saw herself as a soldier's wife. A certain discipline had to be maintained, a degree of self-sacrifice practised.

'What's the matter?' She looked sideways at Guy. 'You've had something on your mind all day.'

'Business.' His tone was almost curt. 'Nothing for you to worry about.'

316

She spoke in French, to suit him. 'Don't leave me out, Guy.'

He slowed the car, put out a hand and clutched her wrist. 'I'm sorry, darling.' His voice was gentler, a lover's voice. 'I'll see that from now on you are left out of nothing.'

She felt ashamed that, for some strange reason, she did not quite believe him.

She pleaded a headache because of the heat when they reached the chateau and she went upstairs to their bedroom and lay down. It was a large, high-ceilinged room, elegantly furnished in the Empire style, with glass doors that opened out on to a tiny balcony that faced south towards the vineyards. She knew nothing of wine or wine-growing, but already she had been impressed by the mystique of it. Here among the vineyards there was none of the exaggerated homage to the grape that she had found with wine buffs she had met in Paris and London, drinkers who had amused her with the veneration of their own palates. Guy and his mother and the workers in the St Cast vineyards did not go in for worship of their product but they left no doubt that they considered they were doing more than just producing something to drink. St Cast wines were a beverage not to be spoken of in the same breath as Coke, Australian sweet sherry and other bottled burlesques. The grape-pickers were out among the vines now and Guy had told her that this year's vintage was expected to be a very good one but not a superb one. She began to wonder what the rest of her own year would be like.

She loved Guy and the love was not all sexual. She had an almost overpowering need for sex; she had been only half-joking when she had told Sally she was a controlled nymphomaniac. But so long as one man could satisfy that need, she would be faithful to him; and Guy did satisfy her. But that was not all: he satisfied her emotional needs. She was not as self-contained as her sisters and other women thought; some of the more sensitive men she had slept with had realized that she wanted more than they could offer with their bodies. She wanted emotional security; never having known loneliness she was, paradoxically, afraid of it. She wanted protection, but she was prepared to give all her love, physical and emotional, to that end. Love, she knew, was a mutual selfishness, but if both lovers realized that and accepted it, then it could endure. She began to wonder for the first time if she was asking too much of Guy.

She dozed off and was wakened by Guy's kiss. 'What time is it?'

'Six o'clock. I have to go out. I'm bringing an old friend back for dinner.'

'Someone I know?'

'No. I knew him in Algiers when I was a boy.' That was the first time she had heard he had spent time in Algiers. 'It's years since I've seen him. I'll be back in an hour.'

At seven, after she had bathed and changed, she went downstairs. Stephane was sitting in the big drawing-room, the doors to the terrace wide open to the still-warm evening. This part of the house faced north, above a long slope of yellow-green grass that ran down to the river. On the far side of the river a long low bluff stood like battlements, topped by a line of poplars that were as still as furled flags. At the water's edge a lone fisherman waited patiently for some sign of life at the far end of his rod.

'One would think that nothing has changed.' Stephane could speak English, but with Prue she never used the language; her daughter-in-law had to speak French or be excluded from any conversation with her. 'I sometimes like to think that before Henry the First left here for England he might have gazed out on a scene exactly like this.'

'You sound as if you wished you had lived in those times.'

'I am a romantic. One always wishes for more than one has at the moment.'

'I'm a romantic, too. At least I think I am. But I'm happy with the moment.'

'But then you have lost nothing, have you?'

Stephane had not turned her head till this moment to look at her daughter-in-law. She was a beautiful woman, at fifty looking no more than forty, only a faint trace of grey in her dark hair; but there was an air of almost too much perfection about her, as if she controlled her beauty in the same way as she controlled her behaviour. She was capable of temper, bias, hate and love; but all those emotions were strained through a cool exterior that chilled everyone but her son. She lived in a past that had not yet been confided to Prue and she would have disappointed Edith, because she had no perspective at all. She hated the present and all that it stood for.

'What have you lost, Stephane?' Up till now Prue had been deferential towards her mother-in-law for Guy's sake; but upstairs in the past hour she had decided to assert her independence. 'Except your husband and that was a long time ago.'

There was no time for Stephane to answer, if indeed she intended to answer. There were voices out in the hall, then Guy came into the room with his old friend. He was a short, very muscular man with black hair cut *en brosse* and one side of his face disfigured by what might have been the scars of a bad burn.

Prue's first thought was that, even allowing for the scars, he looked much too old to have been a boyhood friend of Guy's.

The newcomer went straight to Stephane, bowed and kissed her hand. Prue, all at once alert though for no reason she could name, saw that the meeting had a formality to it that seemed to go beyond the mere greeting of the mother of an old friend. For a moment Stephane was almost regal in her acceptance of the stranger's acknowledgement of her; Prue wondered if, in her romantic mood, she saw herself as the ghost of Eleanor of Aquitaine. Then, like a queen unbending, she took the man's hand, held it tightly and smiled at him.

'Henri, you look so well.'

'I shall look even better very soon, madame.' Then he turned and waited to be presented to Prue.

Guy introduced him. 'Darling, this is our old friend Colonel Henri Raclot.'

He bowed, kissed Prue's hand: but there was less deference to Guy's wife than to his mother. 'Madame, it is a pleasure.'

But Prue knew at once that he was lying: he was not interested in her, wished instead that she was not here. She looked at Guy for support, hoping he would show hurt or indignation at his friend's dismissal of her; but there was no reaction at all from Guy on her behalf. Instead he seemed to have nothing but admiration for Raclot, smiling at the older man with what looked to be nothing less than hero worship.

'I think we should eat at once,' said Stephane. 'Just in case.'

*Just in case what?* Prue looked at Guy for an explanation, but he offered none. He took her arm and they followed Stephane and Raclot across the hall and into the dining room. She could feel the tension in his hand and she looked at him, but he was staring straight ahead, as if ignoring her. Or not wanting to be asked any questions.

The talk at dinner was desultory, not what one would have expected at the reunion of old friends. Prue, the outsider, sensed that the others seemed to be waiting for something. Raclot made a complimentary remark about the de Belfrage wine, but it seemed an afterthought: he was already on his third glass. Once he looked out the window and said, 'It is getting dark.'

'Not really,' said Prue, more to be included in the conversation than for any other reason. 'Where I come from we'd be glad of these European twilights.'

Raclot smiled, for the first time seemed to take an interest in her. 'I am a soldier. No soldier, even your American ones, likes twilight. Or dawn for that matter. They are times when one can be attacked.'

'Not here, surely?' Prue waved at the peaceful dusk settling beyond the windows.

'Ah no, not here.'

'Henri was at Dien Bien Phu,' said Stephane.

'Not just there,' said Raclot and he sounded regretful. 'There were other places.'

Several times Prue had seen him glance at his watch; he did so again now. She looked at her own watch: it was 8.30. Then, on the moment, the phone rang across the hall in the drawing-room. Stephane rose at once, not hurriedly; but Prue, watching her closely, could see the control that held her back from hurrying. It suddenly struck her that she had never seen Stephane go to answer the phone until one of the servants had first taken the call. She saw Stephane turn left as she went out into the hall, which meant she was going to take the call in the library and not in the drawing-room. It was to be a conversation she did not want overheard.

Prue looked at Guy and Raclot. Guy was sitting stiffly in his chair, his forearms flat on the table on either side of his plate; he held a dessert knife in his right hand, turning it slowly round and round with nervous fingers. The colonel looked more relaxed, but that was because he was more experienced in hiding tension. He moved his wineglass slowly in circles, gazing at it as if it were some sort of crystal ball. Then he seemed to become aware that it was empty; he reached for the decanter and poured himself some more wine. He reached across and poured wine into Guy's empty glass, then looked up in surprise as Prue pushed her own glass towards him.

'Pardon, madame. My manners are unforgivable.'

'Are we waiting to drink to something?' she said.

Guy and Raclot looked sharply at each other. Then Guy said, 'What makes you say that?'

She shrugged, wishing now she had said nothing. 'I don't know. I just had the feeling we were going to drink to something. A toast of some sort.'

'We'll try and think of something.' Raclot sat back, relaxing. 'To your President perhaps, madame?'

'We don't seem to drink to our Presidents. I understand it's thought un-American. You probably feel that's strange?'

'Not at all,' said Raclot. 'We Frenchmen don't always drink to our Presidents.'

Then Stephane came back, sat down. She took a sip of wine from her glass, wiped her mouth carefully with her napkin. 'That was from a friend in Paris. There has been an attempt to assassinate the General. It failed.'

There was silence for a moment, then Raclot sighed, put down his glass and sat back. Guy, too, seemed to relax; he picked up the peach from his plate and began to peel it. Prue looked at the wine in her glass, then said, 'Perhaps we should drink to that.'

'To what?' said Stephane.

'That General de Gaulle escaped being assassinated.'

Stephane stood up, stiff and haughty. 'Perhaps you had better explain, Guy. Not everything, but enough to let her know how we feel. Come, Henri.'

She went out of the room and, after a warning glance at Guy, Raclot got up and followed her. Guy stopped peeling the peach, put it down on his plate, the skin still hanging from it like pink crêpe. Prue sat waiting, knowing already that she was about to be told, or half-told, something she would rather not hear.

'You said not to leave you out.' Guy stared at the knife still in his hand. 'I think it would be better if you were.'

'No.' She was in mid-air, had taken the plunge.

He put down the knife carefully, as if laying a place setting. 'My mother is from Algiers. I was born there. My mother's family had a large property there, but no longer. When de Gaulle gave Algeria to the nationalists, we lost everything.'

*Everything but what surrounds us now:* but evidently that did not count. 'Did the – the nationalists take it away from your mother's family?'

'Not exactly.' He seemed to resent the question; as if she should have no questions but just listen to him without comment. 'But my grandparents had to leave the country – their lives would not have been worth a centime. The Algerians had already killed my uncles and cousins.'

'Where are your grandparents now?' They had not been at the wedding.

'They both died within a year of moving here. My mother will never forget or forgive what caused their death. Or who caused it.'

'The Algerians? I don't know much about it, Guy, but I thought that all they wanted was their independence – '

He shook his head sadly: but she had the feeling he would have been angry with anyone else but her. 'You Americans. You think independence is holy, an excuse for everything done in its name.'

'What about Colonel Raclot?'

'His family had been there even longer than my mother's. He went back there to settle soon after Dien Bien Phu. That was till

1958 when de Gaulle gave everything away.'

'What has the colonel been doing since?'

'The only thing he knows – soldiering. For anyone who will hire him.'

'Is someone hiring him now?' *Your mother, for instance?* But she dared not say that.

'No!' He was angry now. 'He believes in what he is fighting for. He is a man of honour – '

Twice in one day: she seemed to be surrounded by men of honour. Or anyway the ghost of one and the physical presence of – how many? She wondered if Guy saw himself as one.

'Are you one of them, too, Guy? A man of honour who seems disappointed because his President has just escaped assassination?' They were speaking in French and this time she was glad; somehow she felt more at ease in it in the circumstances. The subject was too bizarre for the commonplace of her own language: you didn't discuss the pros and cons of a Presidential assassination in Kansas City. 'You're involved in that, aren't you? All of you.'

He slumped in his chair. All at once she saw a weakness in him that had not been apparent before. But then, she asked herself, what had there been up till now to test him?

'I told you it would have been better if you had been kept out of this. It's not for you, darling. You will never understand how we feel.'

'Guy – ' She had to know this: 'Were you and your mother and Colonel Raclot actually involved in the planning of this – this attempt to kill General de Gaulle?'

'No.' But he sounded regretful, as if somehow he had missed out on something. 'Mother and I only learned about it this morning, just before you and I went out to lunch. Henri got in touch with me, to ask us to provide a safe house if some of the men had to hide. There wasn't time for me to get you out of the way, to take you up to Paris. We were afraid you'd be suspicious, acting so suddenly.'

'Oh Guy, don't you know me better than that? I love doing things on the spur of the moment.' But she couldn't laugh at the irony. 'Are the men going to come here?'

He shrugged. 'How does one know? They may all be dead by now.'

He stood up, took her arm and they went across to the drawing-room. Stephane looked up from her coffee. 'Well? Do you understand how we feel?'

'A little,' said Prue, hedging.

'A hundred years ago your Confederate soldiers felt the same, perhaps.' Raclot was sipping cognac. 'After they had been betrayed.'

'Perhaps,' said Prue, suddenly conscious of American history.

Raclot drained his goblet and looked at it; Stephane leaned across and poured more cognac from a decanter. Raclot nodded to her: she was a woman who understood there were times when a man had to drink. To Prue it looked as if Raclot intended doing a lot of drinking during the rest of the evening.

'I understand that you met Guy in Germany at the home of Count von Schnatz. You may have met my late employer there. M. Onza.'

'Yes.' What was it Sally had said about the world being only a collection of small parishes?

'Were you there to buy arms, too?' He laughed, shook his head at the warning glance Stephane gave him. He seemed less deferential towards her now, as if failure of their hopes had reduced them all to the same level. 'Ah, but then Americans don't need to buy arms, do they? Every American has his own gun, isn't that so?'

'Only every second one,' said Prue coolly.

Guy made a belated effort to defend his wife. 'Prue was there with her sister. They were old friends of Madame Onza.'

Raclot raised an eyebrow. 'Really? A beautiful woman, Madame Onza. Beautiful but dangerous, I believe. Did you know her politically?'

'I didn't know her at all.' Prue wondered for the first time if Guy had been at Rudi von Schnatz's to buy arms. Perhaps he had bought the very guns that had been aimed at General de Gaulle this evening. 'My sister knew her in Rome when she was an actress. Before she married M. Onza. She was killed, you know.'

'So I heard. I was in another part of Katanga at the time. That was another failure,' he said to the room at large and took another sip of cognac.

Prue knew that Sally had flown out to the Congo with Michele and that Michele had died when their plane had crashed; but that was all she knew. She guessed there was more to the venture than Sally's claim that it had been no more than a whim, just a spur-of-the-moment decision to accompany Michele. Sally had told her more than she had told Margaret or Nina or their father; but she had obviously been hiding something and Prue had not attempted to prise any more out of her. More than Sally's leg had been crippled: something else, shock, grief, *something* – had changed her. At the wedding in June she had almost succeeded in keeping herself in the background, isolating herself but for the attentive Charlie Luman. Prue wondered if Sally might have met this French colonel out in the Congo. She changed the subject, not wanting to open *that* can of beans, not tonight.

'I don't want to be involved in any of this,' she said. 'I'm still an American citizen and I want no part of it.'

'You are Guy's wife,' said Stephane, meaning *You are my daughter-in-law.* 'But if that is your wish – '

'Can you be trusted?' said Raclot.

'Of course!' This time Guy was not late in his defence. 'You must apologize for that remark, Henri.'

Raclot lifted his glass, said drily, 'Of course. My apologies, madame.'

Prue stood up. 'I am going up to bed. Coming, Guy?'

Guy looked at his mother and Raclot before he looked at his wife. Then he stood up and kissed her on the cheek. 'I'll stay a while longer with Henri. We have a lot to talk about.'

Stephane turned her cheek for Prue's kiss. 'Nothing more will be said about this after tonight. But for now you must allow us our disappointment.'

Raclot got unsteadily to his feet, breathed cognac fumes on to the back of Prue's hand. 'Long live America!'

'Thank you,' said Prue. 'I'm sure we'll manage to do that.'

Upstairs in her and Guy's bedroom she turned over the page on her calendar: 22 August 1962. She had never kept a diary and she wondered if she should now start one. An hour ago a new chapter had started in her life: perhaps it should be documented. But to what end? One purpose of a diary was to sort out one's thoughts: another way of getting perspective. But she had never been one to solve her problems on paper; she acted by instinct and so far her instinct had always proved right. Except, of course, her instinctive judgement of Guy: it looked as if she had been wrong there. It was not a problem she could solve by starting a diary.

She had been in bed an hour, had tried to read and been unable to, was becoming increasingly angry with Guy for not coming up to bed, when she heard the car coming up the long drive. It was not speeding, as she had expected; it came up the drive slowly, cautiously, as if the driver was not quite sure that he was approaching the right house. She got up, put on a robe and, turning out her light, went to the open window.

The car had pulled in below the front terrace, its lights already switched off. Three men got out as Guy went hesitantly down the steps to greet them. Then behind her the bedroom door opened and Stephane and Raclot were silhouetted against the light in the hall outside.

'Prue?' Then Stephane saw her at the window. 'Come away from there! No, don't put on the light!'

Prue moved back into the room. 'What's the matter? Who are those men?'

'Police.' Stephane looked around the dark room. 'We must hide Henri. Here – under the bed!'

'Pardon, madame,' Raclot said to Prue and dropped flat on the floor and rolled under the bed.

'Isn't that rather an obvious place?' Prue had the sudden feeling that she was in the middle of a French farce.

'Sometimes the most obvious place is the best. Get back into bed, pretend to be asleep.' Stephane was at the door, one ear cocked; men's voices, muted but authoritative, floated up from the entrance hall. 'They may go away without searching – '

'I told you, I don't want to be involved – '

'*Please.*' The abrupt change in Stephane startled Prue. She had never expected to see her mother-in-law plead with anyone, least of all herself. And in English. 'It may mean Henri's life. Perhaps – '

Prue did not allow her to finish. She slipped off her robe and slid into bed, pulling the sheet up. She heard Stephane say *Merci*, reverting to French, but she had already turned away, angry and bitter and, yes, afraid.

Then, though he was silent and not moving, she became aware of Raclot lying beneath her. Only in France, she thought; and wondered if Georges Feydeau had ever written tragedies. Because, though this was a bedroom farce, it could only end in tragedy.

She lay, ears strained, waiting for the sound of the car driving away. But that sound did not come: instead, after ten minutes, there was a gentle tap on her door. She wondered what she was supposed to do: wake at once or pretend to be deeply asleep? The dilemma was solved for her. The door was pushed open and the light was switched on. Two men stood there, one in a sports jacket, the other in a nylon windbreaker. Both of them had guns.

Prue sat up, blinking in the light. 'Pardon, madame,' said the shorter and older of the two men, the one in the sports jacket, 'are you the Countess? The young one?'

'Yes.' She reached for her robe. She was still not accustomed to being called the Countess, especially with Stephane in the house. To the servants Guy's mother was still the Countess and when they addressed Prue their use of the title was as awkward as her reception of it. 'Who are you?'

'Police, madame. Will you come downstairs, please?'

Her night-gown was skimpy and revealing; for the first time that she could remember, she felt naked and embarrassed. Which, perhaps, was a measure of her fear. But the two men politely turned away as she got out of bed and pulled on her robe. Then they put away their guns, gestured for her to go ahead of them out of the room. She led the way, all at once feeling a faint lift of hope: they were not going to search her room.

Stephane, Guy and the four house servants were all in the drawing-room. A tall lean man with prematurely grey hair, dressed in a dark blue suit, button-down shirt and black-knitted tie, sat at Stephane's escritoire, writing in a notebook. He looked up as Prue was ushered in by the other two policemen.

'Ah, the American countess. Do you speak French, madame? Good. Then we should get through our questioning very quickly. Take the others out, Jacques.'

'I should like to stay with my wife,' said Guy.

'A gallant thought, m'sieu. But I'm afraid we can't allow it. I've interrogated all of you independently. I can't make an exception for your wife, even though she is an American.'

Guy had taken Prue's hand as she had come into the room and stood beside him. Now he squeezed it, kissed her on the cheek, then followed his mother and the others out of the room. He had tried to tell her something with his eyes and the pressure of his hand, but she had not got the message. The doors were closed and she was alone with the grey-haired man who introduced himself as Inspector Perret.

'Have there been any visitors to the chateau this evening?'

Prue knew that Guy and his mother had been asked the same question; and the servants, too. That was what Guy had been trying to tell her: the answer that he and the others had given. But if they had all been interrogated independently, what answer had they given that had satisfied this police officer? Had they said no, there had been no visitors? Or yes, there had been a visitor, Colonel Raclot?

'Madame? I asked you a question.'

'I heard you, inspector. But I'd like to know what this is all about. Your men wake me, tell me nothing but just order me to come down here – What is going on?'

Perret sighed, ran a finger up and down the side of his long nose. He had dark bags under his eyes and he looked like a man whose bad health did not encourage him to be patient. 'Madame, our President, General de Gaulle, had a narrow escape from assassination earlier this evening. You heard about that, I presume?'

'Yes. Naturally, like everyone else, I was horrified that such a thing could happen – '

'Not everyone, madame. Your husband's mother, the Countess, would not have been horrified. She is an OAS supporter – we have known that for some time. Your husband – ' He shrugged. 'Possibly. Perhaps you would know that better than we do.'

'I am not interested in politics. French or even American.'

'I'm prepared to believe that, madame. When we learned you were to marry the Count, we had you investigated. Our one thought was, did your husband marry you as a possible source of funds for the OAS? You are heiress to a great deal of money.'

Prue somehow kept her temper; but the suggestion shocked her. What if it were true? 'Are French policemen always as rude as you, inspector?'

'Not normally, madame. But this is not a normal occasion. Someone tried to kill our President and we think your husband and his mother know who those men are. Or if they don't, then Colonel Raclot does. Was the Colonel here tonight?'

She could feel herself trembling inside. But she had to take the plunge: 'I have no idea who Colonel Raclot is. I have never met him.'

Perret stared at her and she knew with a sinking feeling that she had given the wrong answer. Then slowly he got to his feet, put away his notebook. 'I'm glad you are not involved, madame. It would have been embarrassing having to arrest an American citizen as an OAS sympathizer. Especially one with your name.'

Prue wanted desperately to sit down, but she dared not move; her legs were hollow, she could feel the sweat behind her knees. Perret walked past her out into the hall. She heard him say something and Stephane replied; but her hearing was as weak as her legs. When Guy came into the drawing-room and took her arm she almost collapsed against him.

'What's happening?' she whispered.

She could feel the tension still in him: he was all bones. 'They are going. What did you tell them?'

'Nothing.' They were both whispering. Then over Guy's shoulder she saw Perret back in the doorway. She raised her voice: 'I'm not used to anything like this – '

'We don't make a habit of it, madame,' said Perret. 'Thank you for your co-operation. Yours too, M. le Comte. We shall be in touch again, probably.'

Then he and his two partners were gone, the servants were dismissed and Stephane came back into the drawing-room. The police visit had had its effect on her: she poured herself a cognac. But she sipped the drink, did not gulp it down: she still had some control left.

'What did they ask you, my dear?'

'If Colonel Raclot had been here. I told them I didn't know him and had never met him.' She was recovering some of her own strength and composure. She went across and poured herself some of the cognac. 'That's the last lie I'll tell for you. And for you too, Guy. I have no sympathy at all for your feelings.'

She was prepared for the hostility in Stephane's face but not for that in Guy's. 'I didn't ask you for sympathy. All I wanted was a wife's loyalty.'

She was still sufficiently wrought-up to be on the verge of hysteria; she wanted to giggle at his pomposity. They were speaking French, but she did not *think* French: she still tended to translate the words in her mind. Then she saw that he would never forgive her if she derided him at this moment. With the arrival of the police he had committed himself fully to his mother's side.

'You have it, Guy,' she said with an effort. 'In everything but this.'

Stephane, first things always first with her, putting a potential marital quarrel in its proper place, said, 'At this moment we have to think of Henri. Where is he?'

'Still in my room, I suppose.' Prue was glad of the interruption: she was in no fit state to begin a fight with her husband.

'Get him, Guy. At once.' Stephane gave orders like a true colonel's wife and Guy went out of the room almost at the double.

He was back in less than a minute. 'He's not there!'

'Damn! Surely he hasn't left the house – they could be waiting for him out there. We must find him.'

Ignored by her husband and mother-in-law, Prue abruptly left the room and went upstairs. She wanted to *run* up the wide staircase, but she knew instinctively that from now on she had to match her own dignity against that of Stephane. For she also knew that Guy would be comparing her with his mother.

She went into her bedroom, took off her robe and sat down on the side of the bed. She was wide awake and she felt that sleep would not come easily; but she did not want any further involvement with Guy and Stephane tonight. She did not want to be there if and when they found Henri Raclot.

Then, looking down as she slipped off her mules, she saw the man's shoe sticking out from under the bed. She started up, then, laughing softly, she got down on her knees and looked under the bed. Colonel Raclot, drugged by too much wine and cognac, was sound asleep snoring gently as he lay flat on his back.

2

As she had expected, she did not sleep well. At her call Guy had come up to the bedroom and woken Raclot; the colonel, grinning foolishly, had been apologetic. Still half-drunk, he had been led away by Guy, who had not come back. Prue had waited for him; the bed had seemed empty without him. But he had not come upstairs again and at last, worn out by a battery of emotion, she had fallen asleep. When she woke she reached out of habit for Guy, but his side of the bed was still empty.

She lay a while, afraid of the day. She tried to will Guy to come into the room, to give her his usual morning kiss. But if there had ever been any telepathy between her and Guy, there was none that morning: the bedroom door remained firmly closed. At last she got up, had a bath; she longed for the bracing sting of a shower, but there were no showers in the chateau. She dressed, put her make-up on carefully: oh, she thought, the helpful masks that Ricci, Arden, Rubinstein can provide. She went downstairs, riddled with apprehension but outwardly calm and confident.

Guy and Stephane were at breakfast, fiddling with croissants and coffee. Colonel Raclot sat between them eating a soldier's breakfast; or that of a hungry man on the run. His plate was piled with sausage, bacon, eggs and potato: it looked as if it would sustain him all the way back to Algiers or wherever he wanted to go.

Guy got up, pulled back Prue's chair for her, kissed her (formally? she wondered) and went back to his place at the bottom of the table. Stephane, as usual, was at the head of the table.

'Croissants, my dear?' Stephane pushed the basket towards Prue.

'Not this morning.' She suddenly felt perverse. 'I think I'd like a little of what Colonel Raclot is having.'

Stephane said nothing for the moment. She rang a bell, a servant came in and was given the order. 'It will take a little

329

while,' she said as the servant went out. 'Has last night's little adventure made you hungry?'

*No, just bloody-minded.* But how did you say that in French? Prue looked across at Raclot. 'I thought you'd be gone by now, Colonel.'

Raclot had a mouthful of food, so Guy answered for him. 'The police are out on the road and also down on the river. They are trying to be inconspicuous, but we know they are there. They must know Henri is still here.'

Raclot seemed unconcerned. He swallowed his food, shrugged. 'We have nothing to worry about, unless they come to search the house again.'

'It will be better if you can join the others in Marseilles.' Stephane was drinking her third cup of coffee, although she had eaten only half a croissant. But even after what must have been at least a disturbed night, she looked as elegant as ever. But there was no light in her eyes: she had laid too much hope on last night's attempted assassination. A true soldier's wife, she said, 'We must re-group our forces as soon as possible.'

Raclot shook his head. 'No, madame. I must re-join the others, yes. But another attempt to kill the General – no. Not for another six months, a year perhaps. They'll be too alert. We'd only lose more good men.'

'He has survived far too long as it is. We have to do something *soon* – '

She is the fanatic, Prue thought. And with dismay saw her marriage starting to collapse: Guy was nodding emphatically at his mother's every word. Suddenly he said, 'Darling, let's go out on the terrace.'

'I haven't had breakfast – '

'The servants will call you when it's ready. Come – *please.*'

She thought of ignoring his request, but common sense told her she would gain nothing by trying for small victories here at the breakfast table. Stephane and Raclot, the latter suddenly stopped eating, were watching her carefully. God, she thought, they were discussing me before I came down! She pushed her chair back angrily and stalked ahead of Guy out on to the terrace.

'Well? Is my loyalty being questioned again?'

He looked surprised, put out a placating hand. 'Darling, after last night how can I say you aren't loyal?'

'Please, Guy – ' All at once she felt dispirited, drained of argument. 'What do you want?'

He gazed at her, long enough for her to search for some love or understanding in his face; but there was none. Then he walked

330

across to the balustrade of the terrace, stood staring down at the long rows of poplars lining the drive that led down to the distant road. The harvesters were at work among the vines and occasionally there was a dull yellow flash as an upturned basket caught the sun. But neither Prue nor Guy saw the workers: all they could see were the invisible police somewhere beyond the trees.

'I am taking the Citroën out in half an hour, going down to the village. The police will stop me and search the car, but they'll find nothing. A few minutes later Mother will go out in the Renault. The police will try to stop her, but she will take off as fast as she can and the police will chase her. As soon as they do, we want you to take out one of the estate vans. Henri will be hidden in the back of it. We want you to drive him as far as Poitiers. From there he can pick up a bus, go across country and pick up another bus or train for Marseilles.'

'No.'

He turned round. '*Please*. Henri is our closest friend. He was one of my father's students at Saumur. He was one of the few survivors when they went into action – it was he who came back and told Mother what Father had done. He was a good soldier for France. For the General, too. He got out of France in 1940, went to London and joined the Free French. He was sent to Lebanon and Syria and he was decorated there for bravery. He came back and was with General Leclerc in North Africa – he was decorated again and General de Gaulle himself pinned the medal on him. He stayed in the army after the war and was sent out to Indo-China. He was one of the heroes of Dien Bien Phu – but nobody really cared any more. He went home to Algeria to settle down, tired of being a soldier – all he wanted was peace. Then the General came back to power and gave Algeria to – *them*.' His mouth twisted, as if he had swallowed a word much more bitter. 'Mother and I can't think of him as a traitor. The General is the one guilty of betrayal – '

*Oh God, why didn't I know this side of him?* Back home she would have known if any prospective husband was a Republican or a Democrat: in the circles she had moved in there had been no other faiths. In Rome she may have met or even slept with a Fascist or Communist; politics had never come up in any of the affairs she had had. But this with Guy and his mother was more than politics; or more than the politics she had grown up with. This may have been how some Southerners had felt during the Reconstruction. Such hatred went beyond politics as she understood them. Even her father, rabid as he was, could never have hated a President so much as to want to kill him. For all her

331

sophistication, she was an innocent in certain passions.

'What if the police don't chase after your mother, if they guess what's happening and wait for me?'

'That's a risk, but a small one. Why should they suspect you of conspiring with us?'

'Perhaps Inspector Perret also believes in a wife's loyalty to her husband. So he would suspect me – '

'What we are discussing is too serious for sarcasm – '

Jesus, she thought, how did he ever hide all this pompousness from me?

'Will you do it for us or not?' His tone could not have been blunter.

A servant came to the door behind her, said her breakfast was ready. She nodded absently, no longer interested in food; she felt sick, felt she would throw up even a mouthful of coffee. She looked at Guy, wondering if she could put this day behind her, forget it forever, and start all over again with him.

'All right,' she said in English, trying to escape in language if in nothing else. 'I'll do it.'

He took her hands in his and kissed her on the lips; she was surprised to find she *suffered* his kiss. Abruptly she swung round and went back into the house. She declined the hot breakfast that had been prepared for her; Stephane nodded understandingly, but Prue was not grateful for her sympathy. Somehow she managed to down half a croissant and some coffee; if she were arrested, only the Lord knew when she would eat next. She was trembling inside and she tried to calm herself by thinking wrily of the headlines in the *Kansas City Star*: Ridiculous French Charges Against KC Heiress. And the *Independent* reporting in next week's issue: The Comtesse de Belfrage, youngest daughter of Lucas and the late Edith Beaufort, has returned from her honeymoon in romantic Martinique to what her husband, the Comte de Belfrage's, compatriots would call *un petit contretemps*.

Stephane said, 'I think we should synchronize our watches. Is is now exactly 8.42.'

Guy and Raclot checked their watches; then all three of them looked at Prue. 'Oh,' she said and looked at her own watch: it had stopped at 4.50. The wry part of her mind took over again: *I'm not meant for drama like this.* But she adjusted her watch, got it going again.

'You'd better leave now, Guy,' said Stephane. 'I'll follow in five minutes. You follow me, Prudence, in three minutes. That will give me time to get the police some distance away from the gates. I'll head north. You turn right when you come out of the gates and head south. Don't dawdle but don't draw attention to yourself by speeding.'

Prue wondered if she should salute. She looked across at Raclot and saw the hint of a smile on his face; but there was also admiration. She wondered if Raclot had a wife; but decided he was a loner. He might love a woman like Stephane, but would never declare himself. His passion was for other things: war, killing a President . . .

Guy kissed Prue again before he went out to the Citroën. 'I love you, darling.'

*Only for what I'm about to do?* 'Be here when I get back. I may need some comfort.'

He searched her eyes and she gazed steadily back at him: they had never been so open to each as in that moment. She was sick to think that she found him wanting. She was about to say she had changed her mind, that she was not going to be part of their wild scheme; but he must have read her too well. He turned away and went out of the house on the run. A minute later there was the sound of tyres on the gravel and the Citroën went past the windows and down the long drive to the gates.

'Damn!' Stephane, pulling on a pair of driving gloves, gesturing to Raclot and Prue to follow her, hurried out through the house to the yard at the back. 'He's so impetuous – just like his father. I'll have to hurry, so that he doesn't get too far ahead of me. We must keep them off-balance.'

She got into the Renault, started up the engine, then held her hand out the car window. 'Good luck, Henri.' He kissed the gloved hand. 'Don't despair. There'll be another opportunity.'

She nodded to Prue, the unranked one in her small army, let in the gears and took the Renault out of the yard. Raclot gestured at the green estate van on the far side of the yard.

'That is ours, madame, Shall we go?'

'Everything is so organized. Stephane didn't make up all of this on the spur of the moment, did she?'

He opened the door of the van, ushered her in. He was smiling and now he was alone with her, she liked him better. 'Stephane never does anything on the spur of the moment. She would have made a better commander than her husband. He was a splendid teacher and a brave man, but he was hopeless once we went into action. He couldn't fathom the difference between theory and practice. The enemy on the blackboard proved to be much different in the field.'

'Have you ever told Stephane that?' She looked at her watch: a minute to go.

333

His smile widened. 'Would you? No, Stephane lives on illusions. One of them is that her husband was perfect.'

Thirty seconds to go: she could feel herself tensing. 'You sound as if you lied to her about Guy's father.'

'No.' He got into the cabin of the van, slid over the seat into the rear. There were several empty casks in the back of the van and he settled himself against one, propping his feet up against another. 'I told her the truth. What I didn't tell her was that he should not have killed himself. It accomplished nothing. It is time we moved.'

She took the van out of the yard, driving cautiously, like a learner. *Which is what I am, a learner in conspiracy.* But as she went down the drive, increasing speed, so did her confidence increase. She peered ahead at the open gates: there was no sign of a police car.

'Right at the gates.' Raclot seemed totally unconcerned. 'Then we'll take the first road on the left. That will take us on to National 147 and we can go straight through on that to Poitiers.'

The van came to the gates. Prue took her foot off the accelerator, waiting for the call to halt. She drove out into the road, arms stiff, palms damp, eyes so strained she felt she was looking both ways at once. The road was empty. She swung the van sharply to the right, there was a grunt from Raclot as he flung up a foot to prevent a cask falling over on him, then they were picking up speed, heading south, unhindered and unpursued.

She drove steadily, paying attention to her driving, only occasionally speaking to Raclot. Once they passed a police car coming towards them and she slowed momentarily; but the police car went past, neither of the men in it giving her or the van a second glance. It took her an hour to reach Poitiers, but at last she brought the van to a halt on the outskirts of the town.

'This is as far as I'll take you, Colonel. I don't want to stretch our luck too far.'

He got out through the back door of the van, came round and stood beside the cabin window. He held out his hand and after a moment's hesitation she gave him hers. He surprised her by shaking it firmly. She was pleased: somehow it seemed more sincere than if he had just politely kissed it.

'Some day, madame, I hope I can be of assistance to you.'

She looked around at what she could see of the town. How much conspiracy had it seen, how many would-be assassins had passed through it since the days of Clovis? The bishops who had

334

questioned Joan of Arc had first met here: she wondered if some unknown soldier had promised assistance for Joan. She blushed at the pretentious comparison; but felt herself surrounded by history that was alien to her. She would never be French, no matter how long she lived or how involved she became.

'No, Colonel. Let us finish here and now.'

'Do not be too harsh with Guy,' he said and she wondered at his insight. Then he stepped back and saluted her, a foolish thing to do, she thought, in the circumstances. 'Good luck, madame. We all need it.'

### 3

'We shan't forget what you have done,' said Stephane.

'I'd rather you did,' said Prue.

They were sitting out on the terrace in the still-warm evening. The workers had gone home from the vineyards and nothing moved in the landscape; the vines stood like ranks of green bowmen fallen to their knees in death. The flat golden light threw everything into sharp relief. The smell of grapes hung heavy in the air and Prue wondered why it should suggest the smell of death to her. Or was it the smell of decay? she wondered, looking sideways at Stephane.

'Another year and you will see our point of view. One can't throw away all the past, as the General is trying to do.'

'I thought he was trying to revive some of the glory of the past. France's glory, I mean.'

'France had an empire once. It was as much part of our glory as any of the things he is trying to revive. It is stupid to give independence to people who are not ready for it. Look at what is happening in the rest of Africa. Henri told me one could not believe the barbarities that happened in the Congo.'

'I seem to remember there were some barbarities after your own Revolution in 1792.'

'The rabble were responsible for that. You don't think I'd have been on the revolutionaries' side, do you?'

'Of course not,' said Prue. 'How stupid of me.'

Then Guy came out on to the terrace, debonair, gay, a man who had had a successful day. He kissed his mother, then Prue.

The proper pecking order, Prue thought. 'I've been talking to Marseilles. Henri got there safely. He picked up a truck that took him all the way. Now we just have to wait for another opportunity.'

'I don't think we should discuss it any more. Prudence doesn't approve of our aims. Or our methods. Which surprises me. One would have thought that Americans understood the need for violence at certain times. It's endemic with Americans, isn't it?'

'Only with immigrant Americans,' said Prue, ashamed of her prejudice, sounding in her own ears like her father. But she was not prepared for a debate such as this and her tongue had grabbed at the first argument that had come into her mind.

'Was John Wilkes Booth an immigrant?' said Guy.

Prue gave him a wifely smile that told him what a son-of-a-bitch she thought he was. 'He was an actor.' *What a stuffed shirt I must sound.* 'They are always unpredictable.'

'How true,' said Stephane, deciding the guillotine had been lowered far enough. 'It's time for dinner. I think we might have some of the '59 as a celebration, Guy.'

'It is already being chilled,' said Guy smugly.

'Good boy,' said his mother and patted his cheek.

Oh Christ, thought Prue.

When Guy attempted to make love to her that night she fell back on a wife's second best defence. 'I have a headache.' For good measure she moved up to her first defence: 'I think my period is coming on.'

'Poor darling.' He kissed her solicitously. 'It's been a difficult day for you.'

'I'm glad you noticed.' She kissed him: remotely, her lips void of any feeling.

Her period did not come that night nor in the next week, when it was actually due. A month later the de Belfrage family doctor told her she was pregnant. She was depressed by the news, but Guy and Stephane were delighted, so much so that they seemed to miss her lack of response.

'We must pray for a boy,' said Stephane. 'To keep the family name alive.'

Prue had no sense of lineage. There were American families, she knew, who counted every generation back as if it were a pearl in an increasingly valuable necklace. She knew, too, that her father sometimes wished that the Beauforts had the depth of family history to be found in some of the Eastern establishment dynasties; before Thaddeus the Beauforts, if not nameless, had had

336

their name writ on some pretty muddy waters. She had not yet adjusted to the idea that she was no longer a Beaufort but a de Belfrage.

'Girls run in our family,' she said, forgetting Nina's son.

'Don't let's be pessimistic,' said Stephane, and Prue wondered if her pregnancy was going to be another organized military scheme.

Matters did not improve over the next eight months. In October the Cuban missile crisis occurred and Prue, worried for the family at home, even though she did not think Kansas City would be a primary Russian target, called her father and sisters every night for a week. Guy and Stephane, with the French disregard for other people's confrontations, thought that Prue, and indeed all Americans, was reacting with typical American panic towards the Russians; the de Belfrages were absolutely certain that Khrushchev was only bluffing. Prue's disposition towards them was not improved when the crisis suddenly petered out. Stephane at one point tried to give her a lesson in military and political strategy, but Prue managed to dodge it.

Guy was attentive over the succeeding months, always on call when she needed him; but too often it was Stephane who told him when he was needed. Stephane herself was all care and concern; but also commanding. Prue bore the regimen with patience, mainly because she could see no way of escaping it. She had come to realize that she no longer loved Guy, but, romantic as she was, she still hoped all love was not dead. Perhaps when the baby came he would stop loving his mother so much and start loving her and the child.

Melanie Stephane de Belfrage was born on 16 May 1963. Guy wanted the child named directly after his mother, but Prue was adamant that that should not be so. Melanie was her own mother's second name and she insisted that the baby be called that. She would have named it Edith except that she had never liked her mother's first name. Stephane, for her part, did not seem to care what the baby was called. It was not a boy, so it could contribute nothing towards the continuation of the de Belfrage title.

Melanie opened her eyes on a world that was growing smaller by the hour. Above her, in the blue-black upper galleries of space, Astronaut Gordon Cooper circled the earth, seeing the world whole but with its imperfections as obscured to him as they were to the innocent Melanie. In the big house in the Loire valley Prue felt as remote from the world as the astronaut high above her. Reading about his mission in *Le Monde* she felt a certain pride in being American, but for all the interest that Stephane and Guy showed, Gordon Cooper could have been an Unidentified Flying Object.

Guy lavished attention on his daughter. Prue watched with approval and hope; but gradually she realized that things had not changed. His spectrum of love had widened from his mother to his daughter; Prue, in the middle, had gone out of focus. He was weak, she now recognized, too weak to bear the burden of a wife without the aid of his mother. A weakness, which Prue also recognized, that Stephane would always play upon.

Nina, Margaret, Sally and Lucas had all come across for the birth of the baby. Stephane was a gracious hostess and in-law and none of the family thought to ask if Prue was happy; Prue was amazed at how they were all taken in by the smiles and the charm, the best French diplomacy used at the domestic level. But once long ago (or so it seemed) she had fallen for the same treatment herself.

'Is the child to be an American or French citizen?' said Lucas, practical as ever, thinking ahead to Melanie's inheritance.

'French, I suppose,' said Prue; but made up her mind that she would not immediately discuss the subject with Guy. She did not understand French law, but she did know a thing or two about a mother's law: 'But I'll see she is put on my passport till she is old enough to have one of her own.'

Lucas nodded approvingly. 'Very sensible. An American passport still counts for something. President Kennedy has improved the American image abroad. He's turned out better than I expected.'

'Will you vote for him if he runs again next year?'

'We'll see,' said Lucas, careful that political fair-mindedness should not be taken as far as folly. He looked down at his latest granddaughter. 'I hope her world turns out to be as good as yours and mine has been.'

'Daddy – do you still have an agency looking for Tim and Michael?'

'Why do you ask?' He was abruptly taut with suspicion.

'I don't know – I suppose it was looking at Nina when she came in to see the baby. I thought she was going to break down. I'm sure she did, but she got out of the room first. Michael would be almost seventeen now, wouldn't he?'

'Yes.' Every year he circled his only grandson's birthday on a private calendar he kept locked in his study desk. 'Yes, I still have an agency on retainer. But they never come up with anything.'

338

'If ever he was found and Nina took him back, Tim I mean, would you accept him? For her sake?'

'Of course,' he said gruffly and left the room, afraid that he too could no longer contain his true feelings.

The family went home to Kansas City. Prue, suddenly homesick, afraid of being tempted to go with them, dared not drive to Paris to wish them farewell. The summer came and went in bursts, wore itself out as a sour memory for the vintners; it was a poor year for wine, one of the worst in a long time. Prue, sour herself now, waited for Stephane to blame it on General de Gaulle; but Stephane seemed ready to write the whole year off as something best forgotten. Even her grandchild, not being male, had turned out to be non-vintage.

Autumn came down from the north almost as a relief. The poplars in the long drive turned to gold and Prue, dispensing for the afternoon with the nurse she had engaged, went for walks, pushing the baby carriage through the crisp yellow carpet of leaves. One morning late in November she asked Guy when they would be moving to Paris.

'I don't want to spend another winter here. The house is too cold.'

'Mother wants us to stay – '

'I don't care what your mother wants. I'm talking about you and me, not her.'

'Darling, be reasonable – '

*Be reasonable:* the gunpowder of so many domestic arguments. She blew up, months of irritation, frustration and disappointment exploding out of her. Guy fell back defenceless: at least, she thought, he has the decency not to go running to Mother for help. She stormed out of the house, taking the baby with her, commandeered the Citroën and took off into the gold-grey day. She drove all day, stopping occasionally on high points to sit in the car and stare out across the countryside, looking for answers that were not to be found in the topography spread out before her. France, for all its appeal, was not her territory. She had never felt so Middle Western as she did today.

It was dark when she arrived back at the chateau. There was no sign of Guy or Stephane, but she made no enquiries of the servants as to their whereabouts. She turned Melanie over to the nurse to be bathed and fed; then she lay in her own bath, trying to make up her mind about the future. Characteristically, she accepted some of the blame for the disaster of the past year and a half: if only because of her own poor judgement of Guy, she must be blamed. She was not quite sure what was expected of a

French wife; perhaps she was lacking there, too: although she could not see Stephane as a compliant wife towards the dead Count. She thought of Guy and saw him now for what he was, the ghost of his father, a shade that Stephane kept alive for her own sustenance.

She got out of the bath, put on a robe and rang for a light supper to be served in her bedroom. Maliciously, she asked for a bottle of the estate's 1959 wine to be sent up; if nothing else had improved during her stay here, her palate had. She ate supper, drank half the bottle of wine, then turned on the television set. It was an American luxury, television in the bedroom, that Stephane had frowned upon, but Prue had insisted on being American in her bedroom if nowhere else.

Later she would not remember the programme she had been watching. Her mind kept wandering, wondering where Guy and Stephane were, wondering what she would do tomorrow and the day after and the weeks and months after that. Then suddenly the programme was interrupted and an announcer, face solemn, voice deep with gloom, flashed on to the screen. It took her several moments to take in what he said. She heard him say 'The President has been shot', and her first thought was, Oh God, they've succeeded at last! She had spent the day pondering the break-up of her marriage and her husband and his mother had been somewhere plotting the break-up of a regime. Then she heard the word *Dallas* and a moment later she knew the news was far worse than she could have imagined.

She sat in the Jeanselme chair in the Empire-furnished room in the chateau on the banks of the Loire, listened to the French voice saying that an era of promise had come to a savagely abrupt end, and felt more American than she had ever felt in her life before. Twice in one day a region and her country had enveloped her in a mood that made her unutterably sad. She began to weep for all the promises that had died that day.

An hour later Guy and Stephane came home. By then, still in her robe, she was downstairs in the drawing-room. 'You heard the news?'

'Yes.' Guy sounded detached, concerned with something more important. 'I'm sorry, if you are.'

'Jesus,' she said quietly. 'You're sorry if I am!'

'We may never know the reason he was killed,' said Stephane. 'But you see? We French are not the only ones who wish our President dead – '

'It's not the same thing! It was some insane crank – it had to be – '

340

But she saw they were unimpressed. The death of President Kennedy proved nothing other than she had judged them too harshly and unfairly. Presidents were legitimate targets; the point of view just depended on who held the weapon. She knew without asking that they had spent the day with men planning another assassination. I have a fierce row with my husband, she thought, and he goes off with his mother to talk about killing his country's President.

'I'm going home,' she said, her voice even and quiet again. 'To Kansas City.'

'What's the point?' said Guy. 'America will be in shock for a week or two. It will be better to visit your family later – '

'Don't be dense, Guy. I'm leaving you and going home for good.'

For the first time since coming into the room Guy lost his look of remoteness; whatever had occupied him during the day disappeared in the sudden realization that his marriage was over. He frowned and Prue marvelled at his obtuseness. Despite all the warning signs of the past months he was now in his own state of shock: she had assassinated his pride.

Stephane, expectedly, was the first to recover. 'Will you be taking the child with you?'

'Naturally. A child's place is with its mother. Isn't that how you've always felt about Guy?'

There was almost a glint of admiration in Stephane's eye. She enjoyed conflict, it kept one honed to an edge. Sometimes she regretted being a woman; she knew she would have been a successful soldier. The one big disappointment of her life had been her son and she recognized now that her daughter-in-law knew it.

'We could get the law to stop you taking the child out of the country.'

'Perhaps. But you wouldn't want the law asking me questions, would you? I might give them more answers than they were expecting.' Stephane's face hardened and suddenly Prue realized she was on very dangerous ground. She retreated from the minefield her tongue had laid: 'Not that I would. I may not be a loyal wife, but I'm not an informer.'

Stephane kept control of her own tongue. She respected the proprieties, one did not threaten members of one's own family, even an in-law, with death. 'Can we trust you to honour that promise?'

'I'm a woman of honour.' Prue, sardonic, coolly composed now she had voiced her decision, was tempted to jump to attention.

'Stephane, you should have had your own regiment.'

'Don't you dare speak to her like that!' For a moment Guy looked as if he might strike Prue.

'That was my parting thrust,' said Prue, glad for once of the French literary style. 'From now on till I go tomorrow there will only be banalities.'

She went up to her room, locking the door against Guy; he disappointed and angered her by not coming to pound on it. Crudely she wondered if he had gone instead to his mother's bed; but though she wanted now to think the worst of him, she had her grudging respect for his mother. Stephane had her moral standards, even if she could find excuses for murder.

## 4

Nina came to meet Prue and the baby at the Kansas City airport in a Rolls-Royce. 'When did you get this?'

'A couple of months ago. I decided I needed something to give me a lift – I was feeling a bit down in the mouth. Does that sound extravagant?'

'Yes.'

'Exactly what Meg said. But she was glad I bought black. She thinks that makes it less conspicuous. She's very much against conspicuous consumption.'

'How does Daddy feel about it?'

'He humours my every whim. He's changed. He humours all our whims now. We can do no wrong. Especially you.'

'You mean my coming home?'

'He couldn't be more pleased. Are you going to tell me about it or wait till we're all together?'

'I don't know that I'm going to tell any of you anything.'

'You sound as if you've become as French as the French – they never tell anyone anything. You came home just in time. Don't you think so, George? Since you've got both ears pinned back listening to what we're saying.'

George Biff, the grey in his hair most apparent now, grinned at them both in the driving mirror. 'Once upon a time you girls shared all your secrets with me.'

'Not any more, George,' said Prue, loving the ageing black man, feeling safe as the big car took them along Ward Parkway, trembling with anticipation and relief as home slid comfortingly towards her and the baby. 'You're too old now to be burdened with them.'

'Burdened? You mean I can't tote 'em any more? Maybe you right. You all old enough to carry 'em yourselves now.'

I'm home, Prue thought. From now on I speak American, think American. One thing could be said for the non-literary style: it was more difficult to be dishonest in it. Lies were more direct and, if you were sharp-eyed as she had once been and hoped to be again, more discernible.

## Chapter Twelve

♦

# Prue

I

Sally married Charlie Luman in the summer of 1964. It was a big wedding and the cream of the Middle West flowed into Kansas City for it; some cream came from the East, Washington and New York, but found it wasn't highly regarded locally and it tended to clot round the edges of the gathering. Ex-President and Mrs Truman came, at Lucas's special behest, and won more approval from the Republicans present than the President had ever done while in office. The ceremony and the reception took place on the estate and the guests, when they had finished congratulating the bride and groom, admiring the ex-President and his lady and covertly criticizing each other's dress, wandered around the grounds and stopped to look at the new house that had been built for the newly-weds and the one being constructed for Prue.

'Lucas has got them all together again,' said one male guest. 'I was glad to get rid of my girls. And I've got only two.'

'I don't think Lucas was responsible for them all coming home,' said Magnus. 'I think they were just naturally homesick. It's in the Midwest blood. Whoever gets homesick for New York or Los Angeles?'

'Native-born New Yorkers or Angelenos?'

'There aren't any. They're all either foreigners or they're from Ohio or Iowa.'

'I'm from Philadelphia originally,' said the other man.

344

'Do you ever get homesick?'

'Are you kidding?'

Prue, Nina and Margaret sat together round a table under a large umbrella and watched Sally moving among the guests, leaning on her stick but never making it too obvious. 'I couldn't be happier for her,' said Margaret. 'And for Charlie, too.'

'I wish Mother were alive to see this,' said Nina. 'She'd have been out of her head with ecstasy. A big wedding at home at last and all of us here to enjoy it.'

'You look like Mother,' said Prue. 'You could be her twin, except for the colour of your hair.'

'I've noticed it, too,' said Margaret. 'You're getting more and more like her as you get older. What are you now – forty? That photo in Daddy's study was taken when Mother was forty. You look exactly like her.'

'I know,' said Nina. 'Magnus remarked on it.'

'Is he starting to court you?'

Nina laughed. 'Men don't court women of forty. They take them to dinner and maybe try to seduce them, but they don't *court* them.'

'All right, is he taking you to dinner and trying to seduce you?'

'Mind your own business. Why do you want to know anyway?'

'Just idle curiosity,' said Margaret, more than idly curious. 'You could do much worse for each other.'

'Stop match-making. You're starting to *sound* like Mother.'

Margaret got up and went away to see that everyone was being looked after. She was acting as matron of honour, a distinction that Nina, though the eldest, had gladly allowed her to assume. Prue looked after her. 'She looks happy and content. Is she?'

'I think so,' said Nina. 'Or maybe she's just a better sufferer than the rest of us.'

'How do she and Bruce get on?' Prue watched Bruce Alburn moving among the guests with the assurance of a man who knew his place was safe in the family.

'They suit each other. He's nice and honest and hard-working, so Daddy likes him, too. But I just wish once in a while he'd show a little ignorance about something. In his own quiet way he's the greatest know-all since St Paul.'

Bruce saw them watching him and he came across, dry smile widening. 'Everywhere I look, beautiful Beaufort women.'

'Bruce darling,' said Prue, 'you old Arkansas hill boys are too flattering. You-all talk to the gals back home like that?'

Bruce grinned. 'We-all don't never say you-all down in the Ozarks. You-all is Southern talk. But you-all is both mighty

345

purty. Any Southern gentleman would tell you that, not only an Ozark hill-billy.'

Prue suddenly felt uncomfortable. 'I'm sorry, Bruce. I didn't mean to be rude – '

He touched her hand gently. 'Prue, it's water off a duck's back. Anyone from Arkansas who's thin-skinned should never leave home. There are more jokes about us than all the other States put together. But we can laugh, which is more than some of the others can do. You never hear a Texan laugh at a Texan joke when some other feller tells it.'

He smiled at them both, then went away and Nina said, 'You see what I mean? He's as nice as they come. But he had to tell you that you-all wasn't hill-billy stuff.'

'I knew it wasn't. I was just testing him.'

'You're as bad as he is. But how did you know it wasn't?'

'I once went away for a weekend with an Arkansas boy.'

'This is not the day to ask the question, but how's your divorce coming along?'

'Guy isn't going to contest it. I think he might have if Melanie had been a boy. His mother would have insisted that he did.'

'What are you going to do? Go down to Arkansas?'

'What do you mean?'

'It's not like you to go long without a man. But I can tell you from experience, there isn't a surplus of unattached lovers in Kansas City. Not good ones.'

'I'll look around. I get the urge every so often, but so far I've managed to control it. Are you on the Pill?'

'I want to know more about it before I risk it. Are you?'

'Not yet. But when I have my next man marked out I think I'll try it. I can't believe all women's messy worries are over.'

'They'll never be really over till you're out the other side of the menopause.' Nina smiled, like a cat in a dairy, not looking at all like Edith now. 'I think I may be a pretty gay old girl once I turn fifty.'

An hour later Mr and Mrs Charles Luman, the one sexually handicapped, the other finding now that she could do without sex, left for their honeymoon in Japan, Thailand and Cambodia. A small war was going on in Vietnam, but it was nothing that would worry a honeymooning couple. Their marriage might have been called one of convenience, but it was also one of love. Sally had waited two years before she had finally told Charlie all about herself; or nearly all. He had been shocked at first, but more understanding than she had expected. It had been another six months before he had asked her to marry him.

346

In that time she had gone to New York to see Cindy Drake. She had not seen or heard from Cindy since she had left Vassar. The taste of first love lingers, an itch in the memory: would I still love him or her if I saw him again? But she had never gone looking for Cindy or tried to write her; not till, some months after she had told everything to Charlie, she saw Cindy's name in a theatre review in *Time* magazine. Cindy was playing in a revival of a Tennessee Williams play on Broadway and had got good notices. Sally went to New York the next day, telling Nina and Margaret that she was going to do some shopping. She got a seat in the third row centre and sat and stared at Cindy all through the show to the total exclusion of the other players. Then she went backstage after the performance, knocked on a dressing-room door, went in and found Cindy with a tall middle-aged woman, handsome and very butch, who bridled at once as soon as Sally came in the door.

Cindy had looked surprised but that was all. 'Sally! After all these years – ! This is Rona Freeman.'

Rona Freeman shook hands with a man's grip. 'Cindy has told me about you.' She looked challenging, feet planted solidly in sensible brogues, ready for any invasion of her territory. 'Are you only visiting New York? You don't live here?'

This is ridiculous, thought Sally. *She's so obvious in every way; how could Cindy have fallen for her?* Then she remembered that Cindy had always wanted protection. *God Almighty, did she ever see me like this?* She smiled disarmingly at both of them, glad now that she had come. The itch and taste were gone. 'No, I'm just visiting. I'm going back to Kansas City tomorrow. I just thought I'd pop in and tell you how much I enjoyed your performance, Cindy.'

'Thank you.' Cindy looked at Rona, as if to ask if it were all right to accept praise from an old lover.

'Kansas City?' Rona Freeman relaxed; her territory was safe. 'Do you have any theatre out there? Or is Buffalo Bill still playing?'

'Only at Christmas for the kids. Good luck, Cindy. Maybe next time I hear of you you'll be in Hollywood.'

'Over my dead body,' said Rona Freeman.

Sally looked at the tall thick figure. 'That should be quite a climb.'

Next morning she went to Bergdorf-Goodman and Bonwit Teller, splurged on a new spring wardrobe, bought presents for everyone in the family back home in Kansas City, where Buffalo Bill was playing pantomime for the kids, and returned to Beaufort

347

Park happy. The following week Charlie, back from an overseas tour of duty to Europe, proposed to her.

So now they went off to start their marriage in the accepted way, Charlie's secret still their own, both of them sure that happiness was going to be theirs. They were relying on more than most couples start out with: knowing their handicap they were determined to make their marriage work. They were not going to rely on just romance and chance.

Prue's house was completed in December 1964 and she moved in in time for Christmas. Liking the style, she had been tempted to have the house built as a copy of a small chateau, but decided that would be thumbing her nose at fate. She was also tempted to furnish it in the Empire period style, but resisted that urge too. So the house became an Italian villa and the furnishings American Modern and once she had moved in she felt at home and comfortable. She engaged a staff of three and a nurse for Melanie, bought herself a Jaguar, went through her French wardrobe and decided it was too good to throw out, accepted all invitations that came her way, went to bed with a brewer from St Louis and an oil man from Tulsa, but stayed the night with neither of them, settled back into Kansas City life and, for the time being anyway, wondered why she had fled it.

Time slipped away into yesterday. Her divorce became final, but she felt no sense of release; she had already experienced that the day she had left St Cast. People began to realize that the Sixties were like no other decade that had gone before. The Beatles released a whole new wave of barbarians on the world, sub-teen Goths who demanded for themselves a whole new territory in market research and were granted it willingly. Permissiveness replaced selection; anything went, so long as you didn't have to pay for it. Four-letter words became a *lingua franca*, as if the newly educated of the world felt they might be tongue-tied by polysyllables. Politicians were shocked to find there were more unbelievers than believers, many of them violent. The small war in Vietnam snuck up on the American public, turned into a big war to the delight of the military establishment but no one else, especially the young men who had to go out and fight it.

Lucas was one of the few among his friends and business acquaintances who saw no future in the war. 'We'll never win it, not out there. And why do we always have to prop up corrupt regimes in the name of anti-Communism?'

'Daddy, you're sounding more socialistic every day.'

'I must be falling under the influence of my granddaughter.'

Margaret's daughter, Martha, was now in her first year at the University of Missouri. She was as beautiful as her mother or any of her aunts, but she seemed to be refusing even to accede to nature. She wore granny glasses which she did not need, covered her face with as much hair as possible without blindfolding herself and wore clothes that looked like the cast-offs of a buffalo hunter's mother. Lucas, looking at her, wondered what the world had come to. But he uttered no word of protest and was more indulgent towards her, her sister Emma and Prue's child Melanie than he had ever been towards his own four girls.

Martha came home for the long vacation in the summer of 1969. She had had her own small private war with Margaret and Bruce and won: she had moved out of the estate and was living on campus. Her only good score with her parents was that, majoring in American history, her professor reported that she was the most brilliant student he had ever taught. It was a pity, Bruce commented to Margaret, that she was only learning history so that she would make a better revolutionary.

She came across to see Prue in the latter's house on her first day home. 'Aunt Prue – ' She was an odd mixture of rebellion and respect; she never attempted to be too familiar with her aunts or her grandfather. 'I'd like to bring home a man I'm going to work for, but I don't know if Mother or Grandfather will approve of him.'

'Who is it? Jerry Rubin or some other revolutionary?'

Martha shook her head, her hair swinging across her face like a wind-blown blind. 'No, he's in movies. It's Fingal O'Farrell.'

'You're going to work for *him*?'

O'Farrell had been in the Kansas City newspapers and on television every day for the past week. He was an Anglo-Irish film director who had made three films that had been hailed for their innovative technique and that had also made money; he was in the Middle West now to make his first American film, one based on the journeys of Lewis and Clark. The newspapers had been full of him and Mr O'Farrell had left no doubt that he was full of himself. Success had gone to his head and anywhere else that it could find space.

'I'm to be a third assistant something-or-other. I'm to help him on research. He said he'd like to meet all of you.'

'You mean he's a social climber? So many of these movie people are.'

'Don't be a snob, Aunt Prue. It's bad enough with Mother.'

'Darling, do something about your hair – it's like talking to a yak. And do you really need those dreadful glasses? If you're

349

going to be a rebel, what's wrong with being a pretty one?'

'You're as bourgeois as the rest of them, aren't you?' But she said it without rancour and somehow managed to make it sound less than insulting. 'Doesn't all our money worry you? Didn't you ever want to rebel against it?'

'No. I don't think any of us ever has. We all rebelled against Daddy, to a greater or lesser degree, but I don't suppose you'd call that a revolutionary movement? No, I didn't think you would. But say no when you disagree with me, darling, don't shake your head. I'm always expecting your hair to fall off. Would you wear a hairband if I bought you one? How about a tiara?'

Martha took off her glasses, pushed back her hair and kissed her aunt. 'I should boycott you, but I can't. Will you talk to Mother about having Mr O'Farrell here? Say for Sunday lunch. Luncheon. He told me he loves to play tennis.'

'I'll strike a bargain. Buy yourself a hairband and I'll see that Mr O'Farrell is invited to luncheon next Sunday.'

'You're a typical Beaufort. Always screwing the workers.'

'Screwing is a word I keep for the bedroom, darling. I never invite the workers in there.'

Prue talked to Margaret and the following Sunday Fingal O'Farrell and his associate producer came to luncheon. Lovett, the associate producer, was a pleasant ordinary Englishman who only seemed to accentuate the flamboyance of O'Farrell.

Lucas was coming across from the main house with Nina when the big limousine drew up in front of the Alburn house. O'Farrell was first out of the car, flinging open the door and bounding out as if about to attack someone. He was six feet tall but looked shorter because of his bulk: he must have weighed at least 220 pounds. He had long thick hair, prematurely streaked with grey, and a Biblical beard, also streaked with grey. He was dressed in a flowing pink kaftan, sandals and pink-and-green argyle socks. His eyes were hidden by huge white-rimmed dark glasses.

'Good God!' Lucas pulled up, turned on his heel. 'I'm going back.'

'Don't be silly, Daddy,' said Nina, although she too was wondering what the luncheon would turn out to be. 'This may be a whole new experience for you.'

'There's no doubt of that. What is he – a transvestite Apostle or something? There are none of our friends coming, I hope?'

'Only Magnus. He doesn't shock easily.'

'If he's not shocked by that apparition, he's finished as the family lawyer.'

O'Farrell took off his dark glasses to greet the family. His Irish charm seemed to Prue to be larger than life; he laid it on male and female alike, only confirming Lucas's view that the man was a transvestite. He seemed never to stop talking, words tumbling out of the Biblical beard as if St Paul were trying to get all his sermons done in one day. Only Martha and Emma seemed impressed.

'Moving pictures were invented by an Irishman, fella named Gilhooley from County Cork. He did it at the instigation of the Holy Roman Church. We've got to have somewhere to send 'em between Saturday confession and Sunday communion, said the priests. Get 'em out of the dance halls and the pubs, they said, there's too much sin in them places. So Gilhooley was put to work and he invented motion pictures. That was back in 1888 – 12 March 1888, to be exact. He photographed the Cork-Dunmanway hurling final. Dunmanway won. They're still running the film in Dunmanway, every year it's the biggest box-office grosser, takes more money than James Bond. It's full of blood and violence – Catholics never think of that as sinful. The colour's fading a bit, but they touch it up every so often by hand. Sometimes fellas come over from Cork and watch the film and afterwards the audience beats the bejasus out of them. But it's all good Irish fun and nobody gets into trouble between confession and communion the next morning. The Church nominated Gilhooley for sainthood. Once the word comes through from the Vatican I'm going to make a film about him. With Sam Goldwyn as the devil's advocate. Are we going to play tennis, Mr Beaufort?'

'Whatever you wish,' said Lucas, glad of anything that would stop the flow of words. 'Did you bring some tennis clothes with you? I'm afraid we don't have anything on hand that would fit you.'

'Not to worry.' O'Farrell hitched up his kaftan. 'I always play in this. Shades of Suzanne Lenglen, eh?'

Prue looked at her father, waiting for him to explode or just keel over in a faint. But he rose stiffly, nodded to Magnus and Charlie and they strode off to change. Everyone moved out of the house and down to the small pavilion beside the tennis court. Tennis sneakers were found for O'Farrell and the four men, Lucas still looking half-catatonic, went out on to the court.

Margaret looked at the associate producer. 'Is Mr O'Farrell always so overpowering, Mr Lovett?'

'Mother!' said Martha.

'It's necessary to ask,' said Bruce, who, like all the others, had said hardly a word in the past two hours. 'Just in case he comes here again.'

'Your mother's right,' Lovett said to Martha. 'Fingal is too much – you'll find that out when you come to work for us. But one has to overlook it because he always produces the goods. Like now.'

Out on the court O'Farrell was proving easily the best man in the match. He served and smashed with a grace that belied his bulk; his backhand was a joy to watch. On the other side of the net Lucas was reduced to angry impotence. Somehow or other he would have to keep it from the River Club that he and Magnus had been wiped off the court by a bearded Irish windbag in a pink dress.

'I think this may be the day Daddy retires from tennis,' said Nina.

At the end of the day O'Farrell had still not won any friends among the older Beauforts; but if he noticed his lack of popularity he gave no sign of it. 'It's been a beautiful day and I've loved the conversation. Talk was the greatest thing ever invented – after the motion pictures, of course – '

'Did the Irish invent talk, too, Mr O'Farrell?'

For the first time it seemed that O'Farrell looked directly at Prue. He laughed, took her hand and buried it in his beard. 'Miss Beaufort, I think you could hold up your end in any talk.'

'I never hold up my end in public, Mr O'Farrell.' Prue looked at him and wondered what sort of man was hidden beneath the kaftan, the surfeit of hair and the flood of talk. She had dropped her married name when her divorce had become final and, like Nina, was a Miss Beaufort once again. Every year she took Melanie to France to visit Guy and his mother; the visits were not something she looked forward to but they were not too much of a strain. Any love she had once felt for Guy was now dead and he made no attempt to resurrect it. She had not fallen in love with any other man, though she had had several affairs that had, as it were, kept her in practice. Now she said, 'I'd like to come and see you at work.'

'Do, dear lady! We move out on Wednesday for Nebraska, a region, I'm told, that has gone backwards since Lewis and Clark passed through it in – when was it, Martha my pet? Never mind. Dates are only spanners in the works of history. Yesterday, today and tomorrow are all the same.'

'Expect me when you see me then,' said Prue. 'I'd hate to confuse you with an appointed day.'

O'Farrell laughed uproariously and Prue flinched, waiting for him to slam her on the back. 'Oh, you and I will enjoy each other,

Miss Beaufort! I'll have my Indian scouts – at sixty dollars a day, isn't it, Henry? – I'll have them out looking for you every day till you arrive. Goodbye, Mr Beaufort. Marvellous day! I've learned so much!'

He and Lovett drove away and Lucas said, 'If he ever comes here again, let me know. I'll leave town.'

'Are you really going up to see him on location?' Sally said.

'Why not?' said Prue. 'I can't believe all that bull he puts out is real. I'd like to see him in his own element.'

'You can keep an eye on Martha,' said Margaret. 'I don't want her raped or scalped by one of his sixty-dollar-a-day Indians.'

Margaret had lost touch somehow with her elder daughter. She tried to stifle the resentment she felt that Prue seemed to have succeeded where she had failed, but it was not easy. Prue, Nina and Sally had remained uninfected by politics; but she now felt as strongly as her father once had. She and Bruce were as conservative in their political thinking as Lucas had been; they had worked hard to have Richard Nixon elected as President and they fully supported him and his policies. She found it difficult to understand how she could have raised a daughter who was radical in her thinking, unpatriotic in her attitude towards the Vietnam war and, her worst sin, seemingly ashamed of being a Beaufort. It annoyed her intensely that none of these things seemed to perturb Prue who, by ignoring them, had gained the confidence of Martha that she herself had lost.

'Mother,' said Martha, 'the Indians are no longer interested in us white women.'

'We're relieved to hear it, darling,' said Prue. 'But your mother was only joking.'

Margaret did not want Prue to defend her, but said nothing. She looked at Bruce for support, but he just gave a slight shake of his head. He had never attempted to play the heavy stepfather and though neither of the girls loved him they respected him. In a climate of women, especially Beaufort women, he had learned the advantages of compromise.

'I think you are the one who should be careful,' Sally said to Prue.

'Of Mr O'Farrell? Men like him are no problem. It's you quiet ones who trouble us.' She smiled sweetly at Bruce and Charlie.

A shadow crossed Sally's face, but no one noticed it, not even the sharp-eyed Prue. None of the family knew of Charlie's disability. Once or twice there had been casual questions as to whether she and Charlie intended having a family, but she had just as casually brushed them aside and lately no one had raised the matter again. Not even her father, though when she and Charlie had first married he had strongly hinted that he hoped they would present him with another grandson.

Charlie gave his own sweet, cheerful smile. He was now a co-pilot on Pan American Jumbos and life, as far as it was possible, had been good to him. He loved Sally and they were happy together; as far as he knew, she was no longer interested in other women. They had worked out a sexual arrangement that satisfied her, though it left him frustrated; but he would never let her know and did his best to disguise it. He would have liked to adopt a child or two, since he loved children, but Sally had been cool to the idea when he had first mentioned it and he had never brought it up again. Sometimes he felt uneasy, wondering if Sally was entirely happy, but he was not a man who met such doubts head-on. He played life differently from the way he had played football.

'Us quiet ones are the ones who stick around, though.' Then the smile suddenly died and he looked at Nina. 'Sorry, honey. I didn't mean that.'

Nina, sitting beside him, pressed his hand. She had real affection for Charlie and she often wondered what was missing in his and Sally's life. She was not offended by what he had said. Everyone's life was like an old battlefield: the odd, forgotten mine lay there to be trodden on by the unwitting foot.

'Charlie, don't apologize. That was all so long ago.' But not so long ago that she had forgotten.

Prue went to Nebraska for two days, not taking Melanie with her. She found movie-making both interesting and boring, the movie-makers the same. They appeared to live in a world even more circumscribed than her own; or perhaps that was just the crew Fingal O'Farrell had gathered about him. The crew knew who she was and treated her with wary respect; the actors couldn't make up their minds whether to be respectful, contemptuous or indifferent. They all aspired to fame and fortune, but particularly secure fame and fortune. Prue Beaufort had no fame in her own right, but she sure as hell had fortune and security. More so even than the two male stars, who were rumoured to be getting a million dollars each for their work as Lewis and Clark.

Fingal O'Farrell had discarded his kaftan and wore fringed buckskins. He looked handsomer and huskier; but was still as voluble as ever. On the second night Prue went to bed with him in his trailer on the location site; the crew and the actors were quartered in motels in a nearby town but Fingal preferred, as he said, to commune with nature after a hard day's work. Going to bed with Prue was evidently part of his communion.

Stripped, he turned out to be all muscle; he was also a magnificent lover when he stopped talking. Next morning he tried to persuade Prue to remain with him. However, with no intention of a lasting affair, she knew the loving had to stop before the gossip got really started. She kissed him goodbye and went back to Kansas City.

Before she left she had a word with Martha. 'I'm not going to ask you what you think of an aunt who spends a night with such a man – '

'Aunt Prue, people don't judge other people by their morals any more – '

'The fact that you used the word *morals* gives me some hope for you. All I wanted to say was that you should not let Mr O'Farrell get *you* into his trailer. He is a social climber, as I suspected. While he was climbing over me last night – don't laugh, darling. I don't mean to be crude, though I suppose it sounds that way. The point is, he'd like to marry money. He's making a great deal of money now, I'm sure, but he has no guarantee that it will go on. I don't think he is the genius you think he is and some day the film backers will wake up to him. So beware. Learn what you can from him, but stay out of his trailer. Goodbye, darling. Socialize with the Indians. I'm sure they're safer.'

She went back home and assured Margaret that Martha was safe and working hard. 'Don't worry about her, Meg. While she's out there she's not going to give a thought to being a radical or protesting about Vietnam. She is, as they say among movie people, working her ass off.'

'Delightful,' said Margaret. 'I wonder what Mother would say? A granddaughter of hers working her ass off for a transvestite poseur.'

'Poseur, yes. But transvestite, no. Take my word for it.'

'You aren't having an affair with him, for God's sake!'

'No. We communed with nature one night, but that's it. And I've warned Martha he's not to be encouraged with any more invitations.'

Martha completed her work on the film and came home without Mr O'Farrell. Nine months later the film was released and turned out to be a savagely extravagant corruption of the Lewis and Clark story. Fingal O'Farrell had as little respect for the figures of history as he had for history itself. Even Martha

355

was shocked when she saw the finished film.

Prue did not see O'Farrell again till the summer of 1971. She had been in France with Melanie, paying their annual visit to St Cast. Melanie was now eight, a pretty child who already showed promise of growing up to be a carbon copy of her mother. She was sharp-eyed and intelligent; her only failing was that she was uninterested in reading anything at all, sex books or anything else. Prue did not regret that she showed no interest in prurient literature, but she hoped that she was not going to rear a semi-literate daughter.

Guy was politely affectionate to his daughter, but no more than that. Stephane was a politely solicitous grandmother. But she still had not forgiven Prue for walking out on her son and the air was always full of her darts on every one of Prue's visits. In 1968, when Prue and Melanie had arrived for their visit two months after Robert Kennedy had been assassinated, the darts had been particularly sharp and poisoned. The failure to elimi nate her greatest enemy, General de Gaulle, still rankled.

Now, on this visit, Prue asked, 'Do you ever see Colonel Raclot?'

'Occasionally, perhaps once a year. He lives in Beirut.'

'Would he be safe there? I thought the Arabs would have him on some sort of list because of his feelings over Algeria.'

'He lives among the Christians there. The civilized ones.'

'Most of whom, I suppose, would have been educated at the American University in Beirut.'

'More probably here in France.'

The darts flew both ways. At the end of her stay Prue thought that she, like the bowmen at Crécy, had come off best. But she determined there would be no more visits. Melanie, acutely observant, had already begun to remark that the atmosphere between the grown-ups was pretty bitchy.

On the way home Prue and Melanie stopped off in London, staying at the Savoy where the Beaufort name still had its cachet. Melanie, who, unlike her mother, liked outdoor sports, said she wanted to go to Wimbledon so that she could tell Grandpa all about it when they went home. Prue called the London office of Beaufort Oil and next morning two tickets to the Centre Court were delivered to the hotel. It did not occur to Prue to ask how they had been obtained; so her daughter would probably grow up believing that tickets for Wimbledon were as easily available as tickets for the Underground. The chief executive of the London office, whose tickets they were, took the day off and watched the tennis at home on television. His wife, who had bought a new outfit for the occasion, got drunk on sherry and cursed all Americans, particularly those who never had a thought for the workers in the outposts of the Beaufort empire.

Fingal O'Farrell and a very pretty English actress were sitting right behind the Beaufort seats. He had trimmed his beard now to a Van Dyke style, but his hair was still long. He was dressed in a white safari suit and a wide-brimmed straw hat. Prue thought he looked like Trader Horn before the African rot had got to him.

'My dear lady!' The players had not yet come out on to the court and he was able to play to the gallery without being told to shut up. He introduced his companion. 'Miss Genevieve Mulligan, who will one day be a big star if she does as I tell her.'

Miss Mulligan fluttered her eyelashes so violently that one of them came loose and she spent the rest of the afternoon trying to set it right again, much to the delight of Melanie who, now that she was at Wimbledon, found tennis was actually *boring*.

O'Farrell treated the three females, as he called them, to strawberries and cream during a break between matches and then invited Prue to a cocktail party that evening at his house in Knightsbridge. 'It's a sort of farewell to myself. I'm off to Australia to do a film about one of their heroes, Ned Kelly. It's been done before but not the way I shall do it. Do come this evening!'

Prue, still suffering the effects of the visit to St Cast, decided that the party might help lighten her mood. The Savoy provided a woman to come in and sit with Melanie and she went off to the big house in a side street in Knightsbridge. When she arrived the party was already bubbling with the lava of gossip, back-biting and self-appreciation.

'Egotism,' said the actor-knight, 'is the only -ism one can truly trust.'

'It's a pity four-letter words have become so chic,' said the publisher. 'Shit equals wit these days.'

O'Farrell, in a blue silk kaftan this evening, welcomed Prue with more show than she wished. But he was intent on demon-strating whom he knew; Prue was to discover that the room was chockablock with fame and fortune. Fingal O'Farrell had to prop himself up with other celebrities.

Prue disentangled herself from him and found herself beside a thickset man with a moustache and an amused, half-wondering expression on his blunt face. 'He's a bit overpowering, isn't he?

I don't know why I got myself mixed up with him.'

'Are you going to Australia with him on his new picture?' She recognized his accent, though she had not met many Australians.

'God knows why. I'm not the art director, I'm something he calls his artistic adviser. He hasn't listened to any advice, I'll bet, since his mother told him to get off her tit.'

'Nicely put. But no compliment to his mother.'

'Sorry. I don't usually talk like that in front of women – the wife would kill me if she heard me. It must be the atmosphere. I'm Steve Hamill.'

Prue introduced herself and he raised his eyebrows. 'I didn't catch your name when he yelled it out. I think I'd turned off.' He sipped the beer he was drinking. 'I knew your sister Nina years ago. She and her husband Tim were my first buyers. How are they?'

'They separated. Nina's all right, but we haven't heard from Tim in ages.'

'They broke up, eh? Who'd have believed it? The wife and I used to think they were the happiest married couple we knew. After ourselves,' he added with a grin.

'Is your wife here?'

'Not a chance. She can't stand our Irish friend. She's hoping that while he's out in Australia the abos will shove a spear into him.'

'My sister still has your paintings. One of them is her favourite. A woman and two small children, done mostly in blues.'

'That was the wife and kids. It was my favourite, too. I almost didn't sell it, but we needed the money in those days. I owe her a painting. She and Tim gave me a thousand quid, told me it was an advance on the first painting of mine that had a thousand-quid price tag on it. I finally got there last year.' He raised his glass to himself. 'You're looking at a thousand-quid-a-painting man. Well, actually two thousand quid. The gallery have put up their prices on me this year.'

Prue took a glass from the tray of a passing waiter and raised it. 'Congratulations, Mr Hamill. Nina will be delighted to know you've made it. But why do you need to bother with Mr O'Farrell?'

'I got sucked in by flattery. It's hard to resist being told you're indispensable, that you're the one man in the world a producer wants. But tonight – ' He looked around him, then finished his beer. 'I think I've just decided I'm dispensable. I'm going over to our Irish friend and give him the two-fingered salute and tell him – ' He grinned. 'No, no more crudity. Give my regards to Nina. And tell her my offer still stands. I'm having a show next month here in London. She can have her pick.'

'Perhaps Tim feels he's entitled to a choice, too.'

Steve Hamill shook his head. 'It was Nina's money, not his. Maybe that was what broke 'em up, was it? Or am I being crude again?'

'Crude but possibly correct. I just wouldn't mention it if you should meet Nina.'

'I'm crude but not dumb. If I were, the wife would have kicked me out years ago. Nice meeting you, Prue. Don't get sucked in by O'Farrell. Oh, this is Clive Harvest. The place is full of bloody Aussies tonight. Watch 'em – they're the greatest free-loaders you'll ever meet. Except for Clive. He's one of our tennis players. I'm a cricket fan myself.'

He moved away through the throng and Prue looked up at the tall blond young man beside her. He was younger than she, handsome, tanned, a male animal with intelligent eyes and a smile that was somehow familiar.

'I'm out of my depth here,' he said. 'Are you an actress or something?'

'Depends what you mean by something. I'm not in movies, if that's what you mean. Very much not in movies. I think I'm what they call a lady of leisure.'

'You don't look – Oh sorry. I thought you said a lady of pleasure. It's a bit noisy here. You want to go out in the garden?'

They drifted round the edge of the crowd and out into the small garden. The sky was still pale blue; some thin clouds were shot with the last rays of the sun that had left London and was heading for the West Country. Prue always found the summer evenings one of the more attractive features of England. But London no longer held the attraction for her that it had when she was younger.

Harvest led Prue to a bench and they sat down. 'I had a two-hour match this afternoon. The legs are a bit tired.'

'At your age? I thought you tennis players could go on for hours.'

'I save my strength for other things. A bloke doesn't want to be playing tennis twenty-four hours a day.'

'What other things? Never mind, don't tell me. I don't want to sound like one of those cocktail coquettes in the house there. Do girls fling themselves at you?'

'Some of them do.' He managed to sound modest.

Physically, if not mentally, he had begun to interest her. Sexually she had been rather quiet over the past six months. A new man had come to town in Kansas City, Roger Devon IV:

he always signed his name that way, a regal touch that looked out of place in KC. Devon money was Boston money and old; it had joined the newer Beaufort money to expand its oil and banking interests. The family was the sort that had scions instead of sons and Roger IV was the scion who had been sent to Kansas City as its representative. He and Prue had been attracted to each other at once, but back East he had a marriage that, if not on the rocks, was close to a rough shoreline. He was a gentleman of the old school, a species she thought had died out with her grandfather's generation. His saving grace was that he was not a stuffed shirt as well. Against the yen of her body she had become a lady of the old school, a condition of which she had never thought herself capable. She was in love with Roger Devon IV and she would wait till he was divorced, an arrangement that was now in the works.

In the meantime she was not in Kansas City, the evening was warm, this handsome young male animal . . . 'Do tennis players eat dinner?'

He took her to a small restaurant in Kensington where the food, the service and the space between tables was much less than she was accustomed to. He did not ask her much about herself, but, prompted by her, told her about himself. He ate as if he were starved and drank almost all the bottle of Spanish wine. She tasted the wine, then, with memories of St Cast on her tongue, told him she was not a wine drinker. Watching the way he ate and drank and remembering his complaint that his legs were gone, she wondered if the evening would progress any further than this table.

'I'll never be Number One,' he said. 'There are too many good players around now. But I make a living and I don't know a better way of making it. If I were back home in an office, would I be taking a good-looking older woman to dinner?'

'I don't know. How old are the older women in Sydney?' At thirty-one she wondered if Australian women were considered over the hill when they left their twenties.

He smiled and once again there was that dim memory itching at the back of her mind. He was at that age, twenty-four or twenty-five she guessed, when his features were just starting to set into their own individuality; he was still young enough to remind her of a dozen faces and expressions. Perhaps he had copied it from some public personality: the world was full of young men smiling like Paul Newman.

'My father's very popular with older women. And some not so old. Your age.'

360

'Thank you. I was beginning to feel senile there for a moment.'

He smiled again: he had a certain charm, not very smooth but agreeable. 'I think Dad and I might compete for you. Sometimes I see him out with a girl and I say Hello Dad, emphasizing the *Dad*. He could kill me, it sets his night right back on its heels.'

'He must love you.'

'He does, actually. He just wishes I'd go into the firm with him, that's all we ever fight about. He's in the import-export business. I'd just find it dull. Well, that's dinner. It wasn't very good, was it? I'm sorry. What are we going to do now?'

She could not invite him back to the Savoy, not with Melanie in the other bedroom in the suite. 'If I were a younger woman, what would we do?'

He shook his head at his obtuseness. He stood up, came round and pulled her chair out for her. Almost a little too late in the evening he showed he could be gallant and attentive.

'I'm sharing a flat with another guy just up the road. He's been knocked out of both the singles and doubles, so he's gone down to the country for a couple of days.'

'Let's be grateful to his opponents who knocked him out.'

In bed she had no complaint with him. He released from her all the pent-up sexuality of the past six months, satisfied her not once but several times. At last she got out of bed, went into the bathroom and dressed there. She felt guilty, the first time she had ever felt that way getting out of a bed.

She did not kiss Clive Harvest goodbye. 'Good luck tomorrow. I hope you haven't worn out all your strength.'

'Are you coming to Wimbledon tomorrow?'

'No, I'm leaving for home. I'll tell you now, so there won't be any complications if we run across each other again – though I don't think it's likely, I'm not a tennis fan. I'm divorced and have a little girl. I'm going home and I hope to be married again within three months. So goodbye, Clive, and thank you for a very nice evening. If we ever meet again, let's be strangers.'

He got out of bed, had the grace to pull on his shorts. 'I won't be stupid and ask if you were having a last fling. It was too good for that, for both of us, I mean. I think I got a little education tonight. And I don't mean just in there.' He gestured at the bed.

She did kiss him then. 'We older women have our advantages.'

She went back to Kansas City next day and in October of that year married Roger Devon IV in a quiet wedding on the Beaufort estate. Lucas, slowed down now but still standing straight and tall, had not felt so happy in a long time. He was certainly happy with his new son-in-law; and with Bruce Alburn and Charlie Luman. And he had hopes that Nina would at last make up her mind about Magnus McKea.

## 2

'It will be a relief to get away from Watergate,' said Roger.

'I'm just glad I'm not going with you,' said Bruce. 'I don't think I'd like to be an American abroad right now. Especially a Republican.'

'Maybe the British have the best idea,' said Charlie. 'I was talking to a British Airways pilot at Heathrow the other day. He said if any Prime Minister had done what Nixon's done, he'd have been eased out before the shit hit the fan.'

'The fan probably wouldn't have been working anyway,' said Lucas. 'Not with all the strikes they have.'

The four men were having lunch, not luncheon, in the private dining room on the top floor of the Beaufort Bank building. It was a ritual that Lucas had started three years ago when he had found that he had two able and likeable sons-in-law working under the one roof with him. He, Bruce and Roger lunched together every Friday and when Charlie was home from his overseas tours of duty he came along to the gathering. The four men liked and respected each other and the meal was one of the main pleasures of Lucas's week.

He was now seventy-four years old and though he owned more than one man's fair share of the world's wealth, it had become a world that held less and less appeal for him. He still looked less than his age, still held himself erect, still played tennis; but the years had eaten him away inside like a cancer. There were times when he woke in the morning wishing he had died during the night.

The standards he had lived by were crumbling. He was not given too frequently to imaginative metaphors, but sometimes he felt he was standing on a jetty the pilings of which were being rotted and pounded by a polluted and vicious sea. He had once tried to incorporate the image into a speech to a bankers' conference in Chicago, but it had sounded too florid for his dry delivery and he had crossed it out from his draft. He had been shocked at what had happened to women's thinking in the past few years; he kept silent because he loved them, but it distressed him every time his granddaughters Martha and Emma came home to Kansas City from their Women's Lib campaigning; he was only thankful that none of his daughters had got themselves involved in such heresies. He no longer had any interest in music, mainly because there was no longer any music, not his kind; Margaret and Nina had tried to get him to symphony concerts, but such occasions were no place for a man who liked to tap his foot to the beat; as for rock or country-and-western he could only suppose that listeners to such trash had ears that should have been closed up at birth. Such caterwauling was a corruption of music: but then perhaps it was only a sound-track to the general corruption all over: morals, politics, law and order. Sometimes he was glad that Edith was no longer alive.

So many of his friends, too, were no longer alive. Their political differences buried, he had become a close friend of President Truman; he had actually wept at the President's death, for the chirpy old man and for an era that, for all its faults, had had certain standards he had respected. He had turned his back on Richard Nixon before Watergate had monopolized the head-lines; he knew nothing of the new President, Gerald Ford, and didn't want to know. Without becoming reclusive like certain other very rich men, he had retreated to the obscurity that he had once enjoyed and now enjoyed again. When the Beaufort name, as that of an individual rather than of the corporation, got into the news it was usually that of one of his daughters. Though only Nina, strictly speaking, was still a Beaufort. She and Magnus, for reasons Lucas never dared to query, were still the best of companions but still not married.

Magnus arrived late for the lunch. He was a regular, like the sons-in-law, but his office was still on 9th Street and sometimes he was delayed in getting across to the Beaufort building. He came in now, sat down and attacked the grilled bass, catching up with the others in a few minutes.

'Man shouldn't rush good food like this. Well, you're taking off tomorrow, Lucas? Wish I were coming with you. I'd like to talk to those Arabs on their home ground. I wonder if they're as arrogant at home as they are when they come over here. They're really screwing us and it's going to get worse.'

'That's why Roger and I are going to Abu Sadar. I think we can persuade the old Sheikh to hold his prices. We're making more money, but all this escalation of price does nothing for the oil companies' PR image. A lot of men in the street think we're in cahoots with the Arabs.'

'Are we?' said Magnus.

'I hope you choke on a fishbone. You're starting to sound like my granddaughters. No offence, Bruce.'

'Meg and I have given up on them,' said Bruce. 'They'll settle down when they reach thirty. Most radicals do, if someone makes them a better offer.'

'I shan't be here. If they don't settle down, don't try and get in touch with me – I wouldn't want Heaven spoiled.'

Next morning Lucas, Roger and Prue left in the private Boeing 707 for the Middle East. It would never have occurred to Lucas himself to have bought the plane for the use of company executives; he saw nothing wrong with travel by scheduled airlines. But Bruce and Roger had persuaded him of the economy and advantages, not least the privacy, of a company aircraft; the privacy such travel provided had been enough to convince him. But he used the aircraft much less than the executives who worked for him.

'Won't you let me come down to Abu Sadar with you?' Prue said.

'No,' said Roger. 'The bargain was that you could come only as far as Beirut. You can enjoy yourself there, it's an interesting town. We'll only be down in Abu Sadar three days at the most.'

Prue smiled at him, did not press her argument. Sometimes she was surprised how content she was with him; she allowed him to run her life with much more compliance than she had expected of herself. He was not a domineering husband, but he had a gift of convincing her that whatever he suggested was best for both of them; Andover and Harvard had given him a well-rounded education but somewhere along the line he had also educated himself in the diplomacy of dealing with women. He was not strictly handsome, but he radiated a quiet sincerity that gave added value to his just-average looks. It was a further mark in his favour that he avoided the usual handicap of a trustworthy man: he was not dull. He was a lover, husband and father who kept his wife and children entertained all the time he was with them.

Prue had not brought the children with them on this trip. Melanie was now twelve and, following her mother and aunts, was at Barstow; Grace was two-and-a-half and had been taken by her nurse to spend a week with her father's mother in Boston. Prue sometimes sensed a disappointment in Lucas that she had not given him a grandson. Michael was never mentioned in the family circle, though she had no idea what conversation went on between her father and Nina about the past.

The plane landed at New York to re-fuel, then flew on to Paris where they stayed overnight at the Crillon. Lucas, said Roger, had to be protected against jet lag, and the old man had not argued. Prue certainly hadn't: a night in Paris, even after a long flight, was always enjoyable. They went to dinner at Roger's choice, Lasserre's, and even Lucas, still a Francophobe, had to agree that the food was good. Each time she landed in France Prue wondered about Guy and Stephane, but she never mentioned them to Roger. He, in turn, never spoke of his first wife. They had each discovered in the first month of their marriage that, though they claimed to be sophisticated, they were both old-fashioned enough to be jealous of previous lovers. Prue, the romantic side of her prevailing, took it as a sign that what they had between them then was true love. She could not remember ever having felt jealous before she had married Roger. She had not, as far as she could remember, been jealous of Stephane. But she did not probe her memory too deeply, not of that period of her life.

They flew on to Beirut next morning and checked into the Hotel St Georges. Prue and Roger had been in their suite only ten minutes when the phone rang.

'Sheikh Zaid sends his compliments, Mr Devon, and asks that you and Mr Beaufort meet his son Sabah this afternoon.'

'Who are you?'

'I am Hassan Burami, Sheikh Zaid's personal aide. We haven't met, Mr Devon, I am new. The Sheikh sent me up here to meet you. In the meantime he would like you to have tea with his son this afternoon. The Sheikh has a house up on the Aley road, as you know.'

Roger didn't know. He had only been to Abu Sadar once before and he had flown there via Bahrein, not Beirut. He did not want to take tea with the Sheikh's son and he knew that Lucas would like the idea even less; but he had a strict appreciation of Arab protocol and manners and he knew that to refuse might offend the Sheikh. He was not concerned whether it would offend Sabah. The son was the sort of Arab who gave Arabs a bad name, a profligate spender who spent all his time and money on pleasure. Roger was only glad that Prue had not been included in the invitation.

'We shall send a car for you, Mr Devon. At three-thirty, shall we say?'

Lucas was not happy at all about wasting an hour or two with a fat Arab young man whose main business was gambling and buying women. 'Dammit, what's the point? The Sheikh won't trust that young slob with any business matter.'

'The point is, Lucas, we've been invited. By the Sheikh himself. He must have some reason for wanting us to see the slob, as you call him.'

'Oh, all right. But you do the talking. I'll just sit and sip that damned awful coffee they make out here.'

The car called for them at exactly 3.30. Arabs were usually not so punctual, but it was just a stray thought that floated across Roger's mind and he did not dwell on it. Prue went down in the elevator with her father and Roger and met the slim young man who introduced himself as Hassan Burami. He was dressed in a well-cut lounge suit, wore dark glasses and had a slight American accent.

'I had three years at Caltech,' he explained. 'Is Mrs Devon honouring us with her presence?'

'No,' said Prue. 'I'm going up to the Rue Hamra to do some shopping. We American wives are supposed to do nothing else but spend our husbands' money when we're abroad.'

'Arab wives are learning to do the same. Very expensive if one has several wives. Which I don't.' He had a pleasant smile, youthful and sincere. 'It is a pleasure meeting you, Mrs Devon. Shall we go, gentlemen?'

Prue touched her father's and husband's hands, a light farewell, and went down the steps into the street. The black Mercedes passed her as she walked along the promenade and she waved, though she could see no answering hands through the opaque windows of the car.

When she returned to the hotel an hour later the ransom note was waiting for her, given to her by the desk clerk with her key.

# 3

'We've been in touch with Abu Sadar,' said Bruce. 'They've never heard of anyone called Hassan Burami.'

'What about Prue?'

'I told her not to move out of her room. I got on to the embassy in Beirut and Bredgar, the ambassador, said he and his wife personally would stay with her till you arrived. Washington has been advised.'

'Has the money been arranged?' Magnus asked.

'Our associate bank in Beirut is getting it together. Five million dollars in Swiss francs – Christ Almighty, the secrets that must be buried in those Swiss banks! That's where they'll send it, of course, as soon as you hand it over.'

Magnus did not look at Sally, who had a secret buried in a Swiss bank, a secret that was now worth slightly more than the ransom being demanded for her father and Roger. She had not touched the deposit since he had arranged the payment to the Belgian missionary Order thirteen years ago; he guessed she never would touch it, it was something she had put out of her mind when she had married Charlie. Even Lucas seemed to have forgotten it.

All the family, plus Magnus, were collected in the drawing-room of the main house. Magnus was dressed for travelling and so was Nina. She had insisted that she should accompany him to Beirut. Bruce and Charlie, bringing up the possibility of danger, had tried to talk her out of it; but Margaret and Sally had agreed that one of them had to go to Beirut to comfort and support Prue. Both Margaret and Sally had also wanted to go at first, but in the end they had listened to reason. Melanie had been told of what had happened to her stepfather and grandfather and she, too, needed to be comforted and supported. Now they were all waiting on word that the private jet, sent from Boston by the Devon corporation, had arrived at the Kansas City airport.

Charlie said, 'I don't know why the bastards haven't made a big splash in the media. Usually terrorists like them are looking for publicity as well as money.'

'They'll make their announcement soon enough. Maybe they just want to be sure the money arrives in Beirut first.'

The phone rang and Margaret picked it up. She felt sick and weak, had not felt like this since . . . She remembered the two occasions well: when she had learned that Tim had disappeared and when they had come to tell her that Frank had committed suicide. Both occasions had been tragic for her and she prayed now that this would not be another tragic event. She said a few words into the phone, then put it down.

'The plane's out at the airport ready to go. We shan't come out with you – all of us out there together might cause some comment. We'll keep it out of the newspapers here till we hear something from Beirut. We mustn't antagonize them. Terrorists too often seem to be psychotic if someone else steals their publicity.'

'Jesus,' said Charlie, 'I'm psychotic, too, just thinking about the sons-of-bitches. Every time you fly an aircraft through that part of the world you're looking over your shoulder for some bastard to hijack you. I think I'll come with you, Magnus,' he said suddenly.

'No,' said Sally. 'I want you here. Just in case – '

He put his arm round her. 'Don't think the worst, honey. All they want is the money and maybe the publicity. They can't have anything against your father or Roger.'

Don't you believe it, thought Magnus. Any American capitalist imperialist would have a great deal against him in the Middle East.

But going out to the airport in Nina's Rolls-Royce, with George Biff driving, he said, 'Are you prepared for the worst?'

'Yes,' said Nina. 'I've been thinking about it.'

He put a comforting hand on her knee. 'Try not to.'

Up front George Biff said, 'I like to be going with you. Mr Lucas gonna need someone to lean on when you get him back.'

Magnus looked at Nina. Each time he looked at her he saw more of her mother in her; but he loved her now for her own sake. 'You see? George is optimistic.'

# 4

Ambassador Bredgar and his wife were doing their best to comfort Prue. One or both of them had been with her ever since the news of the kidnapping had reached them, Bredgar going back to his office only when the embassy called him. Prue appreciated their efforts, but she wanted something more constructive than just comfort. She was relieved when Nina and Magnus arrived.

The sisters embraced each other, both of them holding back their tears. The Bredgars discreetly withdrew and Magnus went out into the living-room of the suite with them.

'They've made their announcement, Mr McKea. An hour ago.' Bredgar, grey-haired, raw-boned, adjusted his horn-rimmed glasses as if he needed a new focus now that the kidnapping was out in the open. 'They not only want the five million dollars. They want a guarantee that Beaufort Oil will withdraw, completely and without any compensation whatsoever, from Abu Sadar.'

Magnus blew a silent whistle. 'That complicates things. I'm in no position to make that sort of deal. I'm sure Mr Beaufort himself would never agree to it, not even if it meant his own life.'

'I regret to say that Washington would never agree to it, either. I've been in touch with the Secretary of State. He's seeing the President now, but he's already given me their answer. They won't allow any American oil company to quit the Middle East under threat. That would only open the way for the same pressure to be put on all the other companies. There are a great number of Arabs, some in high places, who feel very strongly that we Americans are no longer necessary to help them produce their oil.'

'I'll go in with the ladies,' said Mrs Bredgar, who knew when an ambassador's wife should make herself scarce. 'Miss Beaufort might like some coffee or something. She must be worn out after that long flight.'

'You'll find all the Beaufort women very durable ladies,' said Magnus. 'They inherit it from their father.'

'Let's hope he stays durable long enough for us to rescue him,' said Bredgar.

When the ambassador's wife had gone into the bedroom Magnus said, 'Have you made any contact with the kidnappers yet? Who are they?'

'So far they haven't given themselves a name. There'll be some crackpot terrorists who'll be claiming credit in the next hour or two, it always happens. But I don't think these guys are crackpots. Their announcement read almost like a parliamentary decree. None of the usual abuse about American imperialists, stuff like that.'

'So how do we get in touch with them if we don't know who they are?'

'They are going to make another announcement tomorrow morning. I think they're playing it canny. They know the final decision on the withdrawal from Abu Sadar will have to come from Washington, not Beaufort Oil. They know discussion on that will take a little time.'

'In the meantime – '

'In the meantime my security people are doing what they can to find out who this outfit is. I'm afraid we have to be patient, Mr McKea.'

'I think I'd find that easier if it were my own life at stake.'

## 5

The two men sat in the café-bar on the corner of the Rue Hamra and Rue Jeanne d'Arc. The tables out on the sidewalk were occupied by tourists, all of them less arrogant than they had been a few years ago, all of them trying to look friendly, all of them thinking of the approaching winter and wondering if the Arab bastards would raise the price of oil again. The interior of the bar was full of locals: students, merchants, conspirators: an air of conspiracy mingled with the smell of coffee in any Arab bar these days. The two men in the corner had that air about them or anyway they talked in low voices.

Henri Raclot said, 'You heard the news on the radio about the kidnapping of those Americans? Even the super-rich are no longer safe.'

'Yes,' said Tim Davoren.

'I know the daughter of Lucas Beaufort, the old man. The wife of the younger one, whatever-his-name-is. I knew her years ago in France. A very lovely woman. Brave, too.'

'I knew her once. She was very young then. Too young to be brave.'

Raclot sipped his *arak*. He had spent too long in unexpected places and situations to show surprise, even when he felt it. He had shown no surprise when, three years ago right here on the Rue Hamra, he had bumped into Nigel Burgess whom he had not seen since the Congo days. Neither had asked what the other was doing, but had just taken the pleasure of the moment for itself. One hid one's curiosity as well as one's surprise. Raclot knew that it did not pay to be too curious in the world in which they had both lived. And, for all he knew, Burgess might still live.

'I wish I could help her,' Raclot said. 'I owe her a great debt.'

Tim contained his own curiosity. He came to Beirut twice a year to sell opals, but he kept his identity as secure as was possible. This was oil men's territory and he did not want to stumble across anyone who might recognize him and take the word back to Kansas City. He never stayed in any of the better-known hotels, always preferring a small *pension* and never the same one twice. He had thought several times about not looking up Raclot again after their accidental meeting; but he had some good memories of Africa and Raclot was the only man he could share them with. So he would call up the Frenchman and they would meet for a drink and lunch or dinner; they would talk about old times but never about the present and neither of them would ask questions that might embarrass. He still let Raclot call him by the name he had been known by in Africa; he had not told him that he had yet another identity that he used in business here in Beirut and back in Australia. Indeed, he had not told Raclot anything about his business or mentioned Australia at all. He had long ago given up the name Tim Davoren. He would have succeeded in blocking it completely from his mind if it had not been for his son, who would always be there to remind him of the past.

'You could never help her in this, Henri. You're on the wrong side. These chaps are Marxists.'

'You know who they are?'

'I have a fair idea. They approached me last year, when I was here, about buying some guns for them.'

'Did you sell them any?' Raclot asked the question warily.

'I gave that up years ago. I thought of passing them on to Rudi Schnatz – I wonder if he's still in the game? – then thought better of it. There are so many buyers nowadays, it got so that my conscience started to worry me. In the old days you could be pretty certain whom the guns were going to be used against. Not any more. You could sell guns now and find them being used against your own chaps. Like today, for instance.'

'Lucas Beaufort is one of your chaps?'

Tim smiled, pushed back a lock of grey hair that had fallen over his brow. The black moustache had been shaved off the day he left Kansas City; the once-dark hair was now steel grey. Twenty-five years had wrought changes in his looks; he was no longer instantly recognizable as Tim Davoren. He often wondered what Nina looked like now, but it seemed she led a sheltered social life and he had never seen any pictures of her in newspapers or magazines. He had been tempted to write and order a year's subscription to the *Independent*, feeling sure she must be occasionally featured in *its* pages, but he had recognized the danger there in time. He did occasionally see pictures of Lucas in *Time* magazine or in copies of the *Wall Street Journal* that he would pick up on his trips out of Australia. Lucas did not appear to have changed at all.

'I doubt if he'd think of it that way. But yes, we're on the same side. In a way.' He sipped his Arab beer, too light for his taste after the Australian beer he had become used to. 'Henri, would you really like to help Mrs Whatever-her-name-is? Prue.'

# 6

Prue had got over her initial panic. Thirty-six hours had passed since she had received the ransom note and she had slowly but steadily regained some measure of control. She was a natural optimist and hope held her afloat like an unsinkable buoy. But she wondered how she would have stood up to the fear and worry if Nina and Magnus had not arrived.

She was alone in the suite with Nina when the call came from the desk downstairs to say that Colonel Raclot would like to see her. Magnus was at the embassy, holding an awkward three-way conversation by phone with Washington and Kansas City. Bruce, speaking for Margaret and Sally, was all for agreeing to any terms the kidnappers were asking. But Washington was still stalling, still insisting, without actually saying so, that an American presence in Abu Sadar was worth more than any two men's lives.

'Who is he?' Nina asked.

'I knew him in France. I think we'd better get Magnus back here.'

A plainclothes security man from the embassy had been kept in the suite. He let Raclot in when the latter knocked on the door, then looked at Prue for instructions. She asked him to wait out in the corridor for a few minutes and, with a careful look at Raclot he went out, closing the door behind him.

Raclot kissed the hands of both women, expressed concern at what had happened. 'A long time ago, madame, I expressed the hope that I could repay you for what you did for me.'

'I helped the Colonel escape from the police.' Prue saw the intrigued look on Nina's face. 'But that is all I'm ever going to tell you. It's something between me and the Colonel.'

The world must be full of secrets, Nina thought; but she had so few secrets of her own. She was not even privy to the one that still concerned her most: the whereabouts of her husband and son.

'It would be better,' said Prue, 'if you could wait till our friend Mr McKea arrives. He knows what we can and cannot do.'

'As you wish, madame.' Prue had never known Raclot to

speak English before; but maybe mercenaries needed to be multi-lingual. 'Do you ever hear from Guy?'

'Only on my daughter's birthday. Just a card.'

'Still his mother's boy, eh? A pity.'

Magnus arrived in ten minutes, flinging open the door and striding in, his bald head glistening with sweat, as if he had run all the way from the embassy. He still looked and moved like a man much younger than he was, but Prue remarked that he had got older in the face in the past few hours. Things, she guessed, were not going well with Washington.

She introduced Raclot, who explained that he thought he could help. 'I can't make the contact myself. I'm known to be on the wrong side in all the little internal wars that go on in this part of the world. They call me a right-wing Christian Fascist. Which is perhaps what I am,' he said without apology. 'But I have a friend who can make the contact. Or try to.'

'Who is he?'

'I'm sorry, I can't tell you that.'

'Colonel, how do I know we can trust you? There is a great deal of money involved in this – '

'Magnus, please – ' Prue remembered when Raclot had once asked if she could be trusted. History did repeat itself, in cracked mirrors.

The stiffening in Raclot was barely discernible: it disappeared as soon as Prue spoke up in his defence. 'I owe Madame Devon a very great debt, m'sieu. One that has no dollar value on it.'

'I apologize, Colonel,' said Magnus. 'I wasn't really thinking of the money. But I don't want our hopes raised and then find out we've been tricked.'

'I understand, m'sieu. I can assure you that the man I'm recommending is a man of honour.'

'I'll have to confer with our ambassador. Certain things have been taken out of our hands. Will you come with me to the embassy?'

'Of course. I'm *persona non grata* there, but I'm sure you'll vouch for me.'

'Get on to the bank,' Magnus said to Prue. 'Tell them to bring the money to the embassy at once. It will save time, if we get the okay from the embassy.'

'Do you think the kidnappers will settle for just the money?'

'I don't know. But if anyone can afford such a bet, it's the Beauforts.'

He and Raclot went out and Nina said, 'What a callous, nasty thing to say!'

'I'll bet he's already sorry he said it.' Prue was already on to the bank. 'But I think we're forgetting something. This is just as worrying for him as it is for us. In his own way he loves Daddy as much as we do.'

'You have Roger to worry about, too – '

'Yes.'

Prue finished her call to the bank, went to the window and looked out. She put on her glasses, not knowing what she wanted to see; she was still sharp-eyed when she was close to things, but anything distant had now become a blur. The glasses did not help her now: she looked out on a city that hid its secrets so well that all outsiders like herself might just as well have been blind. Then tears produced their own blindness.

# 7

Ambassador Bredgar was waiting in his office with two of his senior men whom Magnus had already met. A third man, quiet, anonymous-looking, stood in the background. 'This is Ben Criska. He heads our security.'

Magnus nodded and Raclot smiled and said, 'M. Criska is the CIA station chief, Mr McKea. I'm on his list of those to be watched.'

Bredgar said sharply, 'Is that so, Ben?'

Criska nodded. 'I think in this case Colonel Raclot can be trusted. He's never been a fortune-hunter and he's certainly not on the side of these guys, whoever they are. They're not a right-wing bunch.'

Raclot's dry smile hadn't altered. 'I must ask you some day, M. Criska, for a personal reference.'

Bredgar, still uneasy, had had enough of the fencing. 'Are you the contact, Colonel? No? Then who is?'

'I'm afraid we have to go on trust there,' said Magnus. 'Mrs Devon knew the Colonel some years ago and she says he is to be trusted. Unless your men have come up with an alternative, I'm afraid we have no choice.'

Bredgar looked at Criska again and the latter shook his head. 'We've made no progress. I think the Colonel can be trusted. The question is, can his contact be trusted?'

'Yes,' said Raclot.

There was silence for a moment, then Magnus said, 'That's it, then. Any instructions for the Colonel to pass on? He's already told me that his contact won't see any of us. None of this satisfies me at all, but as I said, we have no alternative.'

'Colonel Raclot,' said Bredgar, 'you have to tell your contact that my government will not agree to any demand for a withdrawal of Beaufort Oil from Abu Sadar. He will have to convince those terrorists that all they will get is the money he will be carrying. If they ask for more money – ' He glanced at Magnus.

Magnus felt like a man who had no bargaining position at all: the only credit he had was hope and that was not negotiable. 'We'll pay more if they ask. The money doesn't matter. Tell him to tell them that we'd withdraw Beaufort Oil if it was our decision, but it isn't.'

'I'm sorry,' said Bredgar, 'but there are broader issues here than the lives of two men.'

'There always are with governments.' Magnus knew he was being unreasonable: he was not incapable of the broad view. Without governments there would only be anarchy and no man's life would be safe. That was what he had always believed, he knew it was what Lucas believed. But, when the crunch came, one expected a government to have compassion.

Ten minutes later Raclot left the embassy with the money. He had his own car, a small Renault, and he drove out of the city and up the Damascus road to the small house that looked out on one of the finest views in the Mediterranean. He lived there alone, with a Christian Arab woman coming in each day to housekeep and cook for him. He would sit on his tiny terrace and watch the sun go down over the sea, see the ghosts of Phoenicians, Hittites, Arabs, Crusaders in the golden mirages on the water and regret that he had not lived in those days. His own times were as dead as those distant eras, and he would know that, as surely as a man with terminal cancer, he was dying of loneliness and lack of interest. But it was something he would never confess to anyone, least of all to the man waiting for him in the house. But he suspected that Burgess, too, could be dying of the same illness.

I

Tim drove south along the Rashaya road in the rented Simca. The two suitcases containing the ransom money were locked in the trunk. He had not bothered to open the suitcases and check that they contained the Swiss francs and not bundles of worthless paper; Raclot had told him who had given him the money and he knew that Magnus McKea was not one to try and cheat on other men's lives. But as he drove he could not help thinking of the fortune sitting there a few feet behind him. He wondered how kidnappers arrived at the ransoms they demanded. These men he was going to meet had asked for ten times the amount that the kidnappers in Germany had asked for Nina back in 1946. The ransom – or bribe – that Lucas had paid him had been chickenfeed to what was there in the trunk of the car. Perhaps lives had no real value at all: the money demanded and paid was the only real commodity with value. Lucas and Prue's husband, Roger Devon, in the total scheme of the world, perhaps meant no more than the innocent natives he had seen killed in the Congo.

He turned up the road towards Merjayun. He had fought through here during World War II, before his regiment had been sent back to England for the invasion of Normandy. That had been a clean war: no kidnapping of civilians, no ransom demands, just plain wholesome killing of soldiers. Far away on his left he could see the snow-sprinkled peak of Mount Hermon; he

376

had once led a patrol up there looking for a suspected Vichy French outpost. It was occupied now by other troops, Syrians with their guns pointed towards Israel. Once it had been a holy mountain: the Canaanites had regarded it as the seat of the Lord of the Sun and Clouds. But nothing was holy to modern armies: soldiers were the sacrifices given to the gods these days. He felt suddenly tired, sick of the world.

He stopped in Merjayun at the house of a Greek Orthodox, a merchant who made a living in a dozen commodities, including information. Tim had made several phone calls while he had been waiting in Raclot's house and by the time Raclot had returned he knew where he had to go. The merchant, a small wizened man with no politics but a highly developed sense of survival, did not invite him into the house but came out to the car.

'The men you wish to meet, sir, will be waiting for you at the Kefer Tibnit turn-off on the Nabative el Tahta road. Why do you smile, sir?'

'The men I have to meet have a sense of humour.'

'Perhaps, sir,' said the merchant, as if he doubted it. 'I was asked to check that you had not been followed. I am to telephone them.'

'As far as I know, no I haven't been followed. There was a fair amount of traffic on the road, it was difficult to tell. I hope you haven't been put at risk by being involved in this.'

The merchant smiled, showing tobacco-stained teeth. 'One is always at risk in this part of the country, sir. The Lebanese, the Palestinians, the Syrians, the Israelis – one has to sniff the wind and hope that one can tell which way it is blowing. I am just a neutral messenger. I have given you the message. Good luck, sir.'

Tim drove on, wondering if Lucas knew where he was being held and would appreciate the irony. He saw Beaufort Castle away in the distance on his left some time before he reached the Kefer Tibnit turn-off. He drove past the jumble of small houses and stores at the turn-off, swung on to the side road and pulled up beside a stone wall in the shade of a walnut tree. An olive grove stretched away on his left; on the opposite side of the road the ground fell away into a shallow wadi where a peasant was working among some scraggly tomato plants. The sun was dropping down towards the western hills and shadows were already creeping out of the wadis and lengthening themselves out from the trees. He hoped the men he was to see would come before dark.

He sat waiting, unafraid but apprehensive. He was not concerned for his own safety; strangely enough, now that he thought

377

about it, he was philosophical about the safety of Lucas and Prue's husband. He knew their chances of being spared were less than fifty-fifty. He knew from experience that one could never tell how an argument would go with Arabs; he could only hope that their emotion of the moment was favourable towards him and what he would put to them. But he was apprehensive about meeting Lucas and he was not sure how he would handle that situation.

Out of the corner of his eye he saw the peasant straighten up among his tomato plants. Then he came up the wadi, followed by two men with sub-machineguns who had appeared from behind rocky outcrops. They came on the run and were beside the car before Tim could get out to meet them. The two men with guns jumped into the back seat and the peasant, a younger man than he had looked while down among the tomato plants, slid into the front seat beside Tim.

'Hello, Mr Burgess.' Tim had given his old pseudonym, the one he had used when he had been a contact man in the arms dealing in this territory. 'Drive straight ahead, please. I'm sorry we had to keep you waiting, but we had to make sure you had not been followed.'

Tim started up the car. 'My guess was right, Hassan. I thought you were in on this.'

Hassan Kirmani, who had called himself Burami when he had picked up the two Americans in the lobby of the Hotel St Georges, took off the ragged cloth he wore round his head. 'I'm glad they sent you, Mr Burgess. At least we can talk with you. We were afraid they would send some obdurate American from the embassy. One can't talk to American officials.'

*You may find I'm pretty obdurate, too.* 'Have you been talking to Mr Beaufort and Mr Devon?'

'No. The old man has refused to talk to us at all. He's an – ' Hassan smiled. 'An obdurate old son-of-a-bitch, isn't he? Or don't you know him?'

'I knew him a long time ago. He sounds as if he hasn't changed. You're not holding him in the castle, are you?'

Hassan continued smiling. 'It would have been a nice touch if we could have. We Arabs like irony. But we're holding him in its shadow, as it were, so perhaps that's good enough. Turn here, please.'

Tim turned the Simca on to a narrow track that ran up between outcrops of rock, past huge round boulders that looked like the toppled domes of mosques. Over to his left, beyond a deep ravine, he could see the castle. Time and weather had taken their toll of parts of the wall, but it still looked as impregnable as it must have looked to Saladin when he had besieged it. The Christians had always lost out in the end in its defence: he hoped that was not an omen for Lucas and Roger Devon.

Dusk was thick among the rocks when the Simca suddenly came out into a tiny village perched high on a cliff above the ravine. At first glance the village seemed deserted; then Tim saw the armed men on the flat rooftops of the houses. He pulled up the car and he, Hassan and the other two men, who had not spoken a word during the drive, got out. Tim went to the trunk and took out the two suitcases, lifting them out with some difficulty.

'It is heavy,' said Hassan, taking one of the cases. 'It must be tiring to be rich.'

'The world is full of rich men with slipped discs.' Tim wanted to keep Hassan in a good humour, at least until he had seen Lucas and explained what he had to say to the kidnappers. 'I'd like to see Mr Beaufort alone. Is that possible?'

'You don't want to see the other man? All right. You can be alone with Mr Beaufort, but we shall be listening to what you say to him. It is not that we don't trust you, Mr Burgess. It is that we don't trust the old man.'

They went into a house, the largest in the village, that backed on to a cliff that fell sheer to the bottom of the ravine. Tim was led through a sparsely furnished living-room and out on to a small terrace surrounded by a low wall. Geraniums bloomed defiantly despite neglect in two red earthenware pots beside the wall; rose bushes, wild as a barbed-wire entanglement, grew along the back wall of the house. This had once been a home; Tim wondered when the owner had been bought or kicked out. He waited by the wall, looking down at the long drop to the bottom of the ravine, till Lucas was brought out by Hassan. The only escape from the terrace would be by suicide.

'Mr Beaufort,' said Hassan, 'this is your go-between, Mr Burgess. You may have ten minutes together, but we shall be in that room there, listening to your every word. Don't attempt to whisper.'

He went back into the house and Tim said, 'Hello, Lucas.'

The walls of the castle reflected the last of the setting sun: the two men stood on the terrace in a fading golden glow, the colour of better memories. Lucas peered at Tim, but there was no recognition in his face.

379

'It's Tim. I've changed a bit, but I thought you'd never forget me. I haven't forgotten you.'

Lucas shut his eyes and shook his head in disbelief. He opened his eyes again, swayed a little, then sat down heavily on the one rough chair on the terrace.

'Jesus God Almighty.' His voice was little more than a hoarse whisper. 'Is this some sort of revenge or what?'

'You're wrong, Lucas. I'm on your side. I'm here to try and reason with them to let you go. I have the money they've asked for. But I don't know if that will be enough.' He looked sideways towards the open door of the living-room. There were shadowy figures in the gloom there, but none of them moved. 'Have they told you what else they're demanding?'

Lucas nodded, almost absently. 'Yes, yes. But how did you – ? Never mind, I'll believe you're on our side. How's Michael?'

'He's well. You'd never recognize him, either.' He managed a smile, trying to improve the atmosphere between them. *I'm still his real enemy, not Hassan and the others.* 'He's doing all right, Lucas.'

'Does Nina know – ?'

'No. Nobody knows I'm the go-between. Magnus brought the money to a friend of mine, but my friend didn't tell him who I was. I'm not sure that I want them to know. It's been a long time, Lucas. Maybe it's best that it all remain forgotten.'

'I've never forgotten what you did. Nor has Nina.'

'Did you ever tell her what *you* did? Paid me off?' It was a cruel question, but he couldn't help it.

Lucas shook his head, looked away across the ravine. The sun rimmed the top of the castle walls for a moment, then was gone; the castle started to fade into the rising tide of dusk. 'What's that over there?'

'Beaufort Castle. You should look up its history when you get back home.'

Lucas looked at him as if he had made some sort of sick joke. 'You still go in for your goddam whimsy.'

'The last thing I'm feeling right now, Lucas, is whimsical. Forget the past for a moment, will you? Let's concentrate on the present. I've got to get you out of here.'

Lucas stared at him, then at last nodded. He had become resigned to not leaving the house alive: the thought had saddened him a little but not very much. But he was sad for Roger and for his daughter Prue and his grandchildren: they should not be made to suffer because of him. Because he knew that he was the real pawn in this game. 'Am I going to go home? Has Washington agreed to what they're asking?'

Tim spoke to the open door of the living-room. 'You'd better come out, Hassan. You and your colleagues.'

Hassan came out on to the terrace with three other men, all young like himself. None of them carried guns; there were enough guns on the rooftops all around to protect them. Hassan had changed out of his baggy trousers and torn shirt and like the other three men was dressed in a business suit. These were the negotiators, the ones who did not kill personally but just issued the orders. And Tim had no doubt that Hassan would issue such orders if he did not get his way. These men, members of the small Abu Sadar Revolutionary Front, had ambitions that precluded any mercy towards anyone who would get in their way. He was certain now that, if they had to, they would kill him as well as Lucas and Roger Devon.

He said bluntly, 'Washington refuses to negotiate with you, Hassan.'

The bluntness seemed to put Hassan and the others off-balance. They were used to circumlocution: Arabs didn't argue or bargain bluntly. 'Mr Burgess, let's talk – '

'I'm sorry, Hassan. All I'm allowed to offer you is the five million dollars you asked for.' He did not say that he could go higher: that could come later, if it was necessary. 'But there will be no deal on a withdrawal from Abu Sadar. The Sheikh is backing Washington and so are the Saudis.'

'What about the other oil states?' Hassan's expression had not changed, but the other three young men looked angry.

'Iraq is backing you, and Libya. You could expect their support. The Gulf States are sitting on the fence.'

One of the young men, plump and with a neatly trimmed beard on the upper of his two chins, said angrily, 'They know we'll take the money and still kill our two hostages if they don't agree to our terms?'

Tim glanced at Lucas. The old man was still sitting on the chair, one arm draped over the back of it. He was watching the exchange carefully, but his face gave nothing away. He looked at Tim, then nodded and stood up.

'I'm sure Washington understands that,' he said.

'Do *you* understand it, Mr Beaufort?' said Hassan. 'It does not worry you?'

'I'm not worried for myself. But you don't need to kill my son-in-law.' Then he seemed to realize he had a son-in-law standing beside him, one he had disowned – bought off – years ago, one whose death he would never have regretted. 'Roger, I mean. Mr Devon. He should be spared. I'm Beaufort Oil, not him.'

Tim watched the four young men, saw the – obduracy? – in their faces. 'Hassan, what are you going to gain by killing them? Or me – will you kill me, too?' Hassan said nothing, but the answer was there in the faces of the other three. 'There's no way in the world that Washington will ever agree to what you're asking. Take the money – I'll arrange for more, if you want it – and let me take Mr Beaufort and Mr Devon back with me. Kill them and perhaps you'll have the Sheikh's men come looking for you.'

'They are looking for us now.' The plump bearded man had a sort of furious bravado about him. Tim recognized him for what he was, a coward who would do anything to prove he was not. They were a dangerous sort: until you got them alone. But the plump one would always see that he was never alone. 'They mean nothing to us!'

'You might have others.' Tim ignored him, spoke directly to Hassan. 'This is PLO territory, isn't it? They mightn't want outsiders coming in here looking for you.'

'How would they know where to find us, unless you told them where you were coming?'

'I didn't know where you were till I got to Merjayun. But they'd find you.' He hoped he was not putting the old Greek merchant at risk. 'Take the money, Hassan, and let them go. Your other demand is hopeless.'

Lucas, in the middle of the most critical bargaining of his life, the bargaining *for* his life, stayed silent. He realized that Tim's argument carried more weight than his own; Tim knew these Arabs better than he himself did. Lucas for the first time in his life regretted his xenophobia: he had shut himself in, knew too little of what made foreigners tick. Maybe he, or any other American, would never fully understand the Arab thinking; but he could have tried. Tim seemed to have tried and partly succeeded: at least they were listening to him. Lucas became sourly aware of the irony that surrounded him like the dusk: the castle with his name, the son-in-law whom he had banished pleading for his life . . . Twenty-five years were suddenly like a stone in his chest.

Hassan hesitated, then spoke to the other three Arabs. 'We can't make the decision ourselves. There has to be a council meeting – '

'No!' The bearded man clenched his fists, as if he were about to strike someone to get his argument over. 'They left it to us – we did the kidnapping, we were the ones who took the risks – '

'Be quiet, Zaid.' One of the other young men, thin-faced and with a glaucoma-blinded eye, spoke for the first time. They were speaking in Arabic now; but Tim understood what they were saying. He had spoken English up till now and he could not remember if Hassan knew that he spoke Arabic. 'It's too big a decision for us to make. I agree we must go down to meet the council.'

Hassan saw Tim listening to them. All at once he swung round, said to the others, 'Let's go inside. Don't let's argue in front of them.'

The four Arabs went back into the house and Tim and Lucas were left alone again on the terrace. It was almost dark now, they were just a shadowy figure to each other: as they had been for so many years.

'How is Nina?' Tim hadn't expected the question to be so difficult to ask.

'I think she has got over you,' said Lucas. 'But not over the loss of Michael.'

'She never married again. She should have. I thought you'd have persuaded her.'

'I did my best. I think I've at last succeeded. She's going to marry Magnus McKea.'

Tim was surprised at the jealousy that stabbed him. 'He's a good man. Or he was.'

'He still is.' They were silent for a while, then Lucas said, 'Are you ever going to let Michael come back to us?'

'I've thought about it, Christ knows. But I could never come back myself . . . There's a letter in a safe deposit box telling him who he is.'

'Where's the box?'

'Ah, Lucas – ' Tim smiled in the darkness. 'He'll be told where it is when the time comes.'

'Why didn't you send him back to us? I mean when he turned twenty-one. So that he could make up his own mind about whether he wanted what we could give him.'

'I think I was afraid of what your money might mean, in terms of risk. One of your American entertainers, Sophie Tucker–'

'I saw her years ago at the Reno Club back home. Are you going to quote her bit about, "I've been rich and I've been poor and, believe me, being rich is better"?'

'That was it. Yes.'

'She was right, you know. And I'm trying not to sound smug as I say that.'

'I'm not so sure,' Tim said slowly. 'Perhaps being, well, *comfortable* is better. Being poor is hell. I've never been really poor myself, but over the years I've seen more poverty than you've even read about, Lucas. Germany after the war, Africa, here in the Middle East – '

'I don't know what real poverty is, it would be sheer hypocrisy for me to say that I did. I've always had a social conscience about it and I've tried to do something about it through the Foundation. But I'll admit it, I've never had the – courage, I suppose you'd call it – to go out and take a long hard look at what poverty really is.'

'Well, at least you're honest. But that's not what I really started to say. I was worried, for Michael's sake, about the *dangers* of money. Your sort of money. People like you Beauforts are marked targets. Nina was kidnapped because of your money. I didn't think much about that aspect of it at the time – the only thing the kidnapping made me think was how much I loved her.' He was silent for a while in the darkness: old love was there like something tangible. Lucas, sensitive again to his son-in-law, was also silent: he had once loved Edith the same way. Then Tim went on: 'Now you've been kidnapped because of your money – '

'Not just because of the money.'

'No, but your oil interests represent money. There's five million dollars inside there in the house. What if I lived long enough for another day to come when I'd have to carry another five, ten million dollars to buy back Michael? I don't think I could face it. Lucas, I'm the opposite of you – I don't have the moral courage to face up to real riches.'

There was a scraping sound as Lucas moved his chair back to stretch his legs. He looked out towards the castle, now just a dark cliff against the stars. When he reached home, *if* he reached home, he would read the history of the castle; there might be a lesson or two to be learned there. He realized now, at the end of his life, there was so much he had not learned.

'I still wish you had sent Michael back to us, to make up his own mind.'

'That was another thing – I wanted him to grow up to be his own man. Not your man, Lucas. Nor mine, either. He's made his own way.' They were silent once again, then Tim said, 'We made a mistake, Lucas. Both of us.'

384

Lucas nodded invisibly in the darkness; then realized that his silence might have been mistaken for disagreement. 'You shouldn't have done it to Nina. That's what I found unforgivable.'

'Do you think I've forgiven myself?'

It was another quarter of an hour before Hassan and the other three Arabs came out of the house, bringing the tension of their whispered conflict with them.

'We're taking you down to meet our full council, Mr Burgess. All three of you. You can put your argument to us all.'

'A board of directors?' said Lucas.

Hassan chuckled. 'If you like, Mr Beaufort. But more democratic than the board of Beaufort Oil, I'm sure. We'll get Mr Devon and leave at once.'

Tim and Lucas were led through the house and out to where the Simca still stood by the front door. Then Roger Devon was brought out. He and Tim looked at each other, strangers related by marriage to the tall old man standing between them. But in the darkness all they saw was each other's shape: they remained faceless strangers to each other.

'Roger, this is – '

'Nigel Burgess,' said Tim quickly. 'I used to work for Mr Beaufort down in Abu Sadar years ago.'

Lucas hesitated, said nothing. He had no idea why Tim still wanted to hide his true identity; but he knew that, if they got back safely from this situation, he himself would not lie to Nina. He would have to take the risk of telling her the truth, all of it. He could not continue to carry the burden of it any longer. For the time being, however, he would let Tim play it his way.

Roger shook hands with Tim. 'What's happening? Are they releasing us?'

'I'm afraid not,' said Lucas. 'Not yet. We have to go before their board of directors.'

'I'm glad you haven't lost your sense of humour,' said Roger. 'That means you haven't lost hope.'

'Don't be too optimistic,' said Hassan. 'You ride in the Simca, Mr Devon. We'll ride in the other car, gentlemen.'

A second car, a battered-looking fin-tailed Chrysler, had pulled out of an alley at the side of the house. The Abu Sadar Revolutionary Front did not ride in style. Tim wondered how much of the five million dollars would be spent on luxury transport; he had seen revolutionaries in Africa who had let sudden wealth go to their heads. Roger was bundled into the Simca. The suitcases full of money were brought out and put into the trunk of

385

the Chrysler. Tim and Lucas were ushered into the back seat, Hassan and Zaid taking their places in the front seat. Hassan took the wheel and Zaid, now carrying a Schmeisser machine-pistol, sat beside him, turned half-round to face the two men in the back. He still looked angry, ready to use the gun at the slightest excuse.

'We'll have to blindfold you,' said Hassan and got out of the car and went back into the house.

Zaid cursed him in Arabic, calling after him, 'You're getting careless! I'm surprised you remembered a little detail like that.'

Hassan turned back in the doorway of the house, just for a moment losing his control. 'You forgot it too, I notice.'

'I was for killing them, remember? That way their eyes would be shut forever.'

Oh Christ, thought Tim, seeing emotion taking over. If Zaid's mood prevailed when they got to the terrorists' headquarters, wherever it was, no amount of reasoned argument was going to save them. He began to think of escape; but selfishly, only of his own. He could not hope to rescue Lucas and Roger Devon. He looked out at the shadowy figures who had now come down from the rooftops: even the darkness did not hide the outline of their guns against the dim white walls of the houses.

Hassan came back with two pillow cases, handed them to Tim and Lucas. 'For your own safety,' he said; then he called out to someone in the Simca to see that Roger was also blindfolded. He got into the Chrysler, looked back at Tim as the latter was about to pull the pillow case over his head. 'You speak Arabic don't you, Mr Burgess? I thought so. Most of our council don't speak English. You'll have to put your argument to them in Arabic. It had better be good.'

'My Arabic is passable,' said Tim.

'Your argument isn't,' said Zaid. 'Put that pillowcase over your head. Come on, Hassan, let's get moving!'

As the Chrysler went back down the narrow track, followed by the Simca, Tim tried to relax, to breathe steadily in the dark stuffiness of the pillow case. They travelled slowly; evidently it was a track Hassan did not know well at night. At last they came out on to a smoother surface that Tim recognized must be the Kefer Tibnit road. They turned left, then after a few minutes turned left again, were once more back on a rough road, though not a track this time, judging by the speed of the car. He gave up trying to work out their route in his mind; he felt quite sure now that they would not be going back over it. The car abruptly slewed to one side, jerking to a halt, and he put out a hand, felt Lucas's hand within his own. He gripped it, said, 'I'm sorry, Lucas,' but wasn't sure what he was sorry for and didn't know if Lucas heard him.

He ducked as he heard the first shots, falling off the seat and down behind the back of the front seat, pulling Lucas with him. Then the bullets swept through the car, smashing the windows and windscreen; glass spattered them like sharp hail. Still crouched down, he heard a grunt above him, heard the Schmeisser go off in a wild burst. He dragged the pillow case from his head, looked up and saw both Hassan and Zaid, their faces blown away, lying with their heads slammed back over the top of the front seat. The Schmeisser, Zaid's dead finger still clutching the trigger, was ripping the last of its magazine through the car roof.

The lights of the Chrysler were still on, still unsmashed; the ambushers, whoever they were, must be deliberately firing to miss them. The Simca's lights had gone, but they were suddenly replaced by a brighter illumination; there was an explosion and a sudden red blaze as the Simca burst into flames. Tim flung open the door of the Chrysler, afraid that it, too, would go up in flames; he tumbled out into the dirt, yelling to Lucas to follow him. Lucas, pulling the pillow case from his head, did so. But age, the stiffening of his limbs, hampered him. Instead of falling out to lie low on the ground, he stepped out.

He stood up, almost as if stretching his cramped body. There was another short burst of fire and the bullets hit him in the chest. He fell on top of Tim with something that sounded like a gasp of disbelief. Tim rolled out from under him, grabbed him and pulled him away from the car. He rolled Lucas over on his back and crouched above him. Out of the corner of his eye he saw someone get up from beside the Simca and run away into the rocks beside the road; it looked like Roger Devon but he could not be sure. By the glow of the burning Simca he could see the pain and shock in Lucas's face; the old man coughed and blood came out of his mouth. One hand clutched Tim's arm, but there was no strength in it.

'Tim – ' The words were just bubbles of blood on his lips. 'Go home – please – '

Tim pressed the old man's hand. His mind was a whirl, no line of thought coherent. He was wondering who had ambushed them: was it the PLO? He was still crouched down, still with the instinct to survive: if the ambushers were the PLO, he might be no better off than he had been with Hassan and his group. But no matter who the ambushers were, they were of no further concern to Lucas. The old man was already dead; Tim felt the hand slacken in his own. He looked down at the man he had hated for so long and suddenly wanted to weep. Lucas would never know how much he had longed to go home.

Then he heard the men coming out of the rocks across the road. He straightened up, saw the five men with guns outlined against the glow of the burning Simca. He said in Arabic, 'Don't shoot – please – ' Then the bullets hit him and he fell face down on Lucas.

He heard the further shots coming down from the hillside. In the moment before he died he heard the men with the guns, as they turned and raced away, shout something in Hebrew.

2

Lucas's body in a plain coffin was loaded on to the Boeing 707, then Prue, Nina and Roger went aboard. Magnus was the last to go up the steps, waiting for his final word with Ambassador Bredgar and Ben Criska.

'You understand, Mr McKea,' said Bredgar, 'that nothing must be said about this. I'm sorry, but it is just impossible to release the full story.'

'I know,' said Magnus, not attempting to disguise his bitterness, 'there are broader issues.'

'There's no point in repeating how sorry we are,' said Criska. 'I thought we were doing the right thing. We'd had the Israelis alerted from an hour or two after we learned about the kidnapping. If it had come off, you would have been grateful.'

'I think we should have been consulted first,' said Magnus.

'Certain things have to be kept under wraps, Mr McKea.' Criska sounded annoyingly patient, as if he spent all his time explaining to people actions they would never understand. 'We followed Burgess as far as Merjayun – we're pretty sure he didn't see us. Then when he turned up into PLO country, we had to turn back. There wasn't time to come back here to Beirut. I sent a man across the border into Israel and he phoned our man in Jerusalem. The Israelis know that territory like the back of their hand – they even knew where the Abu Sadar people hung out.

388

They had patrols standing by and we had to use them. We had no one else to turn to if we hoped to get Mr Beaufort and Mr Devon out alive. Those Abu Sadar guys were never going to take no for an answer from Washington.

'You've warned Mr Devon not to say anything? About how we got him back from the Israelis?' Bredgar looked embarrassed; twice in five minutes he had taken off his glasses and polished them. 'Not even to his wife?'

'His wife and her sister both know. I told them.'

Bredgar shook his head at the folly of civilians. 'Mr McKea – '

'I owed it to them,' said Magnus. 'They were entitled to know how their father died. Despite the broader issues.'

He had not told Prue and Nina immediately. It was twenty-four hours after Raclot had left to give the money to the go-between before Roger, cut and bruised, a bullet wound in his shoulder, had been brought back to the embassy by Criska and another official. Magnus had been sent for, first being cautioned that he was not to bring the women with him or say anything to them till he had been briefed by the embassy. Worried at what news he was to be given, upset that he had to leave the equally worried Prue and Nina at the hotel, he had gone to the embassy. He had been ushered at once into the ambassador's office where only Bredgar, Roger and Criska were present.

He had guessed at once that the worst had happened, that Lucas was dead. But he was stunned by the story Criska had told him, of the terrible mistake made by the Israeli patrol that had been waiting in ambush for the terrorists.

'They thought Mr Beaufort and Mr Devon were in the second car, the Simca. They only blew it up after they saw the men jump out. That was how Mr Devon got away – he was hit by an Abu Sadar bullet, not by Israeli fire. It was all just a terrible mistake – '

Then anger flooded Magnus and he wanted to hit Criska. It had been Roger who had restrained him. 'Please, Magnus – it won't help. Not now.'

'Where is Mr Beaufort's body?'

'The Israelis left the two bodies, Mr Beaufort's and the go-between's, where they were. The PLO came down when they heard the firing and the Israelis had to slip back across the border. They managed to take Mr Devon with them. We've had to wait to bring him back via Cyprus.'

'What about Mr Beaufort?' Magnus persisted.

'We've already heard from the PLO. We have our contacts,' Criska explained. Jesus, thought Magnus, how do these people work? Do they draw no lines? 'They've taken the bodies down to Merjayun. A Greek merchant there has them. We can collect them whenever we wish.'

'Let's go back to the hotel,' Magnus said to Roger. 'I'll call you in half an hour, Mr Criska. I'll want someone to come with me down to Merjayun. I'd rather it wasn't you.'

It was Bredgar who flushed angrily, not Criska. But Magnus was already on his way out of the office with Roger.

Back at the hotel Prue and Nina, prepared for the worst, took the news of their father's death stoically. Later they would both break down, but for the moment they kept control of themselves and took relief and compensation in the safe return of Roger. Newspaper and television correspondents were clamouring for a press conference, but the hotel had kept them all down in the lobby. A doctor was called for Roger, the bullet was removed with a local anaesthetic and he was put to bed in the suite; he refused to go to hospital and Prue, wanting something to do, some distraction to keep her from thinking just yet about her father's death, said she would take care of him with the aid of a nurse sent in by the doctor. Nina, also wanting to keep herself occupied, said she would handle the calls from Kansas City. In the meantime both sisters wanted their father's body brought back to Beirut as soon as possible.

Magnus, slipping out of the hotel by a back door, went down to Merjayun in an embassy car, accompanied by a Second Secretary, a young man named Fisher; the embassy car was accompanied by a hearse. Magnus sat without saying anything and Fisher, a big bluff man with glasses and a nervous tic to his mouth, respected his silence. At least, thought Magnus, giving him a side glance, he's a better diplomat than that bastard Criska. Later, much later, he would come to appreciate that Criska had done what he had thought was best; but for the time being he was filled with a bitterness that was like a sickness.

The Greek merchant opened the door to them before they could knock. He had obviously been waiting for them; and so had the small crowd gathered outside the house. Magnus caught a glimpse of two women and some small children hanging over a stairway landing as the Greek led them to a bedroom at the back of the house. He wondered how the women felt at having the corpses of two strangers kept in one of their bedrooms.

The two bodies lay side by side on a double bed, a sheet draped over them from head to foot. 'Who brought them here?' said Fisher.

The little old man shrugged. 'I never ask for names, sir.'

His English was good, with a slight American accent. Magnus wondered by what roundabout route he had come from Greece to finish up in this small town in the Lebanon hills. But then by what roundabout route had Lucas arrived at the same point? And, unlike the Greek's, his journey was finished. Or almost.

He turned back the edge of the sheet and looked down at the dead Lucas. For a moment it seemed that he was looking at a stranger: smaller, older, paler than the Lucas he had known for so long. He put a hand to his mouth, stifling the sob he could feel welling up in him.

'Do you know this man?' Fisher had turned back the sheet on the man who lay beside Lucas.

The man, unlike Lucas, was indeed a stranger. He was about Magnus's age, with thick grey hair; his lean, tanned face was more than half-hidden by a rough bandage that someone had applied. His one visible eye was closed; the nose and mouth and other eye were covered by the bandage. Magnus stared at him, wondering what debt the Beauforts owed him. His death had not been anticipated, probably least of all by himself; otherwise he would not have volunteered. He had probably volunteered for no other reason than out of friendship for Colonel Raclot, the one who owed the debt, whatever it was, to Prue.

'Did they have any papers?' Fisher's tic had increased, as if he was not experienced in the sighting of dead men. 'Passports, anything like that?'

'No, sir. There was nothing on them at all.'

'It figures. I wonder what happened to the money? The five million bucks?'

The old Greek blinked; but Magnus ignored him. 'The PLO probably has it. We can kiss it goodbye.'

'Ben Criska won't like that.'

That fact pleased Magnus, but he didn't comment on it. Instead he said to the old Greek, 'We should like to pay you for your trouble. Do you mind taking American Express travellers' cheques?'

'Sir, there is no need – ' But the old man had already produced a Parker fountain pen, a gold one.

So the body of Lucas Beaufort, worth conservatively two billion dollars when he was alive, was bought back for two hundred dollars. The body of the stranger was a bonus; or so it seemed. The two corpses were loaded into the hearse and the return trip to Beirut was begun.

'We'll keep Mr Beaufort's body at the embassy till you're ready to leave,' said Fisher. 'What about the other guy?'

'I'll see Colonel Raclot as soon as we get back. Would you call him and have him come to the embassy? I don't want him interviewed by any press men. I'm sure he would not want it, either.'

Magnus waited at the embassy till Raclot arrived. He took the Colonel into the side room where both bodies had already been put into plain coffins. Raclot stood a moment with his head bowed in prayer, then he blessed himself and followed Magnus out into the corridor. People were coming and going in the corridor: senior officials, clerks, people asking where to get visas. The business of government did not stop for two bodies in a side room.

'What was his name?' said Magnus.

Raclot shrugged. 'Nigel Burgess. But it could have been anything. He was a mercenary like myself, years ago in Africa. Most of us didn't use our real names out there.'

'Where did he come from?'

'I think he was English. I saw him only once or twice a year, when he came here on business. He never told me his business and I never asked. We tend to be like that. People like us, I mean.'

'We'll pay to have him buried. Where was he staying?'

'I don't even know that. I always had the feeling he had more to hide than I had. Each time he came into Beirut he would phone me and we'd have a drink or dinner. That was it, nothing more. I suppose that sounds strange to a man like you, M. McKea, always surrounded by friends and business acquaintances.'

'I don't think anything will sound strange to me after the past forty-eight hours, Colonel. Can I leave everything to you? If you should trace any relatives, a wife, children, please let me know. We'll see they are properly compensated.' He saw the look on Raclot's face and he gestured awkwardly. 'I know, Colonel. Money is no real compensation. I don't always think only in terms of dollars. But if he had a wife and children, I'd hate to think he'd left them unprovided for.'

'I understand, M. McKea. I have no wife or children, so one doesn't think in practical terms like that. You are right. I'll do what I can to see if he can be traced.'

Tim Davoren was buried next morning under the name of Nigel Burgess. Colonel Raclot began at once trying to find some clue that would lead him to the true identity of his dead friend. Because Tim had always been well-dressed and looked reasonably affluent, he made the mistake of going only to the better hotels. He drew a blank there, so he got in touch with a Christian Arab in the police force. The police officer got back to him in a week:

there was no registration of any foreigner named Burgess. Raclot gave up. If Burgess had gone to such lengths to hide his identity when he was alive, what right did Raclot have to try and disclose it now he was dead? Magnus had asked the wrong man to do the job.

The owner of the small *pension* on the Rue Zarif waited for the Australian M. James Harvest to come back to claim his two suitcases; after two weeks he opened the suitcases, took out what he fancied and then told his con to take the cases out and dump them near the Kurd refugees' camp on the Juniye road. The Kurds would soon make use of them and they would never be traced. He did not go to the police to inform them that one of his guests was missing. In Beirut you never went looking for trouble. If trouble was going to happen, it would come to you sooner or later.

The police, after a month, did go looking for James Harvest. But they went to the gem dealer on the Rue Kantari, whose address Tim had given when he had been asked on arrival where he could be located while in the Lebanon. The gem dealer said he had not seen M. Harvest at all on this trip. He was a reputable man, with a thriving business among influential Arabs, and the police had no reason to doubt his word. They asked if M. Harvest had a foreign address and the gem dealer, for the first time looking uneasy, said no. M. Harvest, who had seemed a very honest man and had always traded honestly, came and went without ever giving an address, either here in Beirut or overseas, where he could be located. All their transactions had been in cash; but that was not unusual in Beirut, was it, gentlemen? M. Harvest had sounded as if he were English, but he would probably have had to come from Australia to bring the magnificent opals that he offered for sale. Possibly, said the police, but the immigration records showed that he travelled on a British passport. They thanked the gem dealer and went away and started a file on the missing James Harvest; but a year later, when the Arab-Christian civil war broke out, no further entry had been added to the file and James Harvest had been forgotten. He was not the first and he would not be the last foreigner to disappear in the back streets of Beirut.

Prue, Nina, Roger and Magnus left Beirut for home the day after the stranger was buried. Lucas's coffin had been placed at the rear of the main cabin, screened from those sitting in the forward end by a curtain. The plane climbed into the morning sun, banked and headed west out across the sea.

'All I wish,' said Nina, 'is that he had died at home. I don't think it ever crossed his mind that he wouldn't die in Kansas City.'

Magnus looked back at the snow-topped mountains, at the city climbing the slopes, at the cypress-lined cemetery where the stranger would lie in a grave that would probably never be tended.

'At least he'll be buried at home,' he said. 'Beside your mother. That would please him.'

## Chapter Fourteen

◆

# The Sisters

### I

So we are back in the spring of the present. Time has moved in its own time. The emotions stretch it and condense it; memory has no hours. History, as Prue once remarked to herself, repeats itself, if only in cracked mirrors. Questions are still asked, answers still have to be given. Perhaps history is no more than that: but with one final question to which history has no answer. In the meantime . . .

'Where's Miss Nina?' Margaret said.

'In the drawing-room,' said George Biff. 'With Mr – Mr Harvest.'

Margaret paused in front of the hall-mirror to look at herself: not at her hair or her make-up but at her attempt at composure. She was satisfied, but only just. 'Do you know who he's claiming to be?'

'Yes.'

'How is my sister taking it?'

'Not so good. You don't look no better, Miz Meg.'

'Thank you, George. You've always been a comfort.'

She paused with her hand on the closed door to the drawing-room. She had found it difficult to believe Nina when the latter had phoned her ten minutes ago, as she had come into her house on her return from the tennis matches. Nina had sounded almost incoherent: excited, joyful, yet afraid. And Margaret, too, was afraid. The long-ago past threatened to open up like a pit.

She knocked, went into the drawing-room and closed the doors behind her. Nina was seated in a chair by the fireplace. Opposite her sat the Australian tennis player: Something-or-other (Cliff?) Harvest. He stood up and she saw that he was taller than he had appeared on the court earlier this afternoon. He also seemed less graceful, awkward even. Or certainly uncomfortable.

'This is my sister, Mrs Alburn,' said Nina. 'Or your Aunt Margaret.'

'Not yet, not quite,' said Margaret; but smiled. 'Are you really Michael? Is he?' She looked at Nina, not waiting for him to answer.

'I don't know – ' Nina gestured helplessly. 'Thank you for coming over, Meg. I'm in shock, I guess – my legs feel like glass – '

'It's natural – after all these years.' Margaret sat down, feeling her own legs weakening. 'If you are Michael, Mr Harvest, where is your father?'

'Dead. Or anyway presumed dead.' He hesitated, then sat down on the couch opposite the sisters, crossed his long legs awkwardly. 'He disappeared three years ago in the Middle East.'

Margaret examined him frankly, while she struggled to make her memory, which she had tried to smother for so long, come alive. She looked for Tim in him and, with a pang, saw the resemblance. Not a great one, but it was there: the smile, not quite so ready as Tim's but faintly familiar, the good-humouredly mocking eyes. His face also had some of the Beaufort bone in it; and his hair was the colour that Nina's had once been. But physical resemblance meant nothing. Newspapers, when short of news, were always running pictures of look-alikes of the famous. This man Harvest would not be here if he had not thought he could offer at least some resemblance to Tim and Nina. But she did not examine too closely just then why she wanted him to be an impostor.

Harvest looked at Nina. 'Do you think I'm your son?'

'I don't know. This afternoon – '

'I know. I saw you looking at me – that was what gave me the confidence to come here.'

'I could see something of your – of my late husband in you. But not your antics – ' Margaret remarked Nina's reserve: she was trying hard not to give too much of herself away too soon. 'He was always a gentleman.'

Not always, thought Margaret.

'You *sound* like a mother.' Harvest grinned, a little more relaxed. 'I think you could blame my antics on Dad. In a way.

I was a pretty spoiled kid, till I rebelled against him and we had our arguments.'

Nina sat in silence, studying him, her feelings showing in her face. She wants to accept him, Margaret thought. And determined that acceptance must be put off till she had made her own decision.

Then something Harvest had said a moment ago suddenly registered, like a shot from far away. 'You say Tim is *dead*?'

'Tim? Oh, Dad. He called himself James, James Harvest. I didn't know our name was Davoren till I opened his letter. I have it here.'

Margaret sat as silent as Nina. If Tim was dead, then at last she was free: for she had loved him as much as Nina had. She watched as Harvest handed Nina a letter. Nina read it carefully, then looked blankly at Margaret as the latter held out her hand for it.

'Let me read it.'

'But it's not for you – '

'It was not for you, either. It was for Mr Harvest. Let me see it.'

Nina surrendered the letter. It was typewritten and it had all the correct facts: according to it, Clive Harvest was really Michael Davoren. But Tim had made one legal mistake. She re-folded the letter and handed it back to Harvest.

'You don't look impressed.' He sat up, leaning forward.

'Your father would have made it easier for you if he had signed his name instead of just *Dad*. That signature means nothing.'

'The letter's addressed to me, not to some lawyer. You're not making it easy for me, are you?'

'Don't be sharp with me!'

'Meg – please – ' But Nina did not protest too strongly.

'Jesus Christ,' Harvest said slowly and sank back into the couch. 'All right, I apologize. If I'd known it was going to be like this – '

Margaret glanced at Nina, who was still studying the man opposite her. She wondered what image Nina had built up in her mind of what her son, if he ever returned, would look like. Margaret herself had hardly given a thought to the missing Michael; all her memories, which she thought she had stifled for good and forever, had been of Tim. Perhaps Nina had thought her son would look like this man, but she must be thrown off-balance to find that he was now an Australian. The flat accent, the drawling of one syllable into two ('know-en'); none of it

397

suggested the almost mellifluous voice that had been Tim's. If anything it was closer to the flat Midwest twang, which all the Beaufort sisters had been taught to avoid.

'If your father died three years ago, why did you wait so long?'

'It was a year before I went back home. I've spent most of my time playing tennis in Europe and here in the States. There was nothing to go back to, there'd only been Dad and me. He'd moved twice since I'd left home – so there was no home to go back to. Nothing I could call home. I left everything to the lawyers – they tidied up the estate. They knew nothing about the safe deposit box – that was in a bank in Zurich. I only found out about that by accident. I went back to Sydney eventually and they gave me all Dad's personal belongings. Including a box of papers, business papers. There was an address of a bank in Switzerland, just a scribbled note tucked away in a book about tennis. It was marking the page where there was a photo of me.'

'So you decided to play detective?' Margaret said.

'No, not right then.' He bit his lip, stared at her; then recovered and went on, 'It was only late last year I did anything about it. I was in Zurich for a tournament and I went and looked up the bank. The letter was there in the safe deposit box. There was something else. A quarter of a million dollars' worth of bonds that Dad had bought back in 1949. The bank manager told me Dad came there every year and drew the interest in cash.'

'A quarter of a million?' Nina looked at Margaret. 'Tim never had that much money in his life.'

'Your story sounds less and less believable, Mr Harvest,' said Margaret; then softened her tone as she saw the look on Nina's face. 'But that isn't to say we don't believe you.'

'No?' Again the smile was faintly familiar, a mocking grin in a dusty mirror. 'I only half-believe it myself. Dad was something of a liar – well, maybe not a liar. But he never told the entire truth. Not to me or anyone else, as far as I could gather.'

'Tell us what happened. Everything.'

'My whole life story? I can't do that.'

'Just the outline. Where you have been the past twenty-eight years.'

He clasped his big hands together, held them between his knees. He's ill at ease, Margaret thought: now he has to produce the truth himself. Or what he hopes will sound like the truth.

'You read in that letter what happened when we left here – when was it?'

It was a date Margaret had forgotten, but Nina remembered it: 'August 20, 1949.'

Harvest nodded, as if impressed by Nina's memory. 'I suppose that was it. Dad doesn't mention the date, but you can see when he wrote the letter – twenty-eighth September nineteen forty-nine. We must have gone back to England through Canada – '

'We traced you that far.' Nina's voice was steadier now, she seemed to have regained her composure. Margaret decided to leave the questioning to her. 'Your grand – my father had private investigators working on it for a year. We never found out how my husband managed to get a child across an international border without a passport. You were entered on my passport.'

'I guess there are ways and means. Obviously it worried him. The letter says he had to get forged passports when he got back to England and changed our names. He even had a forged birth certificate for me – I saw it years later. I suppose you can get anything if you have the money.' He looked around the room, but it was evident he was seeing far beyond these walls, right to the very limits of the Beaufort empire. 'We never seemed to be short. Or not by ordinary standards. But then everything's relative, isn't it?'

'That's not very profound, Mr Harvest,' said Margaret.

He gave her a hard stare, recognizing an opponent. Then he looked directly again at Nina. 'Well, after England we went out to Kenya. I grew up there, or I did till I was, I don't know, fourteen, I guess. Dad had a partnership with another bloke in a mining survey firm. He would sometimes be gone for weeks on end. Sometimes I used to think he was into something else, but I was never sure. He could be pretty secretive at times.'

'Why did you leave Africa?'

'Dad never really explained it to me. He just suddenly decided to go – it was after he came from one of his trips, I remember that – and we went.' He searched for something in the sisters' faces, a hint that they were beginning to believe him; but there was nothing. He went on, a listlessness creeping into his voice: 'Sydney wasn't bad. We lived pretty comfortably and he sent me to a good school. That was where I found out I could play tennis. Dad was good and he encouraged me. At first.'

'At first?'

'When he found out I wanted to make a career of it, that's when our arguments started. He wanted me to go into the business with him, but I knew I couldn't face that. I don't think he liked it himself, sitting there in an office all day trying to act like

399

a businessman. I know how much he used to look forward to his trips to the Middle East.'

'Why was he so much against your making a career of tennis?'

'He said I'd never be good enough to get to the top. He was right – ' Again there was the self-mocking smile that nagged like a nerve-end at the sisters' memories. 'I'm number ninety-nine in the world pro listings right now. Next year I could be number one hundred and ninety-nine.

'How degrading, to be ranked like that. Don't you feel jealous of the men above you?'

'Up to a point. That's what keeps me going, trying to beat them any way I can. The clowning helps put some of them off. Some of them. Most of them are getting used to me now.'

'Why do you try so hard?'

'I'll have to retire in a couple of years, I guess. Top-liners like Rosewall can go on till they're old men, but promoters don't give contracts to middle-aged second-raters. I've been on the world circuit for twelve years now. I've got used to the good life.'

Nina stiffened, as if listening: to an echo perhaps? Then she said, 'But if your father left you a quarter of a million dollars, you should be able to afford a reasonably good life.'

'Yes,' he said carefully, looking directly at her, blinkering himself against the richly good life that surrounded them.

Margaret said, 'You said your father was presumed dead. Was his body never recovered?'

'No, he just disappeared. It was three months before I knew of it – we'd often go that long without writing each other. Then one of his friends in Sydney wrote me asking if I knew where Dad was. He had this business, taking rugs and textiles into Australia and taking opals to the Middle East, but as I said, he could have been into something else. I don't mean drug-smuggling. He was pretty cranky about any sort of drugs. Maybe I was trying to glamorize him, but sometimes I wondered if he was in intelligence work.'

'You found no trace of him?'

'None.' All at once he looked sad, as if he had lost something he hadn't known he had valued so much till it was too late. 'I went to Beirut, but I couldn't stay there – I had tournament commitments. And the police weren't very helpful. They had a file on him, half a page, but that was all. I just kept hoping he'd turn up.'

'Beirut?' said Nina. 'When was this?'

'You mean when he disappeared? The end of 1974. Why?'

'Nothing,' said Nina and looked at Margaret.

'There will have to be proper enquiries.' Margaret decided it was time she took over again. 'Our attorneys will need to talk to you, Mr Harvest. How long will you be in Kansas City?'

He stood up, leaving before he was dismissed. 'That depends on how we go in the tournament. If we're put out tomorrow night, there's no point in hanging around. We're due to play in Houston next week.'

'Our attorneys will need more than an hour or two with you.'

'Then we'd better win tomorrow night.'

Nina stood up. 'I'll come to see you play. Good luck.'

'Will you be there, Mrs Alburn?' There seemed to be a challenge in his voice.

'We have boxes for every night. If you have time, perhaps you can meet one of our attorneys informally. Mr McKea. My sister's husband,' she added, watching him carefully.

'I know,' he said. 'It's just that the Beaufort name sticks in my mind. Thanks for seeing me.'

The two sisters went with him out of the drawing-room, Margaret riding hard on Nina to see that she did not suddenly break down and claim him as her son. George Biff was standing in the hall.

Nina said, 'Mr Harvest, this is George Biff. Do you remember him?'

Harvest was either a good actor or his puzzled effort at memory was genuine. 'I don't know. I don't remember this house at all.'

'We didn't live in this house,' said Nina.

That seemed to put Harvest off-balance. Then he recovered and put out his hand. 'Hello, George.'

The old black man was stiff and formal, not the George who had played with a laughing child on the lawns years ago.

'You don't recognize him, George?' Margaret said.

'No, Miz Meg. I know who he supposed to be, but I don't recognize him.'

Nina looked disappointed, but said nothing. Harvest said an awkward goodbye and went out to his car. Only then did Nina say, 'I think I was waiting for you to okay him, George.'

'Don't you recognize him, Miz Nina?' Nina said nothing and after a glance at Margaret, George went on, 'I watched him playing tennis this afternoon. I was standing down behind your box. Unless I remember wrong, he play right-handed. Michael was left-handed.'

Nina abruptly spun round and went back into the drawing-room. Margaret lowered her voice. 'I think you did recognize him, George.'

'No, Miz Meg. We don't wanna drag all that up again after all them years, do we? She nearly forgotten about him.'

Margaret shook her head. 'I don't think so. She's never forgotten him.'

'Still think it ain't gonna do her no good. Or any of us. I think you thinking like me. Ain't that so?'

But she, too, did not answer, afraid of giving herself away. She went back into the drawing-room, closing the doors. Nina stood at a window gazing out at the house that had once been hers. It was Margaret's now, but it was the one from which Tim and Michael had disappeared all those years ago.

'Do you think we should have taken him over to your place? Just in case he remembered something of it.'

'He wouldn't remember anything – there's nothing in it now that was there when you lived in it. He never once glanced up at that picture.' She nodded at the painting above the fireplace. 'That's all you have left of what you had in those days.'

Nina did not appear to be listening, as if thoughts were tumbling through her mind too fast for her to dwell on them. 'Did you hear what he said about Beirut? Tim could have been there when Daddy was kidnapped. I wonder – no, it's too bizarre.'

'You wonder what?'

'If the man who took the money to try and ransom Daddy and Roger was – no, it couldn't have been.'

It could have been, Margaret thought. But her mind was already hardening towards a decision. *It ain't gonna do her no good. Or any of us.* 'That could be part of his story. It was in all the newspapers that Daddy was kidnapped and killed in Beirut. Mr Harvest is shrewd. He hasn't spent all this time making up his mind whether to come to us, without also making up a good story.'

2

'You played very well tonight,' said Magnus. 'Considering.'

'Considering I had something on my mind? The questions you asked me this afternoon – '

'I'm sorry about that. It would have been better if we could have left it till after the tournament – or till you were knocked out. But now you're in the quarter-finals. Have you always been

402

a right-handed player?'

'Is that a trick question, Mr McKea? You're not doing a Perry Mason on me, are you?'

'If ever we get to court, which I hope we shan't, they'll throw questions like that at you. Were you always right-handed?'

'No, I wasn't. I was left-handed till I was thirteen. I broke my left elbow and it was left a bit weak. I learned to do everything right-hand then. How will that stand up in court?'

'Plausible, Mr Harvest. You seem to have most of the answers.'

They were at the party being given by Beaufort Oil, part-sponsors of the tennis tournament, at the Mission Hills country club. The Beauforts belonged to both the Kansas City country club and Mission Hills. Both clubs had limited membership and a long waiting list, but no club ever refused a Beaufort who wanted to become a member; to have refused would have been like a temple barring its senior vestal virgins, though one would have had to allow for a certain degree of defloration.

Talk bounced lightly, like amateurs' balls; a lob here, a gentle volley there, always waiting to be put away by the professionals' cynical experience. Girls left themselves open to love games; mothers fluttered around like nervous line umpires. Fathers, brothers and boy-friends nodded knowingly at the professionals' talk, held their glasses in the John Newcombe grip and were careful of their drinker's elbow, which they had just discovered was similar to tennis elbow. The pros succeeded in hiding their boredom, because this was the affluent life to which they all aspired, for which they were wearing themselves out night after night and day after day on tennis courts across the world. Footballers and ice hockey players and baseballers were never asked to mingle with the rich country club set; that was just for tennis players and golfers and the better class of card sharp. The pros smiled covertly at each other, God's Chosen Jocks.

'I could tell you all to get stuffed, Mr McKea,' Harvest said, looking pleasant and affable to anyone passing by. 'I don't really know if I want to be as rich as all of you. From what I've read, it has its handicaps. There have been two kidnappings in the Beaufort family. That was only because they were rich. Nobody's going to kidnap a retired tennis player who doesn't throw his money around. I could live pretty comfortably if I turned round and walked out of Kansas City. Maybe I'd be more comfortable. I'm not here for the money, Mr McKea. I'm here because I'd like to know who my mother was. Or is. It's a human instinct.'

He turned and walked away and Magnus looked down into his empty glass, feeling properly ashamed. The past two days had

403

not been easy for him. Nina had confessed to him that she *wanted* Clive Harvest to be her son Michael: if only to lay a ghost. But then, almost immediately, she had admitted that the ghost that would be laid would be Tim's. Or would it? he had asked gently: gently, because he had been trying to hide his selfishness. With Michael (if he was Michael) constantly there as a reminder, would Tim ever be laid to rest? The debate had gone on between them, never acrimonious, each of them trying to protect the life they shared; but always round and round, neither of them coming up with a resolution. Even his lawyer's mind had not been able to settle on a judgement. Harvest's story rang true – up to a point: it was like a carillon in which one bell, struck only occasionally, jarred on the ear. He was worried about the Beirut chapter, though he had not confessed that to Nina. Should he have lifted the bandage from the face of the dead Burgess, made a more determined effort to find out who the man really was? If Burgess had indeed been Tim Davoren, would he have gone back to Beirut and told Nina so? In his heart he could not be sure that he would have done so. He wondered if Lucas, who must have known if it was Tim or not, would have told her.

He crossed the room, looking for a refill of his glass. Bruce, Charlie and Roger were standing in a corner, moored to a floating waiter. Magnus took a fresh drink and joined them; the waiter, set loose, drifted away. The Beaufort men, as some women called them though never to their faces, looked at each other, not at all interested in the party.

'We saw you talking to him,' said Charlie. 'He certainly doesn't look worried.'

'What's he got to lose?' said Roger. 'I know the women wish it were over and done with, one way or the other. I'm not speaking for Nina, of course,' he said to Magnus.

'I think they'd better stop talking about wanting this over as soon as possible,' said Bruce. 'There's more to this than just whether Nina gets her son back or not.'

'For instance?' said Charlie. He was still the same cheerful Charlie Luman, but sometimes now the smile seemed a little vacant, worn like a false moustache. He had begun to put on weight and Pan American's doctors had warned him at his last physical examination that he might not pass the next one if he did not take care of himself. He had not taken their advice, had begun to think of retirement.

'For instance, how much control would pass to him in the Trust if he should be Michael Davoren? What would happen if he wanted to draw out his share? No fortune, not even the

Beaufort one, is safe if somebody starts to pull a leg out from under it. He'll get more than any of your or my kids will.'

'Not mine,' said Charlie, and smiled behind his upturned glass.

'Sorry, Charlie. I meant me and Roger.'

Charlie's secret was still his and Sally's. Some Pan Am pilots sometimes wondered why he never took advantage of the opportunities that came his way on overseas tours of duty, but always in the end they put it down to the fact that, being married to a Beaufort woman, he knew how his bread was buttered and did not want to exchange it for a little margarine on the side. He looked across the room now and waved to Sally and she raised her silver-topped stick in reply.

'Margaret and I have talked it over,' Bruce said. With Lucas's death he had become president of the Beaufort banks, domestic and foreign. He was no longer the small-city banker he had been when he had met Margaret; he had his own aura of money now. The fact that he talked more easily of money than of anything else kept a glow on the aura. 'I don't think we should say yes or no to him till every last detail has been examined.'

'Prue won't talk with me at all about it. She says it's Nina's decision and hers only.' Roger was one of the two men, the other being Magnus, who had been absolutely sure of himself, and had remained so, when he had married into the Beaufort family. He still signed himself Roger Devon IV, not with a flourish but with the conviction that he was no one else. His father, Roger III, was still alive; portraits of Roger I and II hung in the Devon house on the Beaufort estate. A month ago Prue had discovered she was pregnant again and if the child should be a boy, it had already been decided that he should be called Roger V. Lucas, if he were still alive, would have been pleased: he at least was part of a dynasty, if only having come in through a side door. 'How do you feel, Magnus? Not as a lawyer but as a husband.'

Magnus sighed, committed himself. 'If Nina accepts him, I'll accept him.'

# 3

The four sisters sat round the table in the luncheon room of the main house. They called it Nina's house, but none of them, not even Nina, really thought of it as hers. They had all been born in it and till it fell down or was demolished they would always have a proprietary interest in it, a substitute for the common womb that had borne them all.

'He's through to the final,' said Nina. 'He told me last night he's never played better in his life.'

'He's cut out those dreadful antics of his,' said Margaret. 'If he stays with us, I shouldn't want him to be remembered for those.'

'There are some people who still remember Grandfather's antics,' said Sally. 'We've learned to live with them.'

'They were financial shenanigans.'

'Which are excusable,' said Prue. 'So long as there are no bad manners displayed.'

Four days had passed and in the Beaufort circle, sisters, husbands, lawyers, there had been no other topic but Clive Harvest. There had been argument, rhetoric, pleas, prevarication and plain gossip. He was well-named: the mere mention of him had harvested an abundant crop of talk.

'I wanted him to come and stay here,' said Nina. 'But Magnus vetoed that.'

'Quite right, too,' said Margaret. 'Nina, for God's sake, don't make yourself so vulnerable.'

'I'm beginning to feel that he *is* Michael. Here in my belly.'

'Bellies, darling, aren't recognized in a court of law.' Prue savoured the *quenelles de brochet*, nodded approvingly. The sisters still treated themselves well at meals. They all had full figures, but their masseur, a man whose hands were familiar with half the women in the country club set, always took care of that extra pound or two. 'But I know what you mean. Love, even mother love, starts in the anatomy.'

So far she had managed to dodge a face-to-face meeting with Clive Harvest, though she knew it could not be put off indefinitely. Old lovers had never worried her in the past: it was as if once they put their clothes on, she gave them another identity. She had almost forgotten Clive Harvest and the night in London (six? seven?) years ago; as she had put out of her mind all the other men she had slept with, including Guy. She was totally in love with Roger, physically, emotionally and romantically; sharp-eyed as she had always been, despite her increasing myopia, she had decided that hers was the most complete and secure happiness of all the sisters. Now she was afraid: no woman could feel secure who had slept with a man who now claimed to be her nephew. Even if he was honourable (was an honourable man different from a man of honour? she wondered, memory glinting like a far-off glass) and kept quiet, there would always be the fear that one of them might make a slip of the tongue. She had begun to pray (who hadn't prayed since she was a child) that Clive Harvest would not be Michael Davoren.

'Has there been any word from Australia?' Sally asked.

'Bruce talked to them this morning,' said Margaret. 'It was around midnight their time. They've been working really hard, he said. They haven't been able to come up with much on this James Harvest. But he lived well – by Australian standards, I suppose they mean.'

God, thought Prue, she's becoming as provincial as Stephane.

'I think they're fairly civilized down there,' said Nina, tongue in cheek seeking a piece of stray *quenelle*.

'The point is,' said Margaret, 'they haven't yet come up with any conclusive proof that James Harvest was Tim.'

Sally, only toying with her food, did not care whether the lawyers came up with proof or not. She was convinced that James Harvest and Nigel Burgess and Tim Davoren were one and the same man; but she was still struggling with herself as to how to express that conviction. As she had been struggling with herself ever since the death of her father, when she had learned that the go-between who had been killed with her father had been named Burgess. She had argued with herself that no harm could be done by telling Nina that she had met Tim in the Congo back in 1961; but she had known the argument was weak. Nina would never forgive her for having concealed the information for so long. It no longer mattered why *she* had been in the Congo: that was a forgotten war and nobody cared any more who had been on whose side. It would be almost impossible to explain to Nina how she had come to make her bargain with Tim there in the Congo bush: she couldn't expect Nina to understand. It worried her just as much that perhaps Charlie, too, would neither understand nor forgive her.

Prue said, 'What have the Australians come up with about Clive himself?'

'Nothing much. He seems to have been a pretty public personality. On the sports pages,' Margaret added, downgrading him socially.

'Have you told Martha and Emma yet? They might welcome a male cousin. Even one from the sports pages.'

'I called them,' said Margaret and said no more.

Martha, married to a history graduate and living in Paris, and Emma, unmarried and living in a commune in California, had been unexcited, almost uninterested, when Margaret had called them. She, who looked upon herself as the cornerstone of the Beauforts, had brought forth two children who had run away from the Beaufort name. Anyone who wanted to reverse the path, Emma had said on the phone, had only their sympathy. Margaret wondered just how much of their respective fathers sometimes spoke in them.

'What about your two?' Sally said to Prue.

'They're all for him. Melanie's thrown out Robert Redford and pinned Clive's photo up on her wall. Grace has done the same. He's replaced the picture of her pony.' Melanie was now fourteen and Grace, Roger's child, was five, both of them as romantic as their mother had been but not as alert and observant.

George Biff, doubling again as butler, came in with the *boeuf en gelée*. These weekly luncheons of the four sisters, held regularly when they were all home, delighted him. Each of the sisters took it in turn to have the luncheon in her own house, but it was understood that George was always to be the butler. The servants in the other houses might resent it, but it had become a ritual, with him as much part of it as the sisters themselves.

'Looks good, Miz Nina. You want me to slice it?'

'I'll do it, George. Just bring in the red wine.'

'No red for me,' said Margaret. Sally followed her lead, adding, 'It brings on the hot flushes.'

George said, 'How about you, Miz Prue? You hot flushed, too?'

'Only with embarrassment that you should ask such a question. Do you put questions like that to all the women you know?'

'Not any more,' he grinned. 'You stick with the white wine. A little red-eye don't hurt no man, but it don't do the ladies no good.'

'You'd know,' said Nina. 'You old reprobate.'

George, on his way out of the room, smiled back at all of them. He knew how concerned they all were with the problem of this feller Harvest; in the past few days he had seen Miz Nina growing older before his eyes. He thought the tennis feller *might* be Michael, but if it was left to him to decide he'd say no. Let bygones be bygones.

'I looked after all you ladies pretty good.'

'Indeed he has,' said Sally when he had gone. 'Maybe we all should have married him.'

The four sisters silently debated that option with themselves, but each of them decided that she was happy with the husband she now had. Even allowing for the fantasy of Sally's suggestion, marrying George, or anyone like him, would have been a problem right from the start. Lucas had never shown any sign of colour prejudice; but then perhaps he had never really been tested. None of his daughters had ever brought home a black lover. Not even Sally.

Then George came back to the door. 'Mrs Alburn. Mr Alburn is on the phone. He says it's important.'

Margaret excused herself, went out to what had been her father's study and was now Magnus's. Little had been changed in it: Magnus had no desire to exorcize Lucas's ghost. But it was a long time since Margaret had been in the room and she felt an almost overwhelming flood of emotion as she looked around. She picked up the phone.

'Meg?' Bruce occasionally allowed his soft dry voice to get excited; today was one of those occasions. 'We've come up with something that our friend Harvest forgot to mention to us. He was here in Kansas City two months ago, for a couple of days.'

'He could have been on his way to some tournament.' She wondered why she was defending Clive Harvest. She looked around the room again, saw her mother's photo smiling at her from the mantel over the fireplace. Why did Magnus still keep that photo here in the study? Had he ever told Nina that he had once been in love with Edith? Oh God, she thought, the secrets . . .

'Meg? Did you hear what I said? Listen to me. He was here to see a private investigator. He engaged him to draw up a dossier on the Beaufort family.'

'How do you know?'

'The investigator came to Magnus and me this morning. He's double-crossing Harvest, but that doesn't matter. He's shown us the list of questions Harvest wanted covered in the dossier. One of them was to find out how much the family is worth and what was in your father's will. The investigator couldn't answer that last question and that was when he decided to come to us.'

'What's the investigator's name?'

'Pedemont. Dave Pedemont. There's no reason you should ever have heard of him.'

4

It was match point in the final set, Harvest serving for the championship. The auditorium was full tonight; the match and the atmosphere had complemented each other. Up in the press boxes the sports writers were honing their clichés; in the television commentary box the clichés had been worn tissue-thin. For the spectators it was simply the best doubles match they had ever seen.

Harvest threw the ball high, called on an overdraft of strength and served as hard as at any time during the match. 'Fault!' cried a line umpire; but the call was so close that the spectators on that side of the court booed. Harvest took his time, bouncing the ball several times before steadying himself for the second serve. He threw the ball high, higher, it seemed, than on the first serve; again he called on that reserve of strength that seemed to have deserted the other three players. The racquet hit the ball at an exact point in the air where everything met: power, follow-through, direction. There probably had not been a faster serve all night: the ball was just a flash across the eyes. It clipped the backhand corner, kept going away, and the receiver had no chance to return it. He flung a despairing racquet at it, got only the rim to it and the ball went ricocheting off into the crowd. The auditorium rose up, looked like lava ready to spew down into the court. The match was over and the Australians, Harvest and Gissing, were the World Professional Doubles champions. And, since money was what they were playing for, each of them was $25,000 richer.

Charlie Luman let out his breath in a long whistle. 'If you're going to win, that's the way to do it. Everybody gets their money's worth.'

'I think I'd rather win six-love,' said Bruce.

Magnus looked at Nina, pressed her hand. 'Well, he's won something.'

'Do we have to have this meeting tonight?' she said. 'It's a shame to spoil all his good feeling over that win. It's the biggest win he's ever had.'

'He's leaving for Houston in the morning.'

'I know. But – ' She looked over her shoulder at him as he helped her into her coat. 'Is that man – the private investigator – do we have to have him there tonight?'

Margaret, beside her, pulled her own coat about her. 'I don't think this is a meeting where outsiders should be present.'

'I'm sorry, girls,' said Magnus. 'But you left it to us men to try and get all this sorted out. We've decided this man Pede-mont could be our trump card – if one is needed. Harvest has always had a plausible answer when we've caught him out on a few things. That point about changing over from being left-handed to right-handed when he was a kid. Not being able to produce a photo of his father because his father was camera-shy. We just want to see how he reacts when we bring Pedemont into the room.'

Going back home in the Rolls-Royce Nina said, 'I'm beginning to wonder how I would have handled this if I'd been alone. An only daughter and still not married again.'

His face closed up, but in the darkness of the car she did not see it. 'Do you resent all our – help?' He wondered if *help* was the right word.

'No, no.' She felt for his hand, held it reassuringly. 'But everyone is – I don't know. So *protective*. You all seem more concerned that I should not be – hurt. More than that I should possibly be happy.'

It took him a moment or two to say, 'You sound as if you would rather take a chance. I mean, on his being Michael.'

'He is Michael,' she said. 'I don't need any proof.'

Magnus said nothing. In front of them George Biff sat stiffly behind the wheel. He, too, had decided that the Australian was Michael. But he could understand how Mr Magnus and the others must be feeling. Let bygones be bygones . . .

Dave Pedemont, the private investigator, was waiting in the drawing-room when Magnus and Nina arrived home. 'I came early, like you said, Mr McKea. Evening, Mrs McKea.'

Nina nodded, not at all interested in the man, not wanting him here.

'I think it best if you wait in the study,' Magnus said. 'We'll bring you in after Mr Harvest has arrived. You're sure you don't mind doing this for us?'

'Like I explained, I felt you had a prior right. I once worked for Mr Beaufort, Mrs McKea's father – '

Nina showed interest in him for the first time. 'What did you do for my father?'

Pedemont knew he had made a slip. He had to keep a tight rein on his memory. He had been trailing this woman's husband, the guy Davoren, *before* he had left her: he had to keep that straight in his mind. 'I – it was when your husband first disappeared, Mrs McKea. Your first husband, I mean. I – your father didn't think I was big enough, I mean had a big enough organization, to go through with the whole investigation. I'm bigger now, of course. Four men working for me. Associates in every State.'

Magnus said, 'Would you come through to the study?'

Five minutes later the others arrived: the Alburns, the Lumans, the Devons. Nina, looking around, once again felt the pang that

411

had become increasingly frequent in the years since her father's death. The Beaufort name was no more. There would still be all the enterprises bearing the name, the empire was still there; but all those brass plates, billboards, letterheads, were now just echoes of Lucas and Thaddeus. For a cold moment she felt she was standing by open graves, the headstones for which had already been erected.

'Do you think he'll put in an appearance?' Margaret said.

'He's here,' said Magnus. 'You mean Pedemont?'

'No, I meant Clive Harvest. Or Michael. Whatever we're going to call him from now on.'

'He'll be here,' said Bruce. 'He's on a winning streak.'

'Jesus Christ.' Charlie looked around him. 'No booze, Nina?'

'Over there,' said Nina. 'I think I'd better say it now. If you are all going to do a hatchet job on him, I'm leaving the room.'

'Hear, hear,' said Charlie.

'I don't think that's our intention,' said Roger. 'In the end it's going to be your decision, Nina. If this family were in different circumstances – I mean if we were all no more than blue-collar workers out in the suburbs – '

'Don't let's stretch our imagination too far,' said Prue. 'We're *us* and there's no getting away from it.'

'That's my point. We're *us*. And us has money. That complicates things. Out on Wornall Road or wherever, in Little Italy, if a missing son came home the decision would be much simpler.'

'You think so?' said Nina. 'You don't know much about women, Roger.'

'Hear, hear,' said Sally, not looking at Charlie or indeed at any of the men. She sat down, laid her stick beside her crooked leg. 'I'm beginning to think we women should have kept this to ourselves.'

'There's some acrimony creeping in here,' said Magnus. 'I don't think our quarrel should be between ourselves. I hope we have no quarrel at all.'

Nina passed by the back of his chair, touched the top of his head. 'Thank you, darling.'

Then they heard the front door being opened. It seemed to Nina that everyone, herself included, froze for a moment, like second-rate actors in a poorly directed play. Or perhaps it was only her imagination. Tonight, everything she saw, heard, thought, felt, came to her through a prism.

It was George Biff who brought Clive Harvest into the drawing-room. The other servants had been told they were no longer needed. Nina knew there was already gossip in the servants' quarters; she did not feel it should be added to by anything that might filter out from this meeting tonight; George would keep his mouth shut. He went out, closing the doors, and Clive Harvest stood there with his back to them, facing the family he hoped to join but which could have been mistaken for a firing squad.

Then Nina went forward. 'Please come in, Clive. Congratulations on your victory tonight. We're all very pleased for you.'

'Thank you.' But he sounded as if he doubted their pleasure.

'I think you've met everyone, haven't you?'

'No. I still haven't met Mrs Luman and Mrs Devon.'

'Oh?' Nina was surprised. She had assumed that everything had been taken out of her hands by everyone. But somehow Sally and Prue had been overlooked. Or had wanted to be overlooked. She smiled at them warmly, recognizing now that they, at least, were on her side. 'I'm not sure how to introduce them. I mean, if they *are* your aunts – '

Harvest shook hands with Sally first, then with Prue. There was no recognition in his eyes: he looked at Prue as at a stranger. 'I can see you're all sisters – '

'Families do tend to resemble each other,' said Prue. Looking at him carefully, but for another reason than the one she stated: 'I'm looking for the resemblance in you. You do look familiar.'

'It's there,' said Sally. 'A bit of both Tim and Nina. Does that make you feel better, Mr Harvest?'

'A little.'

But he seemed unworried by their scrutiny. He was less awkward, more at ease than the first time he had been in this room. He's still deaf from the applause at the finals tonight, Margaret thought, he's a champion. *I wonder if he is going to turn round and walk out on us all?*

'Mr Harvest – ' Magnus came forward with a drink. 'Beer is your favourite, isn't it? Well, do we get down to business or do we prolong this meeting?'

'Magnus,' said Nina warningly. She too, thought Margaret, looks much more confident than that first afternoon in here. The champion's mother. Or her son's champion.

'Sorry. All right, Mr Harvest. I think if we had more time this matter could be settled, I mean without any doubts on our side – '

'I'm not the one in a hurry. I've wondered for twenty-eight years who my mother was. A few more months won't matter. You're the ones in a hurry, Mr McKea. Because you're afraid I'll go to court, get the family a lot of publicity it doesn't want.'

413

Oh, he's so confident tonight, Margaret thought. And felt the trembling unease weakening her. Because the only way they were going to puncture that confidence would be to bring in Dave Pedemont.

'He's right,' said Nina.

Magnus spread a surrendering hand, as if a judge in court had upheld an objection by defending counsel. 'Were you expecting to go into court, Mr Harvest?'

'Why?' For just a moment the confidence wavered.

'Excuse me.' Magnus went out of the room, returned with Dave Pedemont. 'Mr Harvest, I believe you know this gentleman.'

Harvest looked as if he had been aced. He stared at Pedemont, then slowly looked around the room at the others. 'Money buys everything, doesn't it?'

'We didn't *buy* Mr Pedemont, as you put it,' said Magnus. 'You made a mistake, Mr Harvest. There aren't very many private investigators in this town. You went to the one who worked for Mr Beaufort years ago, who actually was engaged to look for Tim Davoren.'

Margaret was studying Pedemont, waiting for some glance of recognition towards her; but there was none. She doubted if she would have recognized him if she had passed him in the street. He was bald now, had put on a lot of weight, wore square-framed, gold-rimmed glasses; he looked prosperous, more like a business-man than the struggling private detective who had come to see her (here in this very room, she remembered with a start) all those years ago. But then, she bitterly remarked, prying into people's private lives had become a business, a very successful one, in the past few years. Or had he become a successful black-mailer, found other women with secrets that had to be kept?

'Do you want to repeat to us, Mr Pedemont, what Mr Harvest asked you to find out?'

'There's no need for him to do that,' Harvest said slowly. 'I'm sure he's given you a full report. Do you double-cross all your clients like this?'

'No,' said Pedemont.

Liar, thought Margaret. For a moment their glances met. *He knows I remember whom he double-crossed.*

'Like Mr McKea has said, my first duty was to my original client, Mr Beaufort.'

'You could have told me that when I first came to see you. You took my retainer.'

'You'd have been suspicious if I hadn't. Here it is, in full.'

414

Pedemont took a cheque from his pocket. 'I've made it out to cash.'

Harvest hesitated, then reached out and took the cheque. Then he looked at Nina, ignoring everyone else. 'I'll admit to all the questions I put to him. I just wanted to find out what sort of family I might be coming into.'

'Including how much it was worth,' said Bruce.

Nina, without looking at Bruce, held up a silencing hand. 'Go on, Clive.'

'All that you people seem able to think about is money. I think about it, I like having it – but it's not the be-all and end-all of everything. I don't pick my friends or the girls I fall in love with – ' His glance fell on Prue for just a moment, passed on. 'I don't pick them by how much money they have in the bank.'

'We're not talking in the same money terms,' said Magnus, but said it almost kindly. He was watching Nina, knowing what he had to accept for the future. 'The Beaufort money has power. A lot of it.'

'Oh, you don't have to tell me that. I've worried about it ever since I learned of it. I don't know that I want to inherit any power, it means too much responsibility. The life I've led since I left school, all I've been responsible for is myself. *That* was why I put all those questions to Mr Pedemont here. I just wanted to find out how much responsibility I was going to inherit with the money.'

'Plausible again,' said Bruce.

'Lay off him, Bruce,' said Charlie, on his second drink.

'It doesn't worry me, Mr Luman,' said Harvest. 'I couldn't care a damn now. I'm Michael Davoren, I'm sure of it. There were times when I had my own doubts – but not any more. My father was Tim Davoren and my mother is Mrs McKea. But I don't care any more. Bugger the lot of you!'

He put down his half-empty glass of beer, turned and had opened the doors of the drawing-room before Nina said, 'Wait!' He looked back at her without turning round. 'I'd like a moment alone with you.'

He stood very stiff and silent, then he nodded. 'Okay. I didn't mean to include you in that last remark.'

Nina went out of the room, closing the doors after them. Those that were left looked around at each other.

'Well,' said Roger. 'I said it was going to be her decision in the end.'

'Hear, hear,' said Charlie. 'Or am I repeating myself?'

'You are, darling.' Sally stood up, began to walk around the room, as if to relieve an old pain in her leg. But she was feeling no pain at all, only relief. Perhaps, after all, she was not going to have to tell Nina about the Congo and the meeting with Tim. 'But I think we'd better start accepting him. He's our nephew.'

Margaret looked at Pedemont, wanting him out of the way. 'I think that will be all, Mr Pedemont. Thank you for coming to us. You were very helpful.'

'That's a private investigator's job, Mrs Alburn. To be helpful.' There was still no sign from him that he had ever met her before. But perhaps he had become successful in more ways than one: at hiding his intentions, for instance. 'Maybe I can be of help some other time. You have my card, Mr McKea.'

'Yes,' said Magnus. 'Send us your bill.'

'No bill, Mr McKea. I got well paid a long time ago. Good-night, all.'

Magnus took him out to the front door and Roger said, 'Well, he's more honest than I expected. Giving Harvest back his retainer, not billing us – '

'He'll be looking for business in the future,' said Bruce. 'It might be good policy to use him now and again. Just in case – '

'Don't you ever trust anyone?' said Prue. And wondered how much, in the future, she could trust the lover who had turned out to be her nephew, who had told her a moment ago that he had loved her, if only for one night. 'Let's go home, Roger.'

'We can't go yet. Not till Nina comes back.'

In the study Nina stood in front of the fireplace, before the photos of her father and mother, looking at her son, trying to climb over the long blank years that had made him a stranger. It suddenly struck her that she had not even touched him since they had met. She closed her eyes, remembering the weight of the baby against her breast, the energetic life in the three-year-old boy in her arms. She opened her eyes and said, 'I wonder what your father would say if he could see us together?'

'I think he'd be pleased. It took me a long time to wake up to it, but he was always lonely. Even when we were together.'

'I might come to envy you, you know. You had more of him than I did.'

'Well – ' He put out a tentative hand, touched one of hers but did not take it in his own. 'I can tell you about him. The things we did – '

'No.' She wanted to touch him, hold him to her. But he was too tall, too big, to hold him to her as the child she had lost all those years ago. She had lost the experience of being a mother.

'There's Magnus. I shouldn't want him hurt – '

He nodded. 'I like him. I think he was on my side. But the others – '

'You'll learn to live with them. They are all nice people – really. They were just trying to protect me, there was no other reason. In case – ' She smiled a little weakly. 'At the start even I wasn't sure.'

He smiled in reply. 'Neither was I. But now – '

Then he took both her hands in his, leaned forward and kissed her softly on the cheek.

There was a knock on the door. It opened and Magnus stood there. 'Well?'

'He is Michael,' said Nina.


# 5

Walking back across the lawns towards their own house, Margaret took Bruce's hand. 'Cold?' he said.

'A little.' With ghosts from the past.

A security guard, doing his rounds of the estate, passed them. 'Night, Mr and Mrs Alburn. Beautiful weather.'

'Everything all right, Walt?'

'Yes, sir. Everything's secure.'

No, thought Margaret, her grip on Bruce's hand tightening. *Nothing is secure. Not while there are secrets to be kept.*